TURBULENCE

E. J. NOYES

BELLA
BOOKS
2017

Bella Books, Inc.
P.O. Box 10543
Tallahassee, FL 32302

Printed in the United States of America on acid-free paper.

First Bella Books Edition 2017

Editor: Cath Walker
Cover Designer: Judith Fellows

ISBN: 978-1-59493-561-9

Other Bella Books by E. J. Noyes

Ask, Tell

Acknowledgments

There are always so many people to thank for the smallest things while writing a book, but if I started on a list that includes the barista for keeping me caffeinated and every one of my friends who accepted my vacant "I'm writing in my head right now instead of joining in a social gathering" stare, this section may never end.

Thank you, BFF extraordinaire Kate for reading everything I write, picking it all apart, and for your willingness to talk through the weirdest plot and character things with me. I promise I'll write you a non-romance one day, even though I'm still a little bit mad at you for not naming your only daughter after me.

Thanks to Ash, my Americanis(z)ation expert. Sorry about all the random, often greeting-less messages and for your patience with all my questions.

Unending gratitude to my editor, Cath who makes everything so much better, and who has tried so valiantly to teach me the right usage of *lay* and *lie* and what nouns and verbs are.

Thank you to the team at Bella for making the second try as smooth as the first.

Most importantly, I'd never get a word down if it wasn't for the support, encouragement and love from my partner. Pheebs, we've had eleven years of clear flying, and there's nothing but endless blue skies ahead.

CHAPTER ONE

For the first time in months, the hand fondling my breast was not mine. I opened my eyes a fraction, then jammed them closed on the sunrise beginning to peek through partially open curtains. The hand shifted ever so slightly. Something brushed across my nipple, which stiffened a fraction before my body did. Traitor.

Hips snuggled into my ass and breasts pressed harder against my back. "Ah-ha." The voice was low and smooth like buttered whisky. "You *are* awake." The hand moved again, sliding down my stomach before slipping between my legs. A hot tongue danced over my neck. "You never did tell me your name."

Before I go further, I'd like to make something clear. I'm not the kind of girl who falls asleep in the same bed as a one-night stand. Actually, I'm not even the kind of girl who has one-night stands. Standards aside, there was something about the woman who had her hand between my thighs that had made me throw my usual rules out the window.

Cliché? Yes, but true. What can I say? I was lonely and susceptible to a hot woman with a great voice and a knack for flirting. After all, I hadn't been laid since Steph walked out on me months earlier, screaming about how I should try investing in our relationship as much as I did in my company. By "our relationship," she mostly meant her business ideas.

Flimsy reasons aside, there I was in my hotel but not in my room, and in danger of turning one night into one night plus a morning-after romp. I was also in danger of being late for my meeting with my best friend slash business partner, Mark. A night of hot sex wasn't a legitimate excuse for forgetting to set an alarm and potentially missing the meeting, even if he had once used the very same excuse on me. Okay, more than once.

The hand was making progress. Very good progress. Despite my mental protest and rationalization, my clit was running this show. But I had places to be. I stifled a moan and rolled over to put a stop to the proceedings.

Face-to-face with her, I confirmed the woman was every bit as stunning as she had been last night. No booze goggles for me. I slapped a disclaimer down as quickly as I could. "Look. Last night was fantastic. Mind boggling even. Just what I needed." My voice was hoarse from lack of sleep. And four screaming orgasms.

Dark wavy hair bounced around her face and shoulders as she nodded in time with my rambling, her eyes wide and full lips upturned. "I'm pleased. I thought so too." She reached for me again, fingers playing over my hip.

Stay the course, Isabelle. Focus. I twitched away from her. "I have to go. I need to get to the airport." Not that I'd miss my flight. One of the benefits of a company jet.

"Me too. Let's share a cab." She smiled lazily at me. The woman stretched, the sheet slipped and it took every bit of willpower I had to keep my eyes on her face. I failed, miserably, my gaze sweeping over her nakedness. Oh Christ. If this were a cartoon, I would have been drooling with my eyes bouncing on stalks.

Lightly muscled with delicious curves, legs that went on forever, firm breasts that were a little more than a handful—but I do have small hands. Her eyes. Darkest brown I'd ever seen, with laugh lines creasing the edges. Adorable cleft chin and a bone structure that made me want to weep. Nowhere near butch, but not *quite* my usual ultra-femme type. Though, after the things she did to me, I wondered if all this time I didn't actually know my type.

I slid from her grasp and grabbed the phone, pressing the button for the front desk. Phone between ear and shoulder, I fumbled on the floor for my panties. I was sure they'd been tossed in that general direction. An overly-cheerful voice answered after three rings. "Concierge. How may I assist you?"

"This is twelve-zero-one. Can you please arrange a car to the airport?"

"Certainly, Ms. uh…Rhodes. When will you be ready?"

I snagged my panties, or at least the panties I thought were mine. Black lacy thong. Yes, mine. "Fifteen minutes."

"A driver will be waiting for you downstairs. Do you need help with your baggage?"

"No. Thank you." I hung up, tugged my underwear on and stood up. The woman was watching me, still smiling. Temptress. I turned around, certain my resolve would crumble if I kept looking at her. The tingle in my groin had not gone away. In fact it had become more insistent, as had the memory of her mouth on me. Don't think about it, find your things and leave.

My bra was on the television, pantyhose hung over a small black suitcase, blouse and jacket slung neatly over the chair. How clever of me to have the foresight to keep some of my clothes unwrinkled while I had a mouth on my breasts and hands groping my ass. I located my skirt and purse near the front door and began to dress. "What floor am I on right now?"

"Fifth." She rolled onto her stomach and crawled to the end of the bed, chin propped in a hand. Those dark eyes watched me hopping around as I tried to find my second made-to-measure Louboutin and zip my skirt at the same time. "Sure you don't want to stay a little longer?"

Yes, I really did want to stay. Thankfully some sensible part of my brain waded through my lust to take charge. "No, I need to go now. I've got a breakfast meeting before my flight."

"Pity. Aren't you at least going to give me your number?" she asked coyly.

I grinned, tucked my blouse in and bent down so we were inches apart. "No. I don't live anywhere near Oklahoma. We're never going to see each other again."

She closed the gap between our lips and gave my mouth a casual exploration with her tongue. Mine responded without permission, as did my hands which reached to tangle in her hair. The throb downstairs dialed itself from a six to an off-the-chart thirteen. Dammit. I moved away first and took a step backward, otherwise it was going to be fuck the meeting to stay and fuck the girl. Again.

I slid toward the door and glanced around to make sure I hadn't forgotten anything. I hadn't, but I wished I could leave my arousal behind so I could think straight. "Have a nice day. And um…thanks."

I closed the door on her response and raced along the hallway, nearly crashing into a bellboy setting breakfast outside a room. I called an apology over my shoulder as I raced to the elevator. While it rose to the top floor, I checked my appearance in the mirrored walls.

It was the appearance of someone who'd consumed a number of gin and tonics the night before, got thoroughly and deliciously fucked for four hours and slept less than two. I tried to tame my hair between floors seven and twelve and gave up just before the elevator doors slid open.

Mama would surely scold me for running, in a skirt suit no less, but I imagined some part of her would approve of the way I handled turns in my four-inch heels. It was a skill I learned back home running from my forced and unfortunately male date at the ninth grade dance. Scott Devery.

No. Thank. You.

Since I was six years old, I'd been telling Mama I liked girls. At sixteen, she'd gently asked if maybe my girl thing was *just a phase*. At twenty-six, when I'd lived in New York with a woman after college, Mama realized it wasn't going away. Now that I was almost thirty-six, she'd fully accepted that my being a lesbian was here to stay and was rather pleased with the idea. Aside from wanting me to be happy and all that, being the mother of *the lesbian who left town* made her stand out in a dull community. And Mama sure loved being different.

I barged into my suite and hastily repacked the bag I'd barely unpacked, given this was only an overnight trip and the overnight was spent in a room other than my own. Teeth brushed, world's fastest shower, makeup fixed, fresh suit, hair… barely passable. I was checked out and in the lobby waiting for my car with forty seconds to spare. That was forty seconds I could have spent kissing hottie on the fifth floor. Damn.

I made it to the airport by six fifty and was in the terminal, handing over my lounge membership card by six fifty-two. Eight minutes to spare. I could have squeezed in a fifth orgasm. Double damn. The desk clerk frowned. "I'm sorry, Ms.—"

"Isabelle Rhodes." I spelled both my names for him.

"Ms. Rhodes, that card doesn't appear to be registered in our system."

I hiked an eyebrow skyward. "Swipe it again, please. I was here two weeks ago." It came out a little bitchy, a by-product of annoyance and a headache starting to slide from last night's gin into caffeine withdrawal. Not a place I wanted to be. Not a place the world would want me to be.

Ever so slowly, he dragged my card through the reader again, shaking his head. "I'm very sorry, it's still not coming up."

I lifted my finger to stop him saying another word and fished in my handbag for my phone to rectify the situation immediately. "Mark, I'm stuck outside the lounge. My card isn't working. Can you come out and help me, please?" The pitch of my voice rose along with my indignation.

He chuckled. "Calm down, Belle. I'm sure it's just a glitch."

"This *glitch* is keepin' me away from coffee and breakfast." I cringed at the drawl creeping into my voice. Cool it, Isabelle and pick up your dropped g. After more than ten years in New York, my South Carolina accent had almost disappeared, though it slid back out whenever I spoke to Mama or was stressed. Both occurred quite frequently.

The sharp sound of Mark's shoes on the marble floor approached. "There's my little pocket rocket. Stop tapping your foot, it makes you look like you need to pee."

I hung up as he appeared adroitly behind the clerk, now happy to accept me into the lounge as Mark's guest. His appearance was of a man who'd slept for ten glorious hours, then had a massage and maybe a blow job before coming here. I hated him for it, all too aware of *my* appearance. Adding to the misery was the knowledge that my hair had gone from passable to misbehaving, evidenced by blond tendrils falling across my face.

Mark's hazel eyes were amused. "Late night." A statement, not a question.

I narrowed my blues at him. "Don't start."

My friend laughed and took my suitcase, leaving me to follow him. I was assaulted by the smell of coffee and I made vague gestures at the barista as we passed. Gestures I hoped would convey that I needed an espresso, pronto, before things got ugly. She'd worked this lounge for a few months. She'd remember me, know what I meant and what I wanted. Or rather, she should.

She caught my eye and I caught her slightly panicked expression before she plastered a smile on her face and nodded. I shrugged out of my suit jacket and lowered myself onto the plush recliner, crossing my ankles demurely.

Mark glanced at his watch. "We're scheduled for eight, so we'll need to head through around ten to."

Another benefit of our own jet was avoiding security hassles. "Mhmm."

"Did that new client sign yesterday?"

"Yes. Yours?"

"Yep." He rolled his neck and it cracked disgustingly. "How did it go with Shane Preston last night?"

Even the sound of that client's name tightened my neck with annoyance. I yanked my laptop out and flipped it open. "I managed to get him up to fifteen, but I don't think he's going to budge from that." Even then, that extra three mil was begged and cajoled and flattered out of him.

Mark gulped his full-fat caramel latte then set it back down with what I swear was a smug look in my direction. "Twenty is his hard limit? If he wants the growth, he's going to have to put in."

"No shit, Mark. What do you think I've been trying to do for the past five years?"

He grunted. "I spent most of yesterday trying to talk that new client out of overextending. Maybe he'll listen if he goes bankrupt. Wanna swap?"

Tempting. Mark and I were equal partners, but we handled separate client portfolios. "I'll try Shane again, but you know how cautious he's been ever since his brother-in-law started to give him advice." I made air quotes. "Three trips this month alone, trying to get him on board. I'm about ready to give up."

And I was getting sick of his insistence on late meetings and then dinner, because he "liked to really know who he was dealing with." The whole thing made long days even longer and after half a decade, I'd have thought he knew me pretty well. I yanked my hair from its loose ponytail and into a messy topknot, almost elbowing the life-saving barista. She set my coffee on the table.

"Thank you so much. Also, I'll have an egg white omelet, please. Spinach, mushroom, tomato. Hot sauce. And another espresso, thank you."

She nodded amicably. "Sure thing, ma'am."

Ma'am. Ugh. Before she'd even turned around, I'd dumped two packets of sweetener into my black coffee and swallowed a gulp, temperature be damned. Mark spoke slyly. "Belle, I can't help but note your appearance. It's been a while, so I gotta ask... who and *how* was she?"

Play dumb. "How was who?"

"Last night's bedmate. Not like you to pick up a random."

I snorted. "Why would I tell you?"

He raised an incredulous eyebrow. "Belle, you tell me everything, including when you have your period."

"No I don't." I pressed my lips together.

"Please. How many times have you swanned into my office dramatically proclaiming how bloated you are and how you, and I quote, 'are not going to fit into your dress for tonight'?"

Oh. Right. "Well…we're friends."

Mark popped a gun finger at me. "Exactly. And friends share, especially details of their first lay in over four months since their god-awful ex left them." He gave an exaggerated shudder.

My phone sounded a text alert from Clare, my PA. *Meeting this afternoon canceled.* Glorious. I swallowed the rest of my coffee. "Preston ran late, as usual, and I didn't get back until almost ten. Wasn't tired, so I headed to the hotel bar. She bought me a drink, and I've got no idea who she is."

"And how long did it take her to get you into her room?"

"Forty-five minutes." Actually it was thirty but I didn't want to sound too eager.

Mark threw his head back and barked out a sharp laugh.

"Shh!" I crossed my legs, leaning back. "If you'd have seen her, I bet you would have taken even less time."

"Oh really?"

I nodded smugly as another coffee and my breakfast were set on the low table in front of me. Caffeine now coursing through my veins, I turned a full-toothed smile on the server. "Thank you so much, I really appreciate it." I shook hot sauce over the plate.

Mark made a swirling motion with his forefinger. "Come on!"

"Come on what?"

"Elaborate. You can't drop a snippet like that and not tell me details."

Mark stared as I ate a delicate bite of my breakfast, deliberately taking my time chewing and swallowing. I wiped the edge of my mouth. "About my age, five-seven or eight. Delicious, funny and extremely—" I raised an eyebrow. "Talented. Responsive. Athletic, but not butch." As I made my list, I became all too aware of my arousal raising its hand. Goddammit. Really? Again?

Mark wrinkled his nose. "Well, isn't it nice to be you? I fell asleep alone at eleven, watching *Bridesmaids*."

I put a little extra sarcasm into my response. "For the life of me, I do not know why you're single."

"Me either," he said ruefully. "But the bed was wonderful, almost makes up for staying in a hotel."

I mused noncommittally. After last night, hotels were suddenly a whole lot more appealing. Still, I knew the chance of a repeat was unlikely. Overnights were rare and only at times like this when Mark and I had clashing meeting schedules. He would rather wait and stay in a hotel than fly on a jet that wasn't *ours*. The guy was like a kid with a toy.

We talked business over another coffee and my restorative breakfast. By the time we left to board, I felt ninety percent human. All I needed was a decent nap and maybe a round with my Rabbit to get rid of the persistent tingle that popped up every time I thought about last night. I slipped oversized sunglasses over tired eyes and walked briskly across the tarmac, rolling my bag behind me.

Out in the sun, a headache poked spikes through my skull. I knew that once I was on board our hostess, Georgia, would supply me with water, Advil and everything else I needed to get back to the office in one piece. Including eye candy. Every now and then, I fantasized about taking her in back and engaging in a little mile-high extravaganza. If it wasn't so gross—being that I signed her paychecks, and that she was straight and attached—I might have seriously considered it.

As I approached the boarding steps, movement in the cockpit caught my eye. I looked up and got a glimpse of dark hair, high cheekbones and a familiar cocky grin. Something electric slid down my spine. I couldn't see the pilot's eyes but it didn't matter, because even behind her aviators I knew what they would look like. I knew, because I'd spent hours shyly staring into them last night while my fingers not-so-shyly explored other parts of her.

Jesus H Christ ridin' a bicycle.

My stomach flipped and I was given a Technicolor reminder of her legs spread wide, heels digging into my back and begging me to let her come. The stomach flip turned into confusion. Why was my one-night stand sitting in the pilot's seat of my private jet?

Sunglasses were lifted, both in the jet and on the tarmac. I paused, and for a moment we simply stared at one another until the cocky grin turned into a brilliant smile, making me totter on my very high heels. My jacket fell from where it was hooked over the suitcase. Wonderful. Let me be clear about something else. I am not a clumsy person, yet there I was stumbling, fumbling and bumbling like the nerd who was about to ask the hottest girl at school to the dance.

Heat crept into my ears as I tried to bend down in my tight skirt and heels to retrieve my jacket. My briefcase slid from my shoulder to join my clothing on the hot tarmac. Perfect. Just fuckin' perfect. I only just managed to stop a string of expletives. My cheeks clearly thought my ears were lonely and warmed with a flush too.

Mark stopped halfway up the steps and turned around. "You all right, Belle?"

"Just a moment," I called. When I finally managed to pick up my things and straighten again, I found my gaze drawn back to the cockpit window. She was still grinning. At me.

CHAPTER TWO

My cheeks were still burning as I climbed the steps. What the fuck was happening? I glanced around for hidden cameras. This had to be a prank, right? Georgia greeted me cheerfully as soon as I made it into the cabin. "Good morning, Ms. Rhodes. May I take your jacket?"

I hate being called Ms. Rhodes but Mark insisted on it from all the employees. He liked to set stupid standards. I thought it made me sound like a kindergarten teacher, but I guess it was a small step above being called *Miss* or *Ma'am*. I passed her my jacket, mumbled my thanks and immediately chastised myself. Though I could be abrupt and demanding, I'd always prided myself on treating employees respectfully. Did orgasms count as respectful employee treatment? If so, color me super-respectful.

I inhaled through my nose, stuck a smile on my face, and tried again. "Thank you, Georgia. Did you have a nice evening?"

Vigorous nodding. "I did, thank you. I love Oklahoma City." Georgia loved everything. She would have had dinner at an inexpensive restaurant then gone to the movies and spent approximately fourteen dollars at the snack bar. After years of signing off on her expenses, I knew she was a woman of habit. She was also a woman of great moral integrity, never coming anywhere near our employee's two hundred and fifty dollar per day allowance for nights out of town.

I settled in my usual seat over the left wing, and glanced at Mark who was getting in a last minute phone call. My pulse thudded in my skull. I couldn't tell if it was from a hangover or the revelation that the only time I'd ever had a one-night stand, my lover was actually my employee.

Could I not just have one thing where my work and my private life didn't bleed together? For a terrifying moment, I wondered if Mark hadn't set it up as a *get back on the horse* scenario. Quickly, I dismissed the idea—he wasn't that kind of person. I stared toward the front of the cabin. The cockpit curtain was closed, hiding her from view.

How had I not known who she was? How long had she worked for us? I took a mental trip backward through yesterday morning's flight. I worked for most of it and rushed off the plane with my earphones still in, calling out my thanks to the pilot as I walked past. All I'd seen was a mass of dark hair in a neat ponytail and assumed she was a relief pilot because both our staff pilots were sick or something. I'd been up working for most of the night before, and I still hadn't had my midmorning coffee. Nobody is their most attentive or observant under such circumstances.

I decided to give myself the benefit of the doubt, concluding I really couldn't have known, because I hadn't seen her face or heard her voice. Georgia stopped in front of me, bending down slightly. "Can I get you anything, Ms. Rhodes?"

An explanation and the pilot, thanks very much. Stop. Exactly the sort of thoughts you are not allowed to have, Isabelle. Still, my eyes went to the front of the plane again before I disciplined them to look up at Georgia. "Some water and a couple of headache tablets would be great please."

"Of course."

She returned promptly and I tried a casual, "The pilot. Is she a relief? I haven't seen her before."

Georgia flashed me a four hundred-megawatt smile. "No, she's not a relief pilot, Ms. Rhodes. Yesterday was Captain Graham's first day flying for Rhodes and Hall, and I believe she's now employed full-time on the A roster." The smile dimmed to three hundred and ninety-seven megawatts and she snuck a quick glance at Mark, still on the phone. "It's my understanding that Captain Ackerman has moved on." Her eyes shone and in any other circumstance, I'm sure she would have vomited gossip all over me.

I nodded, trying to process the fact that my one-night-never-see-you-again stand was not only fifteen feet away but apparently working for me. Surprise! My life was a joke. The cockpit curtains slid open and I caught sight of *Captain Graham* twisting around in her seat. She smiled at me again and my stomach turned in on itself. I should probably have asked Georgia my new employee's first name. I reached over and snapped my fingers at Mark to get his attention. Mark ignored me.

Captain Graham's voice carried through to us. "Good morning, Ms. Rhodes and Mr. Hall. We've received clearance to depart so if you could make sure everything's stowed safely and you're belted in, I can get you on your way back to New York. Georgia, secure the door please."

I blinked. Her professional voice was even sexier than her bedroom voice, if such a thing were possible. I pinched my thigh gently. Not dreaming. This is real and it is awkward as hell.

The takeoff was smooth and uneventful—clearly she was as skilled a pilot as she was a lover. Once we'd leveled out, I opened my laptop and connected to our wireless Internet. While market updates loaded, I leaned toward Mark. "What happened to Ackerman?"

He didn't glance up from thumbing through his phone. "I fired him."

I turned Grams' engagement ring back and forth on my right ring finger, the diamond catching the light with each twist. It was the only piece of jewelry I never changed, and my stylist had long given up trying to get it off my finger because of clashing issues. "Why? You didn't think it necessary to tell me?"

Mark laughed. "Belle. Come on. You have zero interest in that sort of thing."

That he was right was beside the point. Along with the intricacies of running the business and managing the office staff, I found handling the schedules for our team of limo drivers and two pilots tiresome and tended to leave that sort of thing to Mark. Still, I would have thought firing one of our pilots would rate a mention. I drummed my nails on the armrest. "I'd still like to know why."

Mark's voice was low. "He was being inappropriate."

I lowered my voice to match his. "Why isn't Schwartz taking over the A roster then?"

"Because he declined. You know he's thinking about retiring." Captain Schwartz was in his sixties and handled the B roster, which was basically when the A pilot was on vacation or sick.

I jerked my chin toward the front of the jet. "I bet I know why you hired her." The accusation was obviously unfair.

"Actually, I only looked at her credentials. Tamara did the interview."

Of course she did. Tamara, his PA, was so in tune with his needs and wants, it was almost like having a second Mark. I slipped my heels off and tucked my legs underneath me. No matter how hard I tried, I couldn't stop my eyes from straying forward. My mile-high fantasy turned from Georgia to a noisy cockpit session with Captain Graham. Don't be stupid, Isabelle. There's no room up there, you'd have to drag her into the cabin. On second thought, maybe not. I already knew how flexible she was.

Evidently, my face wasn't as neutral as I'd hoped. Mark cleared his throat and when I looked at him, his headshake was emphatic. "I know what you're thinking," he murmured.

I shrugged, lowering my voice. "Oh, I'm well beyond just thinking." We held eye contact until his mouth fell open in realization. Yeah, me too, pal.

He shifted his focus to stare intently at the closed cockpit curtain. I could see the wheels turning, connecting my description of last night's bedmate with the appearance of the pilot flying us back to New York. I turned back to stare out of the window and heard Mark splutter. There was no way he'd push the subject here so I left him to let his imagination run wild.

I should have worked but instead I did some thinking, mostly about my current state of affairs. Or the lack of. Eighty-plus hour weeks and being almost constantly at the beck and call of clients meant sacrificing some things. Like relationships, as I'd found out numerous times. In the last ten years, my longest was Steph at a record four years, eight months and twenty-four days.

Apparently I had trust issues and used my work as a way to keep people at a distance. I'd never been able to shake the fear that women only wanted me for my wealth, so it was easier to keep them away. Especially after Steph proved me right. I longed for an easier time when my only concern was getting my homework in on time or if I should crimp my hair.

My therapist used a lot of buzzwords, such as "fear conditioning," "meaningful relationship goals," and "defensive posturing." I kept going back to her, so maybe she was on to something, or she was really good at bullshitting. Maybe I was just a gullible idiot who needed a guru. I certainly needed something.

Perhaps the thing I really needed was someone casual. A regular fuck buddy. Someone I could call when I wanted a little relief. No emotional attachments, just a woman who knew what I liked and vice versa. Someone, like Captain Graham, who figured out pretty quickly that when she—

Ahem. No.

Sleeping with her again would cause too many issues but still, I planned to spend a fair amount of time fantasizing about her. On one of my glances to the cockpit, I accidentally looked at Mark. He raised an eyebrow. I averted my eyes quickly. To someone who didn't know him, he would seem fine. But after over twelve years of friendship and nine of those as business partners, I could read him like the news. Anxious and frustrated with an undercurrent of annoyed curiosity. Goody.

I sighed. He had every reason to feel that way. The fact I'd slept with an employee—albeit unknowingly—could be a disaster waiting to bite me in the ass. Sexual harassment lawsuit, bad publicity, lost clients. Closing my eyes, I chanted to myself *I didn't know, I didn't know.* Hopefully my truthful explanation would hold water if it ever came to it.

Georgia passed us to knock on the paneling behind the cockpit. "Can I get you anything, Captain Graham?"

"Coffee, same as yesterday. Thanks so much."

Her voice did strange things to me. Oh lord. My stomach twisted, pulse increased, thighs clenched. Oddly enough, I wondered how she took her coffee, suddenly wanting to know this little detail.

The curtain remained open while Georgia fixed coffee, but Graham didn't turn around again. I kept my attention out the window to stop myself from watching her, and spent the rest of the flight trying desperately to figure out if there was a way I could see her again. Such a bad idea. For all my thinking, I came up with exactly zero usable solutions.

As we began our descent into Teterboro, the small private airport just a relative stone's throw from Manhattan, I took a toiletries bag from my leather tote and slipped past Georgia who was playing a game on her phone. She dropped it in her lap, looking up at me guiltily. "Can I help you, Ms. Rhodes?"

I shook my head gently. "No, it's fine. Go back to crushing candy or whatever you're doing." Honestly, I didn't give a shit that she was on her phone. I had no issues with her reading or texting her law school boyfriend or even writing a damned porn novel while we were in the air. It was nice having her around, but really I was just as capable of making coffee and fetching booze or snacks for myself.

In the beginning, I'd argued against needing a hostess but Mark was insistent. It looked good when we traveled with clients, blah blah blah. A few years ago, I'd finally managed to convince Mark that Georgia didn't need to come along when I took the jet for personal trips. He'd put his foot down when I pushed him to allow me to fly without her when it was just me for business, because *a client might see*. Oh the horror. He was a showman, all about image and how we presented ourselves, whereas my talents sat more with the actual money-making side of our business. Over the years, Mark and I had settled comfortably into roles that played to our strengths.

I slipped into the lavatory and thoroughly brushed my teeth, then gargled with mouthwash. Twice. Even as I did it, I wondered why I was bothering. It wasn't like I could grab Graham on my way out, shove her against the wall and kiss the hell out of her. Still, the thought sent a pleasant warmth through my chest. And lower.

A glance in the mirror told me that my hair was still beyond fixable. It had just enough curl to have a mind of its own. Someone once described it as just a little kinky, a description with which I was strangely okay. I blew a strand away from my face. After rummaging in my bag for a hair stick, I gathered, twisted and stabbed my hair fiercely. I gave myself a quick respritz of perfume and fresh swipe of lipstick. All set.

As I returned to my seat Mark made an exaggerated show of sniffing the air. "Trying to impress someone, Belle?"

My answer was a slow eyebrow raise. Pretty sure Captain Graham was already impressed.

Back in our hangar, Mark jumped up and rushed toward the door. His cheek muscles bulged. "You coming?"

I fiddled with my laptop. "You go on, I'll be there in a minute."

Mark rolled his eyes, and I knew I'd be in for it as soon as he could get me alone. I'd better make sure he didn't any time soon. I popped a piece of gum in my mouth, wasted time gathering my bags and strolled toward the door. Georgia flashed me a cheery smile. "Enjoy your day, Ms. Rhodes!"

"You too, thanks again for your help."

"You're welcome."

This is it. I stopped beside the cockpit, tilted my head slightly and made eye contact with the woman I now knew to be Captain Graham, first name still a mystery. "Thank you, very much."

"It was my absolute pleasure," she said evenly. She held my gaze for a moment until my eyes dropped to her lips.

"Thank you," I repeated dumbly before turning to walk down the steps. Very articulate, Isabelle. I hoisted my laptop bag onto my shoulder and strode toward our waiting car.

There was a sound of footsteps behind me, followed by that delicious voice. "Excuse me! Ms. Rhodes?"

I paused and turned. The woman smiled. A hand was offered. "I don't believe we've been *formally* introduced yet. I'm Audrey Graham." Her eyes slid downward to linger on my breasts for a moment before returning to my face. "I'm very excited to be working for you." I had no idea how she managed to look like a respectful employee while ogling my tits, but she did.

As I took her hand, I wondered if it was sexual harassment if your employee had done all the propositioning, or you didn't know they worked for you. Something to look into. "Audrey," I repeated.

The smile wavered. "My mother really likes Audrey Hepburn movies, particularly *My Fair Lady*." The way she said it made me think that she explained her name every time she introduced herself. She let go of my hand, but not before her thumb brushed up and over mine.

I bit my lip to stop the smile tugging at the edges of my mouth. "It could have been worse. She could have named you Doolittle."

Audrey laughed like it was funny instead of the lamest joke ever. Leaning against the step railing, she folded her arms over her chest but it wasn't defensive. It made her look even more confident. And sexy. Very, very sexy. Despite the change in appearance—hair pulled back neatly, lightly made up with uniform clean and sharply pressed—she was still the woman from last night.

Audrey nodded, slow and thoughtful. "Doolittle. Well that would certainly be in direct conflict of my work ethic." She leaned closer, lowering her voice. "As I'm sure you'll remember."

All too well. Even thinking about it made my heart race. Before I could help myself, the old fear crept in. The one that would sit in the back of my mind and tell me women only wanted to be with me for what they could get, not because they cared about *me*. I lifted my chin. "About that. You really had no idea who I was? I find it hard to believe you didn't see me yesterday morning." I worked hard to keep my tone neutral, professional.

Her forehead wrinkled. "No, Ms. Rhodes, I didn't. I was far too occupied with my first day at a new job. I'm sure you can understand that noticing a blonde with killer legs while running postflight checks isn't the same as being able to recognize their face at a bar." Audrey snorted. "Besides, what idiot would knowingly sleep with their employer the first day?"

She was right, and she had me with the compliment about my legs. What can I say? I have as much ego as the next person, if not a little more. I clamped my teeth down on my lower lip and decided to let it go. She leaned a little closer, close enough that I could smell the faint trace of her perfume. Not floral, but something clean that had me imagining a rainforest. The scent dragged me back to last night. My groin sent a pulsing reminder for good measure, as if it thought I'd forget about what she could do. She'd turned me into a ridiculous, horny mess.

Audrey passed me a card from her pocket. "Here. In case you need to contact me."

I studied the text and held it up between two fingers. "In case I need to contact you for what exactly?" Dial-an-orgasm service sounded like the best reason.

"Anything, Ms. Rhodes."

Bad idea to call her. I tucked the card into my purse and lifted my eyes to meet hers. "Well, I hope you enjoyed your first experience working with us."

Her face lit up with another smile. "I certainly did, Ms. Rhodes though I'm sure you'll understand that you've set very high workplace standards."

CHAPTER THREE

When the regulation chauffeur-black Bentley pulled to a stop in front of our building in Lower Manhattan just after one p.m., I slid from the backseat, hoping to lose Mark before he could pin me down with a barrage of questions. I rushed to the elevators, punched the button to close the doors in his face and congratulated myself the whole way up to the fifteenth floor. The second elevator pinged as I opened the glass doors of our office and I turned back just in time to see Mark stepping out. Shitshitshit. I hurled breathless greetings at everyone, accepted a handful of messages and was practically running by the time I got to my office.

I dropped my bags on the plush carpet and as I was closing the door, a hand grabbed the wood and stopped me. "Nice try, Belle." Mark closed the door calmly behind himself. He would never raise his voice or slam a door when people were around. Image you see. But after a whole flight and car ride to think about it, he'd be tumultuous.

I told him frequently that bottling up emotions was unhealthy. He'd probably have a heart attack before he was fifty. No heart attacks for me—I made sure to take the cap off my emotional bottle on a semiregular basis, releasing anger by griping at incompetent people. Mark's a damp match, constantly trying to get lit. I'm a firecracker. Burn hot and bright then go out. Really, I'm not a bitch. Just occasionally bitchy.

Mark spun around to face me. "Isabelle." My full name, not his usual shortened version. He was serious with a capital S. "What the actual fuck? Did you sleep with her? How?"

"How? You want a lesson in the logistics of lesbian lovin'?" I grinned at my alliteration and deft sidestepping.

"Belle."

"Fine." I lifted a forefinger. "I did, but I can explain. It's quite simple really."

"I'm sure it is."

I made sure to enunciate. "I. Didn't. Know."

"How could you not know?"

I ticked off my defense as I walked across to my desk. "You hired her, her back was to me when I walked past and I worked with earphones in the whole flight." If I'd heard her voice, I would have recognized it in the bar immediately. It was as delicious as she was and I was pretty confident I'd heard her entire octave range, right from deep whispers of dirty things in my ear to muffled screams.

Mark grunted and my explanation picked up speed. "I'm serious, Mark. I was drinking at the bar and she approached me. We had a few more drinks and went up to her room. Do you really, honestly think I'd have fucked her if I knew? Like, really?"

"No, I don't but—"

"But nothing. When I left the jet she assured me she was unaware of who I was. And you know what? I believe her." I dropped the handful of crumpled call notes next to the phone and rested my ass against the edge of my heavy mahogany desk.

He waved a dismissive hand. "Whatever. So…no more? It's out of your system?"

Eyes wide, I clamped my lips together and gave him a very noncommittal gesture. It was *not* out of my system. Not by a long shot. Mark stuffed his hands into his pockets and walked over to me. "If you're going to sleep with her again, you need to talk to HR. We need waivers. And no, we can't fire her just so you can screw her again, Belle."

I gave him a hard stare. "I know that, you fucking idiot." I'd already been through all the possibilities, including that one. Thinking of the crescendo as she came, I was tempted to do it anyway and risk being sued for unfair dismissal just so I could have my tongue inside her again. "Look, I don't plan on sleeping with her again, but I'm allowed to have *thoughts*, Mark."

His cheeks puffed. "Fine. But talk to Tom so if she sues your ass for sexual harassment because of last night, we're prepared."

I glared at him. "I'm fairly sure consensual sex between two adults isn't considered sexual harassment. Especially if the sex, mind boggling as it was, happened before these two adults were aware of any employer-employee connection." Still, a small part of me wondered if I might actually be in trouble.

Mark's hands came up to make half-closed fists before he let them drop again. "I just don't get how you could make a mistake like that."

"You don't get it. Hello?" I leaned forward and tapped the air with a forefinger. "Is this microphone on? I feel like you can't hear me. I didn't realize who she was!"

"Very funny," he said drily.

"I don't understand what the problem is. I spent one night with her. It's not like I'm going to force her to lick me every time we take a trip if she wants to keep her job." It was an appealing thought. The licking, not the forcing in order to keep her job. "Anyway. Stop being so damned self-righteous. You dated one of our interns, or have you forgotten that?"

He ignored me and barreled on. "This is completely different."

"No it's not," I muttered under my breath, my back to him as I walked to my chair and dropped into it. His mention of a waiver had darkened my mood, and the fact that he was right darkened it further.

I could just picture the scenario. Can I sleep with you again? Will you sue me if I do? Please sign here and I'll see you out back in five for a quickie. Fuck. I kicked my heels off.

Mark started to gather his things. "So the sex was really that good?"

I spun my chair around, pushing off the carpet with my bare foot. "You've seen what she looks like, right?" The chair made a full revolution.

"I have."

I arched a perfectly shaped eyebrow at him. "Take that, multiply it by the four screamingly good orgasms she gave me and you have your answer."

* * *

By burying myself in work, I managed to push Audrey Graham into a deep recess of my brain, ready to drag out again as soon as I got home. I set a reminder to call Tom, the company attorney, in the morning to see if I really was in any sort of deep legal trouble. He would relish the chance to bill me for preplanning how he would yank me out from under a potential harassment lawsuit. It would make Mark happy to know we'd been proactive. A happy Mark was a quiet Mark and a quiet Mark meant a happy Isabelle.

My frustrations weren't helped by a twenty-minute call with one of my clients trying to reassure him that a dip of thirty basis points in his portfolio wasn't a catastrophe. He was slightly mollified when I pointed out that the last time this happened, I came back with a two percent increase for him. Lord save me from people who don't trust.

If it wasn't for the high commission I'd negotiated from the very beginning, I may have been tempted to tell him to take his shitty whiny attitude elsewhere. In a nice way of course. By the time I ended the call there were hard indents in my legal pad from angry doodling. Mentally drained, I decided to take a break outside the office. I gathered my things, tugged my heels back on and started to walk toward the lobby.

"Ms. Rhodes?" Clare scurried up beside me, tucking her shiny black bob behind her ear. "I've just sent your meeting schedule for next week. And here are the ideas from Christopher for Saturday's gala and the benefit on the eighteenth." She passed me two folders, both with my name in my stylist's extravagant penmanship.

"Thank you." I tucked the folders under an arm and as we walked, opened up my schedule on my tablet. Two meetings in Dallas Monday, late meeting in office Tuesday, Chicago Thursday, lunch meeting back here on Friday. Four flights, four opportunities to see Audrey Graham. Excellent. No, not excellent. No touching. "Please call Christopher and tell him I'll make a decision on the final two outfits for Saturday's gala by five today. He can come to test and fit tomorrow lunch time."

"Of course, and I already have Saturday's hair and makeup scheduled for two."

"Great, thanks." I flipped through a few of the stylist's notes, bored and uninspired by the gowns.

"Rick Elliot called about this year's list issue. He wanted you to know that despite what's rumored, they're doing it in the same format as always for the top ten."

I nodded. "Whatever they want, wherever you can fit it in." It would be my third year running on the magazine's NYC Wealthiest Self-Made Women list, which meant a photo shoot and an interview.

Wordlessly, Clare held out her hand and I passed the folders back. She hovered. "I'll leave these on your desk. Have you eaten lunch, Ms. Rhodes?"

Food. Shit. I glanced at the clock, noting it was almost three. "Not yet. I need some air. I'll pick something up and be back in an hour. Send calls to my cell, please. Oh, and Clare, can you arrange another airport lounge card for Oklahoma please? One that won't demagnetize in the first month."

I hurried out of the building and down the street toward Lou's, my favorite eatery on Ann. It was warm, the sun was shining and I resolved, as I did at least three times a week, to spend more time outdoors.

Lou held his arms wide, his already protruding belly protruding even further. "Blondie. I've missed you. The usual?"

"Yes, please." I dumped my purse on the counter while Lou started working on my ham, Swiss, tomato and mustard on rye, chattering about his son's upcoming wedding. People were staring at me like a woman in a four thousand-dollar suit and shoes that cost two grand waiting for a sandwich near a back alley was an anomaly. Maybe elsewhere, but not in Manhattan.

I'd been propositioned by men at Lou's who either thought I was a high-class escort or I was lost. The truth was far simpler—I really liked Lou's sandwiches and I liked sitting at his counter listening to him talk.

I ate there for the same reason I wore torn dirty jeans, rode the subway to see a movie or go bowling and volunteered some scant free time at the animal shelter. Because I liked the normalcy. I liked people treating me like a regular person, not calling me Ms. Rhodes, or climbing up my ass, or trying to get something from me.

I realized then that was why I felt so drawn to Audrey. She had treated me like a regular person. Every woman I'd dated knew who I was before we started out. They knew me as Isabelle Rhodes: stockbroker with a net worth comfortably in the hundreds of millions, philanthropist and member of various pointless A lists. Not Isabelle Rhodes: ex-middle class social misfit, secret reality television addict and lover of quiet nights at home with a cup of tea.

For the seven perfect hours I was with Audrey, I was just me and me was someone she wanted. Even after she discovered who I was, she looked at me the same way she had the night before, as much as she tried to hide it behind the thin layer of deference.

Lou set my sandwich down on the counter, complete with two pickles sliced into spears. He always gave me two. I smiled up at him. "You're too good to me."

He shrugged, but I could tell he was pleased. "Eh, I just know what you like, Blondie."

"Tell me more about this wedding. You got your suit ready?" I picked up my sandwich, took a bite and listened to him talk.

* * *

I left work at seven and was in the private elevator up to my Tribeca penthouse by seven twenty. Peeling out of my clothes, I took a moment to admire the faint bruising and suck marks peppered along my collarbone and over my breasts. Closing my eyes, I finally let my thoughts run rampant. *Do you like that… you taste so good…fuck, you're gorgeous…I'm going to come…right there…oh, God…don't stop.* I opened my eyes, shuddered and let out a long breath. Christ.

Though it was the last thing I felt like doing, I spent forty minutes running on the treadmill and another thirty doing Pilates in front of the television. After an NYC men's blog named me sixth most eligible bachelorette a few years back, I'd developed a weird sort of vanity.

It was like a subconscious part of me feared that this was as good as it would get and the moment I hit forty, everything would go to shit. The ego boost of being included on the list barely outweighed my annoyance at them not even performing a basic background check, because as far as I knew, my sexuality was no secret. I'd spoken about it in interviews and there were a number of photos on the net of me at events arm in arm with women. I knew this for certain because after therapy or a few glasses of Sav Blanc, I Googled myself.

Still sweating from my workout, I picked through a freezer full of nothing but Lean Cuisine boxes and pints of ice cream I saved for guilty pleasure television night. I checked messages, tossed a random meal in the microwave and trudged upstairs to shower. Moments after I stepped out of the glass cubicle, my cell started ringing on the kitchen counter. The unique tone announced Mama was calling. I raced downstairs and snatched it up. "Hello?"

"Is-a-belllle." My name lasted a full five seconds.

"Hi, Mama. How're you?"

"Why'd you take so long to answer?" Indignant.

"I was in the shower."

"Well, why didn't you just leave it then?" Incredulous.

I stifled a sigh. Telling her *because then you'd complain about me not answering* was not productive. "I was almost done and I thought it might be important. Plus I haven't talked to you in a couple of days. What's up?"

Mama's tone softened. "Just checking in with you, Bunny. You eatin' right?"

"Yes, Mama. I stopped for sushi and salad on the way home." Behind me, the microwave dinged loudly. I cringed, waiting for her shrill admonishment.

Mama did not disappoint. "Isabelle Renee Rhodes! I heard that awful machine. You lyin' to me aside, microwave meals are *not* an acceptable way to nourish your body. And those things are never heated long enough, they're just dyin' to make you sick."

I popped the door of the microwave to stop it beeping again. "Sure they are. What do you call reheated leftovers?" I didn't have the heart to tell her that I sometimes ate a handful of pistachios and drank a glass of wine for dinner because I couldn't even be bothered heating a precooked meal.

"Lord knows why you do not just hire yourself a personal chef. They don't care if your schedule's all over the place. Do I need to come up there?"

A personal chef was a whole new level of elite that I had no aspiration to achieve. "Of course not. I'm sorry, I shouldn't have fibbed. I've had a busy day, Mama. I'm hungry and Steph left a couple of those meals in the freezer." Liar, liar. "You needn't worry about me, I've got restaurant bookings all weekend." Pants on fire.

"Mhmm and you think I'll believe you after what you just tried to pull over me?"

"Call the office in the mornin' and ask Clare if you don't believe me." My voice was pure innocence as I leaned over the marble countertop for my work cell, shivering as skin made contact with cool stone.

"I might just do that."

I sent a one-sentence email. *If my mama calls, I have 2 dinner bookings this weekend.* Clare would know exactly what I meant when she saw it and wrangle Mama appropriately. "Was there anything you wanted, Mama? I'm naked in my kitchen and my dinner is getting cold."

"Well, nuke it again in that danged contraption then," she said drily. "Only phoned to see how you were doin'."

I smiled. "I'm just fine."

"Okay, I hear you. Go on before you catch a cold. I love you, Bunny."

"Love you too. Talk soon."

I dropped my phone back on the counter and stared at my dinner. It looked okay, but could you see bacteria? I'd put it in for the same amount of time I always did, it'd be fine. I poked the surface. Hot, but I did not have time to be attacked by *E. coli*. To be sure, I sent it round for another bacteria-killing minute.

CHAPTER FOUR

The next morning I was up and in the office by six thirty, having only thought about Audrey Graham four times while being driven in. Not bad. Certainly down from the seven times while I was showering and getting ready. I had a problem.

Technically, the office didn't open until seven thirty but I loved being in before everyone else, and made it my daily routine. There was something about the absolute silence that appealed, being able to work with nobody around needing me. The lights were already on, and the coffee machine humming quietly, thanks to building staff who slipped in like magic elves before me each morning. I gave the machine a loving pat. It perhaps worked harder than anyone else at Rhodes and Hall.

The offshore markets had shifted downward quite a bit overnight. I jotted notes and had my day planned by the time I'd poured my second coffee and eaten breakfast at my desk. People started to come in around seven fifteen, and Mark barged into my office as I was cleaning my teeth in my bathroom. I spat toothpaste. "Morning."

"Trying to disguise your pussy breath, Belle?"

"Don't be gross." I eyed him in the mirror. His lighthearted joke annoyed me because no, I wasn't but I wished I was.

"You're calling Tom and seeing HR today, right?"

I nodded, wiped my mouth and pushed past him. "Fear not, friend. The piece of paper will protect me."

Mark followed me. "Stop being so flippant. What if you do it again?"

"Well, I haven't thought about that." All eleven of my earlier fantasies came rushing back to make a liar out of me. I tugged on slingbacks and my voice suddenly grew wistful. "But if it did, does it really matter? Don't I deserve to enjoy myself?"

He couldn't argue. "There're other options, Belle and besides, if she agrees then she's unprofessional too."

"No. Don't even start with that shit. You're getting ahead of everything, as usual. I slept with her once. Well, one night. We're not dating, we won't be dating. If anything happens it'd only be sex." Hot, erotic and extremely satisfying sex. I couldn't help smiling at the memory.

His cheeks puffed for a moment before he let the air out in a noisy sigh. "All I'm saying is be careful. Not just with that poor sensitive heart of yours, but for all we've built here."

Hypocrite. It was all right when he'd done it. I pushed my irritation aside and dismissed him with a wave. "If you're done acting like a broken record, I have work to do."

My morning was spent on the phone trying to put out the usual forest fires. The moment markets moved down, people panicked. I was tempted to make a recording of myself and leave it playing on loop. *Ladies and gentlemen, everything is fine, your money is fine, we're all fine.*

Christopher arrived after lunch with the two gowns I'd chosen, and boxes of shoes on a cart that he wheeled into my office. He kissed my cheek, handed me a gown and shooed me into my bathroom to change, muttering at my dishevelment. I studied myself while climbing into the dress. He was right.

It took me ten seconds to realize this was not to be the gown, and it took my stylist even less time. He held up his hand, shielding his eyes as though the very sight of me caused him physical pain. "Ugh, take it off and put the other one on."

I swapped dresses and came back out to an approving nod. "Better. Pop your feet into these."

Christopher steadied me as I slipped into a pair of Manolos, then offered his hand to help me climb up onto the low box to be pinned. He ran a tape measure over my body, checking nothing had changed since last time he'd fitted me. It hadn't. The lining of the dress was silky, almost sensual. It felt the same as Audrey's hair sliding over my skin as she pressed wet kisses to my stomach. Focus, Isabelle.

My reflection in the mirror confirmed I looked great in this gown, that is if I ignored my hair and the tiredness seeping from behind my makeup. I ran a forefinger under my eye. "I've looked over your suggestions for the benefit. I'm loving options six and fourteen."

"Excellent choices." Christopher pinned something in back. "I've got you in on the eighth for a fitting."

Mark passed by the open door, smirked and kept going. I glared after him, not that it did me any good because he was long gone. Christopher tsk'd me. "Frowning gives you wrinkles."

"It's easy for him to be such an asshole. He just has to rotate through suits and tuxedos."

"But he doesn't look anywhere near as stunning as you do, darling." Christopher moved around to the front, checking the neckline. "Speaking of tuxedos…the ARF fundraising dinner is next month."

I grimaced, thought of wrinkles and let my face relax. "Ehhh, I'm not sure."

His eyebrow moved fractionally. He must have been due for a Botox top up. "Sweetie, it works for Angelina."

"Angelina has about four inches on me."

"Doesn't matter. You've got all those lovely curves just begging for a fitted jacket." He dropped his hands to my hips and sighed happily. "You're such a study in perfect proportions they should teach you in math class. Though you're right, another few inches wouldn't hurt."

I never thought I'd be so pleased by a compliment comparing me to something mathematical. "I bet that's not the first time you've said that," I shot back, twisting slightly to examine myself in the mirror.

"Very amusing, my love."

I gave him a self-satisfied smile. "Thank you."

"You know, Isabelle, I have to say it. Aside from this general…" He indicated my face and hair with a forefinger. "Hobo hair and no sleep thing you've got going on, you're surprisingly radiant. Have you found some little secret you're not sharing with me?"

"Perhaps."

He stared some more, then burst into a brilliant smile. "Noooo. You got laid," he trilled.

"Shh!" I glanced around nervously. The last thing I needed was for my staff to hear.

Christopher brought his hands together and looked to the ceiling. "Oh thank you, mystery sex woman." He grabbed my forearms. "You know I'm only saying this as your friend but honestly, since Steph left you've been acting a little, well, deprived. Whoever she was, you need to hit it again, and quick."

I ignored his jibe. "It's complicated."

"Darling, assembling Ikea furniture is complicated. Making cronuts is complicated." He lifted a finger to shush me and I would have been annoyed if it wasn't one of my most used gestures. "Sex is not. Make it uncomplicated, Isabelle." Lecture complete, he unzipped the dress. "Okay. I'm done."

I twisted around. "Not too much cleavage. It's a charity event, not a hook up."

"Yes, yes," he said distractedly.

"I mean it."

Christopher stood outside the bathroom door to take custody of the dress the moment I'd shimmied out of it, and by the time I'd redressed his cart was packed. "I'll have this dropped at your place tomorrow morning, along with the latest wardrobe additions, and I'll see you on the eighth." He kissed my cheek and imparted one final gem on me. "Remember, sex is the fountain of youth, my sweet. And you're not getting any younger."

Thanks.

Halfway along the hall on my way to the kitchen, I met Clare. She held out a fresh coffee and we performed a swap, full mug for empty mug. The woman needed a pay rise. Every day, I wondered how I'd managed to do anything before she became my assistant. Attentive but never obsequious or overbearing, she had it down to a fine art. I performed an about-face back toward my office. "Thank you. Did those settlement papers come through?"

"Yes, Ms. Rhodes, I've got them right here." She passed over a manila folder.

"No problems?"

"None."

"Great." I set the mug on my desk and grabbed my tablet. "I sent you my speech. Have you had a chance to look over it?"

"I did. It looks good but if I may, I'd suggest changing line twenty-three 'life stability, job and home security and external support networks' to something punchier. Make it a catchphrase." She twinkled fingers near her temple, standard brainstorming gesture for her. "Something like, uh…stability, support and security?"

I tried the phrasing out, mumbling, "With your generous donations, WHSF is able to provide these women much needed stability, support and security." Hmm. "You're right. Can you make the change and print for me, please. But make the order security, stability, support."

Clare smiled, apparently pleased that I'd taken her suggestion. "Will do."

I slid the stylus over the tablet screen. "Debbie hasn't called about the share offer?" It was a pointless question. If she'd called I'd have spoken to her or had a message to return. But I was feeling out of sorts because of Audrey-sex-on-legs-Graham and Mark's pushiness about the whole thing. Early on in my therapy career, I learned that when I felt out of control, I got picky and a little overbearing. Okay, fine. A lot overbearing.

My assistant held her tablet against her chest. "No, Ms. Rhodes. Would you like me to call her?"

"Not yet. We have two days until it closes." I tapped my stylus against the screen but the tablet remained asleep. Frustration bubbling over, I tapped harder. Get a grip, Isabelle. Stop acting like a child, throwing a tantrum because you want something and can't have it.

But why wasn't I allowed? Audrey wouldn't be promoted by sleeping with me, and I'd checked that generous pay increases were already written into her contract. If we scrawled our names on a HR document we could be having satisfying, soul-shattering sex by the end of the week. I was making a big leap by assuming she wanted to. But judging by the way she looked at me yesterday when I'd spoken to her on the tarmac, she wanted to.

Clare leaned over cautiously and pressed the side of the tablet. It blinked to wakefulness. She looked at me a moment, probably taking in my unruly hair, glasses over tired eyes instead of my usual contacts, two-inch heels instead of three or four and my nitpicky demeanor. "Ms. Rhodes, shall I book you a massage?"

I sank into my chair. "Please. As soon as possible."

I heaved a heavy sigh and called our lawyer. Briskly, I laid out what had happened, skimming over the intimate details. Tom seemed unconcerned—though it did take a lot to rattle him—and reminded me that should the opportunity arise for another dalliance, it would be prudent to have Audrey sign that dreaded declaration.

Adding a contractual agreement to my personal life was such an appalling thought that I decided, perhaps out of sheer petulance, that I wasn't going to pursue anything with her. Arriving at a firm decision usually made me feel relieved but this time, I couldn't shake the niggling feeling that I'd made the wrong choice.

* * *

My weekend adhered strictly to Einstein's Theory of Relativity. Every minute felt like an hour because of my desperation for it to be Monday. Audrey Day. The day of just looking, no touching. Burying myself in work on Saturday morning didn't help and by the time my dress was delivered that afternoon, along with my regular Christopher-approved hair and makeup team, I was about ready to explode with frustration.

I was made-up, hair straightened and styled, glued and zipped into my dress then shoved into a car where I ran over my speech again.

Mark met me at the venue, dressed in one of his damned easy tuxedos. Before we posed out front for photos, I had to straighten his bowtie. Inside, I fell right into more photos and endless networking. I delivered my speech to a mercifully attentive audience and rousing round of applause. I drank a little too much, tried not to be outwardly obnoxious and mostly succeeded. Mark had a keen sense of when Inappropriate Isabelle was about to appear and would deftly steer me away from whomever I was on the verge of inadvertently insulting.

I couldn't help myself. Pompous and pretentious, the majority of people at these events only came to get their picture in society pages rather than opening their wallets. Infuriating. It wasn't like they couldn't give and I intended to remind them of the fact. One of the best ways to push donations was to guilt people. To accomplish that, I had to suck up and I had to brag. I hated sucking up and I hated bragging.

I plucked another champagne flute from a passing tray, staring at a group of three men nearby. Real estate money, lottery money, inheritance of great-aunt's fortune money. Easy. I tended to avoid pushing old money into donations because I could always sense their disdain. Old money usually didn't take kindly to new money like me bossing them around.

A quick check that all my assets were in order, tongue run over my teeth and I was ready. Mark grasped my arm. "Don't."

"Don't what?" I responded, adding a touch of innocence.

"You know what I'm talking about, Belle. I see it in your eyes. They gleam when you're about to devour someone." Despite his lecture, he was smiling. He enjoyed watching me eviscerate.

"They deserve it. Are you coming?"

Mark sipped his scotch, ice chiming against the glass. "I'm good here, thanks. I'll watch. Please behave."

"Suit yourself. Maybe you'll learn something." No mention of behaving, or not.

Real Estate Money Philip was someone I knew reasonably well. There was my in. I waited for a lull in conversation then carefully inserted myself next to him. He turned and placed a soft hand on my shoulder. "Isabelle. Brilliant speech."

Smiling broadly, I touched his arm. "Thank you, I'm pleased you liked it. I'm very sorry to interrupt, gentlemen. Philip, will you introduce me to your friends?"

As he introduced me to Lottery Money and Great-Aunt's Inheritance, he kept his arm around my waist, high enough that I wasn't particularly bothered by its location. We made standard small talk, laughing and flirting gently before I decided I'd had enough and it was time to dig in.

Over the years, I'd learned this situation worked best when I relaxed my usual rule and reconnected with my southern roots. In all my years attending fundraising events, I'd found it was a rare man who could resist cleavage, flattery and a honeyed drawl. Shallow and underhanded, yes but there were causes that relied on me to do what I had to in order to get funding for them.

I turned my charm up to an eight point five. "Now tell me, gentlemen. Have y'all written a check to help these women out yet?"

Their exchanged looks told me they hadn't. Philip chuckled. "Hmm. Well things are a little tight at the moment. Sales are down and as you know, the market's been a little slow."

Or you're just greedy. "Really? I could have sworn I saw you arrive in a new Maserati GranTurismo." I tugged his tuxedo sleeve. "Come now, Philip. Ladies love a generous man." I hoped ladies loved generous ladies too. "I've already donated one hundred thousand dollars, so there's your benchmark."

He laughed, not seeming at all embarrassed at being caught out. "Isabelle. You don't miss a thing. All right then. Come on, boys. Let's go give these deserving ladies some money."

I giggled and hated myself for it. "Thank you, gentlemen. We sure do appreciate your support."

When they'd moved out of earshot, I gulped champagne. Something touched my back, startling me.

"Isabelle?"

Fuuuuck. I turned in the direction of the voice, arranging my face into a smile. The fakest of all fake smiles. I leaned in and exchanged double-ugh-cheek kisses with Wendy Hayward, Steph's best friend. "Wendy. How are you? It's lovely to see you." It wasn't lovely. It was nauseating.

She looked me up and down, light blue eyes cold and appraising. "You're looking well," she said, voice smooth and still with the trace of an affected British accent.

I know. "Thank you. And you. I adore that dress." I gestured with my champagne glass. "Very flattering."

A muscle in her cheek flickered. "That was a wonderful speech. I was quite moved."

"I'm pleased you enjoyed it." Already tired of the conversation, I swept my eyes around the room before coming back to her. "I assume you were *moved* enough to donate."

Wendy smiled tightly. "Not yet."

I raised both eyebrows, exaggerating my surprise. "No? Well, be sure to write out a check before you leave. I'm sure you can spare twenty grand or so." I ran my forefinger under my nose and sniffed to emphasize my point. Wendy had a small cocaine problem.

Cold blue eyes got colder. "I'm surprised you haven't asked me how Stephanie is." Nice subject change, very smoothly done.

"Well, I haven't asked because I don't really care," I responded airily. The universe kindly sent Steph to Europe in the days following the breakup so I wouldn't have to see her at these functions week after week. I hoped it was permanent.

Wendy couldn't hide her sneer. "You know, I'm not surprised. I always wondered what she saw in you." Though she didn't say it, the *because you're an uncouth middle class nobody* was clear on her face. Wendy always thought I was trash because I hadn't been born into money.

It was on the tip of my tongue to tell her how good I was in bed. I tilted my head. "Wendy. Please, don't bother trying to understand. Stick to what you're good at. Drugs and oral sex in hotel bathrooms." Leaning closer, I reminded her, "You do remember how I helped you out with that little misunderstanding you had, don't you?"

She would have hated to still be in my debt, not that I'd ever collect. At Steph's request, I'd interceded, calling in a favor from Christopher's boyfriend who knew the journalist that caught Wendy in the bathroom doing blow and giving a blowie.

For a moment I thought she might strike me. Instead she looked down at my perfectly pedicured feet. "Great shoes. They almost bring you up to a regular woman's level."

Bitch. God, I hated her voice. Why hadn't I ever realized how nasal it was? I smiled sweetly. "Enjoy the rest of your evening, Wendy. Do remember your donation."

CHAPTER FIVE

Sunday was spent sulking and working. The working was typical. The sulking was not. I slept fitfully and on Monday woke looking like one hundred and fifteen...okay, fine, one hundred and seventeen pounds of shit. Of course I did, because I was going to Dallas. Being flown there by Audrey. Thank you, Murphy and fuck your stupid law.

I cold-compressed my face while simultaneously having a session with the magic bullet, hoping to relax. Perhaps a bad idea, because all it did was highlight the fact that the battery-operated thing supplying my orgasm was not Audrey Graham.

I arrived at the airport early and tried desperately to calm my nervous flutter before boarding. It was like being fifteen all over again. No, it was worse because now I knew all the implications and possibilities. I thought about passing her a note: *Casual Mutual Orgasms? Y/N? If Y, please indicate when you will be available. Like now?*

Georgia pounced as I came through the door, taking my jacket and inquiring about my weekend. I responded, added a question of my own to be polite and turned to the open cockpit. "Good morning, Captain Graham."

She was cool and professional, but it didn't stop her eyes roaming as she greeted me. "Good morning, Ms. Rhodes."

I dragged my last ounce of professionalism from the depths of my brain—where it was trying desperately to stay afloat in a sea of dirty thoughts—nodded and walked to my seat. I could do this. I could be near her. I could do my job, let her do hers and we'd all be fine.

My resolve crumbled about thirty minutes after takeoff when Georgia asked if anyone wanted coffee. Audrey responded, a little too loudly, that she'd like some with sugar because she was in the mood for something sweet this morning. She turned around and stared at me, those full lips formed into a seductive smile.

The flight was perhaps one of the most uncomfortable experiences of my life, and I wondered idly if every flight from now on was going to be me with my thighs jammed together, trying not to think about what I knew was hidden under her captain's uniform.

We landed at Dallas Executive Airport just before nine a.m. and I fled from the plane like my ass was on fire, throwing a hurried thank you toward the cockpit then rushing down the stairs. If I'd lingered, if I'd looked at her, if she'd given me one indication, then I would have been lost. I turned to stare out the window as we drove off, craning my neck to catch a glimpse of her. I saw nothing.

My client took me to lunch and I endured hours of mind-numbing conversation, unfunny jokes and mediocre wine that I barely touched. A long time ago, Mama instilled in me the art of feigning interest, and I'd fine-tuned my social skills to a point where I could rise to the top of most situations. In this case, Mama's insistence on manners meant I ended up walking away with another three mil to play with and an increase in my commission. Not bad, but I was still out of sorts for the rest of the day. I kept my earphones in and the music loud for the midafternoon flight back to New York and threw my thanks at Captain Graham as I half-sprinted from the jet.

Back in the office, I stared aimlessly out the window at the evening sky and tried to figure out what was wrong. Everyone but Mark and me had left for the day and the peaceful atmosphere should have been soothing. But it felt lonely. I came to the conclusion that my problem was that I was unhappy with my decision to stay away from her. All day, every time I thought I'd pushed Audrey aside, she climbed back up into my consciousness. I was electrified by her, electrified by thinking about our night together.

My stomach curled. Dammit. At this rate, I'd be spending my increased commission on batteries for the Rabbit.

Mark poked his head through my doorway. "Come downstairs for a drink?"

It was on the tip of my tongue to tell him I didn't feel like socializing, but something in his expression stopped me. He seemed almost contrite and a little sad. Both things were strange. I nodded. "Sure. Meet you down there in five." I batted down unruly hair, checked makeup and left the office for the bar on the ground floor of our building.

I spotted Mark at the end of the bar, and after picking my way around staring men in suits, I climbed up onto a stool to the drink he'd ordered for me. "Thanks."

Mark spun his beer glass on the bar. "So…how's things?" he asked after a few revolutions.

Arching an eyebrow, I responded, "Fine." I plucked the cucumber garnish from the rim of my glass and popped it into my mouth. "Why'd you ask?"

"You seem tired and kind of not like yourself." Mark gulped half his beer.

Gee, thanks. Why not just say *you look like shit, Isabelle*? "Well, I'm always tired, Mark." I ignored his allusion to being out of sorts. Discussing why would turn into another back and forth about Audrey, and I wasn't in the mood. I wished we were still just two friends talking about a hook up.

His thumb traced a zigzag path through the condensation on his glass. "I just wanted to make sure you're all right. We've got some…big things coming up."

I frowned. "Nothing more than usual." Dipping my head, I tried to catch his eye. This whole thing was strange. Though we were very good friends, Mark and I didn't check in with each other's emotional well-being every few days. Unless it was something big, we tended to just float around each other.

A handful of pieces clicked into place and I had a sudden thought. "Are *you* all right?" Over the past few months he'd been uncharacteristically moody and erratic. Until this odd not-quite-meeting I'd put the change down to nothing more than stress, knowing full well that I could be the same when I was overwhelmed with work. Now I wondered if he wasn't trying to tell me something. My heart tripped. "Are you sick?"

His head snapped up, smile already fixed in place. "Of course not, Belle. I'm fine." Mark glanced at his watch. "Shit. I'm meeting someone in fifteen minutes, I'd better head off." He stood and poured the rest of his beer down his throat.

"Okay." I didn't even bother to hide my surprise. Usually *let's get a drink* lasted for more than five minutes and a brief confusing conversation. This whole thing seemed like a complete waste of time. Mark bent to kiss my cheek and then weaved through the bar toward the exit.

I watched him push out the door, then ordered another Hendrick's with cucumber. Something felt wrong. I sipped and pondered until halfway through my drink a familiar scent came to me, followed by a familiar voice. "I'm starting to think you have a thing for drinking gin in bars, Ms. Rhodes."

I took a steadying breath before turning toward her. "I didn't expect to see you here." Great non sequitur. Engage your brain, Isabelle.

Audrey set her wine on the bar next to my glass. "I'm here with friends who work nearby." She dragged her stool closer, so close that I could feel her body heat when she sat down. "How was the rest of your day?"

I paused. "Productive. Yours?"

"Uneventful but possibly looking more productive now." She held my gaze for a moment before her eyes dropped to my lips.

Staring at her, I found things I hadn't noticed before. Deeply etched lines fanned out from dark eyes, marks of a woman who laughed and smiled a lot. It made me think of my own laugh lines, their progress halted these past few years by stress, Steph and sleep deprivation. Audrey had a small ring piercing the helix of her left ear, something I didn't recall seeing during work hours. My eyes were drawn to her hands cradling her wine. Clear polish from a recent manicure. Long fingers, made for reaching places regular-sized fingers couldn't.

"Why would it be more productive now?" I uncrossed and recrossed my legs, trying to ignore the pulsing. This really was ridiculous. I'd never been so affected by a woman, but everything she said and did dripped innuendo. Not to mention the way she looked. Smelled. Tasted. I couldn't be imagining the way she spoke, or that she seemed to have no shame about openly ogling me.

She flashed me a self-assured smile. "Because you're here, Ms. Rhodes."

I winced. "Please, don't call me that. Not here. It's not necessary."

"What should I call you then, away from work when we're like this, or doing something else?" She tilted her head, studying me.

Heat rushed through my stomach as I thought about exactly what she meant by *something else*. My breathing hitched when I whispered, "My name." It was almost laughable to try and hold onto any pretense of professionalism.

"Your name," she mused. "Isabelle…Isabelle." The way she said it felt like she was testing the way it rolled from her tongue. "Such a pretty name. I'd like to use it more often, if you'd allow me."

I shifted my gaze from her lips to her eyes. "How, exactly?"

A slow smile spread across her face. Audrey lowered her voice fractionally. "In conversation, over dinner, screaming it as you lick me."

If I wasn't sitting on a stool, I would have melted to the floor. Audrey placed her hand on my wrist. "Why don't you finish that drink and come back to my place. Or we can go to yours." The woman oozed confidence and sensuality, every word had me on edge.

Despite all I felt, I couldn't stop thinking about complications. Consequences. That damned piece of paper we'd have to sign. I spun my glass between my fingers. "I really shouldn't."

She grinned. "I do a lot of things I shouldn't, Isabelle." Her teeth found her lower lip. "I'm willing to bet you do too."

"Sometimes," I admitted, closing my eyes briefly. "But still, I don't think it's a good idea."

"You and I have different opinions on what constitutes a good idea."

I shook my head. "I need time to think. I'm…unsure about what I want." It wasn't exactly true. I knew what I wanted, but I needed a strategy.

"I'm not. I want you," she said simply. "And from the way you're acting, I think you want me too." She swallowed the last of her wine, stood up then leaned down and kissed my cheek. "Enjoy the rest of your evening, Isabelle. I'll see you soon."

She left me sitting there with two body parts pounding and only one able to be tamed.

* * *

Seeing her on the flight to Chicago later that week was incredibly awkward. It was all my doing, because I tried not to act like all I could hear in my head when I looked at her was the way she'd told me *I want you*. During our brief conversations I was flustered, a new experience for me—she was cool and very suggestive.

By the weekend, I'd slid slightly more to the "what's the harm?" end of the scale. The feeling amplified until I was about ready to crumble and text her for a hook up. Somehow, I managed to hold onto the tiniest sliver of self-control. Only just. My phone was unlocked and my hand in my purse, fumbling for her card, when I realized the implication of what I was about to do. HR nightmare. Gossip. Angry business partner. I set my phone down. My willpower could have been bottled and sold to people all over the world about to make bad decisions.

I slipped Audrey's card back into my purse and wondered what it was that she really wanted. She was the kind of woman who could find a bedmate anywhere, so why me? Sure, we'd connected on some basic, sexual level but aside from that, what was there? Pessimistic Isabelle crept in and I went from near manic desperation to fuck her, to certainty that she didn't really want me for *me*. Of course she couldn't really want me. She didn't even know me.

For days, I wavered between wants and needs, and stupid self-defeating notions. By midweek, I was almost certain I could move past my desire and leave her to find her climaxes elsewhere while I did the same. I had plenty of toys and now that I was no longer a one-night stand virgin I could surely have a few more. Fuck her. No, not *fuck her*, fuck her.

I may have been more convinced by my decision if it weren't for her smile when I boarded the jet on Wednesday. Or the tiny inflection she put into her greeting, low and sensuous. The small innuendo she injected into seemingly innocuous comments about our flight plan. She made my skin tingle. My stomach tighten. My heart race.

Why couldn't I let her go? The sex had been great, but was I weighing it more heavily because it had broken a one hundred and twenty-two-day drought? I raced through my memories of that night like a kid sprinting past a house they thought haunted. I was scared that if I lingered on her body on top of me, hard nipples in my mouth and her busy tongue, then I'd break. It was great sex. I wasn't imagining it and of course I should want more. A lot more. Any sane person would.

It was just me again for a trip to Lexington and I was grateful for the chance to be a basket case without Mark in my face. Especially now that he'd apparently picked up on the fact that something was off. I stuffed my earphones in, turned up Daft Punk and tried to work while Audrey was overseeing refueling.

Georgia hovered, apparently anxious that I didn't actually need anything from her. "Very sorry, Ms. Rhodes," she said. "It seems there was an issue with one of the fuel trucks and they're a little behind."

"It's fine, Georgia. Honest."

During the fifteen-minute delay I'd composed one email, and was taking details from printouts on the table in front of me while drawing lines through obsolete stocks. I clamped the pen between my teeth, ignored Mama's voice in my head telling me to "get that pen outta your mouth 'fore you chip your teeth!" and started another email.

I startled when Audrey stepped back into the cabin. Our eyes met as she walked toward me instead of to the cockpit. I slowly reached up to pause my music and tug one of the headphones from my ear. She stopped and leaned down to purr into my ear. "Ms. Rhodes, may I caution you against putting writing implements in your mouth once we're in the air? Just in case we start bouncing around. I wouldn't want you to damage your mouth." Her gaze strayed to my lips.

Before I could respond, she straightened and moved toward the front. My eyes followed her ass. Her. Followed her. Georgia stood near the cockpit, hands clasped loosely in front of herself. "Is everything in order, Captain Graham?"

"Everything's fine, thank you. Can you secure the door please?" Audrey stepped into the cockpit and pulled the curtain closed.

I bent forward, opened my mouth and dropped the pen into my hand. Bouncing around. The same way I'd bounced as I rode her, skin slick with sweat, our breasts pressed together, her mouth on my neck, fingers…

Fuck. I stared at the closed curtain, all too aware of the heat on my neck. She was doing it deliberately, and despite how inappropriate the innuendo was, I couldn't be annoyed. Because I wanted it.

CHAPTER SIX

As we taxied into the hangar at Teterboro after my day of meetings, my main driver, Penny called. I'd barely managed a greeting before she rushed to explain that the car had mechanical problems and the other company car was currently on its way to Stamford, dropping Mark off for a personal matter. AKA, a booty call. It'd be at least two and a half hours until it could make a turn around to come fetch me.

"Ms. Rhodes, I'm so sorry. The Triple-A truck is just loading it up now, but there are no auto shops open at this time of night. I'm close to the airport, and once it's on its way, I'll take a cab and come get you." Penny and I had a relationship that resembled protective aunt and niece. I liked it. The effort she wanted to go to in order to escort me home was very sweet, and also amusing because I was perfectly capable of catching a taxi without assistance.

My heels tapped a sharp rhythm on the hangar floor. "Don't even worry about it, Pen. Can't be helped and I'm fine. I can catch a cab home myself." Quicker to do that than try to arrange another limo company at this time of night and such short notice.

"Are you sure, Ms. Rhodes?"

"Absolutely. You go home and see if you can catch the end of the game."

"Well…okay then. If you're really sure. You take care and I'll see you tomorrow."

"You too, good night." I continued through into the terminal building where I was assaulted by the smell of coffee. One wouldn't hurt. After a pit stop for takeaway caffeine, I made my way toward the door leading out to the cab rank.

"I hope that's decaf, Isabelle." Audrey Graham had stealthy appearances down to a fine art.

My head snapped up to where she was standing a few feet away, carrying a small backpack and staring expectantly at me. "Decaf? No. That goes against my moral code."

"Really? I suppose you're right. I seem to recall you have no trouble falling asleep."

Actually, I did lately and it had everything to do with the non-stop Audrey Graham sex show in my head. My tongue was stuck to the roof of my mouth so I settled for shaking my head. Audrey hiked the backpack up onto her shoulder. "Is everything all right? I would have expected you to be on your way home by now."

"Oh, yes. Just some car troubles. I'm going to catch a cab."

She frowned slightly. It was on the tip of my tongue to ask her to join me, but before I could she gestured toward the doors. "Can I walk you out?"

What would be the harm? It's not like anything could happen between here and just outside the doors. "Sure. I'd like that."

Audrey grasped the strap of my laptop bag, her fingers brushing mine. "Can I carry this for you?"

My hand stilled. "You can but, uh you don't need to. It's not necessary, I mean I can carry it myself."

She studied me, smiling again as though she was amused by my waffling. "I know. Bag carrying is definitely not included in my contractual duties. But I have a free hand, so why not?"

I weighed up pros and cons, and released the bag. "Thank you."

We walked together silently, stopping a little way outside the exit. Audrey stared down the street then back at me. "I'd offer you a ride home but I only have a motorcycle and one helmet, and you don't have any gear." She looked legitimately upset about it, and it was quite possibly one of the cutest things I'd seen.

"You have a bike?" Great question, Isabelle. She just said she did, but she didn't seem the type. I was beginning to look and sound really fucking dumb. It was like she sucked all my IQ points out of my ears whenever she looked at me. Or sent blood from my brain to other, greedier parts of my body. Parts that were picturing her on a motorcycle, her long legs gripping it. Leather-clad. Controlling the rumbling machine. I made a mental note to explore the fantasy at a later, more appropriate time.

"I do. A Triumph Speedmaster. How did you think I get to work? Or did you think I flew my plane to go fly your plane?" Her eyes creased with glee.

"You have a plane of your own?" Keep it up, Isabelle and someone is going to make a dumb blonde joke.

She nodded. "It's only a small light sport aircraft, and the bank still owns a third of it, but yes." Audrey fiddled with her backpack, seeming suddenly shy. "I just really like flying."

"Wow, that's so…" I searched for a word. "Interesting." I imagined someone standing beside me giving me a slow clap. Bravo. Great conversationalist.

"It can be." Audrey stood close enough to be considered impolite under normal circumstances, but right now it wasn't close enough. She turned to face me, mouth slightly open as though she was going to say more.

I looked up at her, grasping her arm gently. "Something wrong?" The muscle in her forearm flexed under my fingers.

"No. I forgot what I was going to say." She held my gaze for a moment, flicked hers down to my mouth then looked away.

The laugh I forced was weak, more of a strained chuckle. "I know what you mean." Consciously, I forced myself to let go of her forearm. Mark always says I'm a grabber, something I tried to suppress around Audrey but it was getting harder.

"I meant what I said the other night, Isabelle." Her eyebrows were jammed down, expression serious. "I don't care if it's only for one more night, once a week or every night until you've had enough. I want you and I'm not going to stop saying it until you tell me to stop."

I ran my tongue over my lower lip and moved fractionally closer. "I don't want you to stop."

Her eyes widened. "No? Good, becau—"

A taxi pulled up to the curb, effectively cutting off whatever delicious and potentially dangerous thing she was about to say. Nice fucking timing. Audrey stepped around me, opened the door and gestured for me to climb into the backseat. I ignored every instinct to throw myself at her and kiss her, and slid in.

Audrey passed me my laptop. "I'll see you later. Try to get some rest, in case you happen to engage in any unexpected bursts of activity over the weekend." She smirked, closed the door and walked off, leaving me to stare after her.

The cab driver sighed. "Miss?"

I startled. "Hmm? Pardon?"

"Where to?"

"Oh…uh…" That's right, you have to tell cab drivers where you want to go. I blinked and turned to face forward again. "Tribeca thank you."

I leaned back against the seat, letting out a long breath. It was painfully obvious that Audrey was baiting me, patiently waiting until I cracked. And crack I would, like a shitty set of gel nails from a two-dollar manicure place.

* * *

The next day I had an appointment with my therapist, Dr. Baker. She was dressed in what I'd come to think of as her uniform, a brightly-colored loose-flowing tunic paired with chunky jewelry—usually a memento from one of her many vacations. Her honey-blond hair was always up in a loose French twist, held in place with an elaborate clasp.

I'd always thought part of the reason I'd lasted so long with our sessions was that she was the perfect mixture of sweetheart and hardass. Dr. Baker had a way of fixing me with her large brown eyes that made me feel like I had no choice but to answer, and no matter what I said, it'd be okay.

As I always did on entering her office, I took a moment to glance around and see if anything was different. She had a habit of shifting her many plants and paintings around, almost as though she loathed spending her days in an unchanging space. To break up the beige walls she'd swapped the dwarf potted lemon with the ficus and added another painting, a cliff landscape.

Once I'd settled opposite her, she opened a fresh pad of paper and stared expectantly over the top of her glasses. I guess I looked like I had a lot to say. Poker face failure. The only thing I wanted to talk about was what happened with Audrey. And talk I did, for almost forty minutes, fidgeting with the weird statuette thing she had sitting on the side table.

Dr. Baker spoke cautiously like I was a horse about to spook. "Let me see if I've got this right. You had a one-night stand with an employee who you didn't know was your employee."

I twirled the ornament between my fingertips, staring at its garish colors. "Yes."

"And she's indicated that she'd like to continue a sexual relationship with you?"

"Mhmm."

"Okay. So, Isabelle, consent and legality aside, you're interested in what she's proposed but concerned?"

At times like this, I couldn't believe I paid her three hundred and fifty an hour for her to parrot what I said. I nodded and tried not to look incredulous. I probably failed. "Yes."

She scribbled. "Where do you think this vacillation comes from?"

Vacillation, good one. I'd have to add it to my list of buzzwords. "I'm not sure."

Dr. Baker raised an eyebrow. After seven years, the woman knew when to call my bluff. "Let's go with the negative thoughts about the situation."

I laughed drily. "Oh, they're the same as always. She could fuck anyone she wanted. What could she want from me aside from money, etcetera ad nauseum."

"But, you've said it yourself. You both seemed to enjoy the sex. Isn't it possible that really is all she wants?"

"Maybe."

"Then this *is* only about sex and not a romantic relationship. You made a mutual connection with her on that level before she knew anything about you. If there's nothing outside of sex, what's the problem?"

I set the statuette down. It really was ugly. "I don't want to have to sign HR paperwork just so I can see her."

Dr. Baker removed her glasses, spinning them around slowly by the arm. "The paperwork you mention is fairly standard in this situation? It's not something designed especially to inconvenience you, Isabelle. Using the relationship declaration document as an excuse feels like a pulling away strategy." Buzz phrase number two. "Forget about the waiver and let's think about the deeper issue here."

The deeper issue was that my whole life was full of paperwork and contracts. Why couldn't I just have something without this sort of shit getting in the way? I chewed the inside of my lower lip, thinking on what she'd said. She was right of course—I was being a baby. Shoving thoughts of the declaration aside, I focused on what really frightened me. If there was no relationship outside of sex, what was there to worry about? Rejection. Deception. Being used. The thought of any of those was unbearable, especially after what Steph had done.

After her father refused to back her latest likely-doomed-to-fail business, Steph turned to me for a loan. When I'd told her no, because it was not a sound investment, she just dumped then badmouthed me. Classy. I wondered what she'd have done if I'd told her what I really thought—I agreed with her father, and the string of commercial ventures in her wake, that she was terrible at running a company.

It wasn't that I was stingy, or hated spending money. It was the opposite. I enjoyed giving and did so frequently, and in large amounts. I'd backed a few small start-up ventures—people who actually knew what they were doing, unlike Steph. It was the thought of being seen as nothing more than an endless ATM I couldn't stand. Stop it, Isabelle. What can Audrey take from you?

My therapist held both hands up, stopping my runaway inner monologue. "All I'm saying is, while you've obviously thought this through, I think you're not giving both sides a fair stake in the argument."

"Maybe." I was a few steps away from petulant teenager.

"This is obviously causing you anguish, and that anguish needs to be addressed. You've got the control here, Isabelle. It's on you to keep the relationship in the zone where you want it. It's time to stop this self-sabotage." And there we had buzz phrase number three. She glanced at the clock. "Let's pick this up next week. In the meantime, I'd like you to think hard about the underlying feelings at play here."

Thanks, Doc.

Slouched in the backseat while Penny drove me home, I thought more about what my therapist had said. Pretty much the same thing she'd been saying for years. The only way I would be able to form a meaningful, long-lasting relationship would be if I let go, stopped making excuses and learned to trust. I was in control. People couldn't take unless I gave. Repeat until it sticks. She was right, and I was tired of being alone. It'd been a sparse decade of unsatisfying relationships. It was up to me.

I knew exactly what my problem was, because we'd discussed it at length many times. Apparently, the reason I had so many trust issues was because of my daddy. I hadn't seen or heard a peep from him in over thirty years. I fact, I barely remembered him. He'd decided that he just wasn't cut out for family life and skipped out on Mama and me. Not good enough for my daddy, so not good enough for anyone else. Sometimes I really hated my subconscious.

When I began to make a name for myself, I fantasized about him coming to find me. Reconnecting, having daddy-daughter days and all that shit. I mentioned it casually to Mark and he made an off-the-cuff and unintentionally hurtful remark about my father only finding me because he wanted to share in some of my money. The thought had stuck with me ever since and of course, warped into a misguided negative thought process about all my intimate relationships being based on a lie.

Once home, I indulged in my post-therapy routine. I opened a bottle of wine and typed my name into a search engine. Really, it wasn't narcissistic. I just wanted to know if anyone was saying anything mean about me. My reasoning was that I'd already been emotionally eviscerated at therapy so why not get everything out of the way at once?

Dressed in threadbare gray sweats, a baggy Wonder Woman tee and Ugg boots, I lounged on the couch. A few months back, I'd been asked if I would do an interview, one of those annoying "Glamour businesswomen relaxing at home" things where the accompanying spread shows a perfectly clean house, and someone fully made up and dressed up posing in their kitchen.

I'd laughed and politely declined, telling the journalist exactly what I changed into the moment I got home. He'd tried to charm me until I dragged out Bitch Isabelle to tell him I had no intention of turning my safe haven into a bullshit image to sell his magazine.

There were pictures from the gala Saturday night up on a few sites. Some of me talking with patrons, laughing and looking like I was enjoying myself. One of me midspeech, gesturing emphatically and another of Mark and me side by side. If nothing else, we made an attractive faux-couple. Him tall, light brown hair and swampy hazel eyes. Me, not tall and very blond and blue-eyed. I swear it was natural blond. Well... ninety percent. Okay fine. Eighty percent.

I read the captions. *Isabelle Rhodes, patron of WHSF, gave an impassioned speech about the importance of...* I scrolled *...wearing a stunning...business partner, Mark Hall...*

As I stared at the pictures, I found myself inserting Audrey in Mark's place. She was darker than him, both hair and eyes. Obviously far more attractive. We would photograph nicely together. I topped up my glass and started reading the comments, mentally correcting spelling, grammar and text speak.

Whos this woman. Hows some money manager relevent?
Great speech tho saw it on you tube.
Hot AF!!!!
Thought she was a dyke. Who's the guy?!
Bitch can afford to donate! U kno what that dress costs? Hey, I need a new car U kno.

Unimpressive, except for the 'Hot as fuck' comment. I backtracked and opened another site, this one a gossip column. I searched and scrolled and tried to ferret myself out but there was nothing juicy. Relieved, I tossed the tablet onto the couch, tucked my feet up and finished the glass of wine.

CHAPTER SEVEN

Friday after work, I was on a mission. A *Say Yes to Audrey* mission. I was tired of trying to keep myself from thinking about her, from wondering about all the what-ifs. Most of all, I kept thinking about what my therapist said about being spiteful to myself by using the waiver as an excuse. The decision had been cemented that morning as I lay in bed, after a self-induced orgasm with my arousal still coating my fingers. I needed to get laid. Regularly. Preferably by Audrey.

Before I made the call, I ran to try and work off some nervous energy and masturbated in the shower to work off some sexual energy. The tee I put on after showering was one of my favorites, like a friend who never tired of seeing me. Steph hated this shirt. Maybe it was the holes. Maybe she hated the Dandy Warhols. Maybe she just hated me. I never found out and realized with relief that I was long past caring.

But I needed some advice before I called Audrey. Mark was out of the question so, slumped onto the couch with a cup of tea, I called my best friend from college. We'd roomed together at Cornell and stayed in touch as much as we could with ridiculously busy lives.

When Nat answered, she sounded out of breath. "Rhodes! To what do I owe this pleasure?"

"Did I interrupt something…or someone?" I teased.

"Ha! I wish. Jill's still at work. I'm out for a run."

"Damn your west coast weather."

She huffed. "You know I hate California."

True. Nat was from Alaska and one of the few people I knew who lived for bleak, snowy weather and genuinely hated summer. We spent a couple of minutes catching up, Nat grumbling about how much of a shit her boss was, before I launched into the main reason for my call. "Need your advice with something."

"Well it can't be business advice, I saw R and H's increase in last quarter's earnings. Also saw your name up on the NYC women's list again."

"Yeah, business is great." I sipped my tea. "It's about a woman."

"Oh? Do tell." Her breathing had steadied and I could imagine her strolling back to her Bay Area Queen Anne.

In a couple of long breaths, I recounted the whole story for her—from the circumstances of meeting Audrey, the mindboggling sex, all the way through to Mark's reactions and now my confusion. Nat whistled through her teeth. "Well, Rhodes. You never did do anything halfway."

I groaned. "I know."

"This could just be because I've got a wedding looming and I'm feeling like I want to be frivolous while I can, but I say fucking go for it. Call her. Dates, sex, whatever. There's nothing wrong with some casual entertainment."

"Yeah…I guess you're right." I set my mug down. "Speaking of weddings, how're the plans going?"

"Surprisingly well. Jill's very calm about it all. I keep telling her to just give me my suit, show me where to stand and what to say, and I'll be there with bells on."

"You delicious butch, you."

"Hey! I'm giving my opinions when asked, but seriously who cares if we have white or cream tablecloths?" Nat laughed. "You *are* coming right? Invites go out next month. March eleventh."

My throat tightened. "Wouldn't miss it for anything, babe."

"Good. Remember, it'll be plus one so if you want to bring this pilot…"

"Didn't you hear anything I just said, Nat? Casual."

"I did. But keep it in mind." I could picture her teasing grin.

"Just me," I said firmly.

"Okay then, Rhodes. Whatever you say."

After we'd said our goodbyes and promised to talk soon, I wandered out onto my balcony with my tea, turning Audrey's card over. It was time to face up to what I wanted, and what I wanted was for her to beg me to let her come. There was nothing wrong with that.

As the phone rang I felt a sudden nervousness I hadn't felt in quite some time. Before I could place my finger on exactly what it was, she answered, "This is Audrey."

"Audrey? It's Isabelle…Rhodes." My voice had always been a little high-pitched but when I uttered that sentence I sounded like a child.

There was surprise in her voice. "Ms. Rhodes, Isabelle. What a pleasure." Then concern. "Is everything all right?"

"Oh yes, everything's fine. I was just sitting here, uh, cleaning my purse and your card fell out."

She made a low, throaty musing sound. "Is that so? And my card picked up your phone and dialed the number on it all of its own accord?"

Busted. "Perhaps. You sound busy." She didn't, but I needed to buy some time to think. Get it together, Isabelle. "Is this a bad time?"

"Not at all. How may I help you?"

I pushed the words out in one long exhale. "I was wondering if you'd like to have dinner. I'm free all weekend, which is unusual." Stop over-explaining. My eyes were scrunched tightly closed as I tried to ward off my awkwardness. It'd been a while since I chased someone for a date. A date. No, it wouldn't be a date but calling to ask for only sex seemed rude.

"Dinner?"

"Yes. With me," I clarified. "I figure we've already done the drinks and sex part. It might be nice to backtrack a step."

She laughed. "I would like that, very much. How about I cook for you at my place? Does tomorrow night suit you?"

Her place. Intimate, easy access to a bed. I tried for nonchalant and got squeaky. "Sure, that would be nice."

"Great. You're not allergic to anything, or one of those weird paleo-vegan-organic food only kind of people?"

"No. I'll eat pretty much anything. Except egg yolk. Because it's gross, not because I've got something against eggs."

"Egg yolk. Well there goes my plan of runny boiled eggs and toast."

"You could always scramble them. I can choke scrambled down." I was surprised at how easy it was to banter with her.

"Expect scrambled eggs and toast then. If you're lucky, I'll spring for bacon." She gave me an address in Crown Heights, told me she'd see me at six the next evening and hung up.

This was either going to be magnificent, or a complete and utter disaster.

* * *

I spent Saturday agonizing over what to wear. What to say. What to take. I settled on wine, no flowers. At least I knew she drank white. Fuck, what if what she was making didn't go with white? Take a white and a red then. What if rosé was a better choice? Shut up, Isabelle.

I had no idea what we were going to talk about, though if everything went as I wanted it, most of what we said would be asking for hands and lips to be placed on body parts. For twenty minutes, I sorted through underwear sets. I needed something that said *You're undressing me, this is unexpected, but I came prepared just in case.* Something that implied I wasn't totally desperate. Eventually, I settled for Victoria's Secret instead of La Perla. A nice red set with a little lace. Nothing overly fancy but a long way away from period underwear and bras for around the house.

Audrey's apartment was a thirty-minute ride from my place. Thirty fidgeting minutes. Penny interceded after twenty. "Is everything all right, Ms. Rhodes?"

"Yes, I'm fine thanks, Penny," I said automatically. After a beat, I blew out a breath. "Actually, I'm not. I'm really nervous."

"About anything in particular?" Another reason I loved Penny—her question was phrased in such a way that I could either answer, or be evasive without feeling rude.

"First date," I explained.

"Ah, well I'm sure everything will be fine. You can call me at any time and I'll come back for you." Her kind eyes found mine in the rear view mirror. "Now do you have the exact address for me?" I found it on my phone and when I recited it for her, I thought I caught a flash of surprise in her eyes. When I looked again, it was gone.

Penny escorted me to the door of Audrey's building and waited a polite distance away for me to be buzzed in. Before leaving, she checked the door had locked behind me. Bless her. As I rode the elevator up to the seventh floor, I fiddled with the bottles of wine.

A waft of something delicious and spicy hit me when Audrey opened the door of apartment seven zero five. In faded jeans slung low on her hips and a tight baby-blue tee she looked relaxed and sexy all at once. Once I'd completed my up and down inspection—twice—I practically shoved the bottles at her with a spiel about how I didn't know what we were having and clarifying we didn't have to drink them tonight. Audrey laughed, kissed my cheek and ushered me inside.

Her apartment was small, clean and tastefully decorated with warm inviting furniture, and the kitchen was full of modern appliances. We rushed through formalities and I had a glass of wine in my hand within a few minutes. I drank a soothing gulp and looked around again. "Great place. How long have you lived here?"

"Just under two years. I love Brooklyn, and I was very disappointed I couldn't find anything in Dyker Heights," she deadpanned.

I grinned at her joke, one I'd heard before. "It reminds me of my first place in New York. I lived with Mark and it was even smaller than this." I was over-talking again, trying to compensate for those damned nerves. Maybe it was excitement. Anticipation. I pointed to Audrey's worn faux-suede two-seater. "Actually I think we had a couch just like that."

She spared the couch a quick glance. "Yeah? Did you toss it out on the corner of Franklin and Lincoln when you moved? If so, it might be yours."

I exhaled. "I'm sorry. I'm just—"

"Dribbling words?" She grinned. "I get it. It's kind of what you do. I like it. It's super cute."

I relaxed some. "I know, I'm sorry. I'm so used to talking all day that sometimes I find it hard to stop." I gestured to the framed photographs on the walls, trying to shift the conversation to something more socially appropriate. "May I?"

"Absolutely."

She stood just behind as I walked around absorbing the images. Most of them were of her and some sort of aircraft. Leaning out a cockpit window, grinning as she stood next to a tail or wing. I deduced she had a brother.

On the wall near the kitchen was a large hand-drawn chart with numbered boxes and a small paper plane stuck on a box in the middle of it. When I raised a questioning eyebrow, she seemed embarrassed as she explained, "That's my countdown. Weeks until I fully own my plane."

"How many?"

"Sixty-three," she said immediately.

I smiled and turned back to her portraits. There were a few of Audrey and an older woman, the resemblance so strong that it could only be her mother. I turned around. She was so close I almost bumped her. I lingered on her lips a moment before catching her eye. "And that's—"

"My mom."

"She's stunning." Of course my implication was that Audrey had inherited her mother's looks.

"I'll tell her you said that." Her smile told me she intended to do so. "Dinner's ready whenever you are. I made Thai."

"Sounds wonderful, one of my favorites."

"I know."

My eyebrows jammed down so hard my eyes complained about the intrusion. She held up both hands in a conciliatory gesture. "I'm sorry, I wasn't sure what you liked so I did a search."

Instantly, I felt the back of my neck tighten. "Oh. You could have asked me."

"You're right, I'm sorry. I just didn't want to bother you. I guess I thought if you showed up and I'd made something you liked, you'd be more comfortable." She looked so earnest that I believed her.

Inhale. Exhale. "True. What else did you find out about me?"

"Nothing important." She waved casually. "Just a whole bunch of pages and blogs listing you as a philanthropist, animal rights activist, spokesperson for women's refuges and supporter of multiple charities."

"Mmm." The twist in my gut was a familiar one, the feeling of being known by what people read rather than what they learned by being with me.

"You're a monster, I do not know how you live with yourself." The corner of her mouth was twitching like it wanted desperately to smile. "Not to mention your place on that Hottest One Hundred blog."

"You saw that too?" Though I managed not to groan, I knew my dismay was clear.

"I did. Nice article, by the way, and some great photos. Very hot." Her eyes roamed freely over my body. "I'm going to have to talk to someone about your spot on that list. You should have been number one."

I brushed past her compliment, trying to ignore the thudding of my anxious heart. "So, I guess there's nothing left for me to tell you if you found all that online." I couldn't stop the bitterness creeping into my tone. It was unfair, there were no laws against Google searches but I'd kind of hoped for her to learn things about me the way a normal person would. With conversation.

Audrey tilted her head. "I wouldn't say that, Isabelle. There're a lot of things I want to know about you, and they're all things I'd like for you to tell me yourself." She tucked her hands into her pockets. "You're upset. I'm sorry. I saw the pages and I got a little carried away."

An apology. I swallowed a little of my fear. "It's all right."

"Kinda fell down an Isabelle Rhodes rabbit hole when I saw all those photos of you looking gorgeous." Her gaze was so sincere it was almost burning. "Forgive me?"

I nodded, aware of a sudden pricking behind my eyes. Nobody had ever apologized for making assumptions about me before. "Of course."

She took my hands, thumbs brushing over the backs, leaving a warm tingle. "I know this is weird, Isabelle. I'm not even sure what we're doing. I mean, we don't have to talk. We don't have to have dinner or anything. We can just fuck, if that's what you want."

I bit my lip gently, considering. "I'd like all of it. The dinner, the talking and particularly the fucking." It was an honest answer. I realized I enjoyed being near her, clothed as well as naked.

"Me too. I just thought it'd be nice to be able to have a conversation. You know, you could ask me how my day was. I could tell you it was fine, and explain how I spent the day flying a gorgeous woman around. Then you can look shocked and tell me how that's a huge coincidence because you spent the day being flown around by a gorgeous woman." She made no attempt to hide her grin.

Her sweetness was contagious. I smiled. "Do you always make everything into a joke?"

"Most things, but not everything." The grin was still there. I wondered if it ever went away. Like Georgia, Audrey seemed eternally cheerful but also with an undercurrent of amusement, like her life was just *good*.

I closed the gap between us, stood on the balls of my feet and pulled her closer. Audrey's grin faded when I kissed her lightly, tracing my tongue over her lower lip. Her hands were on the small of my back, steady and sure. I dropped back down. "Let's eat."

* * *

The woman could cook. After a delicious dinner, great conversation and more drinks, we took one of my bottles and settled on the couch. Audrey poured overlarge glasses and tucked long legs underneath herself. "Can I ask you something else?"

"Yes of course."

"Why is it Rhodes and Hall, not Hall and Rhodes? Mr. Hall seems to do most of the upfront stuff."

"Ladies come first. Haven't you heard?" I took a lazy sip of wine, pleasantly buzzed and very aware of her proximity. And the way her hand was running over my thigh.

"I have heard that. In fact, it caused me quite a bit of confusion in my baby lesbian days."

She was so dry, I couldn't help but laugh. "It's because I put up the money for us to start the company from part of my Grams' inheritance, so my name comes first." I took another sip of wine, holding it in my mouth a moment before I swallowed. "You're right though. Mark handles most of the business side of things. My only real talent is talking people into giving me more money and then multiplying it." A whole lot.

In the past ten years I'd worked hard to turn a small initial pool into an extremely comfortable fortune for myself too. Nationwide, my net worth barely rated, but it was substantial and I had far more than I'd ever need. I could help those who needed it.

"You're selling yourself short. I have it on good authority that you have a number of talents." The purr in her voice left no doubt as to which talents she meant.

My nipples tingled. How was it that she could do so much to me with just a look? I was done restraining myself. I reached out to run my knuckles gently over her cheek. She didn't move away, so emboldened, I closed the gap between us and kissed her. Audrey responded eagerly, reaching to grab my waist and hold me in place. Her lips left mine to find my neck, my collarbone, my ear. "It's taken you long enough, Isabelle."

"I know." After denying myself for so many weeks, it was all I could do to not give in completely and tear off my clothing that second. My hands itched to rediscover all the spots they'd found last time, but still I couldn't let myself go. Not yet. I pulled away, breathless and looked at her, my eyebrows lifted to their peak. "God, Audrey. What are we doing?"

"Right now? We're in stage one of making out. Next comes stage two which is hands everywhere and then if I'm lucky we'll skip stage three and go straight to the orgasms."

I smiled but wouldn't be deferred. "No, not right now. Us. I mean, you work for me."

She nodded. "Yes I do. Your observational skills are beyond compare."

"I'm not looking for anything beyond casual," I said seriously.

"I'm not offering anything aside from that," she countered.

I took a steadying breath. "Why me then?"

"Why not you? You're stunning, I like what you do, and I'm pretty sure you like what I do, if the noises you made that night were any indication." She tugged me onto her lap, hitching my leg over so I was straddling her. Her dark eyes smoldered, burning through me. "I've barely thought of anything else, Isabelle. I've never...pursued anyone so single-mindedly, especially not my boss."

"Me either," I admitted.

She brushed her nose along my neck. "When I saw you walking toward the jet the morning after, I was so excited I could barely sit still. When you left my hotel room that morning, you've got no idea how disappointed I was at the thought of never seeing you again. Never touching you again. And then there you were."

When she rocked me forward, I inhaled sharply. "Audrey, you know you're under no obligation to sleep with me, right? I mean, I want to make it clear. You don't have to do any of this, not the kissing or having dinner or the talking. Don't get me wrong, I'm glad you are, glad we are, but..." I trailed off as she began to unfasten my jeans.

"When you put it like that, it's so sexy. Do you always have to put conditions on great sex?"

"It's not a condition. You know what I mean." I let her pull me even closer, stifling a gasp.

"Yes I do. Do you want me to sign something? A waiver saying I'm willingly mixing business with pleasure?" Her tongue flashed along her lower lip. "Because I am *all* about pleasure."

Understatement. "Mmm." We could arrange it later. When I could think about more than how she kept pressing her hipbone against places that desperately needed the contact.

"I will if it'll set your mind at ease. If it means I can keep doing this." Her hand slipped inside my panties. "Because I want you. Because I can't stop thinking about how you taste and the sound you make when you come. Not because I'm worried that you'll fire me if I don't."

I gasped as a finger slid over my clit and began to make lazy circles. Idiotically, I still felt the need to clarify. I wrapped an arm around the back of her neck. "Technically Mark would fire you."

"You're so wet," she murmured, putting an end to our conversation about logistics.

I moved closer for a heated kiss. "Don't stop."

"I won't." She slid a finger into my depths, and not at all gently. The forcefulness of her entry sent my arousal into orbit and I could do nothing but make incoherent noises, squirming under her touch.

Audrey smirked. "Isabelle, I don't know much about the finance industry, but I've heard the secret is knowing when to get in." She slipped a second finger into my wet heat, causing me to buck under the pressure. "And when to get out."

I reached down to clamp my hand around her wrist, holding her inside me. "Don't you dare pull out," I panted.

"I won't," she repeated. Fingers curled to press against my sweet spot and I was lost all over again.

CHAPTER EIGHT

Early Sunday morning, she fell asleep after orgasm three and I snuck out and called for a car. Between orgasms one and two, we agreed that *keeping it casual* meant sleeping over was too personal, too involved. Between orgasms two and three we decided three or four nights a week was a good start. A healthy amount of time to spend together.

William, the driver who picked me up, seemed unsure about how to take my appearance and general languor. I couldn't blame him. I was totally and thoroughly fucked—in the best way of course—and I looked it. When I wished him good morning, William ducked his head, cheeks reddening and rushed his reply. He'd only been my driver for a few months, taking Penny's off shifts, and was evidently still nervous despite my giving him no reason to be. Polite to employees, remember? He reminded me of Frankenstein—tall and bulky, stiff posture but seemingly sweet and harmless.

Back home, I rushed directly to my office, logged onto our work servers and found the document I wanted. Sighing,

I printed it. "This isn't an inconvenience, Isabelle. It's a smart thing to do. It's necessary. You will not self-sabotage, because you have to treat yourself better than that. And you're talking aloud to yourself. You need to go to sleep." I scrawled my name and stuck some *sign here* flags on the paper then left it on my desk. Upstairs, I fell asleep on top of my covers, still dressed and with my contacts in.

I woke an indeterminate time later to my phone sounding a text alert.

Audrey Graham. *Brunch?*

I replied with nothing but my address and rolled out of bed with the intention of showering and attempting to tame my sex hair. Until I made the mistake of checking on some accounts. I was still standing over the kitchen counter with my tablet, unshowered, sex hair intact when one of the building security guys, Carl called up to tell me a Ms. Graham was here and could he send her up?

Ms. Graham waved off my apologies when I rushed across my foyer and unlocked my front door. "Sorry, I meant to tell them to let you come right up." On tiptoes with a hand on her shoulder, I kissed her cheek.

"It's fine. Though it was a little weird to have someone assist me with taking an elevator."

I grinned. "All part of the service, ma'am. I'll let them know you're to be let up without calling from now on." The door closed behind us, locking itself again with a soft click.

She nodded, biting her lower lip on a smile. With a barely perceptible turn of her head, she glanced around like she was trying not to be too obvious. My house style was to have no style, which according to my stylist was a style. How stylish of me.

I loved my floor to ceiling glass windows, distressed reclaimed hardwood floors and mezzanine sleeping area. The space was a mismatch of retro furniture pieces I'd found in my weekends trawling garage sales or antique stores. My walls were full of art and photographs, and I'm the first to admit that the general vibe of my penthouse was clean but disorganized. I knew where everything was, and that was…just sitting everywhere.

My cleaning lady had learned long ago to dust around the piles of books on the bedside table and floor beside my bed. She ignored plastic wrapped dry cleaning that had stopped to rest over the back of my couches, or the *couch-robes* as Mama called them. Laundry I left in the dryer was folded then piled neatly on my bed, where it usually stayed for a few days until I got around to putting it away. Only my office was spotless, everything orderly and always set in its rightful place.

I made a vague gesture. "Feel free to look around, or I can give you the tour. It's fairly standard. My sleeping area is up top." I pointed toward the glass paneling that bordered the top level. "Down here are guest rooms, kitchen, great room, atrium, office etcetera."

"You have the whole top floor of the building?"

I opened a section of the door leading out to my balcony. "Mhmm. Just under five thousand squares. Four downstairs and one up. And then almost two thousand for the balcony. Kind of wasted for just me," I admitted.

She pointed to the covered hot tub overlooking the Hudson. "Do you use that much?"

"Only when I have company."

Audrey flashed me a knowing smirk and leaned her forearms on the railing. "Wow. Nice view."

I shrugged and plucked a dead leaf off one of my plants. "It's okay. I'd rather the ocean."

"You're too hard to please."

I laughed. "Actually, it's more that I'm rarely home at a time to just sit out here and enjoy it. At least with the ocean I'd get the great smell." She didn't move when I stood beside her, close enough that I could smell lotion and the clean scent of her shampoo. I'd pick those over ocean any day. "If you remember, I'm actually quite easy to please."

Audrey pushed her sunglasses up to rest atop her head. "I do remember that."

Dangerously close to restarting something we'd finished only hours earlier, I took a step backward. "Give me a few minutes? I kind of passed out when I got home and haven't even showered. Can I get you a drink?"

"Sure, and no thanks. I'm good."

I leaned over, kissed her cheek and left her on the balcony while I went to take a quick shower, brush my teeth and change. My contacts were well past feeling like a handful of glass in my eyes, so I took them out and slipped my glasses on.

Audrey had moved to the kitchen in my absence and she pounced as soon as I came back. "You wear glasses?"

"Is that a problem? Do you only sleep with women who have perfect vision? Because I can get Lasik, you know," I teased.

"Not at all. It's incredibly hot, like a very sexy secretary."

"Don't get too used to it. I hate them but I'm so tired that I don't think I could keep my contacts in, even if I used a tube of KY."

"Do you even have KY? You are the moistest woman I know."

"Really? That word?" I wrinkled my nose. "It was a figure of speech."

"Dampest? Most lubricious?" She stepped closer, hands seeking places they'd left only hours before. "Wet. Hot."

I groaned. "You're going to put the brakes on going out for brunch if you keep talking like that."

Her lips met my neck, hands slid to cup my ass. "I think I need to check the situation so I can come up with the perfect adjective."

A low purr built at the back of my throat. "A fine idea." I reached up to take my glasses off but Audrey stopped me.

"No. Leave them on. In a few moments, I'm going to need to think of an adjective for myself…" She leaned in to kiss me, but I froze as soon as her lips touched mine. Audrey straightened. "Something wrong?"

Suddenly that document in my office was the only thing I could think about. My mouth worked open and closed until I managed to find the words. "I have to ask you to do something, and it makes me feel really awkward." Last night she'd said she would sign such a thing but when faced with uncomfortable reality, people often changed their minds.

Her left eyebrow rose. "I'm up for almost anything if you are. I love a little bit of... experimentation."

Good to know. "It's not a sex thing. But we can talk about *that* later. Wait here a minute?" I slipped out of her embrace and went to retrieve the Declaration of Conjugal Relationship that I'd printed before falling asleep. The two pages felt as heavy as bricks.

Wordlessly, I slid it across the kitchen counter to her. Audrey glanced at it, eyes moving back and forth over the title before she picked up the pen. I stood back, stomach fluttering, as she gave the document a cursory read and applied her signature where indicated.

I stared at her name on the page. "You barely even read it."

The pen bounced then rolled off the edge of the counter. Audrey bent to retrieve it. "I don't need to." She was quiet, serious. "I told you last night I'd sign a waiver or whatever if you needed it for HR. I'm not letting a piece of paperwork stop us from enjoying each other, Isabelle."

"You should have read it," I said, deliberately monotone as I slipped around to her side.

"Why?"

I bit my lip. "Then you would have seen the clause I added about minimum orgasm quotas for the week."

"Oh? And what happens if I'm in breach of contract?"

I looped my arms around her neck and kissed the corner of her mouth. "It's my discretion but I'm thinking a little spanking to keep you in line." My voice dropped an octave.

"You know when you tell me that, it guarantees I'll do what I can to break the rules."

I gently pressed my finger to the crease in her chin. "I'm counting on it."

She swallowed visibly. "Well then. Before that necessary interruption, I believe we were discussing lubrication."

Instead of going out, we had each other for brunch, hot and frantic on my couch. Eventually, we ordered in for a late lunch and she left midafternoon after five minutes of shoving me against the wall beside my elevator. The goodbye was a thorough exploration of my mouth, like she'd forgotten how I tasted in the two minutes since she'd kissed me.

Leaning against the wall after she left, I tried to recover. It took me a couple of minutes to calm my fluttering heart and redirect my blood flow from my clitoris to my brain. Despite the number of times I'd come in the past eighteen hours, I still wanted more.

I worked for the rest of the afternoon, fell asleep on the couch around seven and woke up early the next morning to see her again, albeit this time at work. Spending most of the weekend with her hadn't eased my desire. It had ignited it. Solidified my decision. I needed her body like I needed oxygen.

Just before ten on Monday morning, I climbed into the jet and greeted my pilot. Not by a flicker of emotion or words did she betray that less than twenty-four hours earlier, she was screaming my name as she came in my mouth.

Flying to Phoenix, I alternated between working and texting her. When we landed, she would open her phone to a barrage of my text messages, each one dirtier than the last. After my meetings were done, I looked at my phone and saw she'd reciprocated. Five long texts, detailing everything she wanted to do to me, and what she wanted in return. Graphic details. I skimmed over the words again, excitement building. I felt like beetles were skittering across my skin.

...bend you over, slip my fingers inside...ride my face, with my tongue buried deep...tasting you...make you scream my name...bite my nipples...your fingers on my clit...

Fuck. My reply was a simple *My place ASAP*. Audrey gave me a knowing look as I walked past the cockpit and arrived minutes after I got home. For hours we made each other scream in pleasure, doing everything we'd promised in our messages. And then some. She snuck out after I fell asleep, leaving me to wake up alone.

We settled into a routine. We went to one another's house and fucked, then snuck out to go back to our own place. We screwed on couches, the kitchen floor, in beds, in the hot tub, on the stairs and my balcony. She had me in the shower, on her kitchen table and the floor just inside her door because we couldn't make it any further.

The second week after we'd agreed to our casual sexual thing, she asked me one night if I wanted her to bring dinner around. It was late, I'd hardly eaten all day, I agreed. She arrived with sushi. We adjusted the routine. She cooked at either of our houses, or we'd arrive with takeout. Then we fucked.

We got to really know one another. I learned how long to finger her for before going down on her for maximum explosive effect. She discovered quickly that when I'm shitty about work I like it rough, to be flipped over and entered from behind with teeth hard in my skin, but when I'm tired I like it gentle and sweet. I became attuned to the sound she makes at the exact moment before she starts to come. She realized just how much I loved to be picked up and held against a wall, and the exact pressure to use on my nipples to drive me toward an earth-shattering climax. Together we tested each other's toys.

I learned to compartmentalize, figuring out how to talk to her when she was working without feeling like I might slip up and give us away. As the days went by, I became less frightened of Mark finding out. He seemed oblivious, apparently satisfied that his speech had had the intended effect and I'd moved my attentions elsewhere. Not quite, buddy. Nowhere near it.

Donna in HR had nodded her understanding when I'd delivered the signed waiver weeks ago and asked her not to inform Mark of its existence. He didn't need to know every intimate detail of my life. More than that, I didn't want him to treat Audrey differently simply because we were casual bedmates.

The word *casual* was starting to feel a whole lot less appealing.

* * *

Saturday morning, Audrey left my place sometime between one and five without me noticing. Though I couldn't pin down exactly why, I felt strangely off-balance when Penny arrived to take me grocery shopping before lunch. Whenever I needed to go to the store, she always insisted on accompanying me and would liaise with me and adjust her finishing time accordingly. I'd learned via the company grapevine that she'd basically forbidden any of the other drivers to take me.

Wandering through the aisles of Whole Foods together, I imagined we looked fairly odd. Me in faded weekend jeans and worn Lacoste sneakers, hair unbrushed and pulled back messily, glasses on. Her in suit and tie pushing my cart around, insisting on lifting anything heavier than two pounds. People always stared, probably trying to figure which celebrity I was, out with my tall female bodyguard.

Pen was ex-Army and looked it too. I sure as shit wouldn't mess with her. She was imposing but underneath her usually sternly-set features and stiff bearing, she was kind and sweet and fiercely loyal. Though her job was only to drive me, I was sure if need be, she'd take someone out for me. And no doubt love every moment.

We talked about missing football season, our shared love, and Penny stacked bottles of wine and gin into the cart. She smiled knowingly when I asked her to grab two different cases of beer as well. Audrey sometimes liked beer.

I picked out vegetables, choosing only the best and dropping them into the sacks Pen held. "Got plans for the rest of the weekend?" After she'd dropped me off, Pen would be done with her shift, passing the baton to William.

Her smile was broad. "It's our thirtieth anniversary."

I brushed my fingers over her bicep. "Oh geez, I'm sorry. I didn't know." I felt awful that she was working. "Congratulations, Pen. I'm really happy for you."

She mentioned her partner, Loretta, on the odd occasion but was mostly reserved about her private life. I almost asked if she had any plans for marriage, but stopped myself. That was a little too personal. I fished in my purse for my phone and made a note to mark the date for next year so she wouldn't have to work. "What are you doing?"

"I'm taking her to dinner and a show." She seemed obscenely pleased with herself.

"But the Yankees are playing!" If football was Penny's true love, baseball was her religion.

"I know. We'll record it." Penny smiled down at me. "Sometimes you have to compromise. That's part of what makes things work, Ms. Rhodes."

I leaned against the cart. "So that's the secret? Compromise."

Pen nodded slowly. "Yes indeed. Along with honesty and trust."

On the drive back to my place, I was quiet and Penny let me be. I couldn't stop thinking about what she'd said, though it felt silly to be comparing the advice of a woman celebrating thirty years of partnership to the casual thing Audrey and I had.

Penny took all my groceries up to my penthouse, using a dolly that was in the car for that very purpose. Once everything was in the kitchen, I said goodbye, asked her to give Loretta my best and started unpacking.

When Steph and I were together and she lived here, she cooked because she had time and liked to feel like a housewife. I guess years of having house staff waiting on you would make you yearn to just make a meal for yourself. When she left me, I made dinner maybe one night a month and existed on Lean Cuisine and takeout salad or sushi. The fridge dwindled to olives, pickles and four different kinds of mustard. Pantry stock was crackers and pistachios.

Since Audrey, my fridge and pantry had changed. I bought few frozen meals and more raw ingredients. I'd cooked once and she'd laughingly requested that I never do it again—my lack of culinary skills was a huge bugbear for Mama, but a teasing point for Audrey. Snacks Audrey liked sat with snacks I liked. Her choc chip cookie dough ice cream lived in the freezer with my salted caramel fudge swirl. Beer nestled alongside wine and champagne.

I could have moved the beer to the bar area in my den to live with gin and mixers but I liked seeing it when I opened my fridge. The reminder of her in my life. A few days ago, I'd noticed gin and bottles of tonic in *her* fridge. Cucumbers for garnish. I'd never told her that's what I liked, but she seemed to know. She always seemed to know.

After working at home for the rest of the day, I arrived at Audrey's place for our usual dinner-and-sex-night Saturday. She had a movie playing and casually asked if I minded if she kept it on. I didn't. We watched Netflix as we ate dinner, then we fell into bed. The routine was tweaked again. If we were home or in a hotel out of town, we'd eat dinner and watch a movie. Then we'd fuck.

Along the way, when I watched her scrawl notes for herself, I discovered she had atrocious handwriting. She learned how much I hated rom-coms and that I had a slightly age-inappropriate crush on Kristen Stewart.

And I got an inkling that maybe, just maybe, she wanted more from all of this when my period arrived perfectly on schedule—I'd always been diligent about being on time—a few weeks after our first movie night. She had been due to come over after work. I'd meant to send her a text during the day, let her know I was out of commission for a short while. Meant to but was so busy I forgot. There was no point in her coming over. Of course she wouldn't want to if there was no sex.

Half-asleep in the car being driven home, a text message landed. *Let me know when you're home.*

Ah shit. I tapped out an evasive response. *Sorry, was going to call. Need 5/6 days…*

Her response was almost immediate. *Oh. Gotcha.*

After a few minutes, another message came through. *I could bring dinner over? Watch a movie?*

We'd stopped outside my building, but I made no attempt to collect my things. I was stuck, staring at her message, trying to work it out. Come over, have dinner and watch a movie. No sex. My fingers tapped an irregular rhythm against the back of my phone case. Why would she want to come over without the prospect of getting laid?

The car door opened. "Ms. Rhodes?"

"Right. Sorry." I caught William's eye and smiled my apology for keeping him waiting.

He escorted me to the door. "Have a nice evening, Ms. Rhodes."

"Thanks. You too."

I waved to Carl as I stepped into the elevator—he knew by now that I didn't need an escort—and juggled bags so I could press the button for my penthouse. Just dinner and a movie. The sort of thing friends would do. Were we friends? I gave in and called her.

Audrey answered after the first ring. "Iz. Hi."

I couldn't deny the warmth that spread through my body at hearing her voice. "Hey, how are you?"

"Delightful. You?"

I stepped out of the elevator into my lobby, phone wedged between my ear and shoulder. "I'm fine. Uh, you really want to come over?"

"I do. *How to Train Your Dragon Two* is on Netflix and your TV is bigger than mine."

I smiled at her adorable childish enthusiasm. "I never saw the first one."

Audrey gasped. "Isabelle! I can't believe you said that. I've got it on DVD. I'll bring it over."

Two movies and dinner. No sex. I felt like I should be more bothered by it, by the breaking of rules. The thought of sitting on my couch and mindlessly watching television with someone, with her, pleased me more than I cared to admit. "Well, all right then."

"Great." Her voice grew deeper, more serious. "Just to clarify, it doesn't bother me, Iz. But I get it if you're feeling unwell and want to be alone."

What was she saying? She didn't mind that I had my period, and that sex would be okay, or she didn't mind being around me without the prospect of sex? I cleared my throat. "No, it's fine. It's good. I'd like you to come over. I just got in, so whenever you're ready."

"I'll be there in an hour."

She arrived sooner than that. The moment I was in reach, I was grabbed and hugged, takeout bags pressing against my back. Her kiss was gentle. "Hi," she said, still barely an inch away from me.

"Hi yourself." I tucked a loose strand of hair behind her ear and stepped aside to let her through into the kitchen.

We settled on my couch to eat and watch the TV. Halfway through the first film, I nudged her gently. "You're right. This is cute."

Audrey caught my eye and gave me a *told you so* look. We'd moved so I was sprawled against her, my legs stretched along the couch. Her arm was over mine, thumb rubbing over the fabric of my long sleeved tee. Back and forth constantly, rhythmically.

By the time we started the second movie, it was a little after ten. We'd shifted even more to lie on the couch. I was practically lying on her, my head against her breasts listening to her steady heartbeat until the credits started. I craned my neck. She was asleep.

I couldn't wake her to send her home at midnight. Staying on my couch wasn't against the rules, was it? I made an executive decision, something I was good at, and decided sleeping on couches was allowable under such circumstances.

Ninjas worldwide would have envied me as I slipped off her, and out from under her arm to fetch a blanket. Those same ninjas would have made me their queen when I covered her and bent down like a sappy idiot to brush my nose over her hair, and she didn't even stir. I closed my eyes and inhaled the scent of her shampoo then took one last look at her face, softened by sleep, and went to bed alone.

I couldn't fall asleep. I spent an hour lying awake thinking about her asleep on my couch. Fretting. I should have woken her up and moved her into the spare room. Or in my bed. Audrey was gone when I woke in the morning, a neatly folded blanket on the couch the only mark of her presence.

* * *

It was Wednesday when we next saw each other, exchanging short polite work sentences and nothing more when she flew me to Syracuse and back again. Wednesday was enforced night apart. Awful. Thursday I had a fundraiser and she had painting class. Friday dinner with clients. Saturday morning catching up on work. I drifted through my engagements until it was Saturday night and I was at her apartment.

We attacked each other with a ferocity borne of forced abstinence. Begging harder, faster, deeper and more, always more. On her couch, at her table, in her bed. Limp and satisfied, I closed my eyes to gather my thoughts and woke well after dawn, confused. Audrey was spooning me, an arm under my neck to cup my breast and the other wrapped tightly around my waist. Legs tangled, breath on my neck. It felt like the first time I'd awoken in her arms, also accidental. It felt like a different lifetime. I trudged through memories. A month ago? I tightened up my calculation. Thirty-nine days ago.

Arms came snugly around me. "Morning."

I rubbed my eyes and my mouth. No doubt I'd drooled. "Sorry, big week," I apologized in a sleep-hoarse voice. "I didn't mean to fall asleep."

She released me to stretch, her limbs quivering. "Don't worry about it, Iz."

So I didn't.

The next change to the routine happened organically, with no words exchanged. We started bringing clothes in overnight bags. Toothbrushes and some clothes were left behind. Spare contacts and solution sat in her bathroom cabinet. I gave her a pass so she could use my garage space in the building for her vintage-looking motorcycle, and told security she could be let up even if I wasn't there. The night driver told the morning shift if they needed to fetch me from Audrey's apartment instead of my penthouse.

We talked, we ate, we laughed, we fucked and we slept intertwined. But Audrey Graham and I were not dating.

CHAPTER NINE

About a week after menstrual movie night, I sat home waiting for Audrey to arrive. An hour or so before she was due, I received a text. *Sorry, still out with friends, won't make it over tonight. Tomorrow?*

Disappointment stung before I could clamp down on my feelings. I tapped out a quick reply. *I have that interview and photo thing, not sure when I'll be done. Friday?*

Sounds great.

Have fun.

It was okay to say that, right? I could express an interest in her enjoyment of activities unrelated to me? After a moment, I realized my phone was clenched tight in my fist. I released it and dialed Nat.

My friend picked up where we'd left off last week. "So you're still seeing her?"

"Yeah." I cringed, waiting for a smart-assed response.

"Seven weeks, Rhodes. She must be a fucking great lay."

"She is." I flung my arm over my eyes. "Nat...there've been sleepovers."

"Sounds like it's moving into more than that casual you've been ramming down my throat every time we talk."

"Yeah," I said softly. "I like her a whole lot. She's smart, funny and so fucking sexy I get wet just looking at her."

"Why do I sense there's a *but* coming up?"

I smiled. "But, we agreed not to date. Just sex and enjoyment."

"But?" Nat prompted again.

"But, I think I just got upset about not seeing her tonight."

"Rhodes, I love you so much but you need to get some balls. I know you're scared of what might happen but if you don't throw your line in, you're never going to catch a fish."

"I know," I whispered.

"There's nothing wrong with being cautious. However, you need to start being honest or you're going to lose what you've got. Honey, I gotta go. Jill just got home, and she'll kill me if I don't help her bring groceries in. I'll try to call tomorrow and we can talk more."

"Give Jill my love."

"Will do."

I swapped my cell for my tablet. My week was ridiculous. Tomorrow in Toledo by myself then back for dinner with an old client. A client who'd left Rhodes and Hall but still insisted on inviting me to dinner parties. I always went, and made sure to drop in hints about how well my current clients' accounts were doing. Meetings all day Wednesday and Thursday. Phoenix again Friday with Mark. Saturday free, fundraiser planning lunch Sunday. I was tired just thinking about my schedule.

Now Audrey wasn't coming over, my evening looked bare and uninspiring. I ate a banana for dinner and passed time by making small changes to my personal portfolio and trying to plan a vacation. Though it was still over six months until February, when I usually spent two weeks somewhere tropical, it wouldn't hurt to start a shortlist. Beaches, booze and bikinis—both wearing and looking at other women in them—did wonders for my mental health. This year I'd vacationed in the Caribbean, next year was as yet undecided.

After hours of research, I narrowed it down to Song Saa in Cambodia or Bedarra on the Great Barrier Reef. Mark had been there a few years ago and said it was great. Translating *great* from typically understated Mark-speak meant it was fucking amazing. I emailed my travel agent and asked for details about each destination. For one person and also for two. Audrey might like a vacation too. Or Mama. Whatever.

I went to bed alone and woke every few hours. A slow kind of wakefulness, the sort where I couldn't figure out why. Okay, maybe it was because I was starting to get used to not being alone in my bed. Used to being tangled in her long limbs with soft, rhythmic breathing beside me. The smell of her when I'd roll over and burrow into her.

I was not all together when Penny picked me up just before seven. My eyes were heavy, stomach churning with that nauseous hardly-slept sensation. Maybe we talked about an upcoming Yankees game on the drive to the airport. I'm pretty sure I thought about the dinner I had to attend that night.

My feet were heavy on the jet's stairs. The greeting I gave Georgia felt a little forced, but under the circumstances, it was the best I could do. Audrey was already in the cockpit and aside from a polite hello before she turned back to do whatever it was she was doing, my interaction with her was zero. I couldn't help it—I felt put out. She's working, I told myself. She's working for you, trying to get you somewhere safely, not socializing.

Buckled into my seat, I waited for the announcement that we were ready to depart. My work cell rang with an unknown number. "Isabelle Rhodes."

"Ms. Rhodes? It's Richard." Auditor. Interesting.

"Richard, how are you?" I examined my manicure and made a mental note to ask for the same shade again.

"I'm well, thank you. And yourself?"

I hated back and forth greetings like this. I'm good, you're good, everyone's always good. I stared out the window at a small jet taking off. "I'm good. What can I do for you?"

"I'm sorry to bother you, but there's an anomaly with Mr. Hall's quarterly report and I can't reach him. I've been trying now for nearly a week. His phone keeps going to voice mail and he hasn't returned my messages. Your office says he's *unavailable*."

An anomaly. I unbuckled, stood up and moved toward the aircraft door. This conversation wasn't one I could have here, where I'd be overheard. "Richard, honestly I'm not sure what's happening or why he hasn't had returned your calls."

"Yes it's very odd, Ms. Rhodes."

From behind, I heard commotion and Audrey's voice calling, "Ms. Rhodes?"

I spared her a glance but continued down the stairs onto the tarmac. Ms. Rhodes, Ms. Rhodes. Ms. Fucking Rhodes. I kept walking away from the jet. "Richard, what kind of anomaly are you talking about?"

He paused. "I would prefer to discuss it with Mr. Hall first."

"If there's a problem, I need to know about it. What's going on?"

"All I need is for you to get Mark to contact me. It doesn't concern you." He was so condescending, he may as well have added *Little Girl* to the end of his statement.

I was not Mark's fucking PA, or one of our receptionists. Sucking in a breath, I tried desperately to keep my temper in check. I was about seventy percent successful. "Of course it concerns me! Mark and I are equal partn—"

"Ms. Rhodes, I cannot have this conversation with you. Have Mr. Hall return my calls." Then the bastard hung up on me.

A firecracker of rage exploded in my brain. Typical misogynistic bullshit. It was always there, lurking in the background of this testosterone-driven financial boys' club. It was all right for me to bring in more revenue for the business than Mark, but God forbid I should worry my pretty little head about something like an audit *anomaly*.

"Fuck!" I slashed my fist through the air. I did not need this right now.

"Ms. Rhodes," Audrey repeated behind me, voice calm.

"What!" I turned around, feeling the heat of anger on the tips of my ears and my neck. When faced with Potentially Explosive Isabelle, most people chose one of three options. Flee, climb up my ass with flattery, or approach me like I was rabid. Audrey chose none of those. Her posture was confident but not aggressive. I was suddenly struck by how she didn't look at all wary.

Instead, she looked amused, almost sympathetic. "It's not safe to be using your phone out here," she said.

I shook my head, lifted the phone again and asked it to, "Call Mark."

After two rings, he answered, "Yes, Belle?"

Turning away from Audrey, I lowered my voice. "It's me. Richard just called me. Firstly, what's this anomaly he mentioned and secondly, why are you avoidin' his calls?" I paused, grinding my teeth. "What the fuck is going on?"

"Oh, that," he said lightly. "Nothing to worry about. I screwed up the date range on my first report and must have sent that through instead of the correct one. I'm not avoiding him, I'm busy, Belle and getting around to calling him back."

I grunted, not at all mollified. "Well, get around to it soon. I don't appreciate being used as your fucking secretary." The volume of my voice rose with my temper. "If he wants to do that, he can damned well fill me in on what's going on because I'm just as important and entitled to information as you are."

"Nothing's going on," Mark said instantly. His voice was calm and even, and I believed him. But his explanation didn't take the edge off my anger at being treated like a silly girl who was just playing at being a stockbroker. He sighed. "And I'm sure Richard didn't mean anything by it."

The fact that Mark didn't understand how I felt made my temper peak again. "Of course. Silly me. Maybe I mistake the fact that he always addresses you and not me in meetings, yeah? It's clearly my imagination that despite the fact my accounts outperform yours, he thinks you're some sort of fucking stockbroking god."

"Belle…"

"I have to go," I spat out. "The jet's waiting." Surprisingly, the screen on my phone didn't break when I slammed my finger down to disconnect the call.

I pivoted back toward the jet. And Audrey. My anger had carried me beyond rationality and now I was faced with the prospect of trying to regain my composure in front of her. A woman who'd seen me laid bare physically, and now emotionally. A woman who certainly didn't deserve to be ignored and spoken to the way I feared I was about to. A woman about whose opinion I cared a great deal.

Audrey's shoulders lifted, her gaze on me. "I'm sorry, Ms. Rhodes but it really is dangerous to use your phone out here, particularly if we're refueling." She made a little exploding gesture, a small smile on her lips.

Most people would agree and then apologize. Not me. Not now. I held up my hands and looked around in mock confusion. "I don't see any fuel tankers." I hated this part of myself, the inability to just let go and turn my annoyance off. It was my most shameful trait, needing to hold onto the indignation until I'd wrung it dry. I couldn't even blame PMS. I couldn't blame anything but me.

Audrey said nothing. Just watched me, her face impassive. I raised my chin in a silent challenge. Here I am in all my pushy, nasty control freak glory, being rude to you because I can't stop myself. Come and get it. Do you still want me?

Audrey's response was a slow smile. A head tilt. In that moment, I felt she understood me better than anyone else. "Ms. Rhodes, if you'd like to board again, we're ready to depart when you are."

* * *

For the rest of the day, I hid behind my shame and lingering annoyance. After Audrey's calm handling of my outburst, I didn't get a chance to talk to her again. She'd responded to my apology text, assuring me everything was fine, but I wanted to talk to her. Needed to.

My dinner ran late, too late to visit her afterward. I went home to my empty bed and swallowed half an Ambien from an old bottle at the back of my medicine cabinet. Despite drugging myself, I kept waking worried and then worried about being worried. Why was it so important that she think well of me?

Somewhere around two and three a.m. I had a revelation. I cared about her and I cared about what she thought. *Caring was more than liking.* Fuck.

The deeper I delved into my realization the more I knew it was my own fault. Little by little she'd been sneaking up on me, breaking me down. I knew exactly what she was doing and I let it happen. More than letting it happen, I welcomed it.

In the beginning, I wondered what the harm was in giving and taking a little more. Meals, movies, sleeping over. They wouldn't hurt in the long run, right? As we spent more time together, I found myself looking at her differently and now that I knew why and how I felt, it scared the shit out of me.

All day Wednesday my body was one tight knot, so tense and tired I could barely concentrate. Mark was acting like nothing was wrong, and I assumed he'd taken care of his report to the auditor. I snapped at him when he tried to make a joke about how I needed to get laid again, coming within a microsecond of telling him I had been thank you very much.

After the office emptied, I ran downstairs and instructed William to take me to Audrey's apartment. Enforced night apart be damned. I had to see her.

My stomach felt like it was trying to crawl up my esophagus as I pressed the button for her apartment. I should have called. Maybe she'd gone out with friends. Or somewhere to pick up a nicer, less-prone-to-outbursts casual fuck buddy. William stood a few feet away, waiting to see that I'd been admitted and for a moment, I wished Penny were there. She'd be attempting to get me to relax, talking about the Yankees latest win or something equally as engaging.

Finally the intercom buzzed. "Hello?"

My mouth was so dry I could barely talk. "Audrey? It's me. Can I come up?"

"Iz? Absolutely."

The door clicked and I rushed to it, spurring William into action. He held it open for me, standing awkwardly like he was trying to avoid the bubble he'd deemed my personal space. "Is everything all right, Ms. Rhodes?" Eyebrows furrowed, eyes worried. I wondered what his expression would be if something bad actually happened.

"Yes, thanks for waiting."

He flushed. "It's my pleasure, Ms. Rhodes. I'll see you tomorrow."

I heard him tugging the building door to check the lock as I walked across the lobby. Both he and Penny did that now and the thought of their collective concern filled me with such deep comfort that I thought I might cry. I'd almost cried when flowers had arrived from a client that morning.

Coupled with losing my shit over the auditor's call, I'd concluded that obviously I was feeling a touch emotional. Maybe it *was* hormones. Note to self: tell the doctor about it at your next physical. Second note to self: book overdue physical. As the elevator climbed, I practiced what I wanted to say to Audrey. Sometimes I yell at people. I don't really mean it. I'm sorry. Please don't hate me.

As I stepped out of the elevator, she was already standing in her doorway. Cue instant nerves. She was clearly standing there so she could block me from coming in to her apartment. But why let me up instead of telling me to fuck off? Audrey grabbed my arm as soon as I was in range, bending to kiss the corner of my mouth softly. "Hey. Come in."

Her unexpected greeting made me pause a moment. I stepped into her apartment but made no move to remove my coat. "I'm sorry, I know we weren't going to see each other tonight."

"It's fine, Iz. How are you?"

"I'm good. You?"

"I'm good too. So that's good. Can I take your coat?"

"I wasn't planning on staying." Yet I'd let the driver go.

Both eyebrows rose. "No? Why's that?"

"I wasn't sure if you'd want me to," I said softly.

Her smile was uncertain. "Why wouldn't I want you to stay?" She held out her hand for my coat.

I hesitated a moment then slipped out of it and passed it to her. "Thanks."

She wasn't to be deflected. "Why would you think I wouldn't want you to stay?"

My heart raced like I'd just run a hundred meter sprint. "Because of yesterday. Audrey, I came here to apologize. For what I did, and said. I wish I could say it was just a bad day but truthfully, that's not really all there is to it."

"I see. Come sit down. Do you want a drink?"

Apparently I had no say in what I wanted, my body made decisions for itself. My feet took themselves to her couch and my mouth said yes to her offer of a drink. After she handed me a glass of white I had to apologize again. It sounded even more pathetic, made worse by her gentle patting of my knee.

Audrey shrugged as if she couldn't care less, but still managed to make me feel like what I was saying wasn't being dismissed. "I get it, I really do. I know it wasn't directed at me." She smiled and upended her beer.

"It makes me feel horrible, but I just get so urgh!" I shot her an embarrassed look. "You know. Like I have a mini-Hulk out and can't stop myself."

She laughed. "Everyone deals with stress differently. Personally, I prefer a more naked approach." Seductive eyes looked in my direction. "But, whatever works for you."

I grinned, relaxing some. "Well that is one way. Maybe next time you could drag me under the jet and we can try the naked method?"

"Maybe I will." She raised a sly eyebrow for a moment before her expression grew serious. "Why exactly do you care if I witness you being angry with someone?"

"I'm kind of…I don't know." I didn't want her to think badly of me, but it seemed stupid for me to be thinking that. Stupider for me to verbalize it. For some reason it was important that she thought well of me as a person, not just as a lover. It's not like I went after people for sport. I had standards to uphold, and hated being treated like I didn't matter. I'd spent years in New York trying to build myself up as a woman respected for her ability, but one offhand comment could tear it all down like a house of cards.

I took a calming breath. "I was worried you'd think I might lose my temper at you." Good enough. That explanation worked. The truth was right there but I just couldn't get it out of my mouth—*I care about you.*

Audrey wore her thoughtful face. Eyes downcast, right eyebrow dipped. "No," she said finally. "I'm not concerned about that. I don't think you would."

I scrunched my toes up inside my boots. "I'm relieved to hear you say that. It's important to me that I treat my employees well."

She reached for my free hand, holding it between both of hers. "I know, and I've not heard anyone say anything otherwise, Iz. Honestly. I mean, apart from Mr. Hall, I only really see Georgia or Penny and sometimes Schwartz but they're always talking about how kind you are."

Evidently Georgia missed my tantrum yesterday. There was a weird stinging sensation in my nose. One that didn't go away when I rubbed it. "I feel really stupid coming here to tell you this."

"I'm glad you did." Audrey ran her tongue along her lower lip. "I know this is just casual, but I'm glad you thought this important enough to be open with me."

"You really don't seem bothered by it."

"If your little outburst had been directed at me, then I'd be hurt but it wasn't. So I'm not." She shifted fractionally, seeming suddenly uncomfortable. "My father had a temper, Iz. I got good at defusing it after a while."

I chewed the inside of my lip, the word *defuse* playing over in my head. "I don't want you to feel like you should have to defuse me. Like I'm a fucking explosive device. I mean, I am. But I'm not."

"That's not what I meant. I just meant it doesn't concern me. I'm not afraid of you opening the steam valve here and there. I trust you." Audrey's eyebrows came together. "Like I said, I've known one or two tigers in my time, Iz. You're just a housecat hissing because someone petted you the wrong way. It's justified and you're serious about it, but you're not going to scratch anyone."

I smiled at her cat analogy and rested the wineglass on my knee. "I don't mean to dissect it and go over and over what happened. I just felt like I had to explain myself."

"You don't owe me any explanations. We're not in that place, the place where we need to justify and explain or tell each other exactly what we're thinking." She fiddled with the label on her beer bottle, picking at its edge.

For some reason, her statement bothered me. *We weren't in that place.* Where were we then? I took a sip of wine, swallowing quickly. "It'll no doubt happen again, though hopefully not around you."

She was silent, still peeling off the label. When she spoke again, she was calm. Gentle. "Isabelle, I know you care deeply about what people think of you. As a person. A boss. A professional. But, I'd rather you were honest with me rather than holding it in."

I nodded slowly, teeth clamped around my lower lip until I was ready to speak. "I hate being treated like Mark's secretary, just because I'm just a woman and he's the guy. It frustrates me that I get frustrated." I laughed at the absurdity of my statement.

"I get it, really I do. And you're right, it sucks. When I first started out, I had so much shit heaped on me by the guys. I thought it'd go away but it was always there in the background, wearing me down." She looked up and caught my eye. "It's part of the reason I left the commercial industry."

"Really? You don't...seem like that sort of thing would bother you."

Audrey seemed surprised. "It does. And it bothers me that it's happening to you."

I leaned over and kissed her quickly. "You're so sweet and perfect, why hasn't someone snapped you up yet?"

She shrugged, smiling. "Just wait a little longer and you'll see how not perfect I am. I mean, you know I laugh at inappropriate things and can be really messy. Sometimes I get pushy, or upset about things I shouldn't. I jump into the deep end and don't think things through, especially not important things. I get caught up in weird thoughts. I mean, the other day I spent an hour online researching how refrigerators work. Everyone has their shit."

"Mmm."

"I guess what I'm trying to say is that you don't deserve it, and it's bullshit. From where I sit, I see someone who works hard and gives freely. Someone who earns respect and is well-liked and trusted. Someone who's beyond capable and deserves her success."

My words echoed in the wine glass as I lifted it to my mouth. "From where you sit, all you see is sky." I had to make a joke about it or I might cry at her gentle affirmation.

Audrey grinned. "Funny. You think you're so damned funny." She took my hand and kissed each one of my knuckles. "Stay the night with me, or else I'm not going to see you for a couple of days. I've missed you."

As I murmured my agreement, my stomach growled audibly. Lunch was an apple almost six hours ago between constant phone meetings. Audrey clambered over me to kiss my stomach through my top. "First, let me make you dinner. Let me take care of you." She scrambled off the couch before I could protest.

CHAPTER TEN

A few days later, Audrey arrived with sushi right in the middle of a phone argument Mark and I were having about some of his clients' portfolios. I gestured that she should get a drink and start eating without me, and moved out onto the balcony. The city sounds below rushed up, tunneling through my brain and hammering at the ache behind my eyes.

"When you ask for my advice, Mark and then practically do the opposite, it really pisses me off. Especially when it turns out to be a bad buy."

"Belle, quit riding me about it." He was almost whining.

"If you were doing what you should, I wouldn't be fucking nagging you. You're making me feel like my mama."

"I don't need to be babysat." I could feel him pouting, even through the phone.

"Yeah, maybe you do. I hate to say it—"

"No you don't," he countered.

I drove over the top of him like I was a tank. "Honey, I don't know what's going on, but you seem distracted." For the past few weeks he'd been ducking out of the office at odd times, and had long periods where he was completely uncontactable. I'd overheard someone in the ladies' room asking if he was all right because "he seemed so weird."

"Isabelle." His tone was a notch below a warning.

"I'm worried about you. That's all." I turned to look back into the house, watching Audrey bent over in my fridge. She turned around, caught me staring and grinned. I grinned back. Guilty as charged.

Mark exhaled. "I know. But you're my best friend, not my wife. Or my mom."

"I'm the closest thing you've got to a wife, darlin'."

"I can't even begin to express how depressing that is."

"I'm bringing this up as your friend but more importantly as your business partner, Mark." There was no way I could word it that wasn't accusatory. "I feel like you've been missing things you shouldn't. And then that trouble with the auditor. Things are dragging on your end, and for someone so concerned about our image, your…ineptitude makes us look bad."

There was a long pause. So long that I had to ask if he was still there.

"I'm here." The sound of a lighter sparking came over the line. His deep inhalation. "I told you the auditor stuff was just a fuck up of a report I sent, and I sent an amended one through."

"Yes. A fuck up," I said pointedly. "You were late sending the figures through last quarter too, and I had to chase you up."

"Goddammit, can't I just relax for once and enjoy the fruits of my labors, Belle?"

"Of course you can, but if you're not careful you're going to end up cutting down the fruit tree. And then we're both screwed." I slid the balcony door open and stepped inside. "Just think about it?" I decided to leave it there, sensing that mentioning more of his mistakes now would tip him right over the edge.

"I will."

"Good. I've got to go. I'll see you in the morning."

"Yeah okay. Bye."

I tossed my phone onto the counter, stretching over to kiss Audrey. "Hi. You smell amazing." The knot of tension in my shoulders relaxed a fraction.

"Hi yourself." Despite my indicating she should start, she'd waited.

Standing a few feet away from her, a familiar feeling came over me. The one I had when we were looking at one another, still slick and panting as we came down from our climax. Or when she calmly fixed the toothpaste in her bathroom after I'd used it because she squeezed from the bottom of the tube and I didn't. The feeling I got when she'd tell me about something of her day, something I would have found annoying but she would laugh about.

Looking at her, I knew what the feeling was and it frightened the shit out of me. *Comfort*. I stuffed it down where I wouldn't think about it. Audrey extracted sushi and a bottle of white from the fridge and we moved around the kitchen in a routine we'd perfected. Wine glass filled for me, plates and cutlery set out, a second beer for her. When I winced, she brushed her fingers over my cheek. "Is everything all right?"

"Yeah, all fine. Give me a moment?"

"Sure."

Upstairs in my bathroom, I tossed two Advil into my mouth, then rushed back down and swallowed them with a gulp of wine. I started chopsticking sushi onto a plate. Audrey stepped behind me, massaging my shoulders. "Sure you're okay, Iz?"

"Mhmm." I turned to face her. "You don't need to do that."

"Do what?"

"Dig into what's up, try to help me." Buzzwords: defense mechanism. I wanted to tell her why I was feeling out of sorts but it wasn't appropriate. It had only been a little over two months. With our work dynamic, the conflict of me telling her about my issues with Mark was landmine territory. But I wanted to share, and the dilemma confused me.

"Sure thing. Then I won't." There was no defensiveness in her statement, just quiet acknowledgement.

Contrition flushed my cheeks. "I'm sorry, that came out bitchily. I'm just tired." Whenever I said that, I often wondered why nobody ever countered with *you're always tired*. I smiled tightly. "You know what? That's a lie."

"It is?"

"I'm tired but I'm not that tired." I pushed my plate across the counter. "What I really am is confused."

"What about?" Her question was relaxed, inviting me to share.

"I'm confused about us." Tapping the end of my chopsticks on my marble counter, I elaborated, "Dinner and movies. Spending time together. It's confusing for me because of what we said in the beginning."

Audrey's gaze was steady, dark eyes locked to mine. "I know."

"I like it, don't get me wrong but I don't know what it is," I admitted.

"What it is? I assumed it's two people spending time together. Like friends would."

"Friends." The word tasted strange in my mouth. It tasted wrong, like it wasn't going to satisfy my hunger.

"Mhmm." A flicker of unease crossed her normally calm face. "It's not unreasonable to consider us friends? With benefits of course."

I grinned. "No. I don't think that's unreasonable."

"Good." She placed a hand on the side of my face and kissed my temple. "Come on, let's eat."

After dinner, as we slouched watching a movie on my L-shaped couch, I pulled her legs up onto my lap and began to massage her tight calves. My earlier frustration and anxiety had dissipated, evaporating like steam. It was her. Her gentle humor and sweet words. Her presence. She settled me in a way I'd never felt before.

Audrey's default state was calm amusement, along with an almost feline laziness as if nothing was particularly important. I envied and admired her for it. The only time she got frazzled was when we were making love and she was excited but I denied her. Then she would become frantic as though she thought I might disappear before she could do what she wanted to.

There I was, bitching and basically telling her to butt out, yet she somehow snuck up behind me and managed to change my mood anyway. She handled me expertly but I never felt handled. In our short time together, she'd become a master Isabelle Rhodes wrangler. I glanced at her, then back to the television.

Audrey wiggled her toes. "What?"

"Seriously, why aren't you bothered by my moods?"

"Where'd that question come from?"

I held onto her legs and bent forward to retrieve the remote from beside her. Brad Pitt paused midsentence. He looked surprisingly unattractive, possibly for the first time in his life. When I didn't speak, Audrey continued, "We've talked about this. What's going on? Really."

I took a deep breath, letting it out slowly. "I guess I'm worried you'll get sick of it. Sick of me."

Her leg tensed ever so slightly. "No. I don't think that's going to happen."

I exhaled. Again, the words were right there, filling my mouth and threatening to choke me. I care about you. *I think I'm falling in love with you.*

Our silence became the silence that feels like it should be awkward but is really the most natural thing. With others I'd have felt the need to grin, or do something to turn the feeling from seriousness to light. Not with her. She broke first. "I don't want to be anywhere else, Iz."

My response was barely above a whisper. "Me either." I carefully extricated myself from under her legs and climbed over to straddle them. She sat perfectly still as I slid her shirt up and bent to press my lips against the firm, tanned skin of her belly. I ran my nose over her bellybutton, inhaling the sweetness of her. Underneath me, her legs were moving, sliding her feet along the fabric of the couch.

I slid my tongue in an experimental lick along her hip bone and she tensed. I did it again, feeling the jerk of her knee under my ass. We hadn't said anything, nor had she touched me since I'd moved. I looked up. Her arm was slung over the couch, expression soft but desire shining clearly from those dark eyes. I pushed hair from my face. "You're awfully subdued." My fingers took the initiative and unbuttoned her jeans, sliding her zipper down as slowly as I could.

"I'm enjoying watching you work," she murmured.

"Oh, I haven't even clocked in yet."

"Will you be putting in overtime?"

"Absolutely." I slid backward, still pressing kisses over her stomach. When I hooked my fingers in her jeans, Audrey lifted herself to let me tug them down to midthigh, exposing her dark blue boyleg underwear. The woman had no underwear loyalty, and undressing her was like unwrapping a gift. Sometimes she wore boyshorts, sometimes a thong and other times something scant and lacy. She did whatever made her feel good and comfortable and I envied her ability to be so at peace with her self-image.

Her breathing caught when I dropped my nose against her, inhaling the unmistakable scent of her arousal. My throat tightened. Saliva welled. I wanted to taste her so badly. Instead, I crawled back up, slipped my leg between her thighs and pressed myself against her.

"You're a tease," she complained. Still, she didn't touch me. It was as if she was seeing how long she could hold out.

"I know." I pushed her shirt up and tugged the soft fabric of her bra down to expose gorgeous breasts. My lover finally broke when I took a nipple in my mouth, her hands coming to tangle in my hair as my tongue played over hard peaks. Still fully dressed, and more than fully aroused, I ground against her leg as she bucked underneath mine. I shifted, just a little to reach between, sliding my fingers inside the cotton barrier of her underwear.

Audrey lifted her hips when my fingers made contact with her slick clitoris and I felt the tug as she took another handful of my hair. She was so wet. I drew a slow breath, trying to reset, to find a more comfortable place where I could concentrate. I was overwhelmed by the feel of her on my fingers, tight nipples under my tongue, the scent and sound of her making me whole.

"Come up here," she practically demanded. "Kiss me."

I held firm and pulled away. Not kissing her was torturous—I was denying myself as well as denying her. Every time she begged, every time she moaned or sucked in a rough inhalation, another wave of arousal pulsed through me. From experience, I knew I could settle on the other section of the couch and have perfect access to the treasure between her legs.

Slowly, I dragged off her underwear then made my way down again, tantalizingly close to her glistening folds. "What do you want?" I murmured against the soft skin of her inner thigh.

"I want *you*, baby. Lick me," she begged. "Please, Iz."

Hands on her hips, I held her down and finally tasted her.

CHAPTER ELEVEN

Monday, I enjoyed a boozy lunch meeting with a potential client at Le Bernardin. It was one of those depressing smoggy NYC days, the claustrophobia of people and cars everywhere. The kind of day that made me long for the oppressive humidity of my unsophisticated rural hometown where the dominant sounds were neighbors four-wheeling, insects and people drinking on porches while swatting those insects.

I came back to my office, finalized an account and started spinning around in my chair—my favorite way of brainstorming. I placed a stockinged foot against the edge of my desk and pushed off for another revolution. I had an idea, perhaps because of increased intellect from the redistribution of blood to my brain. Maybe it was the booze from lunch. I stood up, wobbled from the head rush and shoved my feet back into heels. My head was still spinning as I rushed out of my office, startling my PA.

I smiled an apology and launched in with, "Clare, I'd like to visit Mama for the weekend. Can you check Mark isn't using the jet and organize it, please?"

My idea was a damned good one, I thought. A high five-figure salary, all expenses and a rarely-invoked contract clause meant our lead pilot could be called on at any time, including for personal trips. I happened to be involved with the lead pilot. Perhaps she might like to see a little of my hometown.

Clare made notes in her neat handwriting. "Of course. When would you like to depart?"

"Around five Friday afternoon. Back Sunday night no later than eight."

"I'll arrange it," Clare assured me.

"Thank you."

Forty minutes later, I was finalizing a buy when Clare knocked on my open door. "Ms. Rhodes?"

"Yes?" I glanced up, shoving hair off my face.

"Your three o'clock meeting Thursday has been brought forward to two and you're all set for Friday afternoon. Penny will be here at four, and Captain Graham will meet you at Teterboro at four forty-five. Then you're scheduled to leave at six p.m. Sunday."

Happy days. "Great, thanks. And you've—"

"Booked accommodation for Captain Graham? Yes, the only available was the bed and breakfast on York."

Good. Hotels in my hometown left a lot to be desired. I grinned. "This is why I keep you, Clare."

She gave me a casual wave, but I could tell she was pleased. "I know. Your updated schedule through to the end of next week is on your calendar."

"Thank you. Oh, can you send through a statement of my personal account for the month, please."

"I'll get right on that." She slipped out, leaving me to check my schedule. My Wednesday meeting in Maine had been moved to tomorrow. Jesus. I had a fundraiser planning dinner tomorrow night in the Upper East Side, one I'd been dreading for weeks and I wanted to get a massage in the afternoon. I rushed out of my office, tablet clutched in hand. "Clare."

She stood up at my approach. "Yes, Ms. Rhodes?"

"This schedule's not going to work. I can't do tomorrow in Maine and be back for my massage." Usually I'd be borderline steaming but I was surprised to feel my frustration struggling to break the surface, like it'd lost buoyancy somehow. When had I become so mellow?

She nodded calmly. "You may have noticed Adrian's agreed to move his meeting forward to ten. You'll be back in the city by three and on the massage table at four."

I ran through mental calculations. "Great. Thanks. Sorry."

"I've just sent through your statement, including this weekend's charges. Shall I tell the driver you're ready for your appointment?" Clare glanced at the gold watch on her delicate wrist. "You'll need to leave in ten minutes."

Therapy. Fuck.

* * *

I clarified my position the moment I sat across from Dr. Baker. "I've been out to lunch with a client. I may be ever so slightly inebriated."

My therapist smiled, leaning forward slightly so the multicolored glass beads of her necklace clinked together. "So you're relaxed and open to talking, then?"

"Aren't I always?"

She laughed. I laughed. Oh we were so funny, making light of my occasional reticence. I settled back in the chair and crossed my legs. My Jimmy had slipped off my heel. I balanced it on my toe and bounced the shoe, curling my toes so the back kept hitting my freshly pedicured foot. If I were Dr. Baker, I would have told me to stop it.

She didn't. I guess she wanted to make sure I'd keep coming back. I did a quick calculation. She could have bought a car with all the money I'd paid her for therapy. Maybe a low-end Maserati. Certainly a high-end Lexus. Low-end Lexus and a boat?

She interrupted my runaway math. "So, what's been going on?"

What hasn't? I word-blurted for fifteen minutes, skating past everything except my rage at Richard treating me like a hired hand last week, the argument with Mark about his audit report and my resulting nastiness with Audrey. When I was done, I sat limply. Talking about it made me feel worse, rehashing everything. I stared at my therapist. "Couldn't you just give me mood stabilizers or something? A lobotomy?"

Dr. Baker smiled. "I feel that would only mask the issue. Let's talk about the deeper feelings here."

I only just managed to stifle my groan. "Okay."

"In all our time together, you've never mentioned any anger issues directly involving girlfriends or lovers. In fact, you've said having them near usually triggers your emotions into a more neutral place."

"Mhmm."

"Why do you think you had trouble earlier this week with Audrey?"

I rubbed my finger on the arm of the chair. "I was annoyed. My day had already been moved around and time was tight. Then when I got that call and the auditor treated me like an idiot and Mark brushed my feelings aside, it just…compounded everything."

"That's an issue with something else, Isabelle, not with your lover. I'm talking about why you felt you couldn't calm down. You said…" She glanced down at her notepad and quoted something I'd said during my earlier blurting. "I ignored something she said. I was sarcastic to her. I was rude and I hated it but couldn't stop."

My spine tingled uncomfortably as my nastiness was handed back to me. "That's correct."

"Isabelle, honestly, this feels like a classic getting in first behavior. You're showing all your cards at once, putting it out there and hoping you can push her away before she can leave you."

Screw her and her stupid fucking logic. "Maybe."

Dr. Baker gave me a knowing look. "Think about it. You do the pushing and she's gone before you can get attached and hurt. It makes perfect sense. How long have you been sleeping together?"

"Almost nine weeks."

Scribbling. "How do you feel about her?"

"What kind of question is that?"

"A fairly straightforward one. How do you feel about her?"

Every muscle in my back tightened. "I enjoy spending time with her."

"What about the sex?"

My cheeks puffed with air for a moment before I released it. "The sex is amazing." Understatement of the decade.

"Do you do anything other than have sex?" She spared me a quick glance, her expression clearly telling me she already knew the answer.

I paused. "Yes."

"Like what?"

"We eat in or I help her cook. Watch movies, uh, talk. That sort of thing."

"To an outsider, it looks a little like you're dating. Do you go out at all?"

There was a longer pause. "Yes, I can see how someone would think that." I chewed the inside of my cheek. "And no, we don't go out."

"Why not?"

"Because I don't really want to advertise what I'm doing. Not right now."

She scrawled something on her pad. "Have you told Mark or any of your friends that you're seeing someone?"

"No." I held up a hand. "Wait, actually, I did tell my friend from college but she's in California."

Dr. Baker peered at me over the top of her glasses. "How do you think Audrey feels about the secrecy?"

Frowning, I answered honestly, "I really don't know. She hasn't said anything so I assume she's fine with it."

Lacing her fingers together, Dr. Baker let them rest on the notepad. "I'd really like to know why you haven't told your best friend you're seeing someone."

"Because I'm not seeing someone," I shot back childishly.

"Isabelle."

"Fine, okay. Because I don't want him to treat her differently because we're seeing each other outside of work. I'm afraid he's going to be an asshole because Audrey is just...wonderfully Audrey and not one of these *elites* he thinks we should surround ourselves with to boost our image." My eye roll was so huge, I felt like I'd torn an eyeball muscle.

"But he's not seeing her. You are. Is his opinion really that important?"

"He's my friend," I said simply. "In the long run, I guess I want him to approve. Or maybe not approve but I want him to see what I see in her. She's such a good person and I...care about her."

The quirk of her mouth was unmistakable and followed by a long scribble. "He can't do any of that unless you tell him," she said pointedly.

"True. But then I'd have to change the Audrey rules. Again."

"Why do you think it's so important that you keep firmly within these borders you've made for yourself, even as those lines are clearly shifting?"

We made eye contact. I broke first. "Because I'm scared," I finally said. "Scared to go further. Scared of how I feel about her. Scared she doesn't feel the same way."

Dr. Baker's smile was slight, but revolutionary as if she'd finally discovered the cure for cancer. "I agree, this is a frightening thing. But remember, Isabelle. Nobody can take anything you don't want them to." My therapist peered at me over the top of her glasses. "I'm not talking about material possessions. I think you need to be honest with her and yourself and I think part of that is sharing this thing with the people in your life."

Thanks, Doc.

I decided to put off my obligatory self-Googling to run for a while. Dr. Baker once suggested that I should use meditation as a means of thought processing. She was very polite when I laughed at her suggestion. I could barely stand massage because I hated to be still, but at least with massage I always fell asleep and woke up loose jointed and relaxed. Meditation was just sitting. What a waste of time. We compromised with exercise to work my feelings loose.

Twenty minutes into my workout I had a disturbing revelation. The reason I was so scared wasn't because I was afraid of what might happen. It was because I was already there. I loved Audrey. Maybe not quite *in love*. Yet. But there was love. It wasn't just about sex, it was about how she made me feel. The way she looked at me when we saw each other for the first time that day—like I was the only thing she'd been waiting to see.

It was all the little things I adored about her. She hated e-readers, but was addicted to a popular crime medical examiner series and always carried a cumbersome paperback around. She gave me her pickles, even though she liked them too. She cried during movies but not just in sad bits, she loved it when people got happy endings.

When I'd catch her watching me, our eyes would meet and I would always feel a spark of electricity, like we were sharing something secret. She knew how to make me laugh and constantly tried to tease all my wit from the place I'd buried it. She was fun. She made me feel good about myself. She was an attentive and responsive lover. Warm, funny, caring. I groaned and nearly fell off the treadmill.

I finished my workout, showered and planted myself on the couch with my old friend Lean Cuisine and my tablet. Market updates, nothing exciting. Time to check where I sat on the ol' popularity meters. I found an opinion piece that mentioned my name and praised me in regards to fundraising benefits. It didn't make me feel any better.

I swapped my tablet for my phone and dialed. Audrey's surprised voice answered. Leaning on the railing, staring at the mess of Manhattan lights, I opened myself up to her a little more. "Hey, no nothing's wrong. I just wanted to hear your voice."

CHAPTER TWELVE

Audrey and I hadn't spoken about the trip to Mama's. Not that there was anything to discuss. As my employee, she was simply flying me home and back. As the woman I was maybe sort of unofficially dating, I could suggest that perhaps I could visit her hotel one night. Maybe she'd like to have dinner or a tour of my hometown.

I called Nat the morning of my trip, blurting my plans until she interrupted me with an incredulous question. "Wait, you're taking her home to meet your mother? Isn't that back to front?"

"What do you mean?"

"I always thought you should acknowledge you're dating and then meet the parents, not the other way around." I could hear Nat's laughter bubbling under the surface.

"It's not like that—she's working."

"Yeah right. I know you and I know your mother. If she catches a whiff of what's between you two, she's going to pounce. You know that."

"Nat," I whispered. "I think I'm falling in love with her."

"Rhodes, I swear I'm going to kick your fucking ass if you don't tell this woman how you feel."

I walked over to my full-length office window, staring aimlessly out at the skyline. "I can't. What if she doesn't feel the same?"

"Then she doesn't. No harm, no foul. You're making it complicated when it doesn't have to be."

Someone knocked on my closed office door. I glanced over my shoulder. "I need to go, I've got a meeting."

"Call me and let me know how it goes back home. Tell your mother I said hi."

"Will do." I hung up and held the phone to my chest. Christ, what was I doing?

Penny was waiting for me when I raced through the front doors just before four p.m. She held the car door open, a hand out to take my bags. "Afternoon, Ms. Rhodes."

I grasped her suited forearm. "Pen. How are you? How was your week?"

"I'm good and my week's been wonderful, thank you for asking."

"Glad to hear it."

Pen wore an odd smile, one I hadn't seen before. If I didn't know better, I'd think she knew something was up. Something different. Something important.

En route to the airport, I sent some preemptive emails so I could turn my phone off in the air, decompress and try to transition from Stockbroker Isabelle to Daughter Isabelle. Good luck with that. I checked my appearance in my compact. Who really cares, Isabelle? She's seen you in all stages of dress and undress. I grabbed my purse and climbed out.

Penny was waiting at the bottom of the stairs, having already stowed my bags on board. "Have a lovely weekend, Ms. Rhodes and I'll see you here at eight on Sunday night."

"Thank you, and you too." I practically sprinted up the steps.

Audrey stood beside the cockpit, hands clasped loosely in front of her. "Ms. Rhodes, how are you?"

"I'm very well." I didn't clarify very well, except I couldn't stop my heart from fluttering every time I looked at Audrey because now I knew I loved her. "Yourself?"

"Better now."

Better now. Better now that I was here? The fluttering intensified. "I hope I didn't ruin any plans you had this weekend." Like a date with a person who isn't me. Please don't say that.

"Does Netflix, pizza and a few bottles of wine with you count?" she asked innocently.

"Sounds like a great way to spend a weekend. I apologize for taking you away from those plans. Perhaps I can make it up to you?"

"Apology accepted, Ms. Rhodes. And I'm sure we can talk about rescheduling or how you can make it up to me." She looked me up and down, her left eyebrow dipped.

"Is something wrong?" I glanced down at myself. Jeans, Cuban heels and a scoop neck chosen especially because of how it made my tits look. I admit, it was perhaps a little unfair to show so much cleavage while she was supposed to be working but I was still hopeful of fulfilling my mile-high fantasy.

"Not at all, Ms. Rhodes. Just a little different to what you usually wear while I'm working. I mean suits, dresses and heels are lovely, but…well." She shook her head as if to clear thoughts from it. "I'm very sorry. That was inappropriate."

"Yes it was." I leaned closer. "Feel free to do it again." I swear I could feel her eyes on my ass as I walked to my seat.

"You make it very hard to do my job," she called from behind me.

I settled in my usual seat and crossed my legs. "Then we're even because since we met, I've found it very hard to concentrate on mine. And pretty much everything else for that matter."

She looked ever-so-smug. "Speaking of jobs, our flight plan is filed, fuel is on board. Everything is ready whenever you are."

"I'm ready." I shoved my purse in the compartment beside the seat and buckled myself in.

"If there's anything I can do to help, or make you more comfortable please let me know." The look she gave me left no doubt about how exactly she wanted to help.

I'd promised myself that I wouldn't do anything naughty while she was working but it didn't stop me running through a checklist of everything I wanted. Flying me to Mama's was at the bottom of the list. "Will do, thank you. Just going to catch up on some *Orphan Black*." I crossed my legs, squeezing my thighs together.

She closed the cabin door, the quiet whine of the hydraulics cutting through the silence, then moved to the cockpit, sat in the left-hand seat and reached behind herself to close the curtains. I yanked the seat belt tighter. "You can leave it open if you like. Unless it'll be distracting."

Audrey turned around, headset in her hand. "Ms. Rhodes, you're always a distraction."

* * *

The moment we landed and began to taxi off the runway I turned my phone back on. Staring at the inevitable barrage of voice mails and emails, all the relaxation I felt at spending a few hours off the grid evaporated. One from Mark, two from Clare, three clients, Mama telling me she'd be there to fetch me at seven *on the dot*. I took notes and made a final check of my emails as Audrey shut everything down.

She hovered near the electrical panel. "Are you ready to head out?"

"I am."

"After you."

Again, I felt her eyes on my ass when she followed me down the stairs. She raised the door, made a few final checks to the exterior of the jet and turned to me. "Well, I'm officially off duty."

"That you are."

"May I kiss you now?" Her eyes twinkled under the artificial lights in the rented hangar.

Tempting. I stepped close so we were almost toe-to-toe. "Perhaps once you're out of that uniform. Wouldn't want anyone getting the wrong idea."

Audrey shook her head slowly. "Damn."

We started walking toward the terminal building. "Mama's coming to get me but I can drop you at the hotel? And I should be able to sneak out tomorrow some time if you wanted to uh, hang out or see some sights."

"Iz, this is time to spend with your mother. I'm certain I can find plenty to entertain myself this weekend. I've never been down this way before." She held the door open for me. "I saw there's a Farmer's Market on tomorrow."

The sound of my boot heels echoed through the almost empty building. "Yep, just behind City Hall. We might catch you there." I turned to look at her, trying to make out her expression.

"We'll see how it goes." She was noncommittal. I couldn't tell if she wanted some time alone, or if she was being polite. I knew the reason when she continued, "You can see me any time. This weekend is for your mom."

The automatic doors slid open and we were outside again, at the front of the terminal. I hoisted my laptop back onto my shoulder. "Remember, just take a cab as much as you need, or hire a car. There's a nice place for dinn—"

"Iz." She flashed me a patient smile. "I know how it works."

My reply was interrupted by Mama's Prius screeching to a stop just past us, and from the curb I heard the ratchet sound as she yanked the park brake on. Lord, I hated the way she did that. She flung the door wide and raced toward us, smiling her gap-toothed smile at me. It was the same smile I'd inherited, though Mama insisted on closing the space between my two front teeth with braces. Secretly, I still harbored a grudge. I thought that gap had made me look cute.

Mama glanced at Audrey, the questioning look turning into a smile before she pulled me in for a tight hug. Despite a five-foot eight-inch mother and an apparently six-foot-three father, I only *just* made it to five-foot three. And that was if I stood up really straight. Whenever Mama hugged me, I fit perfectly under her chin, melding into her soft curves as if they were made just for me. I've always loved that snug fit.

"Bunny! I've missed you," she said into my hair.

I cringed when she used the pet name she'd had for me as long as I could remember. It was one thing in private, but to say it in public? Thankfully, Audrey gave no response to indicate she'd heard. Mama held me at arm's length, though her delighted gaze was on Audrey. My mother had no guile. She looked excited because she was. "You brought a friend! Who is this?"

"Mama, this is Audrey Graham. Our new pilot, and a… friend." Also, you know, my lover. Surprise! I made vague introduction gestures. "Audrey, this is my mama, Constance Rhodes."

Mama reached for Audrey's hand, clasping it between both of hers. "Audrey. What a beautiful name. It's a pleasure to make your acquaintance. Please, call me Connie. You'll be stayin' for dinner?"

"Mama, I don't think, I mean, I'm sure she has plans." I turned to Audrey, eyes wide. If she didn't want an interrogation over dinner, she needed to make an excuse right now.

There were no excuses. Instead, Audrey nodded thoughtfully. "Actually no I don't have plans. Just a night of television and room service."

Mama looked aghast. "Pah! Well it's settled then, I insist. We've got pot roast and fixin's. There's always plenty." Understatement.

I wrinkled my nose. "You left the oven on while you came to fetch me?"

"It's only a twenty minute round trip. You worry too much." Mama dismissed me with a wave and turned expectantly to Audrey. "We'd love for you to join us."

Audrey responded with her stunning smile. "That would be wonderful, thank you. It's been a while since someone cooked for me." She didn't look my way, but I knew it was a sneaky teasing dig.

That smile was the exact moment Mama became smitten. Audrey's smile could win anyone over, but coupled with some poor soul who needed feeding? Mama barely spared me a glance. Don't mind me, you two. Mama nudged me. "Bunny, can you drive? You know I hate drivin' at night."

"Sure." I waggled my fingers for her keys.

We played our usual game where she asked teasingly if I even remembered how to drive, while I fumbled with adjusting seats and mirrors. I turned, hooking my arm over the back of the passenger seat to speak to Audrey. "We can stop by the hotel if you'd like?"

"I'm happy to change at the house, if that's okay? Saves you making an unnecessary trip."

She'd be naked in the bathroom while I sat in the kitchen and tried to converse with Mama. Oh boy. I ran my tongue over my lower lip and almost managed to keep the squeak from my voice. "Sure."

My phone rang as I was pulling out of the terminal. I glanced at the ID. Shane Preston. Grimacing, I hooked my Bluetooth headset over my ear. "I'm really sorry, I have to take this." My whole life was one great big apology for taking calls and working at times I should be doing other things.

"Bunny," Mama warned.

"Mama, please don't. I know, okay, but I can't help it. I have to make a livin'." I avoided her stare and answered, "Isabelle Rhodes."

Shane launched right in with his usual rant about market stability. I had ten minutes before reaching Mama's house, and judging by his tone it'd take every damned one of those minutes to appease him. I'd imagine it was odd for Mama and Audrey to listen to only my side of the conversation as I drove toward my childhood home. Also very rude, and awkward.

For the next five minutes, I got in a few musing sounds until finally Shane told me he'd raise his input again. It'd only taken two months to get him there. I exhaled, battling annoyance that he'd chosen now of all times to call and tell me this. Ever heard of email, buddy?

"Shane, I'm pleased you've decided to commit to twenty. As I said last month, it really opens up a whole new level for you… mhmm…I think you'll be more than pleased with the results."

Mama's small car shuddered as I raced over the train tracks. "Coal? No, as I've told you a number of times, coal is a—" My hands tightened on the wheel. "It's really not a safe investment… the market…well, if you insist, but I must caution you strongly against it. No, I know you told me that your brother-in-law… yes. Yes, I know. May I advise only a small percentage?"

I turned onto my mother's street, slowing to a near crawl to prolong my time. Mama would roast me if I stayed in the car with a client on the phone once I'd parked. I was right there with her—I wanted to go inside, open wine and think about Audrey naked. "…Shane, I understand but I'd like to remind you, respectfully, that this is my job. You're entrusting me with your money and I take your trust very seriously. I've been doing this for a long time, we've been doing this together a long time."

Gravel crunched under the tires as I rolled into Mama's carport at a snail's pace. I raised my pitch to max enthusiasm. The ditziest of ditzes would have been envious. "Great! I'm so pleased you're on board. Why don't you call Monday and we'll get into details." I forced a laugh. "You too, enjoy the show tonight."

I waited until I'd heard the call disconnect, made sure he was really gone, and yanked the Bluetooth from my ear. "Fuckin' idiot asshole! I feel like tellin' him to take his portfolio to Mark if he wants to lose four-point-eight goddamned percent. Christ!" I came to a hard stop, slammed my palm down on the steering wheel and pulled the park brake on.

Mama slapped my arm. "Isabelle Renee. Curse words."

There was a snort from the backseat. I inhaled, trying to calm the pounding in my temples. "I'm sorry. I'm really sorry." My eyes found Audrey's in the mirror. "Sorry."

Audrey smiled and gave me a slight headshake. Mama opened the door, illuminating the interior of the car. She fiddled with her handbag and turned to the backseat. "I assure you, Audrey, she does not get that temper from me."

I nudged the car door open with my toes. "No, Mama but I did learn all my curse words from you."

CHAPTER THIRTEEN

Audrey feigned surprise as I closed the door on my childhood room before she could see inside. "Not even a peek?"

"Oh no." I took her hand and guided her toward the bathroom so she could change.

She lingered at the door, suddenly looking like she'd reconsidered the appropriateness of being in Mama's house. "Are you sure it's fine for me to stay for dinner?"

I ran my hand up her arm, feeling her muscle tighten then relax again. "Trust me. Mama loves two things more than anything. Surprise visitors and feeding people. Feeding a surprise visitor will make her week."

"But is it okay for you?"

"Yes. Get changed, I'll see you downstairs when you're done."

I sat at the kitchen table and distracted myself from thoughts of her changing upstairs by pouring a large glass of white. I'd barely swallowed my first mouthful when Mama pounced. "How's work, baby?"

"Busy, same as always."

"You look tired."

I shrugged. There was nothing to say. I *was* tired. Partly from work but also from shortening my sleep hours with what sometimes felt like scheduled lovemaking, wonderful as it was. "No more than usual."

She moved to stand beside me, body warm against my shoulder as she ran her hand through my curls. "I worry about you, Bunny."

Here we go. Countdown to relationship status in three... two...

"Ever since Steph left—" Bingo. "You've been working nonstop. You need some balance in your life."

I twisted to look up at her. "I have plenty of balance, Mama and besides, I've worked too hard to just let it all fall apart now."

My mother gave me her look. The one that told me I was about to be delivered some home truths disguised as gentle guidance. Her style wasn't to jackhammer, oh no. She was water, gently washing at your feet. It felt nice at first, until you realized that she'd rotted away all your foundations and you were about to be carried away by her tide.

She was like a song stuck on repeat. She'd start with gently reminding me how companionship completes a person, then move onto talking about marriage, which would segue into the grand finale of how much she wanted grandchildren. Having children was dead horse territory—the topic could be flogged no more. I'd been adamant for as long as I could remember that I was not interested in kids. Maternal I was not.

Mercifully, Audrey's footsteps on the stairs made Mama abort her strafing run. I was safe, for now. Mama bent to kiss my forehead, picked up her glass of wine and walked away to check the oven. Audrey stepped hesitantly into the kitchen. She'd changed into tight jeans and tighter tank, let her hair down and reapplied perfume. The scent always did strange things to me, made me feel like I was unconsciously gravitating toward her.

Audrey winked at me then looked to Mama. "Connie, that smells absolutely amazing."

Mama's face was part beatific, part smug. "Wait'll you taste it."

I shuffled to the fridge. "What can I get you to drink? Beer, wine, water?"

"Beer would be great, thank you."

"Any preference?"

"Whatever you've got is fine."

I pulled a bottle from the fridge, popped the top and handed it to her. "There you go." Wiggling the bottle of white above my head, I asked, "Mama?"

Wordlessly, she lifted her nearly empty wine glass. I refilled it for her and poured the rest of the bottle into my own. Audrey settled against the counter, watching finishing touches being put on dinner.

"Bunny, can you check I locked the chickens up? I can't remember," Mama said vacantly.

Audrey didn't bother to hide her smirk. As I gently pushed her aside to fetch the flashlight from a drawer, she whispered, "Bunny."

I took my wine and prowled through the garden, wondering what the heck they were talking about in the kitchen. Mama wouldn't hesitate to pry. It bothered me because Audrey and I weren't anywhere near the meeting family, twenty-question stage. Yet I'd still brought her here. Nat was right. Again.

Dual laughter carried out from the kitchen window. I contemplated creeping up under the window to listen. Too stalkerish. The chickens clucked uncomfortably when the flashlight beam hit them. As I'd expected they were locked up, and it confirmed my suspicions that Mama wanted a few moments alone with my girlfr—

Lover.

I barged back inside. The scene was right out of Happy Kitchens magazine, pot roast resting and Mama handing Audrey a spoon to taste test her gravy. The expression on Audrey's face was one I knew fairly well by now. Enjoyment. Pleasure. "Wow," she said, shaking her head. "That's incredible."

Mama nodded. "Told you."

Told her what, exactly? I felt like a third wheel as I dropped the flashlight back into the drawer. "The chickens were in."

"Thank you, baby. This is about done. Can you set the table, please?"

Audrey helped me relocate my laptop, tablet and work phone to the den. I turned them all to silent. Working at dinnertime was strictly forbidden and I didn't feel like incurring any more wrath tonight, especially not when we had company. "I'm real sorry, she can be intense," I said quietly.

"No, not at all." Her eyes flicked toward the kitchen. "She's great."

My grateful hand found hers of its own accord, squeezing gently, and Audrey returned the gesture with warm reassurance. She cast her gaze around the den at the masses of photos adorning the walls and almost every surface. "Mind if I look?"

"Go ahead."

Audrey wandered around, looking closely at each picture. Most of them were of me, doing everything from being grumpy at age five in a ballet outfit, to running track and receiving my college degree. She picked up one of my favorite photos, the one I kept meaning to have a copy printed.

It was taken last year during a trip Mama and I took to Europe. We were standing outside a pub in London and a stranger had come up and very apologetically told us he couldn't help it, but he'd photographed us. I was getting ready to unload on him, until he turned his camera to show me the photograph. My hair was everywhere, Mama was reaching to hug me and we were both laughing because of her confusion about pounds currency and pounds weight. I loved the lightness of the image. The stranger emailed it to me, and I sent him some money in return and a message that if he was ever in New York, to look me up for some work.

Audrey ran a finger over the wooden frame. "This is brilliant." She lifted the picture close to her face, studying it. Then she looked over and studied me as though she was comparing the Isabelle in the photograph to the one standing beside her. Most of the time, the two Isabelles were miles apart. Except when I was with Audrey. She set the photograph down and faced me, expression soft. I stepped closer, already on the balls of my feet to kiss her.

Before I could, Mama's insistent voice carried through from the kitchen. "Isabelle Renee, this table is not settin' itself!" Despite my age, my commercial success and my ability to manage not only my wealth but my clients', Mama still treated me like a child reluctant to do her chores.

I barely suppressed an eye roll. "Okay! I'm coming."

Mama always ate dinner with a fully-set table, cloth napkins and flowers carefully arranged in the center. The habit was one she'd learned from my Grams and I know she wanted to pass this custom to me. When she stayed with me in New York I made the effort, but I'm sure she suspected the moment she left, I was back to eating on the couch or at my desk.

Audrey's eyes widened, ever so slightly, when I started setting cloth napkins out. "It's just how she is, nothing fancy. Promise," I assured her in a low voice.

From the head of the table, Mama suppressed her natural urge to serve and let us dish up our own dinner. She watched me take small portions, eyes narrowed until I added a second scoop of potato. Gravy was poured onto my plate without my permission and I could do nothing when she carved off more meat and placed it on top of what I'd already served myself. If we were alone, I would have protested and loudly but I had to sit and take it. This time.

Audrey took Mama-pleasing portions of everything. Mama slowly turned toward me and gave me a pointed *this is how daughters should behave* stare. I tried to make contact with Audrey under the table, but she stretched a long leg out and trapped mine against my chair leg before I could nudge her.

Mama stopped cutting beef to start questioning. "Audrey, what did you do before you started working at Rhodes and Hall?"

Audrey straightened, wiped her mouth with the cloth napkin and set it back on her lap. "I was a commercial pilot and instructor for some time, then I moved into private aviation."

I silently forked up green beans, eyes moving between the two of them like a tennis spectator. Mama nodded, slow and thoughtful. "Instructor. I can see it. Why not stay commercial?"

Time to break my silence. I reached for my wine. "Mama. Stop bein' so damned nosy." It was out before I could help myself but I made the correction anyway. "Being. Stop being so nosy."

Audrey seemed amused by my outburst, smiling as she shook her head gently. "It's fine," she said to me before turning back to Mama. "The hours and the pay weren't great and a friend mentioned private work. So I did my certifications and never looked back."

"And do you like working with my daughter?" Mama's usage of *with*, not *for* wasn't lost on me. She knew. For sure she knew. I wondered what new and exciting guidance she'd come up with to talk to me about sleeping with an employee.

"Mama."

Audrey ran her foot up my calf and smiled charmingly at both of us. "Yes I do. The company treats its employees very well and the Phenom three hundred is a really sweet aircraft. Handles beautifully. It's almost like leisure time rather than work." She stopped abruptly and picked up her fork. Her cheeks had a faint flush of color. She was adorable when she got excited. I'd never seen this side of her before and I was suddenly conscious of a warm sort of affection in the pit of my stomach.

"Sorry. Once an aircraft geek, always an aircraft geek," Audrey apologized.

Mama smiled. "Nothin' to be sorry about. It's good to be passionate about things. And I'm glad to hear you're treated well." She glanced at me, a hint of pride evident on her face, then back to Audrey. "Now, when you're done with that, I've got pie for dessert."

Conversation flowed easily for the rest of dinner. Audrey had a knack for it, steering and adjusting through the exchanges effortlessly. As I sat there, watching them talking and occasionally interjecting myself, I realized it shouldn't be a surprise. She had an abundance of confidence. But it never slid toward cockiness or arrogance. I clamped a lid down on thoughts of how much I enjoyed having her in my Mama's house, laughing and joking with us.

Though eating dessert went against every cell in my body, skipping was not an option. Mama doled out cherry pie. "Made fresh this afternoon," she told us.

I knew it'd be amazing, but that was beside the point. I put half my portion back, managed to cut her off after one second of cream pouring and yanked the bowl away before she could add another scoop of ice cream. Mama's lips were thinner than paper. Audrey's were trying not to smile. I scraped all the filling out and ate it, and compromised by eating the top crust. It was fucking delicious. My ass agreed and begged me to finish the rest and take seconds. I stood firm and pushed the remainder away. The chickens would eat my leftover pastry. Really, I was doing them a favor.

After dessert we transferred onto the porch with our second bottle to sit and talk. Audrey and I settled on the day bed, pleasantly dulled by wine and food. I was dulled enough that I didn't care when conversation inevitably turned to the things Young Isabelle had done. Academic prizes, athletic events I'd tried, excelled or failed at. The trouble I'd gotten into.

For sure, Mama knew that telling my employee how I'd once worn the same T-shirt for two weeks in protest of my curfew wasn't really acceptable, but she did it anyway. She did it because that's what she did to people with whom I was involved. I knew she knew about us because she looked so damned triumphant when I didn't shut her down.

Near midnight, Audrey started to shift. "I should really get going. Connie, thank you so much for the wonderful meal and company."

"You're welcome, and don't be silly. It's too late to be takin' a taxi back to town, and Bunny, you've certainly drunk too much to drive." She poured the remaining wine between Audrey's and my glasses. "Stay the night, I'll make up the guest room."

Audrey glanced my way, gauging my response. Her expression was feigned nonchalance, but I caught the hopefulness underneath it. She wanted to stay. I wanted her to stay. I shrugged. "I don't have a problem with it," I said and swallowed another mouthful of wine. It was a lie. The problem I had was that she would be right down the hall from me and I was right on the edge of tipsy. Right on the edge of tipsy meant well into horny. The thought of sneaking around having sex and trying to be quiet ratcheted it up even further.

"Well then, I'll see you for breakfast in the morning." Mama kissed my hair and left us to go make up the guest room and, judging by her wink, to give us a little privacy. Things were dire when my own mother was as invested in my relationship as I was.

Audrey and I stared at each other for a few long moments until she spoke, "Should probably go to bed."

"Mmm." I rolled clumsily off the day bed, holding my wineglass triumphantly aloft. I finished it as we walked to the kitchen, making a quick round of the downstairs doors. Not that it would matter if any were forgotten. Mama left doors unlocked all the time but NYC had ruined such casual behavior.

I caught Audrey's arm as she walked past, holding it lightly so she could break away if she wanted to. What the fuck was I thinking? A rhetorical question. I knew exactly what I was thinking, why else would I have brought her here to my hometown? It seemed that she caught on immediately, twisting back toward me. Her mouth was on mine before I could say anything.

Audrey pushed me against the wall beside the refrigerator, her hands on the small of my back, keeping me close. I lifted myself up on tiptoes, groaning as her tongue frantically explored my mouth. She tasted like wine and cherries. My hands took the initiative and slid under her top, making their way up to skim the skin spilling over the cups of her bra. I started to tug her toward the stairs. In that moment I would have taken her on the floor of the kitchen, or the den. On Mama's couch. Anywhere.

Excitement built, threatening to overwhelm me until she pulled away. I groaned, trying to keep her in place. To keep contact with the warmth of her body, the firm muscle and soft curves that were sending shivers through my body.

"We can't," she said breathlessly. "Not here. God I want to, but we can't."

I ran my tongue up her neck and over her ear. "I can be quiet." Besides, Mama's and my rooms were at opposite ends of the house.

"I don't want you to be quiet," she murmured. "I want to hear you scream."

CHAPTER FOURTEEN

I woke before dawn, as was my habit and lazed in bed for a few minutes. I was alone. Last night she'd left me in the kitchen, a wet, quivering and unsatisfied mess. Brushing her lips over mine once more, she'd informed me of her plans. "Sorry, Iz but I am going to be masturbating in your guest room, so you can just think about that." So rude.

She left me to go to bed and help myself, thinking about her barely ten steps away probably doing the same thing. And think about it I did. I came under my own fingers with my teeth in my hand to stifle the sound as I climaxed. Damn her.

The background noise here never changed. The hum of the AC, livestock competing to see who could make the most noise, and the distant sound of trucks making their way to the highway. I slipped from my bed, dressed quickly and headed out for a run. As I passed the guest bedroom I stopped, hand on the doorknob. I had every intention of stealthily opening the door to look at her until I realized just how creepy it would be.

A quick scrawl of RUNNING on the kitchen whiteboard—Mama would worry if she woke and I wasn't in the house—my music cranked up and I was off. I made my way north as the sun started to peek over the horizon, bringing a tentative orange glow with it. I looped around the fairgrounds, bass pounding in my ears to set pace for my feet. For thirty glorious minutes, my head was clear as I ran. Cars were starting to appear on the streets, people on their way to wherever and I raised a hand to greet each and every one that passed.

The air felt moist in my lungs, different to the cool crispness I was accustomed to. It was almost six forty-five by the time I slowed to a cool-down walk up the driveway. The chickens were milling noisily in their coop and rushed out when I opened their door. I tossed out mash for them, gently nudging them out of the way so I could check for eggs. I made a nest in my sweaty tank, scooped up the eggs, and left them on the counter for Mama when she came down to start breakfast.

Mama had exited her room at precisely seven fifteen every morning for as long as I could remember. Her only exceptions were illness, when she pushed it back to seven thirty or the days my granddaddy and Grams died when she didn't come out at all. I had thirty minutes to myself.

My laptop was on the coffee table, still open from last night. I refreshed my market updater and glanced at figures. Then I logged onto the office servers and made a few transfers. Mama came down the stairs as I was stretching on the floor of the den. I craned my neck to look at her.

From my upside down angle, her frown could be taken for a lopsided smile. "Lord, I wish you'd relax when you're here," she grumbled. "I'll put coffee on. Go shower."

There was no indication from the guest room that Audrey was awake. Odd. I knew, from our sleepovers, that she was an early riser like myself. A few steps past the guest room door, I heard a muffled groan. No, she wasn't…she wouldn't. I stopped and strained to listen and I heard it again. Though it was muted, it was a sound I knew well. Yes, she was. Damn her again.

Knowing she was pleasuring herself in the guest room made it very hard to shower without attending to myself. I gave in, leaned my head against the cool tiles and slipped my fingers between my legs. There was nothing slow or sensual about it. It was quick and rough, designed only to ease the pressure she'd caused.

By the time I'd finished my shower with self-service and dressed, I smelled coffee. The guest room was empty, bed neatly made and Audrey nowhere to be seen. Sounds of their conversation carried up to me. The stairs in this house didn't squeak. I could eavesdrop. Laughter. My name. I paused at the base of the stairs. Mama was starting a story about my fourth grade Christmas pageant. It was time to intervene. I bounded down the last few stairs and into the kitchen. "Mornin'."

Both of them looked up, not at all guilty about being caught discussing me. Audrey smiled when I settled opposite her. "Hey." She'd already been issued coffee and fruit, a precursor to the bigger more fried kind of breakfast Mama insisted upon whenever I was in town.

Mama slid a mug of coffee across the table to me. "Have a good run, baby?"

I pulled it closer. "Thank you, Mama. I did." I dropped a teaspoon of sweetener—the only time it was used in Mama's house—into my coffee and turned to Audrey. "How'd you sleep?"

Her smile was slight. "Very well thank you."

Mama started fussing, setting out fruit for me and gathering breakfast supplies. "What did you have planned for today, Audrey?"

Audrey glanced at me then back to Mama. "Uh, I believe there are Farmer's Markets? I thought I might take a look and explore the town a little."

"Great idea. We were going to head on down after breakfast. You're more'n welcome to come with us." Without asking me, Mama starting assembling fillings for my egg white omelet.

"Oh, that's very thoughtful of you, but really I've intruded enough already." She looked to me, eyebrows raised.

I shrugged, sipping coffee. I knew better than to try and change Mama's mind.

"Nonsense." Mama cracked eggs into two bowls, donating my yolks to her and Audrey's. "Now, scrambled okay with you? Bacon? How d'you like your toast?"

* * *

After breakfast, I helped Mama with dishes while Audrey went upstairs to shower. With her out of earshot, Mama pounced. "Why are you keepin' her in a hotel?"

"What do you mean?" I started drying plates.

"You know exactly what I mean." She eyed me shrewdly. "Your new employee, huh?"

Yep, one hundred percent busted. "She is."

"And the rest. I know that look, Bunny, though admittedly I have not seen it in a long while." Mama raised her eyes to the roof, forehead wrinkled. "Not since Jessie Sweaten in college."

Jessie Sweaten. My first real love. Also the first woman to shatter my heart when she dumped me halfway through second semester for a redheaded pre-med. "It's not that easy, Mama."

"So you admit it then!" She grabbed another dishtowel and flicked me with it. "Can't believe you never told me you were datin' someone."

"I don't know what we're doing."

"Well, she looks at you like she's dyin' of thirst and you're a river. Saw it right away last night."

"Mama, please." Despite my protest, I was happy.

"Just callin' it how I see it, and how I see it is my daughter coming alive 'round that woman." She winked at me.

I leaned against the counter, and suddenly had a strange sense of déjà vu. I was nineteen, telling her I was moving to New York and expecting her to be angry. But she wasn't. "You're not gonna lecture me about it bein' a bad idea? Seeing as she is my employee and all."

"You're not dumb, baby. I'm sure you've been through it already." Mama wiped the benches down. "Let her stay here tonight. I'd like to talk to her some more."

Brilliant. "Mama, please. It's complex enough. Be gentle, I'm beggin' you."

She gave me a noncommittal shrug and left me in the kitchen to wait. When Audrey came back downstairs five minutes later she was casual in shorts, a polo and deck shoes. The woman had legs for miles. I kissed her then rushed upstairs to brush my teeth and tame my hair.

It'd been decided at breakfast that we would take two cars—Mama always tired of the markets quickly and Audrey might want to look around. I snagged my keys from the hook beside the fridge. "Mama! We're leaving!"

Mama called back, "Show Audrey 'round town!"

Show her what exactly? There weren't exactly a lot of exciting landmarks. Audrey held the back door open for me. "Do you want me to drive? I can. I mean, I don't know if that's part of my job description, but I'm happy to. Seeing as you don't do it much." She was smirking.

I recoiled in mock horror. "Drive my baby? No, of course not. But thank you for the offer." I actually really liked driving but didn't need a car in New York. I twirled my key ring around my finger as we headed out to the garage where my first, and only, car was garaged.

Audrey helped me drag the door up, metal protesting the entire way. I jammed the peg into a hole in the wall to keep the door from sliding back down. "Can you flip the light, please? Just behind you."

Audrey whistled through her teeth when she spotted my car, a sixty-eight Bahama Blue Mustang Coupe. "Wow. I never would have pegged you as a muscle car kind of girl. Nice."

I grinned at her reaction. The Mustang was a piece of my past to which I clung fiercely. When I bought her, she was midway through being restored before the guy ran out of money and had to sell. Back then, the 'Stang had a mismatched door panel, rips in the leather interior and a passenger window that you had to force up and down. As soon as I could afford it, I'd had her fully restored inside, outside and under the hood. She was a work of art.

I unlocked the driver's door. "My daddy had a Mustang, or so Mama said. I found this one when I was just on seventeen and bought her." It was perhaps the only thing I'd ever done to feel close to the man who'd dumped us eight days before my fifth birthday.

Years later, Mama told me that's what cut her the most about what he did, that I had a birthday without my daddy. I don't remember being concerned. I do remember I got a My Little Pony set and puked after eating too much cake.

I'd been vague when I told Audrey about why he left and I didn't want to elaborate, not now. We'd skimmed over family details around week three. I knew her father had died when she was thirteen, but she'd been vague about the cause. Her mother still lived in Minnesota and her only sibling, an older brother, in Oregon.

I slid in and opened the passenger door for her. "Mama keeps her turning over for me." Still, the engine caught a few times as it always did before she fired up. The deep rumble bounced off the walls, reverberating through my chest. I fished in my purse for sunglasses, then leaned over to dump the bag on the passenger floor. My breast brushed Audrey's arm and my nipples tightened reflexively at the touch. Down girls.

Audrey gave no sign that she'd noticed the touch or the bullet points of my nipples. "This car is really not what I expected."

I grinned. "No? What did you expect?" We were sitting in the garage while the car warmed a little.

"Something fancier, newer. More like a Lamborghini or an Aston Martin or something, but you've still got your first car." She turned to me and her expression turned soft, like she knew something I didn't. "I think I'm starting to get it now."

"Get what?"

"You."

My heart started racing and didn't let up its ridiculous fluttering the whole way to City Hall. My brain kept up a loop of *she gets you, she gets you*, making my words clumsy and slow. I wrestled with telling her that Mama knew about us. In the end, I settled for a not-lying but not-quite-truthful account. "Mama wanted me to ask you if you'd like to come to dinner again."

"She did?" Audrey's tone was neutral.

Mine was not. It was hopeful tinged with fearful. "Mhmm. Says you're welcome to stay the night again too."

"I see. And what about the hotel? It wouldn't have been used. Seems a waste."

"It doesn't matter," I said quietly. In that moment there were few things that could matter less than an unused hotel booking.

She twisted on the supple black leather seat to face me. "What do *you* want me to do, Isabelle?"

I didn't even need to think about it. "I want you to stay."

Audrey nodded thoughtfully. "If that's what you want, then I will. I'd like to."

"Well, all right then." I slowed down as we approached the courthouse. "Shall I give you the Grand Tour?"

"Please do."

I nodded toward the back of the building. "That's where I had my first kiss, in the parking lot. Krista, my best friend at the time, well…she had to go to court for stealin' a bunch of road signs. I went with her for moral support and when we came out, she dragged me around to the hidden side of the building and kissed me. Then ran off and never said a word about it again. Still don't know why."

"Must have been a really shitty kiss."

I grinned. "Undoubtedly. And just up there, that's where I reversed into Maggie Anderson's new car. Only had my license a week and dinged Mama's car too. Worked all summer to pay for repairs."

I pointed at the back corner of the supermarket parking lot. "That's where I saw my first real girlfriend kissing someone else, a guy, and coincidentally where I threw my drink in her face."

Audrey laughed, throaty and appealing. "Seems like you had some great memories here. Why'd you leave?"

I glanced over at her quickly then back to the road. "Wanted something bigger 'n' better, I guess."

"Did you find it?"

I smiled to myself. "Yeah, think I did."

CHAPTER FIFTEEN

We met Mama at the markets near the tea stand, then lost her somewhere between a barbeque stall and the guy doing sketches for five dollars. I needed to regroup with an ice cream and start the search. She could have been anywhere but my guess was the Coopers' blown glass display or one of the food stalls.

I tugged Audrey toward Maureen Barton's ice cream stand. It'd been a fixture at the markets for as long as I remembered and she sold one thing and one thing only—vanilla ice cream she made herself with milk from her own cows. A few years back, she put the price up from eighty cents to eighty-five and it'd caused a huge fuss. She was reluctant but she said it was, "About time to account for inflation."

Maureen leaned over the edge of the wooden counter. "Is-a-belle. How are you, honey? Haven't seen you for a bit."

"Howdy, Maureen. I'm just fine. You're lookin' well. Hello, Hank." I nodded to her husband who sat silently and unresponsively in back, reading his paper the way he always did.

Maureen shrugged. "Can't complain. What can I get you?"

"Two cones, thank you." I dug in my pocket but Audrey placed a hand on my wrist to stop me. She pulled a couple of notes from her wallet and passed them to Maureen, along with the sweetest smile. A weird sensation snaked under my skin. It took a moment for me to connect the dots. Audrey and I *shared*. We both bought meals when we ate together, and now she was buying me an ice cream. I tucked the feeling out of the way to be examined later. While Maureen was sorting change in her quiet methodical way, I asked if she'd seen Mama.

Maureen reached over to drop coins in Audrey's outstretched hand. "Believe I saw her over near Pete Windham's plant stall 'bout ten minutes ago." Audrey tilted her palm to empty the coins into the tip jar.

I added all the loose change from my pocket as well. "Great, thanks. Good to see y'all."

"You too, honey."

Audrey waited until we were a few feet away before launching her attack. "Y'all." The delight in her teasing was clear as day.

I groaned. "I know, it just happens. I can't help it."

"I like it." Her tongue made a lap around the bottom of her ice cream, the slow and deliberate movement making me think of her tongue making laps around other things.

I blinked the thought away. "Please don't."

"I meant the ice cream." Her eyes twinkled. She had her lips clamped together, watching me. "I'm sorry, Iz."

"Why d'you tease?" Ice cream trickled against my fingers. I raised my hand to lick it off.

"Because you're so adorable when you blush that I just can't help myself. And that little crease near your lips drives me crazy." She stepped closer and I thought she was going to kiss me, right there in the open. I found myself leaning closer, wanting it.

Audrey smiled down at me, eyes drifting to my lips. "Come on, let's go find your mom."

After five minutes, we found Mama buying scarves and feigning surprised forgetfulness at having lost us. She was sneaky, I had to give her that. I endured ten minutes of having scarves held against my chest, with Audrey and my mother engaging in a serious back and forth about which ones suited me best. I bought the two Audrey seemed to like the most then we wandered for another half hour, until Mama declared she'd had enough and was going to fetch something for dinner. She hugged both of us and promised to see us back at home. "No later than five, hear me?"

Yep, I was twelve all over again. Audrey and I kept wandering and I thanked every deity—and added in the universe for good measure—that she'd finally given up ribbing me about the uninvited guest that was my renewed southern drawl. We passed by a food stand run by Mr. Gardener, my eleventh grade math teacher. Mr. G had retired last year and now spent some of his free time hawking barbeque at the markets. I waved.

Mr. G beckoned me over. "Isabelle Rhodes, how're you?"

"Just fine, sir. How 'bout yourself?"

"Kickin' along."

"I'm glad to hear it."

He rested his forearms on the counter. "Glad I caught you. Mind if I talk to you quick about my four oh one?"

"Course not. What about it?" I lifted a hand to shield my eyes against the sun.

"Well, I just don't think it's doin' as well as it could." He chuckled. "And I sure as heck don't trust the guy who's takin' care of it."

I grinned. "You know what they say. If you wanna get the best, you gotta have the best."

He tsk'd me, smiling. "Well, I can't afford the best. Just thought you might know someone."

"I do. You're lookin' at her." I tugged a card out of my purse. "You know I'll take care of you."

"Oh, that's real kind but it's just a little fund. Hardly worth your time."

"Nonsense." I shook the card until he took it. "You give me a call next week and we'll work something out."

"Well, all right then. Thank you. Now, you ladies hungry?"

I glanced at Audrey, who nodded. "Sure."

Mr. G—I still couldn't bring myself to call him Lem—started compiling two of his lunch specials for us. "Ten percent off for my best kids." His weathered face lit up. "Math quiz time. How much does that come down to?"

Beside me, Audrey barely managed to contain her laughter. I nudged her, glancing at his prices. "I'm still pretty sure I'll never get anything under an A minus, Mr. G. Six eighty-four." I handed him ten and answered before he could ask how much change I was owed. "And I'll take three 'n' sixteen back."

He winked. "Knew there was a reason you were my star student."

I laughed and dropped the change into his tip jar. "You take care and I'll talk to you next week." I held my plate aloft. "Thanks for lunch."

We settled at the weather-worn plastic furniture under the even more worn awning outside Mr. G's stall. Audrey stared at her lunch plate. "I could live here just for the food."

I nodded, distributing disposable cutlery. "It's one of the things I miss most. Plus, you know, Mama."

We were silent for a few minutes as we ate. I tried not to watch her but found my gaze constantly drawn back to her. She had a habit, I'd discovered last night, of compiling forkfuls that had a little bit of everything on her plate. I hadn't noticed it before, probably because we never sat opposite, always side-by-side. I wondered what other things she did that I still didn't know about.

Audrey wiped her mouth. "Do you always do that?"

I looked up. "What?" Maybe I wasn't being as sneaky with my watching as I'd thought.

"Help like that." Discreetly, she indicated Mr. G.

"Oh." I lowered my voice. "Some of 'em don't have much. It's not right to take more than bare minimum. It doesn't hurt me, so why not?"

She studied me inscrutably. I tilted my head, eyebrows lifted and waited for her to tell me what she was thinking, but saying nothing more she picked up her knife and fork again. I forked up slaw, unable to come up with any way to enquire without sounding intrusive.

As it turned out, I didn't need to ask. Audrey pushed mashed potato into a neat pile. "Just when I think I've got you figured out…"

I swallowed my mouthful. "What d'you mean?"

This time, she didn't answer me, just smiled and shook her head as though it was a secret she wanted to hold on to for now.

After lunch, we wandered for another half hour—her buying a few more things, me being waylaid by townsfolk to chat. Near two p.m. on our way out, Audrey pointed to one of the stalls near the exit. "I'm going to grab a drink—you want one?"

"No thanks."

Audrey came back with a clear cup of tea, condensation dripping down the sides. She took a sip and ran her tongue along her lower lip, making a small sound of delight.

I tried not to think of the way the moisture reminded me of sweat sliding down her stomach. "How's your sweet tea?"

She smiled around the straw clamped between her teeth. "Good." She let the straw drop and offered me the cup. "You want some?"

I glanced at the straw, thought briefly that it'd been in her mouth—lucky thing—and leaned over to take a sip.

"Say sweet tea again," she said in that low, sensual voice I loved. I shook my head and held eye contact with her as I drank again. Audrey smiled at my resistance, handed me the drink and went back to buy another for herself.

Walking back to the car under the beautiful sky with a beautiful woman by my side I had an uncontrollable urge to take her hand. I stuffed my free hand into my pocket to stop myself. "Did you want to look 'round some more?"

"Sure."

This time, I took Audrey for a slower sightseeing tour. As we drove back past the hall on our way home, she turned sideways to face me. "Would you take me somewhere meaningful?"

"Meaningful?"

"Yeah, you know, somewhere you used to hang out."

Without a word, I did a sharp U-turn and started toward the old forest clearing. Slowing the Mustang to a crawl to accommodate the rough dirt road, I drove us toward my old hang out spot. The road was much as I remembered, though it was a little overgrown.

"Should I be worried that you're taking me into a forest?" Audrey glanced at her phone. "A forest that appears to have zero reception."

I laughed. "What are you concerned about?"

"Oh, you know. The usual sinister things one thinks about when being driven into a secluded area."

"Really? The only thing I ever thought about when I used to come here was making out with girls."

"Well in that case, drive on." Her hand came over to rest on my thigh as I negotiated the track. After a few minutes I came to the large, almost circular clearing and parked parallel to the forest. As teenagers we'd come here to make out, drink and listen to music. It looked a lot different during the day.

We sat quietly for a while, listening to the radio, in one of those moments where it feels awkward to ruin the moment with talking. Audrey fussed a little, and eventually murmured, "Today was really nice."

"Yeah, it was. I liked being out with you in public." I turned the ignition, leaving the radio on low volume. One of the questions Dr. Baker had asked pinged around my head. "Does… it bother you that we don't go out more?"

If she was surprised, she didn't show it. "Sometimes, yes. But at the same time, we kind of agreed that we wouldn't be doing that."

"Yes. We did agree on that." It would be so easy to say something, to hint that maybe we could change the rules again, but I was too much of a coward to verbalize what I felt.

"So I guess I'm okay with it then, keeping things secret," she said carefully. The wording was odd, like she was resigned to what we'd agreed upon rather than happy about it. Before I could respond, Audrey wound down the window, leaning out to look around. "So this is your old make out spot?"

"Mhmm."

"And why would you bring me here, Isabelle?" she asked coyly, settling back in her seat.

I unbuckled my seatbelt. "Wanted to see if it was as good as I remembered." I almost lost my virginity in this spot and in the passenger seat of this car. Tamara Hewson came home from college and taught me a few things she'd learned while she'd been away.

Audrey's eyes moved from mine, to my lips, my breasts and then back up again. "I see. Maybe we should test it out again, see if it still feels the same. For science."

I bit my lip. "Maybe."

"I do love a good experiment. Top prize at the science fair three years straight." She grinned, and reached over to fiddle with the radio until she found a classic nineties station. "Better make sure all the parameters are the same."

I leaned closer, my lips a whisper away from hers. "You're such a nerd."

"I think you like it," she said, and closed the distance between us. Our kiss was surprisingly gentle, almost tentative. Completely unlike our usual heated kisses, it didn't feel awkward or wrong but rather, like one of the sweetest moments we'd shared so far.

This wasn't like our usual foreplay, more like we were kissing for the sake of kissing, which has its own joy. Audrey's hands came to my face, fingers against my neck and her thumb rubbing lightly along my jaw. Despite the curl of pleasure in my belly, I didn't deepen the kiss and neither did she.

Needing to take a breath, I pulled away first but not out of her reach. Audrey's hands stayed on my face and she stared at me so intently that I felt as though I'd been stripped naked. Embarrassed by the emotion that was surely evident on my face, I leaned in and kissed her again. I was distantly aware of the song changing from Coolio to TLC, but nothing else registered. It was just her and me and kissing.

Insistent tapping on the window behind me startled me into breaking the kiss. Twisting around, I saw a familiar amused face and a uniform. Perfect. The female police officer sounded like she was about to laugh. "Excuse me, but I'm going to have to ask you both to exit the vehicle."

"Yes, officer. Just a moment, please."

Audrey smothered her laugh, voice high with mirth. "I heard a car, thought it was just another couple."

Less than amused, I checked my appearance in the mirror, and satisfied I looked somewhat presentable, I exited the car. "Officer. Ma'am." Just the right amount of respect for my childhood pal, Mary.

Mary nodded to Audrey, who was standing behind the Mustang, then turned to me. "Isabelle Rhodes. Thought I recognized your car turnin' onto the track. Well, some things just never change, do they? Couldn't even wait 'til it got dark?" she drawled.

I couldn't help grinning. "Apparently not. How're you doin', Mary?"

"Just fine. You?" She hooked her thumbs in her duty belt, rocking back on her heels. It seemed to me she was enjoying herself just a little too much.

"I'm well." I cleared my throat. "How's Scott?" The irony of this small talk with my best friend from kindergarten was not lost on me. All I'd been doing was having a sweet and very vanilla make out session, whereas Mary had done a whole lot more right here with my ninth grade dance date, Scott Devery. If memory served, they were still together and had three kids.

"He's doin' well. Building business is really takin' off."

The back of my neck was uncomfortably hot. "I'm glad to hear it."

"Mmm. Well I'm 'fraid I'm gonna have to ask y'all to move on. Consider this a warnin'. Maybe next time wait 'til dark so nobody'll see you, or use a bed seeing as you're not seventeen anymore."

"Absolutely. Thank you. Uh, tell Scott I said hi."

She flicked the brim of her hat, smiling widely. "I'll be sure to do that."

I turned back to the car and rested my head against the edge of the roof, burning myself on the hot metal almost right away. I straightened and looked over at Audrey, who'd given in to her mirth now that the cop car was leaving. In this tiny insular town I'd be headline news by tomorrow morning. Mama would never let me live it down.

Audrey was shaking with laughter. "That was fucking magnificent."

"It was fucking mortifying is what it was."

"Come on, Iz. It's hysterical. Of course we'd get caught. Of *course*." She wiped her eyes. Despite my embarrassment, her enjoyment was contagious and by the time I'd started the car, I was laughing with her.

CHAPTER SIXTEEN

Audrey and I laughed almost the whole way home while I told her all my stories from the forest. As promised, Mama had been to the market and brought home a haul for me to grill for dinner, which she insisted I start the moment I finished showering.

Ever since her friend Dolores left the gas on for five minutes before lighting her grill and lost her eyebrows, Mama had been scared of the barbeque. Dolores was lucky that was all she lost. Rumor had it you could see the fireball from blocks away.

I could barely concentrate on the task at hand. Audrey was upstairs showering and had been gone ten minutes. I had a fair idea of what she was doing. Damn her. My skin burned with the memory of her lips against mine sharing endless slow kisses. I ran a hand over the back of my neck. Mama dragged me out of my reverie with a warning. "Don't let it get too hot, Bunny."

"Mama, if you wanna grill, then grill. Otherwise sit on your butt and leave it to me."

"Mmm, well all right then." She busied herself filling glasses. "Tell me, how was the rest of your afternoon?"

I tilted my head to check the flame. "Just fine."

Mama handed me a very full glass of wine. "I heard a funny rumor just before you two got in."

"Oh?" I bent my head to take a careful sip.

"Apparently Mary Devery picked up a couple out at the old clearing. The one where you kids used to hang out."

This town. That took all of an hour to get to her. "Yeah?"

"Yeah. Word is they were butt naked and in a *very* compromisin' position."

"We were not naked and all we were doing was kissin'!" The moment the words came out I scrunched my face up, mentally cursing myself. Mama was the only person who ever caught me out like that.

Her eyes glinted. "Well then, isn't that something." Part of the reason for her glee chose that moment to arrive and save me from discussing it further. Audrey accepted an icy beer and stood close to me, peering at the grill. "Sure it's hot enough?"

I gave her a withering glance and it may have been almost convincing, if it weren't for the fact I'd almost collapsed from her freshly-showered scent. "Yes. It's hot enough."

The three of us sat out on the porch, drinking and chatting, and every few minutes I got up to check the grill. Adding this, moving that. Grilling was the one kind of cooking I was good at. Every item had a set amount of time it needed. Turn, wait, done. It was formulaic, not intuitive. Something I could handle.

We ate outside, and the whole time I kept waiting for Mama to say something about me that would scare Audrey off. As the levels in the bottles grew lower and the moon got higher we laughed louder, told more outlandish stories and all grew closer. I learned that Audrey's mom had owned an art gallery for some thirty-five years, and that her father had been absent since Audrey was thirteen. She told us this quickly and matter-of-factly and for once, realizing it was a sensitive subject, Mama didn't push for more.

But it was new information for me, and I wanted to know the details. I wanted to jump over those lines we'd drawn and gather up every part of her—the funny and the sweet and the painful parts of her life. I wanted it all. But I wasn't allowed to ask her for it.

After midnight, Mama stood up and declared she was ready to drag her old bones to bed. I looked up at her from where I was lounging on the day bed. "Night."

She leaned over from behind, took my face in warm hands and planted a couple of kisses on my forehead. "Night, Bunny." Mama stroked Audrey's hair and left us. The screen door closed quietly.

"Are you ever going to tell me how you got that nickname?" Audrey reached over to grab my thigh. Her grip was light, fingers gently stroking my leg.

My smile was so wide I felt it stretching my already overused cheek muscles. "No. Not yet."

Her eyes narrowed, jokingly. "I'll get it out of you. One day."

I shrugged, still smiling. "You think so?" I was too embarrassed to tell her how at age three, I'd climbed into the rabbit hutch and was eating their food when Mama found me.

"Mhmm. You know, you're different here," she mused. "Softer."

I ran my thumb around the rim of my empty glass. "Guess there's nothing spiky here. Don't need my hard shell."

The ghost of a frown crossed her mouth then disappeared. "I guess you're right."

"You ready to turn in?"

"As I'll ever be." Audrey stood and offered me her hand. When I made it to my feet, she tugged me forward to pull me purposely off balance. I grabbed at her and was enfolded in strong arms. Held tight and not let go.

We didn't hug much. Not standing up. Not like this. We'd hug quickly as a greeting or a goodbye. We'd clutch each other as we gave each other pleasure. We slept intertwined and sprawled on each other watching television. But hugging? Nope.

I relaxed into her immediately. My arms stole around her waist and I held onto her like she was the only thing keeping me upright. In a way she was—we had drunk a decent amount of wine—but this was more than that. Whenever I was with her, I felt safe. I felt understood. I felt like me.

Audrey's nose brushed against my hair. When I looked up at her she took my face in her hands and kissed me sweetly. "Let's go inside."

We shared sink space, brushing teeth and bumping elbows. She waited while I applied my nightly skin-firming moisturizer. Wrinkles? What wrinkles? I flipped the lights off and she used her phone to illuminate the hallway.

"Night." Another soft kiss and a brush of her nose through my hair before she turned away.

"Audrey?"

"Yeah?"

"Stay in here tonight?"

She chuckled. "Iz, I can't screw you in your mother's house."

"No, we don't have to." I swallowed a little of my fear. "I meant just sleep in here with me."

Her neutral expression was visible by the light from her phone. "Sleep," she repeated.

"Yes. Really, you don't have to sleep in the guest room. I'd like you to stay with me." If she did, it would be the first time we'd ever just *slept* together.

"Why?" She asked the question lightly but there was weight underneath that single word. She was offering me something.

I drew a deep breath and took what she offered. "Because, I don't sleep right when you're not with me."

She held my face in her hands again, soft fingertips tracing my features. "Then I'll stay."

The routine had been changed again. Our goalposts moved once more. I'd dropped everything in her palm, all my vulnerability and my trust, and she'd taken it then closed her hand to keep it safe.

* * *

My bed in Mama's house was not made for sharing. We were jammed together, intertwined, her arm slung under my neck, hand on my breast. The other arm tight around my waist. Our legs tangled, my ass against her hips and her face in my neck. My arm was lost in the gap between the bed and the wall.

"Wondered when you were going to wake up." Her words were muffled in my hair.

I hugged her arm, stretching. My muscles responded, unfurling like a flag and my shoulder popped. "What time is it?"

She shifted, releasing me a little. "Little after seven."

"Mama will be up soon."

Her arms came tight around me again. "Let's sleep a little while longer."

"Gotta get up." The complete lack of conviction in my statement was evident, even to me. When I rolled over, her eyes were scrunched closed. I kissed her nose and she startled, eyes wide.

I kissed her lips this time. "Now you're awake."

Though Mama protested, once breakfast was done, Audrey insisted on leaving us alone. I gave her the Mustang and pointed her in the general direction of some things I thought she might like to see. Audrey left with a promise to return at four, ready for Mama to take us back to the airport. Mama and I spent the day gardening and playing the interrogation game. She tried to be casual about it, slipping questions in among asking me to yank that weed or dig down a little further. "So, what are you gonna do about this, Bunny?"

"I don't know. I'm confused. I don't know what I want and I don't know what she wants." I snipped dead leaves off her Black-Eyed Susans.

"Have you tried talking to her about it?"

"No. Maybe a little. I don't...I don't know what to say." I don't know was the theme of the moment. The only thing I knew was that I wanted her in my life, and I wanted more than what we had.

Mama looked at me from under the brim of her straw gardening hat. "Well. I like her and I think she's good for you, baby. You're more relaxed than I've seen you in a long while."

I didn't comment but she was right. Audrey *was* good for me. I tugged at a loose thread on my gardening gloves, unable to meet Mama's gaze. "It's complicated."

"I think the only thing making it complicated is you."

She and Nat must have been having secret meetings. I looked up. "Oh, Nat asked me to say hi."

"Well you can tell her hi back."

I cupped dirt into a small pile. "I told you she's getting married?" Mama loved my college roommate. I still smiled when I thought of their first meeting. Mama was so thoroughly charmed by my gorgeous butch friend that I wondered if she wasn't harboring secret tendencies.

"You did not," Mama said accusingly. "Good for her. When's the weddin'?"

"Early March."

Mama shook her head as though she couldn't quite believe it. "Natalie gettin' married. Well I think that's just great." She eyed me shrewdly and pushed herself to her feet.

Back inside, I picked up Grams' ring from where I'd left it on the kitchen table to keep it safe while I played in the dirt. Mama stared at her mother's ring on my finger. "You know, Grams would have liked for you to give that ring to someone, baby."

I fought against the lump in my throat. Mama's mama was the first person I'd told I was gay and when she died in my final year of college, I felt like I'd lost one of the most important things in my life. I wasn't surprised that Grams was so accepting—she'd raised Mama after all. Mama, who did pretty much whatever she wanted, including having me before she married my daddy. By the time I made the declaration about my sexuality, I think Grams had seen pretty much everything and was done fussing about what other people thought.

I covered my sadness with annoyance at my mother's insinuations. "Mama, you're so far ahead of yourself I'm surprised you haven't time traveled."

My mother simply nodded, a slight smile lifting the edge of her mouth. "Mhmm. Whatever you say, Bunny."

CHAPTER SEVENTEEN

Mama chattered the whole way to the airport. Her main theme was that we—emphasis on both Audrey and me—should come back and visit real soon. Mama hugged me for what seemed like hours then planted multiple kisses on the top of my head and forehead. "Call me when you get home."

"Sure will. Love you, Mama."

"Love you too, baby." Mama released me to grab Audrey. "Thanks for visitin' me."

I'm not sure if Audrey was concerned or not by my mother's enthusiastic hugging. It didn't seem so. She looked at me over Mama's shoulder. "Thank you so much for having me, Connie."

"Was my absolute pleasure. Ya'll take care now. Safe trip home."

Once we'd stepped through the door, I turned to give Mama a final wave. Audrey wandered toward the admin area. "Give me a moment? I just need to arrange paperwork."

I took a seat while Audrey did whatever Audrey had to do, and checked the markets.

"Ready to go?"

My head snapped up at her question. "Yep."

We headed out onto the tarmac toward the hangar, so close our hands were brushing. It would be so easy for me to slip mine into hers. To interlace our fingers. It wouldn't be the first time. She often pinned my hands over my head while her lips were on my neck, thighs and hips grinding against me. I swallowed. If she hadn't been in uniform and we weren't in public, I may have seriously considered taking her hand.

"Thanks for being so adaptable with the whole Mama thing. I'm real sorry, I know she's full on."

"No she's not. She's great. I really enjoyed myself." She smiled, so sweet and so sincere that I was suddenly even more desperate to kiss her. We stopped by the jet, and Audrey cleared her throat, an unusually nervous gesture for her. "Thanks for letting me come along this weekend," she said quickly, as if she wanted to get the words out before she could think about it. "I liked spending time with you and your mom."

"You're welcome. I know she liked spending time with you as well."

"And you? How did you feel about it?" She looked away from me, opened the side panel on the jet and input the code to let the stairs down.

I studied her profile. "I liked it too but honestly, that was one of the hardest weekends of my life. Having you around but not being able to have you." Giving in, I reached over and trailed my fingers over her forearm.

It tensed under my touch. "I...I really can't. Not now."

"I know, I know. Work first," I grumbled, extracting my hand. "What if I just helped myself while you're flying me home?" My hand brushed over my breast. The pulse in my groin was reaching fever pitch, nipples painfully hard inside my bra.

Audrey turned to look at me with a pleading expression. "Then I'd be able to hear you and we'd be a plane crash statistic. Please, just let me do my job." The words were clipped, almost strangled.

She was right, I was being unfair. I removed my hand—dammit to hell—hiked my laptop bag back onto my shoulder and grasped the railing with my free hand.

"Go on up, while I keep an eye on things," she said quietly.

While Audrey organized refueling, I responded to emails and confirmed appointments. I was all too aware that once we left South Carolina, we would likely leave something behind. There'd be no more outings, no lighthearted family time. It'd be back to the simple meal, television and fuck routine we'd perfected. And I hated the thought.

Audrey jogged up the stairs and stowed her bags. As she closed the door, she gestured toward the cockpit. "Are you ready to depart, Ms. Rhodes?"

"Ready when you are." I bit down on my lower lip, noticing her reversion to using Ms. Rhodes, and not liking it one bit.

I tried to work but found myself unable to concentrate. My thoughts were filthy, imagining her spread on one of the seats in the cabin. By the time we came in for approach, I'd fucked her a hundred times, every way possible, imagining the sounds she made as she came. I was wet and quivering with anticipation. When we'd landed, I knew I would have her in the jet. I didn't care if it was on the seat, in the cockpit or the galley or on the carpet. I just had to have her.

We taxied into the hangar and I stayed seated until the drone of the engines cut out. I unbuckled, staring at the still-closed curtain separating her and me. Long moments passed and she still hadn't emerged. Discomfort settled in my belly. Maybe she hadn't really missed the physicality of our relationship this weekend. Maybe I'd pushed too hard.

The curtain slid back and she climbed from the cockpit. She stood motionless, studying me with those dark eyes. When she finally spoke, her voice was low and commanding. "Isabelle... come here." The naked expression of want on her face was unmistakable.

Desire and relief made me clumsy, and I almost tripped trying to get to the cockpit, clutching at the entryway. Audrey grabbed at me, pushing me back into the cabin. I was unbuttoning her work shirt, my lips moving on her neck. "This weekend, that flight. Torture."

"Tell me about it," she breathed. "I'm sorry, I'm not officially off duty, but I can't help myself. I want you so badly. I'm sorry," she repeated urgently.

"Shhh it's okay," I soothed her around our kisses.

"You'll make your driver wait."

"Then hurry up and make me come." I finally managed to tug her shirt off, exposing those tight breasts. Fuck she was so beautiful. I unfastened her bra to give myself access and tossed it on the floor. A hand on her hip, head bent to take a nipple under my tongue. Audrey's hand came to clutch my ponytail as I suckled her.

She yanked my top off and pulled me down. Carpet soft against my bare back, her thigh between both of mine to keep me spread. My heels dug into the floor as she trailed kisses over every inch of bare skin, drawing me out, teasing me. I couldn't stand it. Not now after days being close but still without her. "Please...please let me come." My begging was hoarse with need.

Her first lick was so soft and so sweet I almost went into orbit. I bucked underneath her and bit my hand. "More. Harder, please."

She ignored me, making a soft sweep over my throbbing clit before kissing her way back up, tongue sliding over my breasts before coming back to my mouth.

"Turn around. I want to taste you," I mumbled against her lips. Thinking of her in my mouth as she licked me sent my arousal into overtime.

Propping herself up, Audrey glanced down at me with a devilish grin. "Stay."

I lifted my head to watch as she yanked the rest of her clothes off and then crawled over me to settle between my legs. Grabbing her ass, I held her in place and wasted no time burying myself in her heat. So wet, coating my tongue, thick and delicious. She groaned and I felt her tense under my hands as I lapped at her, not bothering with soft or gentle.

Audrey buried her tongue in me, and contrary to my quick and rough worship, she was taking her time, carefully tasting everything she already knew so well. I had no idea how she could go slowly. Having her in my mouth, her fingers parting me so she could lick me, and her hair against my thighs had fanned my desire to a point where I felt ready to explode. I couldn't be slow with her—I needed to consume her.

I could tell by the low groans, the hardness of the muscle in her ass that she was holding off for me. How considerate. Maybe she was thinking about long division to stop herself coming. Probably not. After what I'd learned about her over the weekend and how much she liked science stuff, she'd likely find math arousing. Finally, she stopped teasing and with a few firm strokes, tipped me over the edge. My cries were loud, echoing off the walls of the jet as I came, just before she did.

By the time I'd gathered my wits, Audrey had dressed and checked that everything in the jet was shut down. I dressed and put my hair back up into an impersonation of a ponytail. A very loose interpretation.

"Come here." She took my face gently in both hands to kiss me. "Thank you again for this weekend. All of it."

I raised my eyes to hers. "No. Thank *you*." A weird lump in my throat made my words squeak.

Penny was standing by the car when we finally emerged, only fifteen minutes late. "Good evening, Ms. Rhodes."

"So sorry to keep you waiting." My smile was apologetic as I tried to tamp down my undeniably frizzed sex hair.

Audrey chimed in with a disarming smile. "Late departure," she said smoothly.

"Of course. Not a problem at all." Pen took my bag from me and moved away to stow it in the trunk. The woman knew something was going on, I could see it in her expression. Smug, and also oddly pleased but trying to hide both.

I stuffed my hands in my pockets. "I'll see you later this week?"

"Count on it." Audrey turned toward my driver. "I'll catch you later, Penny. Tell Loretta I said hi and I'll call about dinner during the week." She walked off without waiting for an answer. They knew one another?

Settled in the backseat, I didn't even need to ask before Penny told me, "Captain Graham and I...used to play softball together. It was me who told her there was a job opening at Rhodes and Hall."

"I see." I should give my driver a finder's fee.

"I hope I didn't overstep, Ms. Rhodes."

"Oh geez, Pen. Not at all." I leaned forward, resting an elbow on the back of the passenger seat. "So, is she any good?"

Penny laughed. "She's decent in the field but can't bat worth a damn."

I grinned, finding it hard to believe that lithe, athletic Audrey was bad at any aspect of sport. "Speaking of, did you watch the game?"

My driver seemed relieved by the abrupt change of topic signaling I was done talking about how Audrey came to work for my company. "Sure did. It was brilliant. Are you ready to depart?"

As we drove around the building, I noticed Audrey strolling toward the lot where her motorcycle would be parked. Penny's question startled me from my blatant ogling. "Did you have a pleasant weekend, Ms. Rhodes?"

I dragged my eyes away from my lover's spectacular assets. "Yes. Yes I did."

"I'm very pleased to hear that." She caught my eye in the rearview, then cleared her throat. Penny seemed on edge, which made me wonder if despite my reassurances she thought I was annoyed with her for suggesting Audrey apply for the pilot's job.

The vibe in the car had turned into a weird mix of confusion and discomfort. Rather than add to it by bringing up Audrey and Penny's connection again, I chose to stay silent and think about the weekend. The more I thought, the more I flitted between contentment and panic. What the hell was I doing? I rested my head on the headrest and chanted to myself *casual casual casual*.

As promised, when I got home I called Nat.

"Spill. How was it?" she asked.

"Amazing. Perfect. Terrifyingly so. Nat, she just...fits. You know? Like, everything's comfortable."

"Rhodes, it may be possible that you've found the only uncomplicated and baggage-free woman in the country."

"I know."

"Did you tell her?"

With the phone between my ear and shoulder, I fixed my ponytail. "No. But I thought about it, like truly honestly thought about it."

Nat grunted. "Every single lesbian in the world hates you for being such a chickenshit, you know that right?"

"Mmmm," I agreed.

"So stop squandering it. I'm serious. You've got two weeks and then I'm staging an intervention. Full page notice in the Times. AG date me, love IR."

Laughing, I opened the fridge and pulled a bottle of water from between Audrey's beer and some takeout I'd forgotten to toss out. "I promise, I'm working on it. I just want it to be the right time." I dumped containers in the trash.

"Right time? You're not staging a fucking moon launch, Rhodes. Just tell her."

* * *

Audrey and I didn't see each other until Friday of that week. Functions, dinners, late meetings and Mark taking the jet—and her—for an overnight on Thursday kept us apart. Antsy and out of sorts, I was almost pacing my apartment as I waited for her. When you're used to getting laid nearly every day, five days feels like an eternity. There was no greeting, just hands and lips finding familiar places as we bumped into furniture and the walls on our way to my bedroom, leaving clothing like a breadcrumb trail for when we would eventually emerge.

When we crossed to my bed, I was down to a thong and my stockings. Audrey panties only. She pushed me onto the bed, settling on top of me right away, but not before I reached between us to slip my fingers under the fabric. No surprise, she was wet already. I rubbed lazy circles, lightly sliding my fingers over her clit.

Audrey grasped my wrist, moving my hand up to her lips. With teasing slowness, she took my fingers in her mouth, sucking herself from them. The whole time, as her tongue played over me she kept eye contact. My stomach flipped, heart thumped in my chest, clitoris begged for attention. Then she guided my hand back between her legs and kissed me. I could taste her. Oh God. I groaned.

Our bodies reunited without thought. Quickly, slowly, hard and soft. We cried our climaxes again and again until we were finally spent. Wet with sweat. Satisfied but also totally unsatisfied. I rolled over to face her.

She was serene, breasts rising and falling with each breath. Audrey always breathed deep and slow, as if she wanted to savor every ounce of oxygen. Perhaps not *always*. I could make her breathing quicken. Make her pant and gasp. Her eyes were closed, a little smile on her face. She didn't need to talk, never felt the urge to cover silence with conversation the way I did.

I was better at being still and silent since we'd been together...since we'd started sleeping together, I mean. I rolled onto my back, noting a cobweb over in the far corner of my room. Note to self: talk to cleaner. "How was your week?"

"Great." Slowly, her eyes opened and found mine. "I flew my plane up to Maine to see some friends, caught up on housework. Flew Mr. Hall around. Mundane shit. You?"

"Work and functions," I said bluntly. Propping myself up on an elbow, I stared at her. She stared back until I smiled, caught out. "You know, we never really talk about things we like. Hobbies and stuff." My words were cautious. This could go either way. Either why *would* we or why *should* we. Or we'd agree that yes, we could talk about more personal things.

"You're right. We don't. Do you want to talk about those things?"

I shrugged, trying and probably failing to appear nonchalant. "I guess."

The corner of her mouth lifted and I had to stop myself from leaning over to kiss the curved edge of her mouth. "Hobbies. Let's see…I used to play softball, right when I moved to the city but it's tricky these days. You never know when you're going to be dragged out of town."

"Yeah I know. Penny told me that's how you guys know each other. What position?"

She raised both eyebrows comically. "Second base."

"You didn't even make it to third base? Wow. I find that hard to believe," I kidded.

She grinned. "Funny." The grin faded a little. "Pen said we were just softball pals?"

"Mhmm."

"I'm not sure why she said that, but we go back further than that." The way she said it felt almost like she was digging up a painful memory. After a long pause, Audrey added quietly, "Maybe she didn't know if she was allowed to tell you."

"Tell me what?" I brushed hair back from her eyes, running my thumb along her jaw. "Hey, are you okay?"

"Yeah, it's just…" She looked at me, her eyes wide and unsure. "It's a little awkward."

My thumb moved to the edge of her mouth, smoothing out the lines that had suddenly appeared there. "You don't have to tell me if you don't want to."

"No, it's fine. I want to." She tensed and then relaxed, almost forcefully. "Penny helped me turn into an actual functioning human again."

Confused, I frowned. "What do you mean?"

She scratched her eyebrow with a forefinger. "This might lean into deep and meaningful territory."

"That's okay," I said quickly.

Audrey studied me, as though she was deciding exactly what to say. When she eventually spoke, words I'd never expected to hear rushed from her in a torrent. "My dad died in prison, Iz. He killed himself a few months into the eleven-year sentence he was serving for the attempted murder of my mom." The words lacked inflection, as though she was reading from a script.

My stomach dropped. "Oh…Audrey."

Her smile was shaky. "I told you I had experience with tigers. He'd been emotionally and physically abusive my whole life and one day he, uh took it to a whole new level, stabbed her and then tried to kill himself. I came home from school and—" She cleared her throat. "Well yeah."

I leaned in and kissed her cheek softly, snuggling into her side. I wanted to be as close as possible, to pour my support and compassion into her if I could. Trying to imagine what she'd seen and been through made my chest hurt, like my heart didn't know what to do with all these feelings. "Your mom's okay, right? You're okay?"

"Mhmm, all good." Audrey's arm came around me and I felt her chest expand with her long inhalation. "Anyway, I met Penny when I was eighteen, not long after I started dating her niece Kimberly, in college. Long story short, I was pretty messed up after my childhood stuff, kind of uncontrollable. Penny was like the authority figure I'd needed my whole life. Someone who was strong without stealing that strength from others."

I nodded, knowing exactly what she meant.

Audrey was staring at the ceiling, her voice faraway. "I love my mom so much and she's sweet and nurturing, but she was trying so hard to just deal with her shit with my dad too. I'd run wild for most of my life, had some weird emotional stuff from what happened. Pen helped me in a way Mom couldn't." The rest of her story came out in a rush, the words running together. "Kim and I lived with Penny and Loretta for almost three years and then Kim got cancer and died when I was almost twenty-one."

I blinked at the abrupt ending to her story. What do you say to something like that? There was nothing except another quiet, "I'm sorry." I smoothed my hand down the center of her chest, between her breasts, as though I could soothe some of her past hurts away.

"Mmm." Audrey kissed the top of my head. "So it's more than just Pen and me playing softball together."

There were dozens of questions and emotions spinning through my head but I couldn't make sense of them to say anything other than, "I didn't mean to make you talk about it if you didn't want to."

"It is what it is, Iz." She laughed softly. "Sorry, that sounded funnier in my head. What I mean is, yeah it all hurts but at the same time it was a while ago. People move on, they change."

The silence between us stretched, but it wasn't uncomfortable. Audrey's hand was on my back, sweeping slowly up and down my spine. I pressed a kiss to her shoulder. "Why didn't you tell me about this before now?"

"I didn't know you were curious." She sounded surprised.

I glanced up at her. "I am. I just didn't know how to ask."

She laughed quietly. "You ask by saying, 'Audrey, would you tell me about your past?'"

"I'll remember that for next time."

Audrey leaned back slightly to look down at me. "You know, a couple of days after you came for dinner that first night, Pen called me. I basically got the 'you treat her right' speech." She cleared her throat. "And the 'moving on' speech."

"Moving on?" She'd shifted slightly away and I pulled myself closer to her, conscious of the evenness of her tone as she tried to sound nonchalant. She hadn't shut down but it felt like she'd closed herself off and I wanted to show her I was here with her.

"Yeah. I haven't…dated much since Kim. A few casual relationships here and there. A month or two but never anyone I wanted to spend an extended amount of time with." She shot me a quick glance then smoothed her expression over to a neutral one as though trying to cover up the implication of what she'd just said.

Or was I imagining it? Was she trying to tell me something, or was it wishful thinking? Trying to lighten the mood a little, I said, "I couldn't imagine anyone not wanting to spend time with you."

A short laugh escaped her mouth. "You only get to see the good things. The things I want to show you."

I kept eye contact with her. "You've never struck me as someone who has a lot of bad qualities." Unlike me, who has them in spades.

"No? Well I'm doing a good job hiding them from you then," Audrey teased. Though there was still an undercurrent of discomfort, it felt as though she'd begun to open up again.

I ran my fingers softly over her hip. "I already know you're impatient, sometimes wonderfully snide and occasionally humorous at inappropriate times."

"Guilty." She captured my hand and lifted it, brushing her nose along my palm. "Do any of those things bother you?"

"Not in the slightest," I murmured. After a beat I added, "Thank you for telling me."

Finally, she raised her eyes to mine and the naked emotion in them was like a punch in the gut. "Thank you for letting me."

We lay comfortably together and I tried to process what I'd just learned. Here I was thinking I had father issues. The whole thing made her seemingly eternal good nature even more incredible.

"I can feel you thinking, Iz." There was a note of humor in her tone.

"It's just…you're so calm and easygoing. How do you move past something like that? I'm still shitty at the guy who cut me off in the lobby this morning."

Audrey shrugged. "Supportive friends and family, plus a really good therapist helped me discover what I needed to let go of." She pulled our joined hands to her mouth and kissed my knuckles. "And what I should try to hold on to."

CHAPTER EIGHTEEN

The half-eaten tube of antacid tablets had rolled just out of reach. Stretching over papers strewn on my desk, I managed to flick them toward me. I palmed another two into my mouth, and tried to suck quietly as Shane Preston's panic hit a high note. I should charge him for treating my indigestion. I should charge him for my blood pressure issues. I should charge him for being an annoying wanker.

After a veiled insult about my competence, I crunched the antacids between my molars, not bothering to cover the sound. "Shane, please. Let me assure you everything is fine."

I had to strain to understand his response, babbling and ranting about shit he really didn't understand regardless of how often I explained it. He constantly misinterpreted me. He misinterpreted Mark. He probably misinterpreted breathing. In the end, I gave up and told him I would come see him the next day to show him exactly what I meant. I made a note to slip a commission rate increase into Preston's next contract and buzzed my assistant.

"Clare, I need to be in Oklahoma tomorrow midafternoon, probably returning around ten or eleven p.m." Knowing Shane, he would want to discuss every penny of his portfolio over dinner stretching into late drinks. Goodbye relaxing time with Audrey tomorrow night.

I turned to the window just in time to see all my plans flying out of it. I had a function tonight, would be home late and the last thing I'd feel like doing tomorrow was seeing one of my most challenging clients.

Clare appeared in my office. "Uh, Mr. Hall has a meeting in Portland tomorrow and then he's continuing to Las Vegas for the weekend, Ms. Rhodes. The jet won't be back until Sunday."

Portland? Why hadn't I heard about it? Mark hated Friday meetings. Fuck Mark and his meeting and weekend trip and taking Audrey. Fuck Shane Preston. Fuck everything.

Cautiously, Clare told me, "Your shared calendar should have updated with Mr. Hall's schedule, Ms. Rhodes." She was telling me, respectfully, that if I looked I would have seen that Mark had gotten in first to use the jet for his meeting.

I squeezed the bridge of my nose. "Okay. Can you arrange a corporate jet, please?" There was no other way to work it.

"Of course."

I shoved papers and my tablet aside and grabbed my purse. "I'm going out for a while."

"You don't want me to get you lunch, Ms. Rhodes?" Clare always seemed put out when I went out to forage for myself and I could never quite figure out why. I'd have thought having some extra time without my bothering her would be refreshing.

"It's fine, thank you. I'll grab something while I'm out."

I tugged the collar of my Burberry trench up around my ears. Air. I needed air. Not fresh air because there was no such thing around here. Plain, smoggy, fumey but non-recycled air conditioning Manhattan air would have to do. I don't know why but as I was striding down the sidewalk, I dialed Audrey. We hadn't seen each other since last Friday, six days ago when she'd given me that precious piece of her past. Damned functions and dinners, and late meetings.

She was breathless when she answered, "Hey, is everything all right?"

"Mhmm." Except for the scooter that just cut in front of me. I gave the departing figure a middle finger and rushed across the street. "This isn't a bad time?"

"Not at all. I'm just out for a run."

"Sweaty?"

"Very."

Oh boy. "I just heard about Portland and Vegas."

"Yeah, very last minute. I only got the call an hour ago."

"Yeah. Speaking of last minute, I'm going to Oklahoma tomorrow." My heels sounded angrily on the sidewalk.

"Oh?" There was the blast of a car horn and her muted yell of, "Fucking asshole!"

My stomach lurched. "You okay?"

"All good. People drive for shit in this city. So someone else is taking you. I feel put out." Though her tone was light, the words didn't feel it.

"Tell me about it," I said bitterly. "And I'm pissed at Mark for stealing you away from me for the weekend. He could have made Schwartz take the shift."

Traffic noise made the long pause slightly less awkward but I was still aware of her silence before she said, "Well…it's not like Mr. Hall knew I had plans with you, Iz." It was phrased carefully but I still felt the recrimination, gentle as it was. She cleared her throat, the next sentence rushing out of her mouth. "I know we weren't going to, but can I come around and see you tonight?"

I tucked flyaway strands of hair behind my ears. "Shit, I'd love to, really but I can't tonight. I've got a function." I let out a little gurgle, feeling a sudden urge to explain. "It's been set for months. Didn't I tell you?" Quickly glancing left and right, I rushed across the street and slipped behind a stationary taxi.

"Uh, yeah I think you did. No worries. I guess I'll just see you when you're back. Or I'll look for your picture on the net." Again, she said it lightly but underneath her casual tone it felt forced, with a hint of something I couldn't place.

"But I'll see you Monday night?"

"Mhmm absolutely. I look forward to it. Have fun."

I laughed hollowly. "Trust me, there's nothing fun about mingling with these people."

Her voice grew soft. "I don't know, Iz. You always look like you're enjoying yourself."

Always look like I'm enjoying myself. Always. She followed what I was doing? I came to a stop outside the deli. "It's all an act. Got to keep up appearances and all that. Honey, I have to go. I'm just out to grab some lunch and fresh air between crazy busy work stuff." The endearment had slipped out before I could stop it. I held my breath, waiting to see if she noticed or mentioned it.

"Sure thing," she said. "I'll talk to you soon. Safe trip. Will you text me to let me know this inferior pilot has delivered you safely?"

"I will. And you too. Um, enjoy yourself in Vegas." After we'd hung up, I stared blankly at my phone. There was something off with her, something nestled alongside the pointed remark about Mark being unaware of our…thing. Was it jealousy? I knew I was jealous, that she might find *entertainment* in the place where entertainment threw itself at you, but the vibe was almost like she felt left out. I shelved it to think about later and went in to order my lunch.

Walking back to the office with a paper lunch bag in hand I tried to reconcile Audrey's words and her tone with what I knew. We'd talked about telling people about us, but I thought we'd agreed not to because we weren't actually in a relationship, so her comment about Mark was out of the blue. As to the other thing, I'd never pegged her as someone who was easily consumed with jealousy. I'd probably misread the situation. It wouldn't be the first time. Of course, I couldn't really ask her because fuckbuddies didn't delve deep into feelings behind motivations. Did they?

As I walked through our foyer, one of our receptionists handed me three call notes. Clare had left another two on my desk. In my haste to get out of the office, I hadn't told her to divert calls to me, but she'd obviously taken it upon herself to give me a few minutes of peace away from work. Bless her.

Lunch first. I needed to eat to rid myself of the burning emptiness in my stomach that hadn't gone since my call with Preston. Maybe I had an ulcer. Mental note: tell the doctor at next physical. Second mental note: get Clare to book really long overdue physical you were supposed to book before. A light knock at the door startled me. I swallowed my mouthful of salad and gestured for Clare to come in.

"Ms. Rhodes? Very sorry to interrupt your lunch. You're booked to Oklahoma tomorrow at twelve. And Christopher suggested an appointment for one o'clock Tuesday."

"Thank you." I ran my tongue over my teeth to catch stray greens. "You can confirm Tuesday with him."

"Yes, Ms. Rhodes."

"Did you send that paperwork to the Holscotts? I need them to sign ASAP." A new client. When I'd met him and his wife for lunch a few weeks back, I knew within ten minutes that I had them. She was certainly not all straight and spent most of the lunch practically sitting on my lap, something her husband appeared to indulge. Gross. No thanks.

"I did and it came back while you were out." She pointed to a stack of papers to my left. "There's a copy right there."

"Good. Can you please tell Amber to reprint pages eighteen through twenty-two of Preston's latest contract for me to take tomorrow. He says they look slightly off center." I raised my eyes skyward to let her know exactly what I thought about Preston's petty bullshit demand.

"Yes, Ms. Rhodes. Shall I also have the printer replaced if it's printing incorrectly?" she asked drily.

I swung back and forth in my chair and tried to hide my grin. "If anyone else complains, I'll consider it. That's all for now, thank you."

* * *

After lunch and client calls, I stopped by Mark's office. He was staring blankly at his laptop and grunted his hello when I stepped behind him to massage his shoulder. "You okay?" I asked. "You look like shit."

"Just tired."

I paused my kneading. "Not getting sick?"

"Not sleeping well." He spun around in his chair to face me.

"Oh? Are you taking anything?"

Mark shrugged, nonchalant. "Sometimes. Think it's just stress."

I smoothed the hair at the back of his neck. He needed a haircut. "Are you seeing anyone about it? Talked to your doctor?"

Mark's wave was as dismissive as his explanation. "Don't need to. Why do you think I'm going to Vegas for the weekend? Need to relax with the guys for a few days." Mark's mouth grinned. His eyes didn't.

"Mmm." My unease was starting to build. This wasn't the first time I'd had a gut feeling that something was off, and it felt like more than just *stress*. I added a mental note to keep an eye on it to all the other mental notes stuck inside my head.

A line of numbers on his screen looked odd. Pointing, I asked, "What's going on? Did you miss a buy cut off?"

"Yeah. I got locked up elsewhere and just missed out."

"That's not like you." I tried hard not to sound accusatory but the nature of my statement made it hard. "Mark is incompetent" was beginning to feel like a recurring theme with us these past few months, and it'd been getting steadily worse.

"Come on, Belle. Don't ride me about it, please. I'm busting my balls running this place."

I raised an eyebrow, only just holding onto my temper. He was lucky we were in the office. "Hey! Don't even start with that bullshit. This is you *and me*, not you running this alone. We're equal partners. And I certainly pull my weight. Just look at the figures if you have any doubt about that. We've been in this together the whole time."

He at least had the grace to look contrite. "I know. I'm sorry. Like I said, I'm just a little tired."

Yeah, aren't we all? I bit my lip to stop from snapping at him. "Okay, fine. Well…I'm here if you want to talk."

That easy smile again. "Thanks. I know."

"Seriously though, is everything okay?"

"Yeah," he said quickly, reaching for a clay paperweight his nephew had made him. "You should come to Vegas and have some fun." The misshapen and strangely painted dog spun crazily as Mark tossed it from hand to hand.

"No thanks, I'm not really into weekends with the guys. And I have a bunch of acquisitions to sort through." Besides, following Audrey to Nevada was veering into stalking territory. She had a right to do what she wanted, when she wanted...and with whom she wanted. The funny thing was, no matter how much I told myself that, I didn't feel any better. I felt sick.

I felt that same rush of jealous annoyance at the thought of Audrey checking out someone else. The feeling made me doubly annoyed. I had no right to such feelings, not unless I was open with my own.

"You work too hard." Now he was tossing the paperweight a couple of inches in the air and catching it again. Stupid circus clown.

It was on the tip of my tongue to tell him that one of us had to, but I swallowed the words and took the paperweight from him. I set it down carefully on top of a stack of papers. "Have a good weekend."

He affected a southern accent, which he knew I hated, and drawled, "Yes, ma'am."

I left Mark's office, slipped into mine and summoned Clare. Again. "Can you please talk to Tamara about a suitable time and book lunch for Mark and me as soon as possible? Usual place." I'd take Mark to his favorite restaurant and hopefully find out what was going on with him. Plying him with good food and wine usually loosened him up a little.

My phone vibrated, skittering across the desk, and Mama's special ring tone started. Clare made her quiet exit as I contemplated leaving the call. Bad idea, she'll just keep calling. I picked up my phone and wandered slowly across my office to glance out the window. "Hello, Mama."

"Hello, daughter of mine."

"How're you?"

"Just fine. Missin' you."

I smiled. "I know. I miss you too."

"How's Audrey?" Bingo.

"Uh, she's okay. Why?"

"No reason." She was trying to sound casual, but all her smugness was seeping through.

I spun around and paced back toward my desk. "Nuh-uh. Come on."

"Just wondering how you two are goin'."

"Same as we were last time you saw us." I leaned over and tapped a key on my laptop to refresh market indicators. My blood pressure crept up.

"Mhmmm, so you're good then."

"Yes. We're good," I said distractedly, leaning over my desk to scribble notes. In the back of my mind I could hear all my past lovers accusing me of never giving them my full attention.

Mama's porch door slammed closed. "You two up to anything this weekend?"

"No she's working, taking Mark to Vegas for the weekend and I have work to do too."

"You sound upset, Bunny."

I tossed my pen down on the desk. "No I don't."

Her musing sound told me clearly that she didn't believe me. She took a deep breath. "Do you remember when you were seven and I caught you diggin' in my garden?"

"Yeah." I'd pulled up most of her bulbs and I still had no idea why. Probably just one of those childish whims. I started to walk back to the window then changed my mind and sank down into my chair.

"And you swore up and down you were innocent, even when you realized you had one of my daffodil bulbs in your hand. Couldn't get you to admit it."

"What're you getting at, Mama?"

"Kinda feels like you're doing that now. All the facts are right there in your face and you're ignoring 'em."

Sometimes I wished she didn't make so much sense.

CHAPTER NINETEEN

On the flight to Oklahoma, the temptation to dull the impending horror of Preston's repetitious bargaining with wine was overwhelming, but I abstained. And cursed myself for it. He met me at his favorite restaurant for an early dinner, where I endured a limp handshake and a mercifully dry cheek kiss. I dove into what felt like the hundredth time I'd explained why I thought his insistence on overweighting his portfolio with certain commodities wasn't wise.

By dessert, which I skipped, I thought I almost had him. By after-dinner drinks at his favorite bar I was certain of it. He finally let me go around nine p.m., assuring me he'd think about my suggestions and be in touch. Scratch that certainty. I wondered if he gave his doctor and lawyer as much grief as he gave me, second guessing every little thing. He probably sent his doctor web links with self-diagnosis.

Not quite ready to fly back to New York and my empty apartment, I stayed in the packed bar for another round. Being in a crowd would normally recharge me, but even surrounded by people I realized that I was just as bored and lonely as I would be at home. I swallowed the last mouthful of my gin and gathered my things. On my way out I caught the eye of an attractive, well-dressed woman in the corner. She let her eyes wander up and down my body then smiled at me. I smiled back and kept walking. Lady, you are no Audrey Graham.

Trying not to grind my teeth during the uncomfortable, turbulent flight, I abandoned any notion of working. Antsy and unable to concentrate, I pushed my earphones hard into my ears and scrolled through playlists. Too slow, too upbeat, too electronica. Eventually, I just hit shuffle, knowing full well the only reason I was being so picky was because I was upset about what might be happening in Vegas.

Maybe I should have gone after all. I could catch an early flight in the morning and spend my weekend at the blackjack tables. And in bed with Audrey. I shoved the idea out of my head and slammed the door on it. That's stalking, remember?

As soon as the jet was hangared and the engines cut off, I politely thanked the unfamiliar pilot, and rushed down the stairs and away from my discomfort. I didn't want to admit that not having Audrey up front had made me feel nervous, almost unsafe. Brilliant. I'd become some sort of creepy, codependent passenger. Creepy codependent person, more like it.

Watching the doors of the elevator up to my penthouse close, I was reminded of Audrey again. Our first night together. The way she'd backed me into the corner of the hotel elevator, traced my lips with her thumb and kissed me before I had a chance to say anything. Murmured how sweet I tasted while her hands confidently traveled to places most people wouldn't go after only knowing someone for thirty-five minutes.

I remembered how I'd felt, my excitement and rationalizations about why I should or shouldn't sleep with a woman I'd only just met. All those feelings came rushing back to draw a shiver from the base of my neck right down to my toes. As I walked across the atrium, my personal phone sounded a text alert.

Did you make it home okay?

Shit, I'd totally forgotten to let her know that the inferior pilot had indeed delivered me safely to and from Oklahoma. I tapped out a response. *All fine. Shit flights.*

The phone began ringing seconds later. I glanced at the display and smiled as I answered. "Audrey..."

"Hey. How are you? Sorry to call, seemed easier than texting."

"It's fine. I literally just got home. How's Vegas?"

She laughed. "Vegas is Vegas." A pause. "Crap pilot hey?"

"The worst. Bumpy flights and he was nowhere near as attractive as you." Walking to the kitchen table, I divested myself of my coat and an assortment of bags.

"Did your meeting go okay?"

"As well as it could."

"I'm glad. I wish you were here...or I was there." There was no trace of that strange vibe I thought I'd detected during our call the day before. Instead she sounded calm and thoughtful.

I responded without thinking. "Me too."

"What would we be doing if I was there?" Her voice changed, became that deeper, huskier timbre I'd come to know and love. The way it got when she was horny.

Time to play along. "We'd be naked for sure. On the couch, maybe." I made my way up to my room, and at the top of the stairs shrugged out of my blouse and tossed it in the general direction of the closet.

"I like the sound of that." Fabric rustling, something heavy hit the floor. "No reason to let distance stop us."

"Are you suggesting what I think you're suggesting?" I turned to look at my neatly made bed.

"If you think I'm suggesting we have phone sex then yes, yes I am."

Excitement traveled straight to my stomach, blooming into soft heat. "How many days is it since I licked you?"

"Seven," she answered immediately.

"Mmm, seven days too many." Thinking of her under my tongue made my stomach flutter, and when I imagined the way she fisted my hair and urged me on the flutter moved lower.

"What are you wearing?" Her question was low, sensual.

The naked desire in her voice turned the flutter to low, insistent pulsing. The woman had me totally conditioned to respond to her. "In a moment it'll be just underwear." I stepped out of my skirt, leaving it to pile on the floor.

"Which ones?"

"The red set, you know—"

"With the white. I know exactly the ones. Oh God." Her voice was strained. "Are you touching yourself?"

"Not yet. Soon. You?"

"I am."

The thought of her fingering herself instead of me doing it was almost unbearable. "What are you doing? Tell me. Please." I climbed into bed and settled myself against mountains of pillows.

"I've got my fingers on my clit, Iz, thinking about you licking me, the way your tongue feels on me. In me."

"That's so hot, honey." My thighs were clenched together. Not yet. Not yet. I closed my eyes, picturing her with a hand between her legs. Making soft, lazy circles over her hard clitoris. Christ. The pressure in mine built until I had to bite my hand, stifling a low moan.

"I am so horny and you sound so fucking sexy. God, I want you in my mouth. Take off your bra," she demanded.

I sat up, unfastening my bra to let my breasts spill free. "Where's your hand?" I rasped.

"Your breasts," she panted. "Iz, touch yourself. Please."

My hand slipped up, fingers tweaking my nipples until I felt the tingle running under my skin with each soft pinch. "Audrey," I breathed.

"What is it, baby?"

"I want to come so badly."

"Then do it. Let me hear you."

I could have climaxed just listening to her and thinking about everything she was doing. My legs were trembling as I ran my fingers down...down...down over muscles taut with desire until fingers met hot, wet folds. My clit was throbbing with every beat of my heart and I slid my finger over the swollen flesh, trying to drag the sensation out. My breathing caught. "Jesus. I'm so fucking wet." A finger, then two.

"Spread your legs for me. Tell me exactly what you're doing," she growled.

I pulled out, fingers gliding easily through my thick arousal. "I…I'm fucking myself. God, I wish you were here. I want your fingers, I want your tongue."

Audrey moaned and I heard the hitch in her vocalization. She was so close to coming. "Iz, I fucking *ache* for you," she whispered hoarsely.

Bracing my feet, I lifted my ass off the bed, furiously driving myself toward the edge. I was done playing, done teasing myself. "I wanna hear you come. Will you come for me?"

Her telltale cry as she climaxed broke me and before I could form a thought, my orgasm crested and carried me over the edge. I cried out, jerking in spasms with each delicious pulse.

After a few moments, Audrey made a quiet confession. "Right now, I really miss you."

I let my legs drop, my heels sliding against the sheets. The burn of desire in my stomach eased, replaced by a far less pleasant feeling of gnawing unease. I had to swallow before I could answer. "Me too."

* * *

All Saturday, my thoughts kept straying to those words. *I miss you.* Such a simple phrase. The words were deeper than sexual desire. It wasn't I miss your body, your hands, your tongue. It was I miss *you* and there had been no hesitation in my response. I missed her too. I wanted her. I was addicted to her and not just for sex.

I'd come to depend on her quiet assurances. The way she smiled at me, her gentle teasing. She drew me out, made me laugh more in the months I'd known her than I had in the year before her. When she looked at me, I knew she saw me. Real me, not sort-of-fake me I'd built for presenting to the world.

I'd wanted to call Audrey again, but forced myself to leave her alone. And it felt horrible. Instead, I settled for closing my eyes and reliving the sound of her voice from last night. It didn't help. For the rest of the weekend I thought about her, wondered what she was doing and tried to distract myself by working until I dropped. Saturday night, I fell asleep at my desk and woke a little before midnight to a text Audrey had sent earlier.

Hotels without you are kind of boring.

I typed out a response without thinking. *Home without you is boring.* Just as quickly, I deleted it. Too much. Tapping my thumbs against the screen, I thought of what I could say. After a couple of minutes I decided on a lighthearted response. *You're getting spoilt.* I added a smile emoji for good measure then tossed my phone aside, disgusted with my cowardice.

She texted very late Sunday to tell me she was back, and Sunday night blurred to Monday morning. Mark was reserved when he came into the office, offering no insight as to how his weekend had gone. I sleepwalked through my day until it was time to leave for therapy. Clare walked through the office beside me, taking notes.

A quick glance at my watch confirmed I was in danger of being late. "I'll need that paperwork first thing and can you double check the meeting tomorrow? Last time he got the time mixed up."

"Absolutely. Is there anything else, Ms. Rhodes?" Clare pressed the elevator button for me.

"Have you and Tamara liaised to arrange a time for Mark and I to have lunch?"

"Apparently Friday is the earliest Mr. Hall is available." She gave me a helpless smile when I arched a disbelieving eyebrow at her. Pretty sure Mark had no meetings this week.

I raised a hand and waved my annoyance away. "Okay fine. Book it please and can you hold my calls until four fifteen. I'll see you in the morning."

Therapy sucked. Raw and confused about Friday night I ended up crying when Dr. Baker asked if I'd made any progress with declaring my feelings to Audrey. Around my tears I managed to tell her, "No, not a single step."

"Why are you denying this, Isabelle?" Dr. Baker's question was calm, but determined. It was going to be one of those sessions where she didn't let me make excuses, but forced me to confront my fears.

I propped my elbow on the arm of the chair, resting my chin in my palm. The urge to say *I don't know* and then just get up and walk out was overwhelming. Dr. Baker waited silently, watching me try to find what I had to say. Eventually I said, "Because I'm afraid that if I tell her, it's going to change everything."

"How?" she asked immediately.

"Well, if she doesn't feel the same and just wants to keep being casual there's going to be the awkwardness of her knowing I want more."

Dr. Baker nodded. "Okay. Do you think that knowing that, she'd call it quits?"

"I don't think so, no." I raised my head from my hand. "But I don't know for sure and if she does, it'll be so humiliating."

"From what you've told me, Audrey doesn't seem like the type to mock you, or purposely make you feel bad for being honest."

"No, she's not." I reached around to dig my fingers into the suddenly tight muscle at the base of my neck. "Listen, it's just…I need something uncomplicated in my life. Work is stressful, there's something up with Mark and I just can't handle something else being confusing right now."

"I think it already is confusing, Isabelle." She set her pen down atop the notepad. "In my opinion, clearing the air and letting this go will ease some of your mental burden."

Thanks, Doc.

In the car home from therapy I texted Audrey. Though I'd be at her place in just over an hour, I was suddenly desperate to connect with her. Even as I was doing it, I recognized my need as insecurity, wanting to reassure myself that she was still there, and still wanted me. Still wanted this.

Want me to bring dinner?

I'm cooking. Massaman curry. Arrive hungry.
Always. Be there in an hour.

Penny waited while I raced through showering and overnight bag-packing. I swear that since the first night, every time Penny took me to Crown Heights, she'd grown more and more gleeful. When she stopped outside the apartment building and turned the ignition off, I leaned forward and placed a hand on Penny's shoulder. "Pen?"

"Yes, Ms. Rhodes?" She twisted around as best she could without shrugging my hand from her shoulder.

"Thank you for what you did for Audrey, for…telling her about the job." I swallowed, unable to say what I really wanted to. Thank you for bringing her into my life.

"You're welcome, Ms. Rhodes." Pen dipped her head, seeming suddenly shy. "One of my better decisions."

"Yes," I mused quietly.

As I stepped onto Audrey's floor, I spotted her opening her door as though she'd had an ear trained for the sound of the elevator. Waiting for me. I couldn't stop my smile. The first thing I thought was that she looked relieved. It was so slight I thought I'd imagined it until she murmured how much she'd missed me, kissing me hungrily. Warmth spread through my chest before I could stop it. "Yeah?"

She strung kisses along my jaw, tugging me inside her apartment. "Yeah."

We settled on the couch for the dinner she'd made, facing each other. Audrey wiped her hands on a paper napkin. "A friend of mine is in town just for tomorrow. Would you mind awfully if we saw each other Wednesday instead?"

"Course not." I moved things around on my plate, stabbing another forkful. "Did you have a good weekend?" Not bitter about being left alone for the weekend, no sir not me.

"Absolutely. I won five hundred bucks on roulette and attended a number of fine adult establishments." Audrey widened her eyes. "And I got myself a happy ending lap dance. I contemplated getting a hooker, but couldn't find one hot enough who did women."

I set my plate on her coffee table. "I'm glad you enjoyed yourself." I was quite proud of myself for keeping bitterness from my voice. If she wanted to get fingered by a stripper, who was I to be pissy about it?

Sure, keep telling yourself that, Isabelle.

Audrey took my face in her hands. Her hands were always so warm and soft, and I felt comforted by the gentle touch. "Iz. Look at me," she sighed. "You're so smart, yet so very gullible. You're too easy. I'm teasing. None of that's true, except for the roulette part. Well, technically it was five hundred and forty-eight dollars." Audrey let go and slid off the couch. "I'm not seeing anyone else in any way. It's just you and it's only been you since our first night."

I exhaled. "Oh. Me too."

She kneeled in front of me. "The happy ending was from myself on Saturday night, thinking about how hot it was listening to you making yourself come. But it wasn't all that happy." She took my hand, interlacing our fingers. "I missed these fingers."

With her kneeling and me slouched on the couch we were almost level. I pulled her close until she was jammed against my legs. Her gaze moved between my eyes and my mouth. "You know what else I missed?" Audrey asked.

I shook my head slowly. "No. Please tell me."

Her answer was to kiss me, her tongue searching for mine. She found it quickly and the familiar urge began to build in my stomach when she bit my lip. Audrey's voice got even lower when she continued with, "That tongue."

The kiss turned frantic when we came together again and her hands slipped around my waist to drag me to the edge of the couch. I let out a groan as her hip pressed against me, my legs wrapping around her ass to keep her in place. Fire spread through my belly down into my groin, and I had a *thought*. About us. Bad timing. Stop. I should be thinking about pleasure, not deep things. Instead I was thinking that I could do it, I could do this. I could have all of it. All of her. If she'd have me. I couldn't imagine growing tired of making love to her. I couldn't imagine growing tired of her.

Her hot tongue made its way up my neck to my ear. Teeth grazed my earlobe. "Hold on, cowgirl. It's going to be a wild ride."

I forgot about my conviction, laughing as she pulled me off the couch and onto the floor with her. The laughter died pretty quickly when her hands moved to other parts of my anatomy. Slowly, she pulled the zipper of my jeans down, her eyes locked to mine the whole time. She stared right into me and I was overcome by the sudden desire to slow down. Make love instead of fuck.

Audrey's hands stilled and she eased herself off me and stood. Without a word of explanation, she pulled me to my feet and led me to her bedroom. As though she'd read something on my face, she'd turned from playful and frantic to soft and sensual. Our lovemaking was sweet and slow. Gentle touches and quiet words. She pressed her forehead to my cheek and as she came, I felt the long shudder and her soft exhalation.

For some reason I couldn't fathom—maybe it was our exquisite connection, maybe it was how close I was to telling her how I really felt—but I started to cry. Not full on ugly crying or even sobbing, just letting tears track down my cheeks. Audrey untangled herself. Her dark eyes were soft with concern. "Everything all right, Iz?" She stroked gently along my ribs.

"Sorry. Just tired and worn out from therapy." More like I was worn out from my own internal battles. I pulled a stupid face and swiped my hand over my eyes.

If she suspected the real reason for my distress she didn't let on. "Come here." She held me close with her nose in my hair and fingers tracing patterns on my skin. I fell asleep in minutes.

The next morning, nothing was said about my little meltdown, and for once, Audrey walked me to the door of her apartment. Usually she stayed in bed while I slipped out before dawn to go home and get ready for my workday. She picked up a brown paper-wrapped package from the utility closet and offered it to me. It was flat, about two feet square and weighed little.

I turned it over, running my finger over a taped seam. "What's this?"

She shrugged. "Just something I've been working on in my painting class. Don't open it until you get home." Her cheeks were pink. Deliciously so. I couldn't recall seeing her blush before.

"A painting. For me?" My voice lifted an octave with my question. I bit my lip. "Thank you!"

In that moment, something passed between us. Something I couldn't name. I thought I saw unasked questions in her expression. Maybe it was just wishful thinking but I wanted to believe there was something more. Something deeper. I almost asked her. Blurted it out right then. Spilled my feelings. But then she kissed me and I lost my nerve and instead mumbled, "I'll see you Wednesday."

William took my painting, then passed it back over for me to hold rather than tossing it into the trunk. The whole ride home I ran my fingertips lightly over the wrapping, wondering what secrets were held inside.

The moment I'd closed my front door and dropped my bags, I tore into the brown paper. It was a pale blue canvas, and slightly off center was a naked woman tangled in sheets. It was minimalistic with rough lines and edges but still beautifully clear. The backdrop was done in such a way that suggested the whole canvas was the bed, shadows and faint lines marking edges. Light blue. The color of Audrey's sheets.

I looked closely at the woman in the painting. Her features were vague—straight nose, a smattering of freckles. I ran my fingers over the bridge of my nose. Painting woman had blond curls, an arm slung under her head and stretched off the bed. The way I slept. I looked closer. The outstretched hand had a mark on the underside of the wrist. A small, unique tattoo that I recognized immediately. My breath caught.

It was me. She'd painted me.

CHAPTER TWENTY

Having not heard from Audrey at all Tuesday, on Wednesday morning while eating breakfast at my desk, I texted to make sure we were still on for that night. I was done eating and my teeth were re-brushed but she hadn't responded. Probably sleeping off a hangover from her night out with friends. Poor darling.

Darling…

After a salon appointment over lunch, I went head down and ass up working until a knock on my open office door startled me from calculations. "Ms. Rhodes?" Donna from HR stood tentatively in my doorway.

"Donna." I glanced at her eight-months pregnant stomach. "How are you?"

"Aside from feeling like an elephant, I'm wonderful."

I stood and gestured to the other side of my desk. "Did you want to take a seat? What can I do for you?"

"I'm fine thank you. I've been sitting all day." Donna held out a folder to me. "I'm sorry to bother you, but I can't find Mr. Hall and I need some medical leave approved."

"Is everything all right?" I asked hurriedly, and simultaneously wondering where Mark was this time—this was his side of the business.

Donna laughed. "Sorry, it's not for me. It's for Audrey Graham."

First I'd heard of it. Poor thing probably had the flu or something. She'd looked a little tired on Monday night and going out all last night drinking wouldn't have helped. I took the papers, already thinking about taking her soup or something. "How long?"

"Medical certificate clears her until next Wednesday."

A week for the flu, she'd need at least that. "Sure thing. I'll take a look and have it back to you, ASAP."

"Thanks." Donna smiled gratefully and left my office.

I glanced at the details. Balancing a pen between my index and middle fingers, I flipped it quickly back and forth on the blotter. The rhythmic tapping stopped the moment I read the details on Audrey's medical certificate.

Vehicular accident.

Oh God.

I pushed my chair back so fast it hit the low bureau behind me. "Clare!" I already had my laptop unplugged and tablet shoved haphazardly in my leather tote.

"Yes, Ms. Rhodes?"

Gathering my bags, I scooted around my desk, catching my thigh on the edge. Panic spilled out my mouth in a stream of words all running together. "Call a car around and cancel everything for the rest of the day. I'm leaving." I yanked my coat from the hanger in my small closet near the door. "Please."

"You have that app—"

"Cancel it." I was already rushing through the office, phone in my hand. "Send anything urgent to me, end of world shit only. I'm off the grid." In the elevator I called Audrey and got voice mail. I left a babbling message.

Downstairs, I ran through the lobby as fast as my Ferragamos could carry me, out the front door and to William and the waiting car. "Take me to Crown Heights, please. Quickly."

Queasy fear curled through my stomach as I dialed her. Voice mail again. I left another message. We hit traffic and the thirty-minute drive stretched to almost forty-five. All three calls I made went straight to Audrey's voice mail. All three messages I left were panicked.

Knowing the anxiety attack was baseless didn't stop it. She'd notified HR that she needed medical leave so she was obviously alive. A week off wasn't that serious. Despite constantly trying to reassure myself, I couldn't rationalize. All I could think of was her, hurt badly.

Yanking up my bags and coat strewn over the back seat, I slid from the car before William could come around to open the door. I buzzed Audrey. No answer. I buzzed obnoxiously again and again until finally there was a hoarse and slightly grumpy, "What?"

A gentle flood of adrenaline spread through my limbs. "Audrey, it's me." To my ears, my voice sounded weak and unsteady.

The grumpiness in her voice disappeared. "Iz? What are you doing here?"

"Are you okay? Can you let me up, please?"

The door clicked and I rushed through, throwing a thank you over my shoulder at a bewildered William.

Audrey opened the door of her apartment, holding a hand up to stop me speaking. "It's not as bad as it looks." Her right eye was shadowed above a purplish bruise spreading to her jaw and the side of her chin was raw, like it'd been swiped with a cheese grater.

I stared at her face, taking in every bit of damage. "Well that's comforting, because it looks pretty fucking bad. Jesus," I said shakily. "What happened?"

"Car versus motorcycle. Some prick turned across me on my way home and I dropped the bike. It's okay though." Her eyes were a little dull but her voice sounded much the same as always. "Then he just drove off."

"Are you sure you're okay? Can I just..." Tentatively I slid my hand into hers, desperate for her touch. A reassurance.

She curled her fingers around mine. "Hey relax. I'll be fine. Bit stiff, but it's nothing that won't heal. Come in."

Once she'd locked the door, I pressed myself against her as gently as I could and wrapped my arms around her waist. The accident victim comforted *me*, stroked my hair and murmured soft words I couldn't quite make out. Oh God. I could have lost her. She'd be gone and I'd never have told her. Squeezing my eyes closed on threatening tears, I buried my face in her shoulder.

"Iz? You okay?"

When I was sure I'd be able to talk, I pulled away and very gently, touched the uninjured side of her face with trembling fingertips. Her skin was warm, blood moving around her body the way it should. She was okay, she'd be okay. I swallowed. "Just scared me, is all." My panic steadied a little. "What else is there?"

"Scrapes and bruises, wrenched my shoulder a little, bit of road rash, ruined my jeans. Plus this beauty." She pointed to her face.

"I told you open face helmets were dangerous." My voice pitched so high it was aiming for the stratosphere. "Fuck. And bikes, and—"

"Cars and flying and walking across the street," she teased. "Come sit down and tell me why you're here." Audrey lowered herself down onto the couch, a brief flash of discomfort crossing her face.

I settled on the couch next to her, running my palm over the arm. I loved her couch. The worn cushions and feel of tired suede always relaxed me. "HR told me you were taking some leave. Why didn't you call me?"

"It was late when I finally got home and I…" She looked as though it was the first time she'd considered why she hadn't told me. "I wasn't sure it was appropriate for me to call you about it," she said seriously.

"Of course it is. I care about you, Audrey. I was worried. More than worried, actually," I admitted quietly. "I called but you didn't answer and then I was, well I was terrified something really bad happened."

"I've been asleep. They gave me some pretty hardcore pills. I'm sorry, I didn't mean to scare you." She stood up, wincing slightly. "Are you hungry?"

Now my fear had settled, I could acknowledge there was an emptiness in my stomach. I didn't get around to lunch after my appointment. "A little."

"Good. I'm starving and I don't trust you to cook. I'll get something delivered." Very slowly, mindful of her injuries, she leaned down and brushed a soft kiss over my lips. When she pulled back, she was smiling. "You've had your hair done. It's different. Darker?"

"A little," I whispered.

Audrey tucked a loose strand back behind my ear. "It looks great. Sit tight and I'll grab some menus."

I stayed for the night, helping her shower and making sure she took another pain pill before sending her back to bed. She held the covers up for me to slide naked in beside her and settled them over me. Gingerly, I wrapped my arm around her waist. "Does that hurt?"

"No. Feels good," she sighed contentedly. "I know you're upset. Do you want to talk about it?"

"Not now. Go to sleep, honey."

I waited until her steady breathing grew steadier before I closed my eyes. Connected to her by something I couldn't name, I eventually fell asleep too but all night I dreamed fear dreams— not having a speech ready, cutting all my hair off before an event and then one that jerked me awake. Audrey skydiving without a parachute and landing on the street in front of me. She just lay there, motionless with arms and legs akimbo. All I could do was stare.

I sucked in air, willing my heart to slow. There was the faintest sliver of light through the bedroom curtains. Enough to make out her features. She didn't stir when I carefully traced the smooth planes of her face, avoiding the mild swelling and cut on her chin. She still didn't stir when I slipped out of bed and hid in her kitchen, crying as quietly as I could. She didn't stir when I slid back into bed and held her until she woke.

Despite Audrey's protests, I stayed with her the next day as well, rescheduling meetings and setting up to work at her kitchen table. I couldn't bear to leave her, even to collect fresh clothes. I already had some underwear at her place and she let me borrow a pair of her too-long sweats and a faded Boeing tee.

I took her face in my hands, studying the abrasion on her chin. It seemed less raw, trying to scab over in places. "This looks a little less angry than yesterday." A gentle kiss helped the healing process.

"Feels okay. Feels better when you kiss it."

After breakfast, Audrey napped on the couch while I worked, taking calls in her bathroom so I wouldn't wake her. Around noon, she started moving on the couch, stretching like a cat. She shot me a cheeky smile. "Iz."

"Mmm?" I asked around the pen between my teeth.

"You in my clothes is giving me some pretty confusing, but hot feelings right now."

I took my glasses off, set the pen down and held my hand out to her. "Why don't you come and tell me about them."

She leaned against my chair. "You look so damned sexy, I want to drag you to bed."

Carefully, I drew her between my knees, my hands resting on her hips. "I'm not sure that's a great idea while you're still hurting."

Hands massaging my shoulders, she made her case, "I need to be close to you in that way, Iz. I want to touch you." Audrey closed her eyes and I caught the faintest tremor in her lips.

We made love gently, every touch soft and sweet. Whispered words and light kisses. Smoldering coals kindled into a small flame instead of a raging inferno. One of her hands in my hair, the other joined to mine, she gave herself to me again and again.

The feel of her under my fingertips and tongue, listening to her climax fanned my arousal to a point where I felt myself throbbing with need again. I slid back up and began a soft trail of kisses over her firm breasts.

"Round two?" There was amusement in her question.

"Mhmm, if you're up for it. How're you doing?" I indicated the bruising over her ribs.

"I'm just fine, Iz." She let out a soft moan when my thigh slipped between hers. "More than fine."

I began to grind against her. Hands slid to hold my ass and before I could protest, she'd rolled me over and was on top of me. I was panting with my desire as she spread me apart with her knee, pinning my hands above my head. I bucked my hips, desperate for the contact. Desperate to come again.

"Greedy girl," she murmured against my neck. Her leg was hard against my center, delicious pressure holding me just outside of where I wanted to be. My hand sought her out, but she kept moving away from me and every time my fingers made contact with her wetness she tightened her grip on my wrists. "Uh-uh."

Still, I kept burrowing and Audrey lifted herself off me abruptly, turned me over and yanked me back so I was on my hands and knees. Before I could do anything, she was behind me, her legs inside mine keeping me spread. I felt arousal coating the inside of my thighs and had to grab the bed head to keep myself from collapsing.

Audrey leaned forward, breasts against my back and tongue on my neck. "I thought I said no," she said throatily, fingers finding my clit again.

I turned my head, trying to find her. "I couldn't help myself."

She locked her teeth in my neck and as I cried out, she slid inside me. "You're so wet, baby. Haven't I given you enough?"

I couldn't form words to answer her, she had hands everywhere, dragging my attention in a million directions at once. Rolling my nipples, sliding over my clit and pumping inside me. I was being played expertly. Her mouth on my back, my neck, my ear. I turned my head to watch her and she captured my lips with hers. She pushed me to the brink, riding me roughly then suddenly withdrew. I groaned. "No. Harder, please."

She gave me what I wanted, entering me again, pushing me further and further until my cries reached a crescendo. Then, she pulled out again. I almost wept with frustration until she rolled me onto my back and dove between my legs. I bit the inside of my arm as her tongue brushed over my slit and dipped inside. "Please. Fuck me," I begged her again.

She dropped down a gear, taking me from revving well over the red line to just past idling. Hard to soft. Fast to slow. The change in pace sent me over the edge. Once I'd finished bucking and crying out my climax, she kissed her way back up and rolled us face-to-face. Audrey ran her fingertips over my nose, brushing them along my lips. "God, you are so fucking beautiful," she said softly.

Beautiful. My body went completely still.

We often called each other things while we fucked. Casual things to fuel our desire like *hot* or *sexy*. But beautiful was something different. It was…intimate. It was what I wanted to hear. I ran my fingernails lightly over her back and waited for my limbs to feel solid again.

She slipped her leg over mine, holding me even closer. I felt the thud of her heart against my breast when she spoke. "Iz."

"What?" I whispered. Her midnight eyes were reflecting light, tiny sparks of brightness guiding me home.

"I need you. Please."

"I know." I captured a nipple between my teeth, biting it and then soothing with a soft sweep of my tongue.

Audrey shuddered when I reached between us to touch her, the place I'd come to know so well. "Don't stop…please."

"I won't," I promised.

When she closed around me, I finally accepted what I'd known all along. I needed this. I needed her. I was so stupid to think I could ever just have something physical. I wasn't made that way.

She cried out her climax hoarsely and the things I thought I'd known, the rules we had in place and everything I'd tried to deny left me like an unconscious exhalation. She held me within her, sharing my breath, my skin, my heat and in that moment I was her and she was me. I was ready. Audrey shuddered again, a soft sigh escaping her mouth.

I propped myself up. "Are you okay? Have you hurt yourself?"

Eyes half closed, she smiled. "No. It's fine, just like the last time you asked."

Resting my head on her shoulder, I dug a piece of courage from deep inside. "Audrey?"

"Isabelle." She was still breathing hard, fingers playing absently over my back.

I ran my tongue around the inside of my teeth. "I lied."

My lover leaned back to look at me, her forehead wrinkling. "About what exactly?"

"About this. About us." I took a deep breath, felt it reach the bottom of my lungs. "I don't want casual."

She was silent for so long that I started to panic. After what seemed like several minutes, she spoke and relief seemed to pour from her. "I lied too. I don't want casual either. I never did."

I spluttered a moment before answering, "Then why'd you agree to it?"

She paused, as though weighing her words. "Because it was better than not having you at all."

I took a moment to absorb all that was implied in that simple statement. She'd been waiting at the finish line since the beginning and I'd only just caught up to her. I'd been so blind. "Well, okay then. I'm glad we're on the same page."

That smile again. "Me too."

I pushed sweaty hair back from her face. "What does this mean?"

"What do you want it to mean?"

"It means…I want to date you." I laughed nervously. "Christ, I hate that word. Date."

She laughed with me. "Really? I like how that sounds. Does this mean we can go *out* for meals sometimes now? Be seen together outside of work?" She inhaled a stuttering breath. "Tell people?"

"If that's what you want."

"It is. So much." Her fingers moved from my back to run over my bare thigh, leaving goose bumps in their wake. "What do you want?"

"I want to walk around holding hands with you. I want us to run together, to see movies and go to dinner." I dropped my head to press a line of soft kisses over her shoulder. "I want to take you to events. I want to show you off. It's selfish and stupid, but I want people to be jealous of me when they see you."

She raised a teasing eyebrow. "Image conscious?"

"Maybe a little," I admitted.

She soothed me with gentle hands and gentler words. "I'm messing with you, sweetheart. Honestly, I'm very flattered."

I smiled at her endearment. "You should be. I'm very particular about what hot women I'm seen with."

"Is that so?"

I nodded and started to run my nose over the soft skin of her stomach. "Audrey."

"Isabelle." I could hear the smile in her voice.

I paused my caressing. "I'm worried."

As she sat up, the movement jostled me off her. "What are you worried about?"

"You leaving. My…thing is to push people away. Before they do it to me, that is. It's something I've been working on with my therapy, but I'm not *cured*." I spoke dispassionately, conveying the information as emotionless facts. "Apparently it's because my daddy left Mama and me. Friends leave, girlfriends leave. So now, I get in first."

Her hand made long soothing strokes on my shoulder. "I see. And you're worried you'll start doing this to me?"

"Yes, and I really don't want to."

She smiled serenely. "Knowing you don't want to do something seems like a good start to changing the behavior, I'd think."

"That's what my therapist says."

"Great minds." Audrey laughed softly. "Look, Iz. This is new but we're not proposing marriage here. We're just going to keep doing what we're doing and label it a little differently. I'm still here."

"You're right, it's just…" There were so many things I wanted to say, but I couldn't sort them into their proper order. Instead, I shrugged and mumbled, "You know."

"Yeah, I know. We'll just see how everything goes." She kissed my nose. "If it helps, I'm scared too."

"Really?"

"Yeah, of course. This is important. You're important. I don't want to fuck it up. But, if you push, I'm just going to push right back. I don't want to go anywhere, honey."

So, Audrey Graham and I were dating.

CHAPTER TWENTY-ONE

I expected to feel different when we made love again, then woke as we always did twined together, her arm around my waist and her face in my hair. Or when we said goodbye with sweet kisses and promises to have a nice day. But I didn't. I felt the same as I had since our first night in her apartment. I could have slapped myself for my stupidity, for dragging things out as long as I had.

Clare slipped into my office just after eight with mail and a fresh cup of coffee, while I was exchanging sexts with Audrey and texts with Nat, and being very careful not to mix up the two. A notification pinged on my tablet. "Meeting with Mark Monday at ten a.m." Why was he requesting a meeting Monday when I had a lunch appointment with him in a few hours? Note to self: ask Mark at lunch what's going on. I confirmed it and reluctantly set aside my phone and suggestive banter to do some work.

All my mail had been sorted into work and non-work piles. Offers, contracts, agreements, and there were a few invitations—

each one for Isabelle Rhodes and Guest. Ordinarily I'd take Mark, but the realization Audrey could accompany me pleased me in a way I hadn't thought possible.

I was engrossed in work until late morning when Clare came into my office, hidden behind a bunch of red, yellow and orange roses. She set them carefully on my desk. "These just came for you, Ms. Rhodes." She looked obscenely pleased.

"Who from?"

"I'm not sure. The courier didn't give a name."

"Thanks." There was an envelope of thick cream paper with nothing but my name on the front. I recognized the handwriting immediately. Audrey's scrawl. For someone so meticulous, she had such awful handwriting. Clare made a quiet exit while I opened my card.

I've been dying to send you flowers for months. Congratulations on finding yourself a hot girlfriend. See you tonight.
xo

I read it again, finger running over the words, and leaned down to bury my nose in the soft blooms. Silken petals brushed against my nose, as soft as a caress from the woman who'd sent them. They were beautiful, the scent incredible and I wondered for a moment if they'd been sprayed with something to make them smell so good. Mama would approve of the arrangement. Mama. Shit.

The Band-Aid approach was best for this one. Rip it off, get it out in the open. Still, I felt like I was about to confess to some horrible deed rather than possibly make her day. I could jam a phone call in now and use lunch with Mark as an excuse to get off the phone. The reservation wasn't for another hour, but she wouldn't know that.

She answered almost right away. "Hello, Bunny."

"Hey, Mama."

"Well this is a sweet and unexpected pleasure. How are you?"

"Just fine." Except nervous. Stupidly nervous. I wiggled my toes against the inside of my shoes.

"You got some free time?"

"Yeah. Waiting to go to lunch. Thought I'd give you a call." I stood up and walked over to the full-length window, staring down at John Street. Some guy dressed in what looked like, from this height, nothing but a tutu was walking a dog. New York. "Mama…"

"What've you done, Isabelle?"

"What? Nothin'. What makes you think that?" I shifted my gaze out to the boats docked at the pier.

"You're splutterin' worse than that car of yours when I start it up. Spill."

Goddammit. Head leaning against the window, I confessed, "Audrey and I are datin'. Officially."

Mama's squeal was so loud I had to move the phone away from my ear. They probably heard her at the front desk. "Oh, baby! I'm so happy for you two." She was moving around the house, her shoes echoing on polished wooden floors, then muted on the rugs. "I told you. Didn't I tell you? What happened?"

"I asked and she agreed. It's still new, Mama and we're just trying it all out."

"Well. I want you to think long and hard about this, baby. I like her, she's good for you. Please try," Mama pleaded.

Christ. Like me dating was a math test I had to study for. I swallowed annoyance. Annoyance stemming from knowing she was right. "I will." The words still came out tersely.

"You still doin' therapy?"

I sighed. "Yes, Mama."

"Don't take that tone with me, Isabelle Renee."

"Yes, Mama. Sorry, Mama."

"You know I'm right." She was smiling, I could tell. "You deserve to be happy, but it's not just going to fall into your lap."

I mumbled my agreement, and made my escape. "I have to go. I've got a lunch meeting." After quick I love yous, I hung up before she could sneak more advice.

* * *

Despite my imminent lunch plans with Mark, when I went searching for him, I realized he wasn't even in the office. Tamara had no idea where he was, which was bothersome because she always knew his whereabouts. That was her job. I called him, slightly irritated that he hadn't even come into the office yet, and he was vague about what he was doing. The message was clear. Not interested—lunch was off.

To add insult, the last thing he said before hanging up was, "I can't make the AWL thing tomorrow night. Sorry, you'll have to go stag."

Like hell I will.

Seething, I hung up on him and called Audrey. "Thanks for the flowers, honey, they're gorgeous. How soon can you get to Tribeca?"

"Middle of the day booty call?" she asked hopefully.

All my anger about Mark disappeared on hearing her voice. "No, I'm taking you to lunch."

She met me at the restaurant an hour and fifteen later, in a blue woolen midi dress that clung to every delicious dip and curve. Watching her weave through tables I was conscious of almost everyone else watching her as well. My stomach curled with that wonderful smug feeling of knowing the woman other people were admiring was with me. It was disgustingly shallow because I knew that she was far more than just the sum total of her physical attributes. But her physical attributes were fucking amazing, and all mine.

I stood on trembling legs. "Hello, beautiful."

"Hey." Her cheeks were flushed, eyes wild. The bruising was easily covered by makeup and the graze on her chin was lightly and fully scabbed over.

I kissed her deep and slow. It was a childish gesture of possession but I wanted everyone to know she was with me. I could almost imagine the collective groan of her admirers. When we parted, her eyes were dark with desire and I had a fleeting thought of engaging in that middle of the day booty call after all. "Thanks for meeting me."

She grinned, settling in the seat proffered by the waiter who'd appeared seemingly from nowhere. "Thanks for inviting me."

I waited until she'd been poured a glass of champagne and we were alone again. "Hungry?"

"Yes." Her seductive purr left little doubt about what exactly she was hungry for but something felt a little off. Her usual house cat serenity seemed to have morphed into something more like a jungle cat. She was restless.

I brushed my thumb lightly over the corner of her mouth. "Are you all right, sweetheart?"

She looked startled that I'd asked. "Yeah fine. Just been lying around home, thinking."

"What's on your mind?" I took her hand, squeezing lightly.

"Everything." She laughed softly. "The usual."

"Well I have one more thing for you. How do you feel about attending a gala with me tomorrow night?"

She didn't hesitate. "I feel very good about it."

"Excellent." Despite my pleasure at having her with me, sudden realization caused an alarmed twinge in my neck. Steph was old Boston money. She knew how to act, what to wear and moved easily in my circles because she was born to them. In some ways she fit better than I did. But Audrey…Audrey wasn't used to events with rich and sometimes awful people.

My mouth went dry. "Have you been to an event like this before? It's black tie."

"Yes, I have attended black tie before. I'm also not a complete novice at buying clothes, you know," she said patiently. "See? I'm wearing some now."

I unlocked my phone and quickly sent her a contact. "Go here this afternoon and I'll ring ahead. They'll help you. Put it on my account." I'd slipped into Overbearing Fiend territory.

She didn't even look at her phone which had just buzzed with my message. "Iz. I've got this. Trust me please and stop trying to *Pretty Woman* me."

I glanced at my phone then back to her. "You're right, I'm sorry. I just…" I dropped my phone into my bag. "I just don't want you to feel uncomfortable."

Audrey deftly steered me away from my organizational meltdown. "Iz, with you beside me, I'll never feel more comfortable." She leaned close and kissed my nose. "I love that you're so worried, but trust me. I'll be fine. I've been to plenty of highfalutin exhibition openings with my mom. I can schmooze with the best of them."

"Okay then." A sip of champagne helped to push some of the nerves aside.

"How's your day been?"

"Busy, boring, better now."

She smiled, brushing the edge of her thumb along the pristine white tablecloth. "I…have you told Mark about us yet?"

I set down my glass. "Not yet."

"Why not?" she asked evenly.

"Because we've been dating officially for less than twenty-four hours, and I haven't seen him today."

"Oh. But you're going to tell him, right? He's going to know we're together if I attend this thing with you tomorrow night."

"Yes of course I'll tell him, eventually, when the time is right." Mark wouldn't know anything about tomorrow night because he didn't care enough to check the columns to see what had happened at the latest galas and parties.

Audrey's tongue smoothed along her lower lip. "Is there really a right time? You're not breaking bad news to him."

"No it's not bad news," I agreed.

"Are you ashamed of me?" She brought her thumbnail to her mouth as though she was going to gnaw the corner, then pulled her hand away to rest on the table. "Ashamed of us and what we're doing?" The change in her was palpable, as though she'd turned from a confident woman into a small child desperate for approval.

"Christ, no!" From the corner of my eye, I saw the waiter abort his approach. Big tip for you, pal. Once I was sure he was out of earshot, I tried for something a little more articulate. "I'm not ashamed of us or this relationship, or how it was before. Audrey, I just…I'm not ready." I didn't know how to tell her something that I didn't quite understand myself. There were so many reasons I didn't want to tell Mark, all jumbled up into one great big *do not want.*

Quietly, Audrey said, "You hiding this kind of makes me feel like a dirty little secret."

My mouth gaped open and I spluttered before answering, "You're not that, not at all."

"No? Why then?" Her hands tightened on the neatly folded napkin beside her plate. "I just don't get it, Iz."

I rubbed my eyes, suddenly overwhelmed by tiredness and something that felt a lot like fear. She deserved an answer, so I plucked one morsel of truth from the maelstrom, hoping she would accept it as the full reason. "I don't want him treating you weirdly because we're together." The words he'd said the day after he found out Audrey and I had slept together echoed in my head. *If she accepts, then she's unprofessional.*

"That's between him and me, Iz. You can't control what he does or how he acts." She stared intently at me. "I don't like feeling…unimportant. You know, with my dad, I got used to just being shoved in a room and ignored." At my soft gasp she hastily corrected herself, "Metaphorically."

"You're not unimportant. Quite the opposite." That tingle spread through my limbs again. Not alarm but like it was trying to tell me something, but I couldn't quite nail it down.

"Okay then, maybe you don't understand where I'm coming from? When we were just…casual or lying to ourselves about what we were doing, then it was acceptable, Iz. Because I had no right to ask that from you. But now…"

"No, I get it. I understand."

She straightened, drawing in a breath. "I'm sorry. I shouldn't have brought it up in public. I don't want this to turn into an argument, sweetheart. Especially not here."

I forced a smile. "Kind of feels like it already has."

Audrey took my hand between both of hers, her thumbs playing over my fingers. "No. This is just a discussion." She looked up at me. "The first of many truthful ones I hope we're going to have over the years."

"Years?" I squeaked. I hadn't dared hope but there she was saying it.

"Yes." She offered nothing else and her seemingly unshakable faith that she'd still want me in months and years pushed a little of the uncomfortable feeling aside.

I glanced down at our joined hands. "Okay. If it's important to you then I'll tell him Monday. I promise."

"Thank you." She picked up her champagne, watching me intently. A small smile graced her lips. "What do you recommend for lunch?"

"Everything." I indicated subtly to the waiter and he came over immediately. Suddenly not very hungry, I tuned out as he began a well-practiced speech.

Audrey was right, of course. I needed to tell Mark. He deserved to know. I let a little of my unease come up to the surface and acknowledged that I was afraid Mark would think she "wasn't good enough" or that he might be difficult, and be unable to separate Employee Audrey from Best Friend's Girlfriend Audrey. Because she was always going to be his employee. And just once, I wanted something that he wasn't somehow involved in.

"Iz?"

"Hmm?" I looked up, noting two expectant stares. "Oh right. I'll just have whatever you're having. Thank you."

The waiter nodded and left us alone again. Audrey followed his departure and when she spun in the seat to face me again, she seemed unnecessarily contrite. "I'm sorry that I brought the mood down. I just wanted to be honest."

"No it's fine. Honesty is good. I guess I'm just getting used to this new dynamic and all." I let my hand rest on the table, palm up and she slid her hand into mine.

With her free hand, Audrey reached for her champagne. She made a deft subject change. "Do you think we would be together if we hadn't met in the bar?"

My thoughts sped through the possibilities but I couldn't arrive at an answer. I settled for, "I'm not sure." Audrey said nothing. I exhaled and tried to elaborate. "I want to say no, to pretend I have some shred of professionalism but you're so persuasive I may have given in if pushed."

"Persuasive huh."

"Very." I bit my lower lip gently. "I do know I would have spent all our time together checking you out."

"Of that I have no doubt." Her grin was fully formed now and smug. "You wouldn't have made a move? Propositioned me."

My eyebrows shot up. "Christ, no! Not at all. I would have thought about it constantly, but no. I wouldn't have asked. I… couldn't have. You?"

"Probably, though only if I was sure I had another job to go to. Just in case." She winked.

"Honey, I would never fire you for that."

"Of course not. It's Mr. Hall who does the hiring and firing, right?" she said teasingly.

"Right." Twisting my champagne glass on the blindingly white tablecloth, I looked at her. "I still can't help but feel that you knew right from the start." My statement was matter-of-fact rather than accusatory.

"Knew what exactly?"

"That I'd cave. Give in and want more."

Her answering smile was slow. Audrey reached under the table to run her fingers over my thigh. "Come on now, Iz. Nobody could know that for certain."

I tensed under her touch, trying to focus on what she was saying rather than how high her hand was moving. "Maybe not, but I feel like you got there long before I did."

"I hoped and I wished, but I didn't *know*. Not for certain, but I thought if I just let you be, treated you the way you deserved, showed you the possibilities then maybe, just maybe you'd want more of what I was offering."

"Well it worked." Meeting her eyes, I saw that contemplative glint again. It disappeared when I smiled at her and admitted, "I've barely thought of anything else for the past couple of months except how much I wanted there to be more. I'm sorry it took me so long to find the courage to admit how I felt."

"Well, we got there in the end." This time when she looked at me, her gaze was bright. Expectant. Open.

"Yes we did," I said softly, squeezing her hand. "So we're good?"

She flashed me a genuine smile. "Better than."

CHAPTER TWENTY-TWO

The next day, Saturday, we enjoyed a lazy morning in bed followed by a long breakfast on my balcony. Since we'd made ourselves official, there was lightness in me, something I hadn't felt in a long time. I hoped it would be permanent. Audrey read the paper, and I worked as we poured each other coffee and passed things back and forth.

I looked up from my tablet to watch her drizzling honey over fruit. Her forehead wrinkled with concentration, lower lip captured between her teeth. Audrey caught me staring. "What?" She sucked honey from her thumb.

"Nothing, sweetheart. Nothing at all. Except you're beautiful." I took her hand and filled her in on our plans for the day. "Christopher will be here at three with his hair and makeup girls. If you want, they can do yours too." I worded the offer carefully, not wanting her to think I didn't trust her. "I know you're fine but it takes some of the stress out of getting ready. You can just drink champagne and let them do all the work."

Audrey was silent for a moment, her thoughtful face in place. "You're right. That would be great." She pointed at her face. "They've probably got some pretty heavy-duty concealer."

"You don't need it."

"Flatterer. What are we going to do until he arrives?" she asked innocently. She tried to hide it, but a smirk slid out.

I returned her cheeky grin. "I'm sure we can think of something."

After an hour in bed, we relaxed quietly with limbs intertwined. I rolled onto my side, head propped in my hand. "You know, I'm fairly certain everyone is going to be stuck to your side tonight."

"Yeah?" She drew the word out. "And why's that?"

I climbed over to slip back between her legs, resting my forearms on her hips. "This stunning body, and that gorgeous face." My hands slid up to cup her breasts, fingers sliding over her nipples.

"Just remember who gets to take it home," she said softly. Her thighs closed around me, heels coming to rest against my calves.

I kissed her abdomen, running my nose over her soft skin. "I'm sorry if it's awful."

"What? The oral sex you're clearly about to give me?"

I pinched her nipple gently. "No. The gala."

Audrey ran a hand through my hair. "I don't care, Iz. I'd spend a week making small talk with strangers if it meant I could stand by your side in public."

I glanced up at her, smiling. "Really?"

She gave me a lazy smile of her own. "Really."

Blinking to stop the tears prickling my eyes from falling, I made my way down between her thighs.

* * *

Thoroughly relaxed after hours in bed, I had bottles of Krug waiting in ice buckets when Christopher arrived with "his girls" in tow. Impeccable in Armani, he gave me a double cheek kiss and swanned into the room. His self-appointed role was, under the guise of supervising, to drink my champagne and make me laugh.

He peered around then made a beeline for the booze. "Are you ready, sweetness? And where's my second project?"

I'd sent him a text earlier to tell him Audrey would need hair and makeup too. His response was typically exuberant. *OMG!? Is this THE woman?! Dying. Emoji. Emoji. Emoji.*

My response to his response was short. *Behave.*

Never. Kiss emoji. Very rude emojis.

"She's finishing her shower." I poured myself a small glass of champagne and settled in a chair. Makeup cases were opened, more champagne distributed, compliments swapped. Christopher lowered his voice to just above a stage whisper. "I'm very excited to meet the object of your affections, Isabelle. Though I must confess I have concerns about someone who chooses their own attire."

I leaned close, matching the pitch of his voice. "I'm quite sure she's fine. Not everyone needs as much assistance as I do."

His peals of laughter lingered as he sauntered to the stairs to call up, "Audrey? We're desperate for you, darling." Then a humorous aside of, "Isabelle in particular."

She came down in a silk dressing gown and was immediately handed a glass and set upon by Christopher. He topped up my champagne, waving the bottle in Audrey's direction. "Audrey. I must thank you for everything you've done for my sweetie here." The man had no filter. I swiveled my eyes in his direction as he bustled on. "She's glowing. I haven't seen her skin look this good since the Dead Sea mud mask. That shit was amazing."

I grinned at him. "Are you quite done?"

"Isabelle, I haven't even begun," he responded cheerfully.

As the girls began to work on us, Christopher asked rapid-fire questions and Audrey shot back answers.

"What do you do?"

"I'm a pilot."

"How'd you two meet?"

"Work."

Christopher spared me a glance but recovered quickly. "And your ethnicity?"

Too far. I looked up. "Hey! That is seriously rude."

He shrugged, totally unconcerned by his invasive questioning. "What? I want to know where she gets her gorgeous skin and coloring. Plus those cheekbones. People pay good money for a face like that, you know."

Audrey grinned. "My mother's Italian. My father was Irish, or rather his parents were."

Christopher all but swooned. "Perfect. What's the deal with that bruise and patch of skin on your chin? Botox gone wrong? Bad laser treatment?"

"Motorcycle crash."

"Oooh, a secret leather chick. Kinky."

It went like that until we were ready. When Christopher deemed us perfectly done, Audrey went upstairs to change, leaving me to slip my robe off quickly. My stylist gave me a cheeky finger wave when he spotted the underwear I wore. A brand spanking—if I was lucky later—new La Perla set, something Audrey hadn't yet seen.

I rolled on my stockings, clipped them to my garter belt and was zipped into my dress. Christopher put his drink down long enough to give me a final once-over. "Divine," he sighed. His attention was tugged away from me at the sound of heels on my wooden floors. I could do nothing but stare in the same direction, mouth dry. Christopher reacted first, clapping excitedly. "Oh my goodness."

The girls murmured their approval.

Audrey usually wore low boot heels, sneakers or flats. That night, she wore three inches of stiletto, drawing attention to those fucking gorgeous legs. A midlength royal blue cocktail dress with a tasteful amount of cleavage, which wasn't enough for me, hugged her body like it'd been painted on. Her hair was down, and swaths of silver jewelry offset her dark features. You could have plucked her up and dropped her in the middle of a model shoot and nobody would bat an eye. My stomach did that nervous excitement twist. Oh God.

I was literally speechless and did a mock cartoon mouth drop and then pushed it closed with a forefinger. Audrey smiled, seemingly pleased by my reaction. It took me a few moments before I could speak, "Babe, I am *so* sorry I ever doubted your ability to buy clothing."

Christopher grasped her hand, careful not to spill his champagne. "Audrey, I believe this is the first time I've said this to anyone, but you do not need my help. Spin. Let me look at every delicious inch."

She spun, finishing with a Marilyn-esque pose. "Do I pass?"

"You get an A triple plus." He turned to me. "I'm taking the divine I gave to you and giving it to her."

I grinned. "She deserves it." I drank in the sight of her and held out my hand. "Come here." When she stepped close, I stretched up to whisper in her ear, "There are not enough superlatives in the English language to tell you how fucking stunning, gorgeous and elegant you look."

She turned her head to look down at me, a flash of lust crossing her face. "Ain't so bad yourself, kid."

Christopher sighed happily. "As a man who is one hundred percent comfortable with his sexuality, I have to say one thing. Nothing has ever made me doubt myself more than looking at you two hot femmes." He downed the last of his champagne, and presented both elbows out to escort Audrey and me downstairs.

He ushered us toward the garden in front of my building, posed us and snapped photos on his phone. Before we slid into the waiting limo, Christopher passed something to Audrey then leaned in to whisper in her ear. She looked to me as she laughed and said something in response, her eyes sparkling.

As we settled in the backseat, my phone buzzed with the photos. I sent a particularly good one to Mama and received a jumble of emojis and bad autocorrects back.

Audrey held a business card between two fingers. "He said he wants to put me in a tux with some, and I quote, 'killer fuck-me heels'." Audrey glanced forward to the closed privacy screen then back to me. She leaned close, breath whispering across my ear. "And I told him I hoped you would."

I shivered and apparently satisfied with herself, Audrey sat back and crossed her ankles. She stared out the window while I ran over my speech, murmuring to myself. We rode in silence for a while but after the third time of me checking my clutch for things I knew I had, Audrey's hand slid to my leg, pushing gently to stop the jiggling of my knee. "What's up?"

"I guess I'm a little nervous."

"What about?"

"You meeting these people." Streetlights cast a warm glow on her face, flashing as we drove past. It reminded me of looking at someone who was watching fireworks. "They can be snobbish."

"Honey, you need to stop worrying," she said gently. "I can handle myself."

"I know, I know. I'm sorry." It'd taken me years to feel like I fit in among these people and I knew that if I was suddenly penniless, they'd drop me faster than I could say *nice knowing you*.

She leaned over and kissed me softly. "It'll be fine. Trust me." Her hand rested lightly on my cheek. The way she held my face always made me feel safe, like she was both comforting me and reassuring me that she wanted me at the same time.

"Thank you."

"You're welcome." She brushed her nose against mine and settled back.

I exhaled, letting as much tension out as I could. "Audrey?"

"Yes?"

"You look amazing."

"You said that already." She came back for another kiss, this one more possessive. When I felt her tongue against my lip— thank the universe for smudge-proof lipstick—the familiar need made itself known again. I groaned and she pressed harder, the swell of her breast against mine and her tongue more insistent.

"Babe." I pulled back, trying to reclaim my composure.

"Mmm?"

"You need to stop kissing me like that, or I'm going to ask you to take me here in the backseat before we get inside."

She grinned, but mercifully pulled away.

Inside, I endured double air kisses and expectant glances as we moved through the crowd. Audrey was charming and polite, squeezing my hand reassuringly. From across the room, a couple I knew waved to catch my attention. I stood up on my toes to whisper in her ear. "We've been summoned."

She laughed and let me lead her over. I held the tuxedoed arm of the tall man. "Hello, Gregory. How are you?"

He leaned down to kiss my cheek, just one thankfully. "Isabelle. You look lovely."

I moved back slightly to open up the circle. "This is Audrey Graham. My…" Say it, say it. "Partner." Her hand tightened on mine as I gestured again. "Audrey, this is Gregory Cain and his wife, Jasmine."

Audrey released my hand and offered hers to Gregory and Jasmine in turn, smiling confidently. "A pleasure to meet you."

"And you." Gregory launched right into small talk. "So, what do you do, Audrey?"

"I'm a pilot, currently working private sector but I flew commercial for a number of years."

Gregory straightened, his polite interest suddenly seeming a whole lot more genuine. "Flying. Wow. Now that's something I've always wanted to try."

Audrey nodded, warming right into one of her favorite topics. "I'd be happy to point you in the right direction. I was an instructor and I've been considering doing my private instructor certifications, so if you wait a few months I might even be able to show you the ropes myself."

He seemed impressed. "I may just take you up on that."

Jasmine laughed, tugging her husband's tux sleeve. "Oh please, he doesn't need another hobby."

Audrey joined in, her laughter low and appealing. "Yes, it can be consuming. Though probably more exciting than golf."

As we all chuckled together I felt a sudden swell of pride, and then shame that I'd ever doubted her. Marisa, one of my fellow AWL Board members, appeared on my right and took my elbow. "Isabelle, can I borrow you for a moment please?"

I smiled at the group, lingering on Audrey who gave me a confident nod. I excused myself, brushed my lips against her cheek and left her to talk shop. The moment we were out of earshot, Marisa pounced. "Isabelle Rhodes. Where did you find her?" Apparently I wasn't needed for anything other than a quick bout of gossip.

"Actually, she's one of our pilots. Long story." I grinned, upending my champagne glass lazily.

"She's absolutely delicious, you minx. But you're not concerned?"

My eyebrows came together to hold a confusion meeting above my nose. "By what?"

"Her status." She made the statement as though it was the most obvious thing in the world.

"Her status?" I repeated incredulously.

"Mhmm. I always think ordinary folk find it hard to fit in, you know what they can be like."

Anger came up my chest like heartburn but I forced it down. I couldn't afford to antagonize this woman. "They? You mean girlfriends? Decent people?"

She held up her hands conciliatorily. "Darling, please. I meant no offense."

"No, I know you didn't." Take a breath, Isabelle. This is not the time or place to get into an argument. I glanced at Audrey, still deep in conversation and looking totally at ease. "I'm sorry, Marisa. It's been a long week and frankly, you hit a nerve."

"She's not trying to—"

"No, no of course not! Nothing like that. But I'd be lying if I said I wasn't worried about how people would accept her." I handed off my empty glass to a passing waiter.

Marisa lowered her voice, eyes across the room on Audrey. "I wouldn't concern yourself, Isabelle. I may have spoken too soon. Seems to me she's being accepted just fine."

I followed her gaze to where Audrey, in addition to Gregory and Jasmine, had drawn a small crowd. She seemed perfectly at ease, capturing people's attention effortlessly. "Yes, I believe you're right," I said softly. "Excuse me."

Audrey and I made the rounds, both together and separately. Eventually, I stopped hovering to ensure she was all right and let her do what seemed to come naturally to her. Confident and adaptable, she worked the crowd like a seasoned gala attendee. Apparently there was no aspect of my life that she didn't fit into. Or maybe I'd just been a slow learner when it came to fitting in among the city's elite.

Shortly before my speech, I excused myself and snuck into the bathroom for a quick makeup check. Audrey found me as I was walking back down the hall. "God you're beautiful. Come here," she murmured, grabbing my hand and yanking me around a corner. "For luck." She kissed me hard, tongue running over my lips and hands sliding over my ass. Then she brushed my nose gently with hers and let me go, pushing into the bathroom without another word.

I stood dumbstruck, lips burning with the memory of her tongue lazily claiming them. Marisa came around the corner, sounding frantic. "Isabelle, there you are."

I dropped my fingers away from my lips. "Yes?"

"You're on in ten."

"I'll be right there." Once I'd regained control.

After my speech—given to the usual attentive and appreciative audience—I was caught up in another round of networking. Taking a breather, I stood on the balcony peering down at the crowd until I spotted Audrey. Easily the most eye-catching woman in the room, she was talking to another of my clients, Peter Altman. He had a helicopter he liked to take up when he wasn't working as a criminal defense attorney. It was logical they'd find some common ground.

She was gesturing with her champagne glass, demonstrating something that looked like a plane control maneuver. He was nodding vigorously, and interjecting with his own gestures. Audrey touched his arm and they laughed together. I expected to feel a twinge of jealousy, one of my less attractive traits. Over time, I'd come to recognize it as insecurity and tried dispel it whenever it appeared. But watching her, I was suddenly aware of a total lack of anxiety.

My thoughts drifted back to what she'd said in bed this morning. It was *me* who would take her home. *Me* who would wake up with her arms pulling me close and her legs tangled in mine. It was *me* she wanted. As though pulled by an unknown force she looked up at me, winked and turned back to her conversation.

CHAPTER TWENTY-THREE

Audrey had been swallowed up by the crowd again and wasn't where I'd seen her last. After a few minutes of wandering through masses of people, I caught sight of her on the balcony. Making my way to the staircase, I paused a moment to stare up at her. She stood still and alone, face impassive and cast in shadow to accentuate that fine bone structure. An exquisite statue and all mine.

I was overcome by a sharp stab of desire and the sudden realization that I never wanted that feeling to go away. I wanted to spend the rest of my life in awe of her, loving her more each day. When I reached the top stair, Audrey turned to me, her contemplative expression turning to my favorite grin when she saw me. "Hey."

I kissed her cheek. "Hey. You okay?"

"Absolutely, Iz. Just thinking."

"We're done if you wanted to head home?"

She pushed off the railing and straightened up. "Sure."

I frowned, suddenly stuck on what she'd just said and her expression before I interrupted. "What were you thinking about?"

"You." Her eyes darted around before coming to rest on my face. "I've been watching you all evening, and I'm about ready to orgasm imagining what I want to do to you when we get home."

That was not the answer I'd expected, but it was far more pleasant than how boring the night had been or the *not telling Mark* that I'd braced for. "Really?" I lowered my voice slightly. "What have you been imagining exactly?"

"Oh you know, boring stuff like bending you over the kitchen table and making you come multiple times before we've even made it upstairs." Her slightly bored tone and body language betrayed nothing, and anyone watching would likely assume we were simply having a conversation about politics or the weather.

I swallowed hard. "I see."

"But we can stay here and socialize a little longer, if you don't want me to take you home and fuck you until you can't even remember your name." Though she spoke casually, her eyes telegraphed her lust.

I took her hand. "Let's go."

"Let's," she agreed.

The whole ride home I ran my hand up and down her thigh, a low hum at the back of my throat. She sat demurely, but I could feel the tension in the muscle of her thigh, tell by the way she kept her knees together that she was as keen as I was. She just had more restraint.

I'd never had sex in a limo before, and the way she felt under my fingertips made me briefly consider it. Quickly, I dismissed the idea. There was no way I could be quiet. The moment we stopped and the door opened, I climbed from the backseat and offered her my hand.

Taking it, Audrey led me across the lobby of my building, waving to Carl at the front desk as though it was a perfectly ordinary moment. As soon as the elevator closed, we came together furiously. Tongues battling, hands groping, I was held against the mirrored wall with lips traveling over my neck, a tongue tracing my ear. "I want you so badly," she growled possessively.

I'd been starved of her all night and I couldn't wait any longer. I tugged her dress up, pressed my thigh between her legs and felt her shudder as she ground onto me. I wanted to drag it out but at the same time, wanted her to take me right there against the wall, my leg hooked around her ass and fingers—

At the loud ding of the elevator, I slipped from underneath her and pulled her into my foyer. I fumbled with the lock for an eternity until I finally managed to get my front door open. All my blood had traveled south, pooling in my groin and I couldn't think of anything except undressing her. Worshipping her. I tossed my clutch onto the sideboard and kept walking into the lounge room.

Her footsteps faltered. "Running away?"

"Far from it." I grabbed her hand and led her to the couch. "Spin around." Standing behind her, I slid her zipper down and slipped the dress off one arm to expose the smooth, tanned skin of her torso. My nipples pebbled, desire coiled in my belly. It would be so easy to take her hand and just...no. I pushed my need aside to get her naked, pulled her dress all the way down and left it to puddle on the floor.

Audrey turned her head to watch me. She was a statue while my hands and lips and tongue explored her back and shoulders, but her tremor of excitement was unmistakable. Audrey exhaled in surprise when I tugged her back to me, her ass fitting right above my hips. One arm wrapped around to tweak her nipples, the other trailing lightly downward until I found what I wanted. I bit her shoulder hard and dipped my finger inside her hot core.

"Iz...I'm gonna come if you keep doing that." Her hand wrapped around my wrist, almost tight enough to bruise.

I unlocked my teeth from her skin, kissing the mark lightly. "Maybe that's what I want, baby."

Audrey groaned when I withdrew, sliding my fingers up her slit until I found her clitoris. The groan turned guttural as I made lazy circles over the pulsing bundle of nerves. Her body trembled against mine. "Stop. Please. I don't want to come yet."

"Unfair." I stopped immediately, putting my fingers into my mouth to suck her essence from them. "God you taste so good."

Audrey turned quickly to face me, hands on my waist. "I bet you do too." Her kiss was intense, probing my mouth until I pulled back. She was going to break me if I didn't get away.

"You can test that theory later but first, sit," I commanded, pushing her down gently onto the couch.

The edge of her mouth was creased up, an eyebrow arched. "What are you doing, Iz?"

"Seducing you, obviously." The pleasure was wholly mine, looking at her on the couch, legs spread, wearing nothing but a few pieces of scant black lace.

The grin widened. "You only have to exist to do that…" Her eyes tracked me as I approached and stood astride her leg.

"Oh really?" It was time for her reward. "I'm far too dressed for this. Unzip me?"

Eyes locked with mine, she reached up under my armpit, sliding the zipper down with exquisite slowness. I stepped out of the dress, being careful not to rip it with my heels, keeping eye contact with her the whole time. She broke before I did.

I win.

"What is that?" she demanded.

"What's what?" I asked innocently, turning around to drape my dress over the coffee table and I admit it, show her my ass.

"That," she said hoarsely.

"Underwear?" It certainly was. Scant amounts of blue satin and lace, a garter belt and a balconette bra that pushed my Bs to Cs.

"You've been wearing it the whole night?" Her words pitched high with indignant accusation.

"Mhmm." The lingerie had been a delicious secret. Every time I thought about her reaction when she saw it, another level was added to my excitement. It had been like hours of delicious foreplay. Perhaps not the greatest idea, given I was about fit to burst. "You don't like it?" I asked, feigning surprise.

"I…if I'd known what was hiding underneath that dress, I'd have taken you into the bathroom and fucked you senseless."

She held out her hand. "Come here." Her voice had gotten deep and husky, the way it did when she was aroused.

The change in her set me off, freeing all my pent up excitement from the evening. Anticipation sent an electric current under my skin. I stepped toward her and placed a leg on either side of her thigh, clamping myself in place. Her hands came up to my ass. Audrey finally took her eyes off my body, looking up at my face. "I almost don't want to take them off."

"Then don't," I whispered. "Fuck me while I'm wearing them."

Audrey fingered the suspender clips attaching my seamed stockings and I could sense the change in her. She'd become almost reverent, running her hand down my stockinged leg like it was a piece of art she was scared of breaking. My arms were slack at my sides as I was explored, studied, worshipped.

My breath caught as she bent to kiss my hip, loose hair trailing over the bare skin of my stomach. Her hands were busy, nails scratching softly over my back, fingertips running lightly over my skin. Then, she did the thing that always got me. She slapped my ass and reached between my legs to run her fingers along the length of my wet heat, front to back. A quick pause at my entrance to tease through the fabric, then knuckles slipped over my clit.

I moaned, jerking like I'd been stung. "Again," I begged. "Please."

The second time, the pressure was harder and the pace slower. My breathing nudged toward hyperventilation. There was no way I could remain standing. My hands on her shoulders for balance, I straddled her.

A thumb brushed over my lower lip. "You are so fucking sexy."

I smirked. "Do we need to start a *no you are* argument?"

She shook her head. "I'll win."

My answer was smothered by a hot kiss. Nipples hard against hers, I claimed her tongue. She groaned when I took a fistful of her hair and rocked forward, trying to find something to keep pressure against my aching clit. Audrey took my cue, reaching between us. Fingers pushed my panties aside to touch me, deftly sliding through my folds.

I groaned at her touch, my bundle of nerves sensitive from her earlier teasing. "Harder," I whispered. She gave me what I wanted, circling my clitoris and sending me closer to the edge. Her breathing was ragged, muscles taut against mine. I bit her neck then apologized with a soft sweep of my tongue. Capturing her ear between my teeth, I begged, "Fuck me."

Audrey filled me before I could form another thought, fingers slipping easily through my arousal. I gasped when she burrowed deeper, finding all the landscapes she knew so well. Kisses along my jaw, a tongue tracing over my ear. She added another finger and made another thrust, gentler this time. "Baby, you are so fucking wet."

"Oh God. Oh—"

Audrey wrapped her free arm around my waist, twisted and in one quick motion, I was lying on the couch. Squirming, desperate for her to finish what she started, I tried to pull her back down to me but she was tugging her panties off and unhooking her bra.

I reached for her, cupping her breasts and rolling her nipples between thumb and forefinger. Audrey unclipped my stockings. Teasingly. Achingly slow. I groaned. We'd gone from frantic to sensual in a matter of seconds. Now, she was taking her time, keeping me out of reach. Some distant, rational part of me knew that when I came it would be worth it, but in that moment I was frustrated as all hell.

I moved to kick my heels off, but she held my leg to stop me. "No. Leave them on." The look she gave me sent sparks of pleasure shooting into my stomach. I was dragged forward and spread apart. She hesitated, then slid my panties down, carefully easing them over my heels before flinging them aside.

"What about you?" I managed to ask.

"Don't worry, baby. You're going to give me what I want when I'm done with you."

The thought made my throat tighten and my pulse race even faster. She moved backward, settling her shoulders between my thighs. Before she put her tongue on me, she said one last thing that turned me to a quivering mess.

"Isabelle, I'm going to make you come so hard, you're going to wish you'd worn this lingerie sooner."

CHAPTER TWENTY-FOUR

Monday morning with coffee in hand I strolled through Mark's open door, psyched up and ready to tell him about Audrey and me. Between the success of Saturday night, the hot sex that followed and our sweet, lazy Sunday I was so loved-up that I wanted to shout it to the world. Mark glanced up as I closed the door quietly, but said nothing about my sudden appearance in his office.

Sitting opposite him, I noticed the disarray of his desk. Sales and purchases ready to be finalized, and various contracts among the chaos. He looked tired, but most surprisingly was the shadow of dark stubble adorning his cheeks. I set my coffee down on his desk. "Pierre's closed this morning?"

Mark had been getting his morning shave from Pierre for years, adhering to a strict facial hair ritual. In all the years we'd been friends, I'd only seen him with stubble a handful of times. It was akin to someone forgetting to get dressed in the morning.

"No, I was just running a little late," he explained in a tone that told me I'd get no more from him.

I tried for some levity. "You look swarthy." And also totally unprepared for the meeting we were supposed to be having in less than an hour.

"Good, that's exactly what I was going for," he replied without taking his eyes from his laptop.

Nope, I was being shut down. Fine. "So, I just wanted—"

"Belle, I'm really sorry but I'm trying to organize shit for our meeting." Finally, he gave me his attention. Or part of it. "Can we talk later?"

Frowning, I agreed with a drawn out, "Sure...okay."

"I'll see you in the conference room in forty minutes."

Forty minutes later when I opened the door to the conference room, Mark wasn't there. Instead, I was more than a little alarmed to see not only Tom but also Quentin seated at the large round table. Our corporate lawyer as well as Mark's personal lawyer. One on their own was strange enough, but both together sent a shrill peal of alarm down my spine, and I had a sudden uncomfortable feeling that I wasn't going to like what this meeting was about.

The uncomfortable feeling was quickly replaced by annoyance at Mark for tossing me overboard without a lifejacket. I brushed my hair over my shoulder, switching automatically to polite hostess. "Gentlemen, this is unexpected, but a pleasure nonetheless." Straightening, I crossed the room with my hand outstretched, suddenly grateful I'd put on a pair of four-inch Jimmys this morning. Without the extra height, I'd have felt even more at a disadvantage.

After exchanging the usual handshakes and greetings and ensuring they had a beverage, I added, "I hope you haven't been waiting long. I believe Mark was just getting a few things ready." I set my tablet and phone down and sat opposite them just as Mark walked into the conference room and closed the door.

The men repeated the same handshake, greeting, refreshment-check ritual before Mark sat down on the same side as me, leaving a chair between us. Odd. He made eye contact with each of us in turn. "Thank you all for coming."

There were damp patches on the front of his light blue Oxford shirt. Sweat. In air-conditioning. My business partner folded his hands on top of the table, his knuckles white. "Well. Where to start?"

Inside my head, Obnoxious Isabelle raised her hand and mumbled a snide *How about with what the hell is going on?* I pushed her down. Clearly this wasn't my meeting and I just had to sit and wait and watch. I pulled my focus away from him to look at the lawyers sitting opposite. Their expressions were unreadable so I concentrated on my friend.

Mark exchanged looks with the lawyers before spinning his chair to face me. "Isabelle."

"Mark. What's this about?"

Mark gestured to Tom who pushed a document across to me. I used my fingertips to drag it closer and as I read the first line, Mark said quietly and in a not entirely steady voice, "I would like to sell you my share of Rhodes and Hall."

"Pardon me?"

Apparently he thought my question meant I hadn't heard, rather than the fact I was having a what-the-fuck moment. Mark's face was impressively neutral when he repeated, "I'd like to make you a sale offer for my share of Rhodes and Hall."

"No, I got that, Mark. I just—" I had to stop speaking. There were no words. There was nothing except a strange hum in my ears.

Mark passed me a stack of folders. It seemed that having made his initial pitch, it was easier for him to get the rest of it out. "If you don't find it agreeable, then we need to discuss dissolution of the business. Here is a full valuation, audit and report on our financial position."

"I know our financial position, Mark," I snapped, then clamped my lips together on the stream of anger that was about to spill.

God, I wanted to yell at him so badly but he'd maneuvered me expertly by having two other people in the room, and holding the meeting in our not entirely soundproof conference room. My body was tight with tension, almost trembling with the effort of keeping my fists unclenched and my posture confident but relaxed. I couldn't appear to be anything but in control. Not here. Not now.

"So that's it?" I asked quietly. "That's what this meeting is about?"

His gaze was steady. "Yes."

Tom and Quentin remained silent which made it easier to ignore them. I stared at my old friend. My business partner. A man I thought I knew but apparently didn't know at all. Looking at him answered none of my questions but as Mark stared back at me, the sadness in his eyes was unmistakable. He leaned forward a fraction. "Do you have any questions, Isabelle?"

Aside from why? Nope there's nothing I can say here. I think I'm golden thanks. Shaking my head, I squared my shoulders. "Of course I'll need to have my own lawyer look at this before I can discuss anything further." I barely managed to keep the bite from my voice. My lawyer should have been here with me for this meeting. Mark should have told me that he was considering leaving our partnership. The acid burn of bile turned my stomach.

Tom lifted his hands to rest atop the table. "Of course. We can set up another meeting when you know how you want to proceed."

I nodded my assent, suddenly overwhelmed by a crushing mental exhaustion. Tumbling around my head were all the implications of this maneuver. Either I threw away what I'd worked my ass off to build, or I took the reins.

Mark gathered his papers. "Isabelle has all the information she needs, so I think that's all for now. We'll meet again once she's had a chance to go over things with her lawyer."

Dimly, I registered Mark saying, "I'll see you both out." He touched my arm, startling me into motion.

I stood with the others, and said automatic goodbyes along with firm handshakes. The moment Mark and the lawyers left the conference room I sank into the chair again. The whole thing had taken less than five minutes. Five minutes for my life to be flipped completely on its head.

I turned the document around and flicked through the pages to find Mark's magic figure. Compensation for backing away from everything we'd built together. I scanned the page, and noted right away that most surprising of this whole thing was that what Mark wanted wasn't a fifty percent split. It was more like forty-seven.

The door closed again and Mark crossed the room to me. "I really would rather you buy me out than dissolve everything we worked so hard for."

"I see." I pushed the proposal away, not wanting it anywhere near me. The money wasn't the issue. Taking full control of the business wasn't the issue, although that seemed pretty daunting. The issue was that I'd been blindsided by his announcement. By him. Why didn't he discuss such a life-altering change with me before getting the lawyers involved? "Why now? Why throw this at me without any warning? What's happening, Mark? I don't understand it at all."

"I didn't want you to worry. And I didn't want you to be pissy at me for weeks while I finalized all the details." He smiled, and for a moment he seemed like the twenty-two-year-old beer-loving nerd I met in college. The guy who'd babbled about taking New York by storm with such enthusiasm that I'd been carried along with him. The guy I'd shared an apartment with while we were interning with the two largest companies in the city, working our asses off and both loving and hating every moment. The guy who'd been right there with me as we'd risked everything to go out on our own. "I'm tired of feeling like I can't do anything right, Belle. I love running a business but I don't like being a stockbroker. I can't pretend anymore."

"That doesn't…it…that's not a reason, Mark."

"To me it is. I need a change, of pace and scenery." Both his hands came up placatingly. "Look. I want you to succeed. I know you can do it. While I'm here you're just going to keep doing what's safe."

"Don't even bother, Mark. Don't get all sanctimonious like you're doing this for me." I raised my chin.

He broke eye contact with me and I knew immediately that there was more. How fucking wonderful. I made a *give it to me* gesture. "Spill," I said wearily.

"A client wants to sue." He laughed humorlessly. "Actually, that's not entirely correct because thanks to Tom's excellent contracts, we can't be sued. I should say, the client wants arbitration."

The wording of these contracts flitted through my head, particularly the clause where the client waived their right to litigate, and where it specified either Mark or I as solely responsible for the client's portfolio. But we operated under the umbrella of Rhodes and Hall, and the company should be liable, if not legally, then at least morally. I'd never even considered such a thing possible because both of us had always done the right thing. "What have you done, Mark?" I had to swallow before I could speak again. "Who is it?"

"David Oldham. Mismanagement of funds."

I managed a squeaky, "Fraud?" The bile started churning again. This wasn't us! We didn't do things like that. We were good people, *clean* people and from the very beginning, Mark and I had prided ourselves on that fact.

"Not exactly, no. He's alleging I didn't act according to instructions." He looked up, expression earnest and said firmly, "Me, Belle, not the company."

"Alleging?"

Mark waved a hand. "Semantics. He's right. I fucked up."

"Fucked up how? Or more importantly why? Mark, what the hell is going on? Stop screwing around and tell me."

The silence in the room stretched out uncomfortably but I didn't fill it because there was nothing else for me to say. Mark squirmed. "I missed out on some important deals and lost him a decent amount of money. There's no defense, I just…stopped caring." All of this information was mumbled to the floor.

"I see." I was impressively calm. I didn't look away from him, as much as I wanted to.

He met my eyes. "I was never as smart as you. You have the gift. I'm a fucking snake oil salesman, not a moneymaker. I didn't mean for it to get so out of hand, I swear, but it just slipped away. Then the longer I left it, the worse it got."

"And how does this affect the company?" I needed facts, not emotion.

"It doesn't impact Rhodes and Hall, not legally, because I'm taking care of things. David has agreed to a settlement which more than covers his loss. In return, he won't be pushing for an arbitration hearing which we know would damage the company's image." He drew in a breath, squared his shoulders. "The settlement is coming from my pocket. It's my mistake, and now I'm fixing it."

"Fixing it…" Everything clicked into place. He'd wanted out for a while, he'd screwed up and now he was falling on his sword. For me. Because he felt guilty. But I was furious that he'd done all this behind my back, chosen how to handle it like I didn't even rate being in the loop. We'd done everything together, the good and the bad and now he was going it alone when we should have been dealing with it together. I was even more furious that months ago when I'd asked him if everything was all right, he'd lied.

"With my departure and a non-disclosure cause, I expect fallout for the company to be minimal. Some clients will leave, but that will be because I'm leaving not because they're worried about integrity." He spoke as though it was a done deal, that I'd buy him out instead of dissolve.

"Right, of course," I snarled. "Who'd stay without a man at the helm?" All my insecurity I'd felt before now magnified exponentially. For the past decade, I'd consistently outperformed him but it was like nobody else could see it. How was I going to convince those people that I was far more capable than him?

The muscles in Mark's jaw jumped as he passed me another folder. He ignored my barb, barreling on with his pitch. "I estimate eighty-five percent will move their accounts to you. The breakdown is in there."

His ridiculous assurance that everything would be fine was almost as insulting as this ambush. I stacked the manila folder on top of his proposal and draft contract. "Tell me then, did you fuck up because you're awful at your job, or was it literally just not giving a single fuck about the business? About us?"

"I don't know," he said quietly. "A little from column A and also from column B."

Perfect. I pushed curls away from my face. "So what's going to happen when I buy you out? You're just going to ride off into the sunset and buy a villa in France and put everything we've done behind you?"

"That's really unfair, Belle." The muscle in his jaw tensed again then relaxed. "I'd have thought a little understanding and support was well within your skillset."

I knew I was being a dick, but all my anger and upset was trampling over my concern for him. "I'm sorry, Mark. I guess most of my emotion is tied up in the bombshells you've just dropped on me."

"I'm sorry," he said steadily. "But I'm doing this for you, Belle. At least this way, you still have the company's reputation."

That was something, I supposed. "Be straight with me, Mark. You're telling me it's only one client then? Just one client who bore the brunt of your idiocy?" I crossed my legs, folding defensive arms over my breasts. "I find that incredibly hard to believe."

His silence told me everything.

"How many others?" I asked, dangerously calm.

He refused to meet my eyes. "Three. Maybe. But there've been no repercussions."

"I think repercussions is a really odd way to phrase being found negligent." Leaning toward him, I lowered my voice. "And you're hoping what exactly? They don't notice that their portfolio is suddenly nowhere near projected targets and the issue just...goes away?"

Mark rested his hands flat on the table. "Yes."

"Tell me then, will I be inheriting those potential lawsuits along with the rest of what you're offerin'? Because I didn't notice that under *liabilities*."

"I'll take care of it," he said flatly.

"You'd better." My tablet blinked with yet another notification. I gathered it, my phone and the stack of papers, then stood. "Well, as they say—I guess you'll be hearing from my lawyer."

* * *

Audrey stepped out of my elevator as I was digging in my handbag for my door keys. She approached with an exaggerated sashay, and a sultry, "Ma'am, I have a delivery of one dinner and two orgasms here for a Ms. Rhodes?"

Keys forgotten, I leaned against the wall. "I ordered three orgasms."

"Oh." She pretended to rummage through the takeout bags. "I'm very sorry, there must have been a mix up. I'll happily supply you with credit."

She bent down, and I stretched to meet her halfway for a kiss. "See that you do."

"Count on it." She unlocked the door for us and headed straight through to the kitchen.

I dumped bags on the couch, shrugged out of my coat and tossed it over a chair. "I'm just going to shower."

Audrey set dinner down on the counter. "Do you want me to pour you a drink?"

I was raw enough without adding booze to the mix. "No thanks. I'll be back in a few minutes."

My clothes piled on the bathroom floor and I didn't bother to remove my makeup before stepping into the shower. When I bent over to wash my legs, my eyes drifted closed. Just a moment, just resting them. What the hell was I going to do? It wasn't about the money—I could easily afford to buy him out. But that would mean taking on everything by myself. Could I do it?

I lowered myself to sit on the shower tiles, letting the water cascade over me. I didn't feel cleaner for it. I felt tainted by what Mark had done. Above everything, I loathed myself for not being kinder to him when he needed it. The glass door swung open and the water shut off. "Iz?" Audrey crouched down and tugged my wrist. "Are you okay?"

I glanced around through the veil of water dripping into my eyes. "Yeah?"

"Oh, sweetie. Come on, let me help you up." It was funny how quickly she started slipping endearments into her speech, like they'd been on the tip of her tongue for months and now she could finally unleash them.

The added softness made already frazzled emotions crack and I had to blink to stop myself from crying. "Mmm 'kay."

"You've been in here for nearly fifteen minutes. I got worried. Well, first I thought you were enjoying the detachable showerhead by yourself and I got annoyed. Then I got worried." She helped me stand up and passed me a towel.

I started drying myself clumsily and she bundled my wet hair to squeeze water from it. Audrey gently pulled the towel up to dry my neck. "Have you eaten a real meal today?"

"Not really, no." Despite having subsisted on coffee and a handful of craisins, I wasn't hungry.

"Come have some dinner, then I'll put you to bed. Hate to say it, darling, but you look like shit."

I smiled a tight-lipped smile and hung the towel back up. "Thanks."

She laughed and dropped her hands to rest on my hips. "Tired and looking like shit, you're still sexy as hell."

"Don't you forget it." I kissed her quickly, then trudged out to my bedroom. Rummaging through a pile of clean clothes that sat on the chest at the base of my bed, I found sweatpants and a long-sleeved tee. Audrey was right behind me, so that when I turned around I almost bumped into her. She opened her arms, and I stepped gratefully into her embrace and buried my face in her neck.

Audrey's hand stroked my back lightly. "Seriously, Iz, what's up?"

"I've had a really *really* bad day," I mumbled against her skin. The sound of the intercom put a halt to finishing my explanation. "Hang on." Wearily I crossed to the station on the wall beside the bathroom, and stabbed the button with a forefinger. "Yes?"

Carl's soft voice filled my bedroom. "Ms. Rhodes, I'm sorry to bother you but Mr. Hall is here asking to see you. He's… insistent."

I rested my forehead on the wall. "You can send him up."

CHAPTER TWENTY-FIVE

Given I'd spent the rest of the day avoiding Mark while I spoke to my lawyer and read through those folders, his arrival at my place wasn't surprising. It was also spectacularly bad timing. I needed some time away from him, to talk to Audrey about my day. I needed to rant and cry and then have her hold me while I fell asleep a tearstained, lip-quivery mess.

Audrey followed me down the stairs, then stopped by the kitchen table while I opened the door and waved Mark in with a flat, "Hi."

"Hey." Mark looked past me and his mouth dropped. He recovered quickly but his surprise and alarm were unmistakable. "Hello, Captain Graham."

"Audrey," I corrected automatically, looking to her.

The expression on her face was fleeting but I knew immediately what it was. Anguish. Accusation. Betrayal. I had no frame of reference for any of it until I recalled that I was supposed to tell Mark about Audrey and me this morning. Before he'd dropped a bombshell on me, that is. I'd promised

Audrey I would do something that was clearly important to her, and meant it, but hadn't followed through. She couldn't know the reason why. All she would see was that I'd broken a promise.

A smile slid over the hurt and she raised a hand in greeting. "Hello, Mark." Not Mr. Hall. I took that as a *screw you* aimed at me, reminding me that if I'd done what I said I would she would have called him by his first name.

When I looked to her, trying to get her attention, she pointedly avoided my gaze. I gave up. Rubbing my dry eyes, I asked wearily, "Why are you here, Mark?"

"I need to talk to you."

Audrey took a step backward. "I might go."

I reached for her, my fingers just brushing her arm. "Please don't. Stay and eat your dinner, honey. We shouldn't be long." I stretched up to kiss her cheek and she tensed. When I pulled away she caught my eye but there was no emotion in hers. Just…resignation as she nodded. I squeezed her hand, nabbed a sweater from the back of the couch and gestured Mark toward the doors leading out to my balcony.

The sweater I'd grabbed was Audrey's and the sleeves hung over my hands as I slipped into the hoodie. I zipped it and tugged the balcony doors closed behind me. Mark had five minutes to say whatever he needed to before I booted him out. There was nothing so important that it couldn't wait until the morning, and the fact he'd chosen to invade my private space made me even more annoyed. If that was even possible. The moment I closed the door, the electric whine of the Venetian blinds sounded as they began to lower.

The slats moved, tilted downward so that if I looked in, I could see Audrey but she wouldn't be able to see us. Even upset with me, she was giving us privacy, but making sure I knew she was still there. I hugged myself, tucking my fingers into my armpits. "What do you want, Mark?"

"I thought we could talk."

"Talk? I don't even know what to say. You fucking ambushed me in there today. You gave me no warning, no time to prepare anything. I have never felt more insulted in my life."

"Speaking of ambushed." He gestured inside. "How long has that been happening?" He pulled a packet of cigarettes from inside his coat and held them up.

I waved to indicate I didn't care if he smoked. "Don't you dare turn this around." Despite the hoodie, I shuddered. "You know I honestly don't even know what to say to you. And I can't figure out what I'm most upset about." Partly what he'd done, but also the fact that I'd suspected something was off and hadn't realized what or how serious it was.

Mark lit his cigarette and reached for the ashtray I kept on the balcony. "I'm doing this to protect you, Belle."

"Protectin' me would have been to not fuck up in the first place. Or to tell me sooner, before it got out of hand. To let me know what was happening for you. To let me help you. We're partners." I ran a hand through my hair. "This is...a fucking disaster. How many clients do you think will stay once word of this gets out? Hmmm? You say the company's protected but I'm involved in this because my name is forever tied to yours. And if you can't handle accounts then surely little ol' Isabelle Rhodes can't."

"It won't get out. I told you that part of David accepting my very generous settlement is that he's signing a non-disclosure clause. He can't tell anyone about it. And there's a caveat that he can't come after the company."

"Oh right, silly me. How could I forget?" I tapped my forehead. "Tom's excellent contracts. So you're just going to disappear into the sunset and everyone will let it slide?"

"More or less, yes," he said, calmly drawing on his cigarette.

"You idiot. Nothing is secret in this city, Mark." I jabbed a forefinger at him. "You've screwed me and deep down I think you fucking know it. I'll be purchasing forty-seven percent of nothing."

"I'm sorry, I really am. Like I said, things...got out of hand before I could figure out how to fix it." His voice wavered. "I've just been treading water for so long, and after that thing with the auditor and David Oldham, I realized that I can't do this anymore, Belle. I have to get out or it might actually drown me one day."

I leaned back against the railing, looking through the blinds. Audrey was on the phone, striding back and forth through my lounge room. "Fine." I deflated, suddenly too tired to hang onto my anger. What was the point? It wasn't like it was going to help me. "I'm sorry too, for not being more understanding. And I should have told you about Audrey and me."

"Yeah well, looks like we've both been hiding things," he said carefully. "Why didn't you say anything about her before?"

"Because of the way you looked at her when you saw her here tonight." I inhaled a lungful of cool early November air and pulled the hood over my head, shoving loose bits of hair away from my face. "You're everywhere, and I just wanted something that was all mine for once. Just for a little while."

"I suppose I can understand that." He spared me a smile that seemed genuine enough. "I'm pleased for you, but I admit, I'm still trying to wrap my head around it. I believe you said something like 'I don't plan on doing it again, Mark.' How long did that last?"

"About a week."

His grunt was amused rather than annoyed. "I hope you know what you're doing, Belle."

"Me too." A pang of uneasiness settled in my belly. "I'm in love with her, Mark and I haven't told her yet. And I can tell she's mad at me now."

"She is? Doesn't seem like it." He carefully ashed his cigarette.

"I was supposed to tell you about us. I was going to, that's why I came into your office this morning and then the day just… got away." I turned to him. "Look, I'm sorry for being a bitch but you threw a whole bunch of stuff at me and it was a pretty damned big bombshell."

"I know. Maybe I could have done it differently." He smiled briefly. "Seemed like the best way to approach it."

"Mmm. Look, we can talk about it tomorrow, okay? But I really need to go in there and talk to her. I have to explain what's going on."

His mouth thinned. "Is that wise? Given she's an employee."

I couldn't help glaring at him. "First and foremost, she's my *girlfriend*, Mark. I'm not going to hide this from her. And this whole fucking sale issue is why she thinks I've broken a promise."

The Venetians began to slide up and I could see Audrey's legs, then her torso appear. I moved away from him and to the doors. She stared through the glass at us, and it was clear from her face that something had happened. I opened the door and pulled it mostly closed behind myself. "What's going on?"

She held up her phone, already moving toward the front door with her keys in hand. "My mom is sick. I have to go."

With quick steps, I followed her. "Shit. What's wrong with her? Is she all right?"

Audrey raised her hands, mouth quivering. "I'm not sure, they're still running tests. Sounds like pneumonia with complications." She snatched her jacket from the hook and shrugged into it.

"Oh, honey, I'm sorry. What can I do?"

Audrey lifted pleading eyes to mine. "Iz, I need your help."

The question burst from my mouth without thought. "How much?"

When Audrey's usually open, smiling face closed over I realized right away what I'd just implied. She looked disgusted, and I wanted to step back, away from the loathing expression. Her mouth twisted, opening and closing as though she was trying to get words out. Eventually, she succeeded. "You thought I was going to ask you for money." I'd never seen her look this way before, never heard her sound so flat.

"Well…if you need some, yeah?" It had been a genuine offer, the same way I'd have offered anyone who I cared about.

She folded her arms over her breasts, jaw tight with tension. "I *was* going to ask you to come to Minnesota with me for a few days. I wanted you to be with me while I try to deal with this. Maybe meet my mom in case—" She cleared her throat.

I caught the past tense immediately. Was. Wanted. Fuck. Frantically, I tried to backpedal. "Wait, Audrey please. I didn't mean it like that. Come on."

Audrey stuffed both hands deep into her pockets, shoulders rigid. "No, Iz. You did mean it. You said it yourself. 'How much?' I know you've had some issues with that sort of thing, but I didn't…" She took a shaky breath. "I can't believe you'd think that of me. I've never asked, would never ask, and it's really hurtful that's the first thing you thought of."

When I stepped closer, she stepped back and I felt the pulling away as deeply as if she'd struck me. I couldn't breathe. I couldn't think. "I'm sorry, please believe me."

"I'm sure you are," she said, each syllable clipped. She glanced at the doors leading to my balcony. "I thought you were going to tell him," she said tightly. "Clearly this doesn't mean as much to you as I thought it did."

Ouch. I stepped closer again and this time she held her ground. "Audrey, I tried, all right? You have no idea what the fuck happened today. I tried," I repeated forcefully. This was so strange and I didn't know how to argue with her. My natural instinct to be defensive wouldn't work with her, and I couldn't find the path to resolving this.

She backed away, holding up a hand to stop me. "Please don't, I can't right now and I really have to go. There're things I need to organize." She shouldered her bag, turned around and walked to the front door. Mark emerged from the balcony, closing the door behind him. I startled at the interruption.

By the time I'd looked back to the front door, it was closed. And she was gone. I ran after her, punching the elevator button but it was too late. Standing dumbfounded in front of the closed doors, I engaged in a round of mental flagellation for being such a shitty person. She'd basically just told me her mama might be dying and I'd steamrolled her with excuses about my awful day.

Mark started to speak the moment I stepped back inside and I cut him off with a terse, "Shut it."

I snatched up my phone and stalked down the hall to the great room for a little privacy. The call rang to her voice mail. She'd be on her bike, speeding to wherever. I guessed she'd fly herself, quicker than booking flights. Fresh fear grabbed me like a vice. She'd be in control of a motorcycle and a plane when she was upset. Shit. Don't drive angry. Don't fly angry.

Anything else you'd like to throw at me, Universe? Actually, don't answer that.

I started pacing. "Audrey, it's me. I need to talk to you and explain. I'm sorry. Call me. Please call me."

When I returned to the lounge, Mark was sprawled on the couch, his legs stretched out with his ankles crossed. I set my phone down on the coffee table and stared at it as though I might force it to ring. I couldn't even bother attempting to sound polite. "Can you piss off please? I need some space, Mark. We can talk tomorrow."

He nodded and pushed himself to his feet, walking to the door without argument. Mark stepped into the hall then turned around, holding out his hand to me. "Belley, I love you. I really am sorry."

I took it, squeezing. "I know. I love you too, even when you're a fucking idiot." Squeezing harder, I said, "But I'm still very mad at you for what you did today."

He smiled sadly. "I wouldn't know what to do if you weren't."

Once the door clicked closed behind him I stalked to the bar in my great room, snatched a bottle of my favorite whisky and a glass. I poured two fingers, took a deep breath and chugged it. Sacrilege for a forty-year-old Macallan but at that moment, I just didn't care. The shudder came quickly, followed by the almost eye-watering burn through my throat and nose. I set the bottle back on the shelf, carried the glass to the kitchen and dropped it in the sink.

It broke.

I left the broken glass where it lay and moved to the couch. Pulling the too-long sleeves of Audrey's sweatshirt over my hands, I drew my knees to my chin. My chest was tight with that awful feeling of knowing I'd behaved badly. I'd thrown everything she'd given me back in her face. In as many words, I'd accused her—wrongly—of being a gold digger when she'd never asked me for a single material thing.

Really, this had nothing to do with money. I could almost laugh at the absurdity of it because almost everything else in my life did. Layered above that was by taking so long to reveal our relationship, it had turned into something so huge that it'd exploded in my hands. And then my whole *sorry your mom's sick, but hey I had a bad day too*. I was such a shit. My phone remained silent.

I gave up waiting for her to call me, dragged myself upstairs and climbed into bed, still wearing Audrey's hoodie which smelled like her, as did the pillow on the other side of the mattress. Shampoo, lotion, perfume and something else I could never quite pin down. I curled up, face buried in the softness and scent of her. I'd once admitted to her that on nights she wasn't there I would sleep with my face in her pillow. She'd laughed, run upstairs to get it and made a big show of rubbing her face on it like a cat.

Our fight looped around and around in my head in glorious Technicolor and with each repeat, I felt sicker. I called and left another message for her then around one a.m., I phoned my therapist and left a message with her answering service. "It's Isabelle Rhodes, I need an appointment with Doctor Baker. Urgently."

CHAPTER TWENTY-SIX

The next morning, bleary eyed and upset, I tried to make myself look like I hadn't been awake all night and went to work. Dr. Baker's receptionist called to let me know my therapist could fit me in but not until late afternoon, which gave me all day to dwell on everything that'd gone wrong in the past twenty-four hours before I could talk to someone about it. Super. I managed to swallow coffee but no food because I couldn't fit anything solid in around my nausea.

In my hazy state, I could only deal with one crisis at a time, and given that Audrey was incommunicado, I focused on the one that was right in front of me. Mark's sale proposal. My lawyer agreed to look at the contract immediately so I couriered it over, and we arranged a meeting for the next day. One task completed. A million more to go.

Whenever I had a break, I called Audrey and left voice mails. I sent texts begging her to call me so we could talk. I even emailed, which was such an awful, impersonal way to convey my message but I was desperate. Nothing. She had gone totally radio silent. I was worried about her, about her mama and it didn't help that I couldn't think of how to apologize for the fact that I was obviously a completely irrational bitch who ignored the important things to focus on micro facts.

She didn't call me back.

Paranoia set in, and I started scouring morbid news articles and death notices. For both her and her mother. Mercifully, I found nothing, though an Audrey Graham from Riverside County, California passed away in her sleep at age ninety-four. May she rest in peace.

Then I got angry. Angry at *my* Audrey for ignoring me. The decent thing would be to let me know she was all right. Alive. Even a text would do. But there was nothing. And I was upset with myself for being angry at her when she was possibly dealing with a dying mother.

Late morning, Mark barged into my office, closing the door behind him. "What's going on?"

I didn't move my eyes from my laptop screen and an insistent client email. "What do you mean?"

"HR just sent me a leave request for Audrey Graham, which was emailed at two this morning, and you look like hell."

"I think we can agree I've looked like hell since yesterday's meeting," I mumbled distractedly.

"Come on, Belle…"

I couldn't meet his eyes and settled for staring at his shoulder. "Mark, I've been such an idiot. I've fucked everything up. Audrey. You. Us. The business."

He sat on the edge of my desk. "Tell me." His voice was low and nonjudgmental.

"I can't," I whispered. "Not here." If I opened the gate, I'd never be able to close it again.

Mark's hand landed gently on my shoulder. "Okay. But if you want to talk you know where I am."

"Mhmm." Finally I met his gentle eyes and was undone. Mark lifted me from where I was slumped in my chair, supporting me and holding me tight as I cried and cried.

I hadn't cried at all since she left the night before. It would have been the smart thing, to let a little of the water out of the dam so it didn't burst at an inappropriate time and place. Like my office. With all our staff outside.

My quiet sobbing finally tired itself out and I was left empty, clutching and crumpling Mark's shirt. He released me and his face was so kind that I nearly started crying again. He ran his thumbs gently under my eyes. "My little Belley. It'll be okay. You're okay."

I'd left a very conspicuous patch of tears on the chest of his shirt. My breathing was that awful half-hiccupping, half-hyperventilating-after-crying kind. Ugh.

Mark lifted my chin. "Go and clean up. I'll tell them to hold calls and keep everyone out until you emerge." He kissed the top of my head and left me by myself in my office.

He was right. Time to get your shit together, Isabelle. Step one: fake feeling fabulous by looking fabulous. In my bathroom, I studied myself in the full-length mirror, drew my shoulders back and raised my chin. I'd seen worse, I was fixable. I ran my hands through my hair then retucked and smoothed my blouse. Step two: repair your face.

Clutching my makeup bag, I stared at my face. I could work with this. Red eyes but not swollen. Thank you makeup gods for waterproof mascara. Wouldn't it be nice if everything were as easily fixed as a makeup repair after you'd ruined it by crying?

Back at my desk and admittedly feeling slightly better, I buzzed Clare. When she appeared thirty seconds later, she gave no indication that my appearance was anything other than usual.

"Clare, I need you to check something for me."

"Yes, Ms. Rhodes?"

"I need you to find Audrey Graham and make sure she's okay." Perhaps pushing boundaries, but I had to know and she wasn't answering any of my frantic attempts to get in contact.

The edge of Clare's mouth twitched. "Would you like me to pass along a message?"

"No. If you talk to her just…I don't know, make something up about her time off or something."

"Will do."

Having given Clare a detective mission eased my hurt fractionally, enough that I managed to compartmentalize my personal issues down to where I could focus on what I needed to do at work.

I mulled over Mark's financial offer and arrived at a ninety-nine percent firm decision about what I was going to do. But I didn't feel any lighter for it. Clare brought lunch for me to pick at. I stared at my personal cell, willing it to ring. But it didn't.

Just before four, as I was closing everything down to leave for therapy, Clare rushed back in after a perfunctory knock. "Ms. Rhodes, I found her. Sort of."

I exhaled. "You're wonderful." I didn't want to know how she'd achieved this miracle of Audrey location. If Audrey had answered the phone for Clare but not me, I might actually have a full breakdown. "How?"

"Well, her phone goes right to voice mail so that's a dead end. But when Georgia and I had drinks last month, she told me that Captain Graham was talking one morning at the airport about her personal plane, and that it was cute as heck." Clare shook her head. "Sorry. So I called the airports near the address listed for her mom on Audrey's next of kin forms. Asked some questions, told a few not quite truths…"

I made a *get on with it* gesture. "And?"

She grinned. "Captain Graham's plane is now parked at Lake Elmo airport just outside of St. Paul. Next I was going to ring all the commercial airlines to see if she'd boarded a flight but thankfully I didn't have to because that would have been harder to lie about."

I stood and slung my laptop bag over my shoulder. "Clare, have I told you recently how great you are?"

My assistant grinned. "Yes, Ms. Rhodes. About three seconds ago. Is there anything you need me to do with this information?"

"No thank you. That's all." There was nothing I could do, and I almost felt worse for knowing that Audrey was fine but obviously didn't want anything to do with any of us.

Clare left my office with a little bounce in her step. I made a note on my desk jotter to contact HR. After everything she'd done for me recently, Clare would be getting a five-figure bonus this year.

I stopped by Mark's office on my way out. I'd revoked his access to our servers, client portfolios and company accounts. He was hunched over his desk, chin in palm, staring at his screen. Since his bombshell the day before, it was like he'd shrunk. Not physically, but it was as if all his bravado had deserted him. On the flip side, he seemed calmer, as though losing the stress of managing accounts had actually helped.

When he realized I was in his office, he looked up at me, blinking slowly as though he'd just woken from a too-short nap. "Belle. You good?"

"Yeah I'm okay. I'm headin' off." *Heading*, I mentally corrected myself.

"Oh." Mark fumbled for some papers. "I've still got Audrey's personal leave request here. Did you want to see it? Technically she's not eligible for that mu—"

"No. Sign off on it," I said immediately. Nervously chewing the inside of my lip, I followed with, "How long has she asked for?"

"Two weeks. I'll have Tamara tell Schwartz he's on the A roster. Should we start looking for a replacement? Or just a relief pilot? I'll need to do it soon." He paused to clear his throat. "Or…you can?"

"She hasn't resigned, Mark." After a beat I mumbled, "Not yet, at least." Thinking about her quitting her job because she couldn't stand to be near me yanked the scab off an unhealed wound.

"I don't think she will," he said quietly.

I hoisted my laptop bag back up my shoulder. "What makes you say that?"

"People don't get upset about things that don't mean anything to them, Belle."

* * *

I must have looked really terrible because Dr. Baker actually gave me a hug before guiding me to my chair. The crying began almost as soon as I told her about the past few days. She pushed the tissues closer. "Well then. That's certainly a lot of upheaval. Where shall we start? Audrey or with your work trouble?"

I shrugged. Both were painful and difficult so why did it matter? "It's just so much all at once, you know? Like it never rains, it pours."

"Yes and bad things come in threes." Smiling, Dr. Baker waved dismissively. "I don't believe in superstition. Except when the Patriots are playing," she added with a laugh.

I smiled through my tears. "Sacrilege."

With a smile, she switched gears from personal back to professional. "Let's start with the work stuff. How do you feel about it?"

"Hurt, blindsided, angry, afraid." I sniffed. "I just feel like I don't even know him."

"He's still the same man as before, Isabelle. Still your friend and I think you both need each others' support now more than ever."

"I know. And I feel like a shit for being nasty about it. But I was just so angry at him for the way he went about it. Like he did everything exactly the way he knows I hate, by treating me like I'm not worthy of being included."

"Did he apologize?"

"Yes."

"And have you apologized? Talked about it?"

"Sort of." I sighed. "Today was so hectic that we haven't had a chance to sit down and have an argument about our argument."

Dr. Baker smiled, pushing her glasses back up her nose. "And what about his proposal? Have you made a decision? You don't have to tell me what it is, if you have."

"I have made a decision, yes." If I didn't tell her what I'd decided then how would I work through my turmoil? I dabbed under my eyes before answering. "If my lawyer's happy, I'm going to accept."

"Good for you." Another line of therapist scrawl joined the scribbles on her page. "I think it's obvious where the fear comes from. Mark's been there with you right from the conception of the company. Of course it's unnerving to take the helm on your own, but I don't believe that's all there is to the fear."

"What else could it be then?"

"Honestly, I think that you're afraid taking full control is going to prove all these naysayers right. Everyone over the years who's implied you weren't capable or that you didn't belong. That you're just a small town southern gal who's way out of her depth."

Mulling it over only took a few moments. She was right. "I think that's a fair point."

Dr. Baker penned a few words on her notepad then looked back to me. "You've made enormous progress since we began our sessions, Isabelle, but I think you have a tendency to focus only on the negative 'what if' scenarios."

I frowned. "Doesn't everyone do that?"

"To a degree…" She snuck a peek at the clock. "I'd like to come back to that another time because I think we need to address your other concern today."

"Yes," I breathed.

"I think we can both agree that this situation with Audrey is partly due to spectacularly poor timing, yes?" At my nod, she continued, "Her mother's illness combined with the belief that you'd somehow broken a promise you'd made are likely the root cause of her reaction."

"I know, but she didn't give me a chance to explain. And she's normally so calm that it threw me, and I guess I panicked." I sniffed quickly a few times, trying to stop the fresh flood of tears I could feel trying to escape. "And to not contact me at all? I'm so worried about her and her mama."

"I agree, it's not an ideal scenario and I can see how you're upset about that. I would be too." After another quick scribble, she asked, "Is Audrey close to her family? You haven't met them yet, have you?"

"Not yet. She gets along with her brother and is close to her mother. Her father's dead. He was...abusive." Briefly, I summarized what Audrey had told me.

Dr. Baker nodded thoughtfully. "Sounds like she's a very strong and resilient woman."

"She is. And everything else." I gave up trying to stop myself from crying and reached for another tissue.

"I might be reaching, but based on her past and her reactions, it seems as though what Audrey fears is being *diminished*, made to feel she's not worth someone's time. By refusing to tell Mark, you inadvertently played to her fears."

Turning to the side, I blew my nose and tossed the tissue into the trash bin helpfully placed near my feet. "I didn't mean to do that. Really, I didn't."

"Of course you didn't, Isabelle," she soothed. "It's just unfortunate that your fears happen to play against hers." Dr. Baker leaned forward, her tone gentle. "Tell me. What are you afraid of?"

She already knew of course, but clearly wanted me to verbalize it. I couldn't help my lip trembling. "I'm afraid of needing. And then having the thing I need taken from me."

She nodded. "Yes. And I think that's why you didn't tell Mark. There are other reasons, sure, but I think it was because you didn't want to admit how much you need Audrey, to him and to yourself. In case it didn't work out, or he disapproved, or even just because putting it out in the world means someone can turn it against you."

Thanks, Doc. Really.

Though I knew it was pointless, after therapy I asked Penny to drive me to Crown Heights. Pen pulled over, parked and waited silently while I craned my neck to look out the window. Unsurprisingly there were no lights on in Audrey's apartment. I turned my phone over and over in my hand. "Has she called you, Pen?"

Her hands tightened on the wheel. "Yes, last night just before she left. But not since." Pen's tone told me everything. She knew what had happened.

"I'm sorry, I shouldn't have asked and put you in an awkward position." Rubbing a hand over my prickling eyes, I asked her to take me home.

"Yes, Ms. Rhodes," she said kindly.

The drive home was unusually fast, traffic flowing as though moving out of the way to let me through. She parked and I collected all my things while she opened the door for me. When I stumbled getting out of the car, Penny took my arm to steady me.

"Thanks, Pen. I'll see you tomorrow."

"Of course." After a short pause she spoke cautiously, "Ms. Rhodes…maybe I'm overstepping, but don't write her off. She's not good with rejection, whether it really is rejection or just something she thinks is." Penny smiled softly. "She's a good person and I know she cares about you."

"Thank you, Penny," I murmured, almost to myself. Funny that she'd pretty much confirmed what Dr. Baker and I had worked through during therapy. "Any ideas of what I should do?" I asked, trying to keep my tone light and joking. It came out a little deranged sounding instead.

"Keep trying," Pen said simply. "She can't bear the thought of not being needed. And she wants *you* to need her, Ms. Rhodes."

Before bed I called Audrey one last time. I'd always thought her voice mail greeting was strangely formal, but now I felt the coolness of it like a wall. Telling me she'd get back to me felt like an unfulfilled promise. As I listened to her recorded message, I was struck by an overwhelming sense of hopelessness.

"It's me. Again. Please call me. I'm worried about you and your mama. Hope everything's okay. I, uh…I miss you." I swallowed hard. "A whole lot, and I'm sorry." I hung up before I said what I really wanted to. *I love you.* I didn't want the first time I uttered those words to be in a voice mail. I wanted to look into her eyes, and have her feel how much I meant what I was saying.

I slept a few disjointed hours, dragging myself into the office before everyone else as usual. The day blurred, still without contact from Audrey. My saviors were concealer for dark shadows and eye drops to reduce the gritty redness of my exhaustion. Contacts out, glasses on.

I ate without tasting, putting food in my mouth only because Mark brought lunch into my office and sat with me to make sure I finished. This was nothing like when Steph left. Then, I was relieved, like I'd lanced a boil. With Audrey gone, I was broken.

My lawyer had called as soon as his office opened to let me know he'd read the contract, and wished to make a few changes. Reluctantly, I'd agreed. It was good business, but not good friendship.

Mark's door was partially closed. I knocked, then peered through the gap. "Do you have a few minutes?"

"Sure."

I closed the door, double checked it and crossed to him. Even in the bubble of his office, I kept my voice low. "I've spoken to my lawyer, and there are a few changes I have to insist on before I sign."

He didn't seem surprised. "Okay, lay it on me."

"Firstly, I'm offering you forty-five percent, not the forty-seven you stipulated."

"I see. May I ask why?" He wasn't so much angry as curious.

"Because I'm going to have to take an initial commission cut to sweeten the changeover of your clients. Particularly those three that you've admitted to mishandling."

"Okay."

"And I want an indemnity clause protecting my company in the event of any future legal action from your ex-clients. There may turn out to be more who make a similar claim, once word gets out. If it comes back to bite me in the ass, you have to be financially accountable for it. I love you, Mark but I can't be responsible for your mistakes."

He turned slowly side to side in his chair, his eyes never leaving mine. "I'll have to speak to Quentin."

"Of course."

Mark and I stared silently at one another until he smiled, a slow smile as though he was remembering something pleasant. "Belle?"

"Yes?"

"You're already acting like the boss."

* * *

I called Mama once I'd arrived home, had a short workout and showered. Lying in bed staring up at the ceiling with the phone resting on the pillow beside my ear, I gave her the bare bones version of the past few days. Mama was a mix of upset about Mark and excited, apprehensive and supporting about my transition from equal partner to sole owner.

After five minutes of excited rambling, with me interjecting as appropriate, she paused and said accusingly, "You're not as excited as you'd have me believe, Bunny. What else is goin' on up there?"

I shrugged, even though she couldn't see me, and managed, "Audrey and I fought. She's gone." Then I burst into tears. Again.

Mama tried—and mostly failed—to soothe me as I sobbed and hiccupped, trying to explain what happened. What I'd done. How she'd left and I'd made her do it. I felt like I'd stepped into a leaky dinghy, cut the rope and drifted out into rough seas with no idea how to get back to shore.

Mama's voice was thick with emotion. "Baby, I'm so sorry." There was a long pause and I knew she was weighing her words, trying to figure out how to approach what she knew would rile me. "But you need to stop pushin' people away."

"Don't, Mama. Please don't." I was so defeated, I couldn't bear to have her digging into me as well.

"I'm serious, Bunny and you need to listen. This is about your daddy, and you know it is. You can't stand the thought of someone not needin' you, so you make sure they don't. Easier if you're not attached."

"Please stop. I can't." What she said made no sense because I already *was* attached.

"You can, and you will," she said forcefully. "Just because he left, that doesn't mean shit, baby. He didn't want to be tied down to anyone or anything. It had nothing to do with you and you need to stop this thinkin' you're not worth anything to anyone because of him."

I kept silent, swiping tears that spilled over anew. Audrey and I both had issues with our fathers, so who better to understand the conflict I had about mine? But I still hadn't really told her just how badly screwed up I was about my father skipping out on us. Didn't want her thinking less of me, I guess. Didn't want her thinking even my father didn't want to be around me.

Mama sniffed. "I should have done better, I could have explained more but I guess my pride was too damned hurt, thinkin' I could change him and not being able to. In the end, when I finally accepted it, so much time had passed that I just didn't know how to talk to you 'bout him. All that shit's on him. Not you. Not me. It's him."

"I don't know what to do, Mama." I rolled over and fumbled for the tissues beside the bed. "I can't see a way 'round it right now."

"You gotta apologize and make it right, Bunny. I bet you never even told her all about your daddy." She sighed.

A long pause while I blew my nose. "Not everything."

"Well, there's a place to start. It doesn't excuse it, but it sure goes a ways to explaining it. You're so scared he's gonna come back because of what you got, not who you are. It poisons everything. Makes you hide things."

"She's ignorin' me. What if she's finished?" I choked down a sob. "I've done an awful thing."

"Oh no. She could never be finished with you. I've seen the way she looks at you. You're oxygen. You're keepin' her alive. I bet she's suffocating without you, just like you are without her."

CHAPTER TWENTY-SEVEN

Friday at two p.m., and in the company of our various legal teams, Mark and I signed an updated contract with everything I'd insisted upon embedded within pages of legalese. Congratulations, Isabelle. You're on your own. Panic and sadness were fighting for dominance while excitement stared on, waiting for a chance to jump in and break things up.

Once we'd seen our visitors out, Mark followed me into my office, a piece of paper held delicately between his fingertips. "Tom had this statement prepared. Can you take a look before we send it?"

The release was only one paragraph of standard spin. Personal issues, branching out and wanting new opportunities, strength and ability of the remaining founder Isabelle Rhodes, continued success of the company, blah blah blah.

I passed the paper back. "Looks good. We'll hold it over until Monday, otherwise it'll be calls from reporters all weekend. How many more of your clients do you need to contact?"

"Seven. I'll have it done by close of business today."

"Thank you." I glanced at the time. It was too late to gather all the employees for a formal meeting today but I needed to calm the undercurrent that had been growing in the office. And I needed to do it soon. I knew that they were starting to talk. Gossip was a low hum that seemed to rise and fall as I moved through the office, like someone twisting a volume knob back and forth.

I blinked a few times, trying to clear my dry eyes. "I want to tell everyone here now and shut down any disquiet. Then we'll have a meeting and a farewell of sorts with all the staff on Monday. You'll be there?" After his confirmatory nod, I added, "And we'll need to speak to Clare and Tamara." Assuming Tamara wanted to stay, she would become my second PA. Clare would have to teach her the ins and outs of working for me instead of Mark—including Mama-wrangling.

I ducked out of my office, interrupting Clare who was scarfing down lunch. "Clare? Can you please tell everyone in the office to come to the conference room in twenty minutes? And schedule a meeting here for all employees, including transport staff Monday afternoon at four. Please arrange an open bar and dinner at Ricardo's for afterward, maybe four forty-five."

I drafted an email for those not in attendance, and was standing at the head of the table when the nine office staff filed into the conference room. Some had notepads and pens, but they all had a similar facial expression. Dread. Mark stood to my left, his hands loose at his sides and his face impassive. The announcement would come from me, but he would answer any questions.

There was no point in delaying. I let my fingertips rest on the table top, drew a deep breath and dove in. "I'm sure you've noticed the parade of guests coming and going from the office this week. As of an hour ago, I have taken over Mark Hall's share in Rhodes and Hall and next week he is leaving us. This information has not been made public yet. A press statement will be released Monday, and until then I'd like to remind you of the Confidential Disclosure Agreements you have all signed as part of your employment contract. I know I can rely on you all to understand the importance and sensitivity of these developments." In my haste, the words came out more harshly than I'd intended.

Looking around the room, I caught their stricken faces and tried to soften what I was saying. "I ask that you *please* trust me, and I'll have more information for you on Monday when everyone is here in person. Thank you."

* * *

With every call Mark made to inform his clients, it seemed I received a reciprocal call to either tell me they would be moving their portfolios to me, or apologizing about taking the offer to terminate their contract. After consulting with Tom, I'd decided to offer termination without penalty if clients wanted it. There was no point in damaging the company image by insisting they move their accounts to my care.

By the time I'd finished expressing my regret for those who were parting ways, and reassuring the ones who were staying that their investments were safe and Mark's departure would not affect the company, I was so drained I couldn't have explained to someone how to boil water.

Mark was right, almost eighty percent of his clients decided to move their accounts to me. The relief was palpable, but I also felt the weight of it like something on my back, crushing me. This was it, my do or die moment.

Christopher's text was a bright spot in a dreary day. *All hail the Queen! You. Me. New work wardrobe.*

I have a "work wardrobe" and it's too early for new season's wear.

Zip it emoji. We're going next level. Hold onto your tits. Kiss emoji. Very rude string of emojis.

Nat's call half an hour before the office closed was another welcome relief. "Have you heard from Audrey yet?"

"No." After four days with absolutely no contact, I'd resigned myself to the fact that she and I had broken up. And I didn't know how to feel about it. Mostly I just felt numb, until something would happen that reminded me of her, like the night before when I found her *How to Train Your Dragon* DVD. I sat on the floor, hugging it and crying for ten minutes. The feeling of missing her was so acute that my chest actually hurt.

"Well. Fuck that. I'm sorry, Rhodes."

"Me too. I just wish—" I cut myself off. "Never mind. I don't want to get into it at work, Nat."

"Fair enough. So the sale's all finalized? Got the keys to your shiny new company?"

I'd called her in a panic the night before, because I needed to talk to someone who was out of the fray and who understood. "Yes. We're making the formal announcement on Monday, having a staff meeting and then Mark's leaving."

"High five to stepping up to the plate." A soft tap sounded in my ear. "Come on, Rhodes, lift your hand, I know you haven't."

I tapped the bottom of my phone with a finger. "There. Phone high five, you weirdo."

Nat laughed. "Hey you did it too. You're just as much a weirdo as me."

She was such a goof. A goof who was also a smart and intuitive market analyst. Planting my foot against the edge of my desk, I swung myself side to side. "Tell me, Nat, exactly how much do you hate your boss and California…"

* * *

I'd called in a favor to get a reservation at Per Se, and that night I took Mark out for dinner and a last hurrah of sorts. It didn't feel particularly cheerful. He was reserved, but every now and then something seemed to crack through our tension and it was almost like nothing between us had changed. And then he'd withdraw back into himself. I didn't have the energy to go after him. After dessert, I knew there would be no lingering over coffee or cognac.

He still hadn't told me what he planned to do. He'd hinted at starting a consultancy, or a not for profit or even moving permanently overseas to do who knows what. Mark's complete lack of a solid plan for his future made me uneasy because despite everything he was my friend, and I cared and worried about him.

Mark set his napkin down and pushed his chair back. "You coming now, or staying?"

"I think I might stay here for a little while. Have another drink, practice saying *I'm the boss.*"

"Fair enough. See you Monday." He kissed my cheek, gently chucked me under the chin and then strode out of the restaurant.

I sank back onto my chair and signaled for the waiter to bring me another drink. I'd only swallowed one mouthful when a voice I never thought I'd hear again broke me from my thoughts.

"Hello, Isabelle." Steph swanned around to sit opposite me, carefully arranging her dress before placing her half-full glass of champagne on the table.

I gaped. What was it Dr. Baker had said about bad things coming in threes? I think I would have preferred a car accident, maybe a mugging. There was plenty I could think of to make up my third that were less painful than seeing her again. Note to self: do not ask the Universe if there's anything else it wants to throw at you.

"Steph," I breathed. "What are you doing here?"

"Eating dinner, the same as you and Mark were." She leaned back, crossing a shapely leg over the other. "I hear you're in some shit. What was this then? A last supper?"

"You hear wrong." It wasn't a lie, really. Things were crappy but manageable. "Seriously, why are you here?"

"Because I live here?" She sounded exactly the same, with that low bored East Coast accent.

"I see," I managed to push out, only just stopping myself from grinding my teeth.

Her eyes swept around the restaurant before coming to rest on me. "So, how is Saint Isabelle?"

"Don't." I'd always hated the way she called me that, just as she'd always hated me pushing her to be more of a philanthropist.

At my hard stare, Steph laughed. "You're exactly the same."

Funny she'd say that, because I felt like a completely different person. I reached for my clutch. "I have to go. It was great to see you again, Steph. You look really good."

Steph sighed and put out a hand to stop me. "Look, Isabelle. I'm back from Europe for good now, we're going to see one another around and it would be a whole lot less awkward for all involved if we could just move on." She straightened in her seat. "I was a shit, you were a shit. We just weren't compatible. It's done."

My grip on my purse was white-knuckled. "I know that, Steph and believe me when I say I'm long over it, and you. But it doesn't mean I have to enjoy being around you, especially after your little smear campaign."

She waved, as though waving my words away. "I was angry with you, and I said things I shouldn't have. I'm sorry I did that, but don't tell me you've never said something you regretted."

Her words struck a little too close to the bone. I studied her, wondering why I'd ever found her attractive. She just... looked like money. Physically she was as gorgeous as ever, even having changed her hair—now longer and auburn, and so suited to her fine features that it made me wonder why she hadn't done it earlier. But her light brown eyes were so cold. She *felt* cold, totally different to Audrey. Or rather the Audrey who wasn't ignoring me.

Surprised by her apology, I mumbled, "You know I have."

Steph almost recoiled, placing a hand on her chest and flashing me a look of mock-surprise. "Is that an admission of guilt? Will wonders never cease?" Her smile softened the barb. "Listen, there's nothing sinister at play. I'm here having dinner, I saw you and I thought you could use some support. If the rumors are true, and I think they are."

"Thank you, but I have plenty of support." Maybe. If I could get Audrey to speak to me again. Twigging to everything she'd just said, I backtracked. "Wait, what do you mean *rumors*?"

She smiled slyly, eyes twinkling. "Grapevine says Mark Hall is leaving Rhodes and Hall. And maybe even the city."

"Where'd you hear that?" I demanded.

"You know I hear almost everything." Steph held up a hand to stop the tirade I was about to unleash. "Don't worry, it didn't come from your office. Nothing ever comes from there." She sighed. "Your staff are your Knights of the Round Table. When we were dating I could barely get Clare to tell me if you were in or out for lunch. They protect you like you're a member of the first family or something."

Relieved, I settled back in my seat. Still, the leak had to come from *somewhere*. An overheard phone call David Oldham had made. A client of Mark's who didn't grasp the importance of privacy. I realized with discomfort that I'd probably never know. "Well it's nice to see you're still not above digging in the dirt for information."

Steph grabbed my arm. "Listen. Stop being bitchy because you're pissed about what happened between us. Take what you've made and run that company like a bitch. You've earned it. You're better than him and you know it."

Suspicious, I narrowed my eyes at her. "Why are you telling me this? What do you want?"

She released me. "I don't want anything, Isabelle." Steph raised her left hand to show off an emerald-cut diamond and platinum Harry Winston engagement ring. Nice. "Despite everything, I don't want you to fail, I never did. Call it sisterhood or whatever." She raised a bare, tanned shoulder in a lazy shrug. "And this way I can claim credit when you're sitting at the top of the earnings list."

I smiled, and it wasn't even forced. I didn't hate her so much as I was annoyed by her return to the sphere I'd tried so hard to make my own. "You do get credit, Stephanie. But not the way you think."

"I'll take it." She was such a narcissist. But that wasn't my problem anymore. It was the problem of whoever had stuck that rock on her hand. "Seriously though, Isabelle, try to find some balance this time. I saw those pictures from the AWL gala and she is lovely."

"Noted," I said flatly. It seemed a moot point now.

Steph studied me with a raised, tinted eyebrow. Understanding dawned on her face and I felt a flash of irritation that clearly she hadn't lost the ability to read me. "You broke up with her," she said.

I sighed, turning my glass in circles on the table. "No. Yes. I don't know. She's ignoring me."

Steph heaved an exasperated sigh. "You can be such an idiot. Like I said, I saw the pictures. Isabelle, you were looking at her in a way you never looked at me. If she's ignoring you then you need to do something else. Make her listen. You've always been like this." She emphasized with a dramatic air clutch, like this was the most frustrating thing she'd ever had to tell anyone.

"Like what?" I asked indignantly.

"You're content, Isabelle. Content to let Mark Hall deal with the nitty-gritty parts of running the company. Content to take all those whispers from bitches about where you came from, without standing up to them. Content to just...let this woman ignore you." She drew herself up. "I bet you've done nothing except call and text."

"I emailed," I mumbled.

"Well, that would certainly get my attention," Steph said drily. She could be quite witty when she wanted to be. "Stop being just content and woman up. At work and with your girlfriend. Now Mark Hall's out of the picture, you can either front up or fuck off."

Ouch. "Life *and* relationship advice from my ex. Is this a special kind of hell?"

Steph smiled, more like the woman who used to fall into hysterical laughter watching SpongeBob. "Maybe it is. For both of us. At any rate, it's added something to my karma bank." She glanced across the room, raised a hand in acknowledgement then stood. "When you're top of the list, remember me in your memoirs. But don't put me under mistakes. That's just bad taste." She pecked me softly on the cheek and walked away.

I watched her wind her way gracefully through the restaurant, then picked up my phone and texted Clare. Apologizing for contacting her after hours, I asked her to arrange an urgent flight for tomorrow. When I set my phone back down, I felt lighter and more at peace with myself than I had all week. Damn Steph for shoving me in the right direction.

Even if visiting Audrey turned into a massive clusterfuck of a failure then at least I'd know for certain.

CHAPTER TWENTY-EIGHT

Clare messaged to confirm my flight to Minnesota was set for after lunch on Saturday, the timing planned around when Audrey might be back from the hospital, if in fact her mother was still in there. Or still alive. Before crawling into bed Friday night, I took half a sleeping pill, knowing that Sleep-Deprived Isabelle would make a difficult situation even worse.

I woke feeling mostly human to spend all morning sitting on the floor of my office hunched over the semi-circle of printouts, hand-drawn charts and dot point lists. I had a handout ready for the employees, and was sure I had a strategy for handling both the influx of clients and managing the staff. So far, the strategy consisted mostly of "working a whole fucking lot more."

William collected me at midday, delivered me dutifully to the airport and Schwartz had me touching down at South St. Paul Municipal a little after four. The driver of the waiting car, a polite bashful young man, confirmed the address Clare had given me and then left me alone as he drove. This was it, no backing out.

I stared out the window, vaguely registering the scenery while I tried to think of what to say. Talking was my strong point. I could spin out words to convince people without even thinking about it. But now when it really mattered, I couldn't think of a fucking thing. *Sorry* featured heavily in all my options but it wasn't enough. I needed reasons why, and truthfulness if I was going to convince her of how deeply I felt.

Audrey's mother—Marietta—lived on about an acre of gently sloping land with a long driveway dissecting her neatly-mown lawn. In the fading light I could see the rose bushes escorting us up to a house which was a two story typical of what I'd seen on the drive over, though perhaps smaller. A porch wrapped tightly around three-quarters of the white wooden house, with a gabled roof and large windows dominating the façade.

The driver parked under a large oak tree at the edge of the circular drive and waited patiently while I fumbled for my pocketbook. He fetched my small overnight bag from the trunk and waited again until I'd walked up the path, before he drove off. Now that I was here, on her mother's doorstep, a sudden and overwhelming burst of emotion almost paralyzed me.

But I was stuck, at least until I could call the driver to come back. And I couldn't sit on this porch forever. The worst thing that could happen was she'd ask me to leave, right? I could handle that with a modicum of dignity, at least while in her presence. Just do it, Isabelle. Before I could have a more protracted argument with myself, I pressed the bell, tucked my free hand into my pocket and waited.

Footsteps were followed by a long pause and then the sound of a chain dragging and locks clicking. There was the longest moment of nothingness, like I'd suddenly been pulled into a vacuum. Then the door opened.

Audrey studied me with an inscrutable expression. "Iz. Hey," she said, the faintest smile finally lifting the edge of her mouth. She looked incredibly tired, like she was on the verge of falling apart. Rumpled and mussed in faded sweats and a hoodie, she was still so damned beautiful it made my throat tight. My heart double-timed, both with anxiety and that sweet longing I always felt near her.

"Hey," I responded, the very model of articulation. "Sorry to drop in without calling."

"That's okay." Her fingers tightened on the door.

"How's your mama?" I asked quickly, just to make sure there was no silence.

The smile grew a little. "Mom."

My eyebrow reached for my hairline. "Pardon me?"

"Us Yankees call them moms."

Her gentle humor made me smile in return, easing a little of my fear. "Well then, how is your *mom*?"

"She's doing better." Audrey opened the door wider. "So, you were just in the neighborhood and decided to drop by?"

"Something like that. I've had some rough flying these last few days. Why didn't you return my messages?"

She practically winced. "I'm sorry, Iz. I forgot my phone charger in the rush to leave and I've pretty much just been at the hospital, or sleeping since I got here." She sighed. "I bought a charger a few days ago but...honestly I needed some time to think and cool off. I'm sorry I didn't get in contact with you."

I nodded slowly. Though it was an honest explanation it was still upsetting. "I was really worried."

"I'm sorry," she said again quietly.

Forcing the upset down, I held out the bunch of flowers I'd carried from New York. "These are for your mama."

"Nothing for me?" Audrey asked lightly.

"Only myself. If you'll still have me." My gut tightened. She wasn't cold but she was definitely guarded, and I had absolutely no idea where we stood with each other.

She smiled sadly and pulled the door fully open. "Come in. It's freezing out." She took the flowers from me and placed them on the sideboard just inside the doorway.

I exhaled a puff of warm breath. "Thank you." I slipped inside and she stepped around me to close the door. Audrey stood with her back to me, a hand flat against the wooden door, her head bowed. For the longest time she didn't move.

"Audrey?" I whispered loudly.

She spun, and before I had time to think her hands were caressing my face, her eyes locked with mine. Those beautiful hands were warm against my cold cheeks, thumbs running softly along my cheekbones. She drew in a deep, slow breath. "You said 'if I'll have you'." Audrey stared at me, pulling me into her arms before I could react. "I want you always and forever, Iz. I'm not whole without you."

Audrey held me tightly, like she was afraid I'd disappear or pull away. I slipped back into her embrace as though I'd never left it, and when I tucked my nose under her chin I could feel her heart beat in the pulse at her neck. Burrowed into her shoulder, I wrapped my arms around her and slid my hands under her hoodie to scratch her back lightly. She felt exactly the way I remembered.

I didn't cry. Until she did. Just a little hiccupping sob but it was enough. We shared tears as we held each other in the entryway of her mother's house. I hadn't responded to her words, hadn't told her how incomplete I was without her. The thought didn't worry me, because I sensed that despite everything, she knew. We could have stood in our embrace for minutes or hours—I didn't know, but eventually she pulled back and wiped her face on her sleeve.

I palmed tears from my cheeks and launched in without thinking. "Audrey, I love you. All of you. I love you in your scruffy pair of jeans, and I love your hair and your smile and I love the way you make me laugh and I love that I can only get eye level with you when you're barefoot and I'm in four inches of heel."

Her mouth opened, but I stopped her speaking by putting a hand over it, desperate to get the words out without interruption. My eyes searched hers, trying to gauge her response. "I love the way I feel whenever I'm with you. I love you. I'm in love with you. There, I said it…and now I'm worried because you haven't said anything."

She laughed and moved back, away from the hand I had clapped over her mouth. "Isabelle, you shushed me." Her laughed died away and the playful sparkle in her eye dimmed to seriousness. "Don't you see? I've been in love with you since the first night you came to my place."

Tears welled again and I blinked a few times, trying to force them back. "Really?"

"Yes really." A thumb ran over my lips. "I love you." She held eye contact with me then leaned in and kissed me tenderly.

I fisted her sweatshirt. "I'm not saying it just because we had a fight either. I've wanted to say it for a long time but I've been too afraid."

"Me too. Come and sit down." After another soft kiss, Audrey took my hand and led me up the hallway. Her mother's house seemed to be laid out with a hallway as an artery and rooms branching off on both sides. It was light and airy, the walls painted in differing bright colors and full of vibrant paintings and photos I couldn't quite make out.

Audrey waited until I'd settled on the couch then moved away to poke at the fire and add another log. She carefully replaced the screen and set the poker in its rack. This simple domestic gesture made my chest ache with desperation to move back to what we'd had.

The moment she sat beside me, Audrey drew me even closer so I was almost on her lap, and took my hands. Holding her hands in mine felt like having a lost piece of myself returned. "Audrey, I owe you a huge apology. For keeping our relationship from Mark the way I did and also for what I said about the money thing, for what it implied. I really didn't mean it."

"I know you didn't mean it that way, honey, but I won't lie. It was a crappy thing to say and it really hurt me." She moistened her lips with her tongue. "And on top of you not telling Mark..."

"Yes it was," I whispered. "There's more to it, but I'm sorry."

"I know you are, and I shouldn't have run out the way I did. I wasn't thinking straight and it was just a little too much on top of my mom."

I squeezed her hands, suddenly desperate to clear the air between us. "I was going to tell him that day, I swear I was. I even got as far as 'I wanted' but then he cut me off and dragged me into a meeting. Then he told me he wants to sell me his half of the business, and if I wasn't agreeable, we'd have to dissolve."

"What!"

"Mhmm, and he needs this because he's basically being sued for acting against a client's instruction. And the kicker? The reason he did was because he hates his job so much that he just couldn't be fucked doing it right anymore." I drew in a deep breath. "So, sweetheart, I really am sorry I didn't tell him about us when I said I would. But I got a little sidetracked that day."

She could have been shitty about my slightly passive-aggressive explanation, but instead she brushed a soft kiss over my lips. "That's a whole lot of crap all at once. What's happening then?"

"We haggled a little and I bought him out. Contracts signed yesterday."

"Well." She blinked a few times. "Fuck."

"Yeah. I think fuck just about sums it up." I smiled wryly. "You should really check your emails."

Her expression turned inward and I could almost imagine all the thoughts bouncing around her head. A slow smile blossomed. "So it *will* be you who fires me?" she asked teasingly.

"You shit." I pulled her hand to my mouth and kissed it. "Seriously, how're you? Is your mom really doing better?"

"We're okay, and yeah she came home yesterday. She's still weak but she'll be fine."

"Will you tell me what happened?"

Audrey explained how Marietta's pneumonia was complicated by the lung cancer she'd beaten eight years ago. We spoke in low voices, the conversation eventually coming back to our argument, with no feelings overlooked. There was still so much we had to talk about, more hurts to dredge up, but knowing that we could, that I now had the chance, eased my worry.

"Audrey, I didn't mean to make you feel worthless or like I didn't want to be with you. I just…wanted something Mark wasn't involved in, that was mine alone, that I didn't need to negotiate or discuss. I didn't realize at the time, but my therapist pointed out how hurtful it was for me to do that to you."

"It was, yes," she said carefully. "But I'm not blameless either, Iz. I left and I shouldn't have ignored you the way I did, it was wrong and I own that." Her hand tightened then relaxed against my thigh. "Remember when we were talking about our flaws?"

"Mhmm."

Audrey's gaze was fixed on the fire. "I never told you my big one. The one where I run away when I get scared. I don't like… feeling like I don't matter, and I panicked."

She was so unshakeable that I couldn't imagine her being afraid of anything to do with relationships. "Look at me, darling. What are you afraid of?"

"That you didn't really want me, that it was only about the sex," she said simply. "I mean that's all we had for so long, you know? I wanted more but I thought you didn't, and we'd only *just* decided to go further when we fought. Even listening to your messages asking about my mom, I couldn't shake that overwhelming paranoia that you were only calling because you missed fucking me."

"You do matter," I said forcefully. "You're so important to me, not just in bed, Audrey and I'm sorry I never actually said the words to you."

"I think maybe I knew, deep down," she said slowly. "But I was too scared to really let myself believe it. Fear isn't always logical, Iz."

"Don't I know it," I murmured.

We sat quietly for a while, watching the fire dance while Audrey played with my hair. I closed my eyes, leaning into her and scratching lightly through her hoodie. Through the fabric I felt the muscle of her abdomen tense and relax as my fingers dug for purchase, and I remembered what lay under her clothes, the body I'd loved so many times.

Along with all my other emotions, my desire for her was as strong as ever. But more than anything, in that moment I just wanted to exist with her. Sex, lust—that could all come later. Right now it was about our emotional connection. How far we'd come from a time when we were only about sex.

Her arm stole around my waist, lips brushed my forehead. "So what's next for Rhodes and Hall?"

Groaning, I opened my eyes. "I can't even think about it right now." I rubbed a hand over the back of my neck. "There's a meeting Monday with all the staff. Details in the email."

She nodded. "Okay."

A wave of fear crashed into me. "Are you coming back?" I caught my lower lip between my teeth.

She nodded, seeming surprised I'd asked. "Yes, of course. My brother's flying in tomorrow to be with Mom, so I can fly back tomorrow night or Monday morning."

I climbed into her lap, snuggling into her and suddenly I felt like I could breathe again. She held me, stroking my hair and murmuring gentle nonsensical words. After a time, she spoke words that were as clear as anything. "Are you staying here tonight?"

"I have a hotel. I'll just need to call a car."

"Stay with me?" She held my hands tightly, almost as though she thought I might leave right that instant.

"Of course," I whispered. "But I have to leave early tomorrow, I've got so much work."

"That's okay. Just…stay."

"I will." Leaning in to kiss her, movement at the edge of the room caught my eye. I nudged her knee, jerking my chin in the direction of the stairs.

Audrey bent her head backward to see what I was trying to indicate. "Mom! What are you doing?" She carefully tipped me from her lap to the couch and rushed toward the figure at the base of the stairs. I stood up, uncertain as to what I should do.

Audrey's mom sighed, then dissolved into a short coughing fit. "I heard you talking to someone." She waved Audrey aside and kept walking toward me.

I stepped forward, smiling uncertainly. Audrey gestured for me to come closer. "Mom, this is my girlfriend, Isabelle Rhodes. Iz, this is my mom, Marietta."

In the flesh the resemblance between them was even more striking and I could see where Audrey got those beautiful cheekbones and wide, dark eyes. They had the same hair, thick and dark with just a touch of wave, though Marietta's was gray at the temples.

Audrey's mom lifted her chin to appraise me. "So, you're the girlfriend," she said, the faintest trace of Italian accent kissing her words.

"Yes, ma'am I am. It's a great pleasure to meet you. I'm terribly sorry to drop in like this."

Though she was gaunt, pale and obviously still weak, she came right up to me and enfolded me in a hug. "I'm glad you came, my Audrey has been miserable without you. You are very brave." She felt like a bag of sticks and my return hug was gentle.

Audrey stepped in. "Mom, come on. I think you should go back to bed."

Marietta scoffed, "Stop fussing over me." She squeezed my hands tight then let them go and shuffled toward the kitchen. "Would you like coffee, Isabelle?"

I brushed fresh tears from my eyes with the edges of my thumbs. I was going to need an electrolyte drink with all the crying I'd been doing. "Coffee would be wonderful. Thank you."

Audrey rushed to catch up, like she was afraid to leave me with her mama. "I'll make it."

"No, I want real coffee." Marietta waved Audrey aside and ushered me onto a chair at the kitchen table. I sat and she busied herself with a stovetop espresso maker. "I've been in America almost forty years and I still cannot stand your filter coffee," she informed me airily.

The scent of coffee brewing soon filled the small kitchen as Marietta set out a plate of what looked like homemade biscotti. "Audrey made these. When she wants to be, she is very good at baking."

The small, comfortable kitchen felt oddly familiar and it took me a moment to realize that the feeling was the same one I had when I went back to Mama's. Warmth, comfort, love. Marietta brushed the back of her fingers along my cheek. "You're a lot prettier than your pictures on the Internet."

I shot a quick glance at Audrey, who wasn't doing a very good job of hiding her smirk. I nodded amicably. "Well, thank you very much. It's kind of you to say that."

Marietta sat opposite Audrey and me, then poured the coffee. "You're also my daughter's boss."

"Yes, technically I am." I added sugar and sipped my espresso. Hot damn, it was good.

Marietta spoke like her daughter wasn't in the room. "She says you are a good boss."

"I, uh, I try to be."

"Do you let her be the boss sometimes too?"

Beside me, Audrey cringed. "Mom. Please stop. Before you embarrass me further. Shouldn't you be sleeping?"

"I'm not tired, and I have been in bed for so long already." Marietta shrugged unapologetically then turned back to me. "For relationships to work, there must be balance. If Isabelle is the boss for work then you must be allowed to be in charge other times." She accented my name beautifully.

A warm tingle ran up my spine. "I agree." I patted Audrey's forearm, telling her silently that all was okay. Apparently all mothers were the same when it came to interrogation of new partners and sharing of information about their children. Even if they were recovering from illness.

Marietta laughed, the sound almost identical to Audrey's. "Good. Then you are as sensible as I'd hoped you would be. Audrey has already told me some things about you, but I would like to know more." She topped up my coffee and began a fresh batch.

"What would you like to know?" I reached for a cookie.

"Do you have siblings?"

"No, it's just me."

"Where do your parents live?"

"My mama lives in South Carolina." I set the cookie, now halved, on my side plate. "I'm not sure where my daddy is. He left when I was young."

Marietta tsk'd. "A shame."

Audrey spoke quietly, "Just tell her to mind her own business, honey." She glanced at her mother and raised her voice to regular volume. "She might even listen."

Marietta waved her finger teasingly. "You complain too much, *amore mio*."

I bumped Audrey with my shoulder. "It's fine. Stop fussing." I turned my attention to Marietta. "Tell me about the photograph I saw in the den, the signed one of Audrey Hepburn?"

"Ah yes. It is not real. A print of her autograph, but it doesn't matter. My best Audrey is right here with me."

I reached for Audrey's hand under the table. "I agree."

CHAPTER TWENTY-NINE

It was still dark when I slipped reluctantly out of Audrey's warm embrace, dressed and kissed her goodbye. Clutching my coat sleepily, she'd murmured something indistinct, and then fallen right back to sleep. It was almost like the beginning when we were sneaking out in the early hours, pretending it was what we wanted.

I'd deliberately turned my phone to Do Not Disturb while with her, and when I came back on the grid, the poor thing almost began smoking with all the alerts and messages from clients. And Mama. As Schwartz flew me home, I sorted through the messages ready for my attention when I would get to the office in a few hours.

I arrived back in the city just after sunrise and after a quick stop for a shower and something to eat, it was back to the office. I worked through contracts, and familiarizing myself with my new clients. Most of the inherited portfolios would be easy to turn around. But more than once I found myself shouting to the empty office, "What the fuck, Mark?"

By twelve thirty, I was about to throw myself on the floor like a toddler. I turned my phone to silent, hoping for half an hour of respite, and slipped out of the office for a change of scenery and some food. Tugging my collar up around my ears against the wind, I ducked across the street, raising an apologetic hand to the bike I'd cut off. As I rushed along the sidewalk, I decided it was definitely a greasy burger and fries kind of day.

Waiting for my order, I ignored the missed calls and voice mail notifications, and opened various news sites. There was nothing about Mark leaving yet, so clearly Steph's *source* didn't have too much influence. The relief would be short-lived because after the press statement was released tomorrow, the shit would hit the fan.

Back at my desk, I picked at my lunch and began to draft what I would say to my staff at the meeting tomorrow. I managed a half-page that didn't make much sense and felt a whole lot like a *I'm sorry, please like me* monologue. I'd ad-libbed enough speeches in my time and hoped that I could do the same for what might be the speech that kept my company afloat.

Rolling my shoulders to ease some of the tension, I deleted my last line and rewrote it. Three times. Then I gave up, made some dot points and decided that was good enough. My phone rang right as I finished. I snatched it up without looking. "Isabelle Rhodes."

"Hey." Audrey sounded relieved. "Is this a bad time?"

"It's never a bad time when you call, darling." I made a pointed effort to set my pen down and get up from my desk.

She laughed softly. "I just wanted to see how you were doing, and to let you know I miss you and that my mom hasn't shut up about you."

The tension gripping my shoulders eased. "I miss you too. And should I be worried?"

"About her planning for the next time you visit? Yes."

I blew a raspberry. "That's not worry material. When she starts including Mama, then I'll worry."

"Don't tempt her," Audrey muttered. "Look, I know you're busy as heck, Iz. I just wanted to let you know I'm still not sure exactly what time I'll be back, but I'll see you at the meeting, or whenever you can find some time."

"Oh. Okay then, thanks. Fly safe?"

"Always," she murmured. "Love you."

"I love you too." There was a long pause and then I heard her disconnect. I stood motionless for a time, staring out into the fading light, and had a moment of perfect clarity and an almost unshakeable conviction.

I *could* balance everything. I would always make time for her. The extra work didn't matter and my relationship with her wasn't going to be a second rate event in my life. There were a few things in my life I could cut—attendance at committee meetings and non-essential functions, a workout here and there. But I wouldn't compromise with Audrey.

Finally at home and in bed I turned my phone off. Closing my eyes, I tried to reason with myself. Sleep. Now. Come on. Please. If you just stop thinking, you'll…fall…asleep…

Something touched my cheek. Bug. Fucking bug. I dragged my eyes open and jerked away. No bug. Audrey. She stood beside my bed, backlit by the muted light showing through the hastily closed blinds.

"You're back," I croaked.

"I am." She kicked out of her boots at the same time she unzipped her jeans.

I rolled over, reaching out to touch her leg. "What time is it?"

"A little after one. I decided I couldn't sleep without you and left mom in my brother's capable hands." Audrey lifted her shirt off and slipped out of her jeans, folding both neatly on the antique trunk at the end of my bed.

"Are you staying with me?"

She stripped out of her bra and panties then climbed into bed. "Always."

I clung to her, head on her shoulder and arm around her waist. "You promise?"

"Promise."

* * *

I slept dreamlessly, limbs entwined with hers, right through until my alarm. When I showered, I felt revitalized rather than just-woken groggy. The simplest thing could turn me from a mess to a functioning person again. Sorting through plastic-wrapped dry cleaning I decided on one of my favorite dresses, a black Stella McCartney with colorful embroidered flowers and a mildly indecent front split. A very naked and tempting Audrey stood behind me in the bathroom while I put makeup on.

After some indulgent ogling in the mirror, I turned around and pointed at the doorway. "Out. I can't concentrate with you in here."

"I think you're doing just fine." Audrey ran her hand over the fabric covering my upper arm. "I love you in this dress."

"I love that you love it." I turned around and traced the line of her collarbone with my fingertips, watching the way her skin twitched under my touch. "You know, I thought about a lot of things while you were out of town."

"What about?" She shuddered as my hand slid lower to brush against her breast.

"You, mostly. How much I love you. How much I need you." I drew in a deep breath. "I couldn't do this without you, Audrey. I mean it."

Her expression was serene, almost meditative with eyes half closed and that kissable mouth on the edge of breaking into one of her precious smiles. "Me too."

"Listen, I…things will be hectic and busy and annoying for the next six months or so, but I promise it'll get better." I twisted to set down my eyeliner then took both her hands in mine. "I promise you will always be a priority for me."

"Thank you."

I pressed a kiss to the base of her neck. "Now I mean it. Get out of here before I ravish you."

She flicked her fingers at her forehead in mock salute and backed out of the bathroom. When I emerged Audrey was sitting on the bed, still naked. I moved to my walk-in. "Are you trying to make me late?"

She stood and followed me. "No, just reminding you what's waiting for you when we're done tonight."

I grinned. "As if I could ever forget." I picked a pair of satin slingback Miu Miu pumps and added minimal jewelry. I felt good. Even in those heels and with her barefoot I had to stretch a little to kiss her. "I'll see you for the meeting."

"Mhmm. Love you." Audrey moved aside to let me by, slapping my ass on the way past.

"Tease. Love you too," I called over my shoulder.

Tom called just before eight thirty a.m. to inform me that our statement had been released. I thanked him, and braced myself for the inevitable barrage of calls from reporters. They didn't disappoint. I juggled calls from journalists and clients while trying to work, and I accepted that even if I thought I'd won them over with skill and charm, some of Mark's clients might yet leave.

Shane Preston obviously had a Google alert set up to catch the keywords "Rhodes and Hall." He called me barely an hour after the press statement went live, assuring me that he wanted to keep his account with me, and also congratulating me. I almost choked at the irony of his sudden turnabout from doubter to fan. Of course the one client I would like to lose was the one certain to stay.

I further revised my opinion of him when he said, "I'd like to add another ten million."

It took everything I had not to splutter in surprise. "Well thank you, Shane. I can't tell you how pleased and excited I am to have the opportunity to make that work for you."

"As am I." He ummed and ahhed for a long moment. "Frankly, Isabelle…I'd heard rumors about Mark Hall's competence and I wasn't certain how involved he was in your decisions. With his departure, I now feel very comfortable increasing my base."

I straightened in my chair. "Shane, I assure you that Mark has never had any input in how I manage my clients' portfolios."

"Good," he said firmly. "Now, when can you come for a meeting?"

My revised opinion of him slid down a notch, back toward pain in the ass. Forcing cheer into my voice, I asked, "How's next week work for you?"

Every chance I got, I Googled. The fact that Mark was no longer associated with the company featured on all the financial sites and some gossip columns. Speculation was that he had a drug problem, possibly involved in organized crime, had a penchant for hookers and every other out-there theory in between. Unfortunately, it was all so carefully worded so as to not be libelous. Pity.

Some articles worried about the future of the company. My favorite op-ed piece was titled, "Where will Isabelle Rhodes go now?" Back to work. Duh. A few sites had photos of Mark and me together. Ordinarily, I'd be pleased with their choice. I looked good, but it only highlighted everything that had fallen apart, and that I had to put it all back together again. But I was starting to feel like I really could put it all together.

Clare assured me all staff would be attending later that day, handed me fresh coffee and some papers, and then left me to work. She brought me lunch and made it clear, without actually saying anything, that it would be in my best interest to eat it. I imagined at some stage, Tamara would be getting a run down on the "make sure Ms. Rhodes eats" portion of her new job.

Half an hour or so before the meeting in which I hoped to establish my position as a woman heading up a large, successful financial organization, Mark knocked on my door. "Belle?"

"Mmm?"

He strode over to my desk, his hands behind his back. "I wanted to give you this." He brought his hands around and I had to lean closer to make out the lump in his hand. It took a moment before I recognized it as a piece of our very first office. The night before the construction guys were due to come in and outfit the space, we'd ceremoniously drunk an expensive bottle of champagne then attacked a wall with sledgehammers.

As we left, I'd picked up a chunk of the wall we'd bashed and given it to him.

I raised my eyes to his. "Is that what I think it is? You kept it all this time?" I had to bite my bottom lip to stop it trembling.

Mark smiled and quickly dashed his palm against his eyes. "Course I did. Now you can have it back, to remind you of how far you've come." He set the lump of concrete on my desk, and opened his arms to me. When I stepped into his embrace he leaned down to speak near my ear. "You're the boss now, Belle, and don't let anyone tell you otherwise. See you at the meeting." He released me and walked out without another word or backward glance.

I dropped into my chair, turning slowly side to side and stared at the concrete, mind blank of all thought except the occasional *shit*.

"You can only do what you can do," I mumbled to myself as I wrote "IT'S NOT PERSONAL" on a sticky note and stuck it to the lump of concrete Mark had left me.

Footsteps in the hallway then familiar laughter carried through my open doorway. Audrey. I smiled to myself, and glanced at the time. Meeting in fifteen. A few seconds later, Clare knocked. "Ms. Rhodes, Audrey Graham's here, as is almost everyone else."

"Thanks, Clare. I'll be ready in a few minutes. Has everyone been given the handout?"

Clare nodded silently and melted away. I smoothed down my dress as Audrey stepped into my office, a thin manila folder tucked under her arm. My smile grew. She wore one of my favorite shirts, a sky blue button-down with the sleeves rolled up. Paired with black slacks, a thin belt and loafers, she had an enviable mix of casual and elegant.

Audrey gestured to my desk. "You know, I've never been in your office. It's very you."

"Thanks. I think. Did you need something to drink?"

"Clare already offered, thanks." Audrey crossed to stand beside me. Eyebrows slightly raised and eyes soft, she studied me. "How are you feeling?"

"Good. I'm about ready. Take a seat and I'll be back in a minute."

In the bathroom, I stared at my reflection. Funny how most of the shadows under my eyes seemed to be fading now that she'd returned. A quick lipstick touch-up, a glower at my hair and I was ready.

Though Audrey would be at the meeting as a member of the staff, she was also there as so much more. She was my lover. My partner. My support. My lifeline. We walked through the office, hands brushing and I felt the lightness of knowing that everything would turn out all right as long as I had her by my side.

Audrey gently thumbed the edge of my mouth. "All set?"

"As I'll ever be."

She held my shoulders. "You've got this, darling. You're still here, Iz. You're still standing."

"Shakily," I clarified.

"Yes. But standing nonetheless and I'm here with you." She kissed me quickly as footsteps approached the open door, then she moved to stand just to my right. Staff began to file in, each holding an identical folder. Mark slipped toward the back of the room. I did a quick head count. Showtime.

Everyone fell silent when I shifted my papers. "Thank you all for coming. I'll try to keep this short, I know you're all eager to get to dinner and drinks."

Cautious laughter around the room.

"First of all, I would like to sincerely apologize for the abruptness of the news on Friday, and for any anxiety or uncertainty that may have caused you." Pushing hair back from my face, I continued, "As you're aware, as of Friday Mark Hall ceased to be co-owner of Rhodes and Hall." When I looked directly at Mark, he smiled and winked at me.

A few members of the group nodded, turning to where Mark leaned relaxed against the wall. Others murmured quietly. I glanced down at my dot-point notes. "As I mentioned on Friday, we appreciate everyone's discretion outside of this office. In the next few weeks, Rhodes and Hall will transition to Isabelle

Rhodes and Associates, and a very fine West Coast analyst will be joining us sometime in Q-Two to broaden our reach even further."

Nat had accepted my job offer and when she and Jill returned from their honeymoon, she'd be starting as an associate. I paused, trying to gauge the feeling of the audience. Everyone was quiet, their eyes on me and an overwhelming sensation of panic bubbled up my throat. Audrey's steadying hand made its way to my back and when I looked sideways at her, she held eye contact with me, her expression calm as she nodded. Okay, I was doing okay.

She dropped her hand and without thinking, I reached for it and gently twined our fingers together. I was dimly aware of the statement I was making to my staff about our relationship, and rather than concerned, I felt settled. It felt right. "I'll try to keep any disruption to a minimum, and I would very much appreciate your patience while we settle in the changes. There's an overview in the handout Clare gave you, which outlines the new structure and other basics. Which leads to my next point. There will be *no* job loss. Aside from Tamara who will be joining Clare as my adjunct PA, there will be no other restructuring and certainly no redundancies."

I felt the shift immediately, like the whole room was letting go of anxiety. The tightness in my stomach lessened some as well. "I value all of you very highly, as does Mark. You're part of the reason this company is so successful."

I swept my eyes around the room. "If there's anything you'd like to talk about, please know my door is open." I gave the assembled group a smile. "In the meantime, please feel free to include me in your gossip."

A low hum filled the room but quieted the moment I spoke again, "I think that about sums things up for now. I'll see you all at Ricardo's. Thank you."

The group began to stand and I suddenly remembered the last thing I had to say. "Oh! One more very important thing." Everyone stopped moving. I inhaled deeply. "From now on, no more Ms. Rhodes. Please, call me Isabelle." Goodbye, kindergarten teacher.

There were soft murmurs and more than a few smiles. Audrey squeezed my hand then released me. I moved through the crowd, exchanging words here, shaking hands there, and even receiving the odd hug before we went for dinner and drinks. A small group had gathered around Mark, speaking quietly with him and exchanging handshakes and laughter. Nobody appeared upset or concerned, and with every passing moment I felt better. Stronger. I could do this.

When the room had emptied of everyone but Mark, Audrey and me, Mark walked over clapping quietly. "Bravo, Ms. Rhodes." His eyes twinkled.

"Oh, fuck off," I said good-naturedly.

"Seriously, I'm proud of you, Belle." Mark hugged me then after a pause, opened his arms to Audrey, who stepped into them immediately. After they'd separated, Mark confirmed, "See you two downstairs?"

"Mhmm." I watched him leave the room, then turned back to Audrey. Her dark eyes connected with mine, her mouth lifted in the special smile she reserved for me. The smile of promise and love.

"Ready to go?" I asked.

"Sure am. That was great, just what they needed to hear. They all trust you so much, Iz." We started toward the door.

Trust. Looking into her guileless face, I realized with painful clarity that the thing I'd missed all along was trust. In myself and others. Audrey was the first woman who I'd fully opened up to, who I'd trusted without question. She was also the first woman to place her trust in me, and her trust was worth more than all the money in the world. I was worth it, I was deserving of it.

I cleared the lump from my throat. "I just need to grab my purse."

"Sure." We made our way down the hall to my office, and Audrey leaned against my desk while I gathered my things. Her smile was slightly mischievous when she asked, "So, do I get to call you Isabelle at work now too?"

"No." I stepped around my chair to stand in front of her.

She arched a confused eyebrow. "Well…what do I call you then?"

I turned Grams' ring on my finger. "I was thinking you could call me Mrs. Isabelle Graham. I mean, eventually that… might be great?"

Her eyes widened. Time lengthened, each second dragging out. "That sounds really good," she said hoarsely.

I ran my thumb over her left ring finger. "What do you say?" There was no anxiety. No nerves or fear. Just that trust between us.

"Is this a proposal?"

"I think it is."

The edge of her mouth trembled before a smile lifted the corner of her mouth. Eyes bright, she turned her hand to slip her fingers between mine. "Then I say yes."

Bella Books, Inc.

Women. Books. Even Better Together.

P.O. Box 10543
Tallahassee, FL 32302

Phone: 800-729-4992
www.bellabooks.com